Praise for
the Imperial Radch novels

"Powerful." —*New York Times*

"Awe-inspiring." —*Guardian*

"Mind-blowing." —*io9*

"Assured, gripping and stylish." —*NPR Books*

"A stunning achievement that belongs on anyone's 'must-read' list." —*Los Angeles Review of Books*

"A classic of SF for the ages." —*Library Journal*

"Astoundingly assured and graceful." —*Strange Horizons*

"Richly textured, gorgeously rendered." —*Entertainment Weekly*

"No science-fiction series [is] as *descriptive* of our current political and cultural moment or as insistent that we open our eyes to it." —*Slate*

By Ann Leckie

The Raven Tower

Lake of Souls: The Collected Short Fiction

THE IMPERIAL RADCH TRILOGY
Ancillary Justice
Ancillary Sword
Ancillary Mercy

Provenance

Translation State

TRANSLATION STATE

ANN LECKIE

orbitbooks.net

This book is a work of fiction. Names, characters, places, and incidents are the product of the author's imagination or are used fictitiously. Any resemblance to actual events, locales, or persons, living or dead, is coincidental.

Copyright © 2023 by Ann Leckie
Excerpt from *These Burning Stars* copyright © 2023 by Bethany Jacobs

Cover design by Lauren Panepinto
Cover images by Shuttershock
Cover copyright © 2023 by Hachette Book Group, Inc.
Author photograph by MissionPhoto.org

Hachette Book Group supports the right to free expression and the value of copyright. The purpose of copyright is to encourage writers and artists to produce the creative works that enrich our culture.

The scanning, uploading, and distribution of this book without permission is a theft of the author's intellectual property. If you would like permission to use material from the book (other than for review purposes), please contact permissions@hbgusa.com. Thank you for your support of the author's rights.

Orbit
Hachette Book Group
1290 Avenue of the Americas
New York, NY 10104
orbitbooks.net

First Paperback Edition: May 2024
Originally published in hardcover and ebook in Great Britain and in the U.S. by Orbit in June 2023

Orbit is an imprint of Hachette Book Group.
The Orbit name and logo are registered trademarks of Little, Brown Book Group Limited.

The publisher is not responsible for websites (or their content) that are not owned by the publisher.

The Hachette Speakers Bureau provides a wide range of authors for speaking events. To find out more, go to hachettespeakersbureau.com or email HachetteSpeakers@hbgusa.com.

Orbit books may be purchased in bulk for business, educational, or promotional use. For information, please contact your local bookseller or the Hachette Book Group Special Markets Department at special.markets@hbgusa.com.

The Library of Congress has cataloged the hardcover edition as follows:
Names: Leckie, Ann, author.
Title: Translation state / Ann Leckie.
Description: First edition. | New York : Orbit, 2023.
Identifiers: LCCN 2022045277 | ISBN 9780316289719 (hardcover) | ISBN 9780316290241 (ebook)
Classification: LCC PS3612.E3353 T73 2023 | DDC 813/.6—dc23
LC record available at https://lccn.loc.gov/2022045277

ISBNs: 9780316290128 (trade paperback), 9780316290241 (ebook)

Printed in the United States of America

LSC-C

Printing 1, 2024

TRANSLATION
STATE

Enae

The last stragglers in the funeral procession were barely out the ghost door before the mason bots unfolded their long legs and reached for the pile of stones they'd removed from the wall so painstakingly the day before. Enae hadn't looked back to see the door being sealed up, but sie could hear it for just a moment before the first of Aunt Irad's moans of grief rose into a wail. One or two cousins heaved an experimental sob.

Enae hadn't cried when Grandmaman died. Sie hadn't cried when Grandmaman told hir she'd chosen the time to go. Sie wasn't crying now. Which wasn't necessarily a problem, everyone knew what expressions you should have when you were following the bier to the crematory, everyone knew what sounds a close relative made, and Enae could sob and wail if sie'd wanted to. And after all, among all these aunts and uncles and nuncles and cousins, Enae was the one who'd lived with Grandmaman for decades, and taken care of her in her old age. Sie had been the one to arrange things in the household these past ten years or more, to deal with the servants—human and bot—with their very different needs. Sie still had all the household codes and bot overrides, and the servants still looked to hir for orders, at least until Grandmaman's will was unsealed. Sie had every right to walk at the head of the procession, right behind Grandmaman, wailing for all the town to hear, in these quiet early morning hours. Instead sie walked silent and dry-eyed at the back.

Grandmaman had been very old, and ill-tempered. She had also been very rich, and born into one of the oldest families in the system. Which meant that the procession to the crematory was longer than one might have expected. There had been some jostling in the entry hall, by the ghost door, Aunt Irad turning up a half hour early to position herself at the front, some cousins attempting to push her out of her place, and everyone eying Enae to see how sie'd react.

None of them had lived in the house for decades. Grandmaman had thrown most of them—or their parents—out. Every year she would hold a birthday dinner and invite them all back for a lavish meal, during which she would insult them to their faces while they smiled and gritted their teeth. Then she'd order them off the premises again, to wait until the next year. Some of them had fallen away in that time, sworn off Grandmaman and any hope of inheritance, but most of them came back year after year. It was only Enae who had actually lived in the house with Grandmaman, Enae who, one might think, would be the most affected by Grandmaman's death.

But for the past week Enae had let the aunts and uncles and

nuncles and cousins do whatever they'd wanted, so long as it didn't trouble the household unduly. Sie'd stood silent as Aunt Irad had changed the cook's menus and stood silent when the same aunt had raged at Enae because sie'd told the cook to disregard any changes he didn't have resources for. Sie had done and said nothing when, the very first day of the funeral week, an actual fistfight had broken out between two cousins over who would have which bedroom. Sie had remained silent when sie had heard one uncle say to a nuncle, *And look at hir, fifty-six years old and sitting at home sucking up to Grand-maman*, and the nuncle reply, *Well look at hir father's family, it's hardly a surprise.* Sie had walked on past when one cousin had surreptitiously slid a small silver dish into his pocket, while another loudly declared that she would be making some changes if she were so fortunate as to inherit the house. And in the meantime, sie had made sure that meals arrived on time and the house was kept in order. That had been the trick, all these years, of living with Grandmaman—keep calm, keep quiet, keep things running smoothly.

Grandmaman had told Enae many times that sie was her only remaining heir. But she had also said—many times— that Enae was an embarrassment. A failure. As far as the Athturs had fallen since Grandmaman's days—look at all those grandchildren and great-grandchildren and nephews and nieces and niblings of whatever degree abasing them-selves to win her favor in the desperate hope that she'd leave them something in her will—as pathetic as they were, Enae was worse. Nearly sixty and no career, no friends, no lovers, no marital partners, no children. What had sie done with hir life? Nothing.

Enae had kept calm, had not said that when sie had had friends they had not been good enough for Grandmaman. That when sie had shown any sign of wanting to do something that might take hir out of the house, Grandmaman had forbidden it.

Keep calm, keep quiet, keep things running smoothly.

At the crematory, Grandmaman's corpse slid into the flames, and the funeral priest sang the farewell chants. Aunt Irad and three different cousins stepped forward to thank him for officiating and to suggest that they might donate money for future prayers for the Blessed Deceased. Enae could feel everyone else glancing toward hir, yet again, to see hir reaction to others acting as though they were the head of the family, the chief mourner, the now-Matriarch (or Patriarch or Natriarch, as the case may be) of the ancient family of Athtur.

"Well," said Aunt Irad, finished with her loud and obvious consultation with the funeral priest, "I've ordered coffee and sandwiches to be set out in the Peony Room." And marched back toward the house, not even looking to see if anyone followed her.

Back at the house, there was no coffee and sandwiches in the Peony Room. Aunt Irad turned immediately to Enae, who shrugged as though it wasn't any of hir business. It wasn't anymore—technically, Grandmaman's will would have taken effect the moment her body slid into the flames, but the habit of ordering the household died hard. With a quick blink sie sent a query to the kitchen.

No reply. And then someone dressed as a servant, but who

Enae had never, ever seen before, came into the Peony Room and coolly informed them all that refreshments had in fact been set out in the Blue Sitting Room and their collective presence was requested there, and then turned and walked away, ignoring Aunt Irad's protests.

In the Blue Sitting Room, another complete stranger sat in one of the damask-upholstered armchairs, drinking coffee: a lanky, fair-skinned woman who smiled at all of them as they came in and stopped and stared. "Good morning. I'm so sorry for your loss."

"Who the hell are you?" asked Aunt Irad, indignant.

"A few minutes ago, I was Zemil Igoeto," said the woman as she set her coffee down on a mother-of-pearl inlaid side table. "But when the Blessed Deceased ascended, I became Zemil Athtur." Silence. "I don't believe in drawing things out. I will be direct. None of you have inherited anything. There wasn't anything to inherit. I have owned all of this"— she gestured around her, taking in the Blue Sitting Room and presumably the whole house—"for some years."

"That can't be right," said Aunt Irad. "Is this some kind of joke?"

Grandmaman would have thought it a joke, thought Enae. *She must have laughed to herself even as she was dying, to think of the looks on everyone's faces right now*. Everything had seemed distant and strange since Grandmaman had died, but now Enae had the feeling that sie wasn't really here, that sie was watching some sort of play or entertainment that sie wasn't terribly interested in.

"Fifteen years ago," said Zemil Igoeto—no, Zemil Athtur— "the Blessed Deceased found herself completely broke. At the same time, while I had plenty of funds, I wanted some way to gain access to the sort of influence that is only available to the oldest families. She and I came to an agreement and made it legally binding. In, I need not tell you, the presence of authorized witnesses. I would purchase everything she owned. The sum would be sufficient to support her in excellent style for the rest of her life, and she would have the use of all the properties that had formerly been hers. In return, on her ascension to the Realm of the Blessed Dead, I would become her daughter and sole heir."

Silence. Enae wasn't sure if sie wanted to laugh or not, but the fact was, Grandmaman would *very* much have enjoyed this moment if she could have been here. It was just like her to have done this. And how could Enae complain? Sie'd lived here for years in, as Ms Zemil Athtur had just said, excellent style. Enae couldn't possibly have any complaints.

"This is ridiculous," said Aunt Irad. She looked at Enae. "Is this one of the Blessed Deceased's jokes? Or is it yours?"

"Mx Athtur has nothing to do with any of this," cut in Zemil. "Sie had no idea until this moment. Only I, the Blessed Deceased's jurist, and the Blessed Deceased herself knew anything about it. Apart from the witnesses involved, of course, whom you are free to consult as confirmation."

"So we get *nothing*," said the cousin who had declared her intention to make changes once she'd inherited.

"Correct," said Zemil Athtur, picking up her coffee again. She took a sip. "The Blessed Deceased wanted to be sure I told you that you're all selfish and greedy, and she wishes she could be here to see you when you learn you've been cut off with nothing. With one exception."

Everyone turned to look at Enae.

Zemil continued, "I am to provide for Mx Enae Athtur, with certain stipulations and restrictions, which I will discuss with hir later."

"The will," said a cousin. "I want to see the will. I want to see the documents involved. I'll be speaking with my jurist."

"Do, by all means," said Zemil, and Enae felt the itch of a message arriving. Sie looked, and saw a list of files. Documents. Contracts. Contact information for the Office of Witnesses. "In the meantime, do sit and have a sandwich while the servants finish packing your things."

It took some time, and a half dozen looming servants (who, once again, Enae had never seen before), but eventually the aunts and uncles and nuncles and cousins had left the house, picked their luggage up off the drive, and gone elsewhere, threatening lawsuits all the while.

Enae had remained in the Blue Sitting Room, unwilling to go up to hir room to see if hir things were still there or not. Sie sat, more or less relaxed, in a damask-upholstered armchair. Sie badly wanted a cup of coffee, and maybe a sandwich, but sie found sie couldn't bring hirself to get up from the chair. The whole world seemed unreal and uncertain, and sie wasn't sure what would happen if sie moved too much. Zemil, too, stayed sitting in her damasked chair, drinking coffee and smiling.

At some point, after the house had quieted, Grandmaman's jurist arrived. "Ah, Mx Athtur. I'm so sorry for your loss. I know you loved your grandmother very much, and spent your life attending to her. You should be allowed to take some time to yourself right now, and grieve." He didn't overtly direct this to Zemil, sitting in the armchair across from Enae, but his words seemed intended for her. Then he did turn to her and nodded in greeting. "Ms Athtur."

"I am fully aware," said Zemil, with a faint smile, "that I'm tasked with providing for Mx Athtur, and I will."

"I would like some time to read the relevant documents, please," said Enae, as politely as sie could, and braced hirself to argue with an angry refusal.

"Of course," said the jurist, "and I'll be happy to go through them with you if you need."

Enae, at a loss for some reason, said, "Thank you."

"You'll see, when you read it," said Zemil, "that I am obligated to provide for you, as I said. How I am to provide for you is up to me, within certain parameters. I have had years to consider what that might mean, for both of us."

"Your provisions will meet the requirements of the will," said the jurist, sharply. "I will be certain of it."

"I don't understand." Enae suppressed a sudden, unexpected welling of tears. "I don't understand how this happened." And then, realizing how that might sound, "I didn't expect to inherit anything. Gr...the Blessed Deceased always said she would leave her houses and money to whoever she wanted." *Watch them gather around my corpse when I'm gone*, she'd said, with relish. *Ungrateful, disloyal while I lived, but watch them come the moment they think they might get something from me.* And she'd patted Enae's hand and made the tiny huff that was her laughter, near the end.

"As I said," said Zemil, "the Blessed Deceased was facing bankruptcy. Her income had declined, and she had refused to alter her way of living. It took several years to negotiate—our ancestor was stubborn, as I'm sure you know—but ultimately she had no choice if she was to continue living here, in the way she was accustomed to."

Enae didn't know what to say. Sie hardly even knew how to breathe, in this moment.

"I wanted the name," said Zemil. "I have wealth, and some influence. But I'm a newcomer to wealth and influence, at least according to the oldest families. An interloper. Our ancestor made sure to tell me so, on several occasions. But no longer. Now I am an Athtur. And now the Athturs are wealthy again."

Another unfamiliar servant came in, to clear the food and the coffee away. Enae hadn't eaten anything. Sie could feel the hollow in hir stomach, but sie couldn't bring hirself to take a sandwich now, knew sie wouldn't be able to eat it if sie did. Grandmaman's jurist waved the servant over, muttered in her ear. The servant made a plate with two small sandwiches, poured a cup of coffee, handed both to Enae, and then took the rest and left the room.

"Have you dismissed the servants?" Enae asked. Sie'd meant to sound casual, curious, but hir tone came out rough and resentful.

"You are no longer the housekeeper here, Mx Athtur," Zemil replied.

"I was until this morning, and if I'd known people were going to lose their jobs I'd have done what I could for them. They've worked for us a long time."

"You think I'm cruel," said Zemil. "Heartless. But I am only direct. No servants have been dismissed. None will be who perform their jobs well. Does that satisfy you?"

"Yes."

"I will do you no favors," Zemil continued, "leaving you in any misapprehension or uncertainty. As I said, what I wanted in this transaction was the Athtur name. There will be some reluctance on the part of the other old families to accept my legitimacy, and that will be made more difficult if you are here as an example of a true Athtur, one who so loyally cared for hir Grandmaman for so long, and rightfully ought to have inherited—in contrast with my false, purchased hold on the name. But I am also obligated to support you. Understand, I bear you no ill will, and I have no objection to providing for you, but I need you gone. I have, therefore, found employment for you."

"Ms Athtur…" the jurist began, reproachfully.

Zemil raised a forestalling hand. "You may stay here for another month, to complete the time of mourning. And then you will take a position with the Office of Diplomacy. Your assignment is already arranged. You will find it congenial, I assure you."

"You could just leave me my allowance," said Enae. "I could move out."

"Would you?" asked Zemil. "Where would you go?"

"I have a month to figure that out," sie replied, not sure sie had understood anything anyone had said for the past five minutes, not even sure what sie, hirself, was saying.

"Let me tell you what your position would be in the Office of Diplomacy. You have been appointed Special Investigator, and a case has been assigned to you. It is a situation of great diplomatic delicacy. Perhaps we should discuss this in private." She glanced at the jurist.

"I'm not going anywhere," he said, and crossed his arms very decidedly.

"You don't work for Mx Athtur," Zemil pointed out.

"No," he acknowledged. "In this matter, I represent the interests of the Blessed Deceased. And consequently, I will be certain that her grandchild is appropriately cared for."

"If she were here..." began Zemil.

"But she's *not* here," said the jurist. "We have only her expressed desire, and your agreement to that."

Zemil made an expression as though she'd bitten into something sour. "All right then. Enae, you've been assigned..."

"Mx Athtur," said Enae, hardly believing it had come out of her mouth.

To Enae's shock, Zemil smiled. "Mx Athtur. You've been assigned, as I've said, to a matter of some delicacy. Some years ago, the Radchaai Translators Office approached the Office of Diplomacy to request our help in tracking down a fugitive."

Radchaai! The Radch was an enormous, multisystem empire, far enough away that no one here in Saeniss Polity felt immediately threatened by them—especially now, with the Radchaai embroiled in their own internal struggles—but close enough and powerful enough that Radchaai was one of the languages the well educated often elected to study. The Translators Office was the Radchaai diplomatic service. Enae felt the itch of files arriving. "I've sent you the details," said Zemil.

Enae blinked the message open, read the opening summary. "This incident happened two hundred years ago!"

"Yes," Zemil agreed. "The Office of Diplomacy assigned

an investigator when the request first came in, who decided the fugitive wasn't here in Saeniss Polity or even anywhere in this system, and what with one thing and another the matter was dropped."

"But…how am I supposed to find someone who's been missing for two hundred years?"

Zemil shrugged. "I haven't the least idea. But I rather imagine it will involve travel, and a per diem on top of your wages. On top of your existing allowance, which I have no plans to discontinue. Indeed, the Blessed Deceased was quite miserly in the matter of your allowance, and I believe I'll be increasing it." She turned to the jurist. "There, are you satisfied?" The jurist made a noncommittal noise, and Zemil turned back to Enae. "Honestly, no one cares if you find this person or not. No one expects you to find anything at all. You're being paid to travel, and maybe look into an old puzzle if you feel like it. Haven't you ever wanted to leave here?"

Sie had always wanted to leave here.

Sie couldn't think. Not right now. "I've just lost my grandmother," sie said, tears welling again, sie didn't know from where. "And I've had a terrible shock. I'm going to my room. If…" Sie looked Zemil directly in the eyes. "If it still is my room?"

"Of course," said Zemil.

Enae hadn't expected that easy acquiescence. Grandmaman would never have tolerated her acting all high-and-mighty like this. But what else was sie supposed to do? Grandmaman wasn't here anymore. Sie blinked, took a breath. Another. "If your people would be so kind as to bring me lunch and coffee there." Ridiculous, sie was still holding the sandwiches the servant had handed to hir, but sie couldn't even imagine eating them. Not these sandwiches, not here, not now. "And I'll have supper in my room as well."

"They'll be happy to help you any way you wish, as long as you're here," said Zemil.

Enae rose. Set hir untouched food back onto the sideboard. Sie turned and nodded to the jurist. "Thank you. I...thank you."

"Call me if you need me," he said.

Sie turned to Zemil, but found sie had no words to say, and so sie just fled to hir own room.

Reet

There were any number of people on Rurusk Station whose work could be done at whatever hour seemed best to them, so long as the work was done in a reasonable time. Reet was not one of them.

The private consultant he was meeting with presumably *was* one of them, but e had been inflexible enough that Reet had been tempted to refuse to meet at all. There was, after all, very little a consultant of any sort could have to say to him that could not be conveyed just as well by a text or voice message. But when Reet had begun to suggest so, the consultant had insisted. The meeting must be in person, and it must occur. Intrigued despite himself, Reet had agreed to the least ridiculously impossible time.

And now he stood here, in this...this facility, which had looked like nothing remarkable at the entrance (aside from an actual human keeping the door, instead of a bot, or people just coming and going freely as they did in most other places) but had turned out to be some sort of private lounge, filled with low tables and thick padded chairs and benches. And waiters, quiet and discreet, bringing food and drinks to the people sitting there talking quietly. Human waiters, not mechs or bots. Just like the guard at the door.

"You're late," said the consultant, when Reet presented himself. E lounged in one of the chairs, another person—a man, round-featured, brown-skinned with light, close-clipped hair—sitting in the seat next to em. An empty bench faced them both.

"I messaged you," replied Reet, not entirely able to keep exasperation out of his voice. "There was a pipe break. I couldn't leave until it was repaired." Surely they could smell the musty whiff of the pipeways on him—he had stripped off his thin coverall and shoved it in the recycler, but he hadn't stopped to shower, because he'd known he was late already and didn't want to be even later.

He could have showered and just gone home. He could be in his tiny room, sitting on his tiny bed, eating takeout dumplings, watching *Pirate Exiles of the Death Moons*.

"Come now, Mr Hluid," the consultant replied. "These state-mandated jobs are all make-work. Engineers fix the pipes by mech, surely, or the bots can do the repairs themselves."

Reet considered several answers, but rather than speaking he turned to leave.

"Wait!" cried the consultant.

The man sitting beside em laughed. "Perfect!" he chortled. "Absolutely perfect. You are certainly a Schan, all the way through!"

Reet stopped. Turned back. "I'm a what?"

"Three hundred years ago," said the consultant, "in Keroxane System, Lovehate Station was destroyed in…" E glanced at eir companion. "Let's call it a particularly violent civil dispute."

The man beside em frowned. "A dispute? It wasn't a *dispute*! The Hikipi rebelled against their Phen oppressors!" The consultant made a placatory gesture.

"I'm aware of what happened on Lovehate Station," Reet cut in. And was suddenly struck with the disturbingly appealing vision of stepping forward, grabbing this man by the neck, and biting into his cheek, teeth sinking into flesh. Impulse followed vision, but Reet kept himself standing straight and still.

"Records were lost in the destruction," said the man, eagerly, his agitation gone as soon as it had come. Reet imagined peeling off the man's skin, as though it were one of the cheap coveralls he worked in. What would he see?

The man continued speaking, oblivious. "Centuries of history, of culture, of genetic data, of nearly everything—gone. All that's left is the records of a few of us whose ancestors left Lovehate Station years before. And of course, the Schans, the ancient Hikipi rulers of Lovehate Station, were supposed to have been destroyed long before that. But there have always been rumors that some escaped that destruction. Imagine if we could find them, the descendants of the Schans. What would that do to the struggle against the Phen?"

"Please sit down," said the consultant. Reet did not, and the consultant went on with a small shrug. "You arrived here as an infant, an orphan refugee, some three decades ago. No family, no adults claimed you."

"I'm not related to any of the families on this station," said Reet. "Hikipi or otherwise. They checked my genetics."

"The Schans were always very secretive about their genetic data," said the man. "I'm Heroth Nadkal, by the way. President of the Siblings of Hikipu here on Rurusk Station."

"The Schans," said the consultant, "were very much their own clan within Lovehate Station when they were in power. They're rumored to have made alterations to all their members—by birth or otherwise."

"You could always tell a Schan," said Mr Nadkal. "By their manner, certainly." He indicated Reet with one hand, smiling. "But there were other ways. What those ways were…we think we have discovered."

"Your route to this station, what we know of it, fits with someone who might have come from Lovehate Station," said the consultant. "And your genes are distinctly odd. I would even say those oddities are unique."

"I'm aware," said Reet shortly. He took a breath, willing the disturbingly attractive images of skinless Nadkal away. "If those oddities had been even remotely connected to any of the Hikipi families here, surely you would have claimed me before now." He should have gone back to his room after work and ignored this appointment. He should never have taken it to begin with. He should leave, right now.

"But no one was looking for a *Schan*, were they," replied Nadkal, as though that disposed of the matter. "This is the result of decades of research, and careful piecing together of what fragments of information and tradition we might have." He laughed. "Just seeing you stand there—you're a Schan. I'm convinced of it." He nodded. Turned to the consultant.

"I've transmitted your fee. Well deserved, I do say. And you"—he turned again to Reet—"Mr..." For some reason, Mr Nadkal hesitated.

Reet suspected he knew what that reason was, but maybe not. Maybe it was something else. Maybe it wasn't because Reet's family name—the parents who had adopted him—belonged to what most Zeoseni would consider the wrong ethnic group. "Mr Hluid."

"No," said Nadkal. "Mr *Schan*. Depend on it. Heir to a long and glorious history. And there may not be any other Schans, here or anywhere else, but you have, I assure you, the friendship and support—and family!—of the Siblings of Hikipu. Come to our next meeting, Mr Schan." Mr Nadkal chuckled, and rubbed his hands together. "Mr Schan. At long last, at long last. Come to our next meeting, Mr Schan, and discover what it is to be part of a community. You aren't on your own anymore. You know who you are now."

It was too much to handle all at once. Reet stared at Mr Nadkal, his gut gone sickeningly tense, as though Mr Nadkal had threatened him. When it was Reet who had been imagining taking him apart. When Mr Nadkal had, in fact, just offered Reet the thing he had always wished for and always known he could never have: a history. An identity that was part of something else, not just Reet, solitary. Alone. It was too much.

There would be blood under the skin, and muscles. And if those were stripped away...

"Fuck this," said Reet. "I'm going home and having supper."

Nadkal laughed again. "Schan!" he cried. "You're a Schan to the core!"

* * *

Reet bought dumplings and then splurged on a tiny milk jelly, and took it all back to his room. He had friends, or at least friendly acquaintances. Some of them (most of the people he'd known as a child) had fallen away somehow over the years. Others—well, Reet found he was in no mood to share anyone's company, let alone try to explain what had just happened. He sat on his bed, back against the wall that a former occupant had painted with a scrawled stick figure of the goddex of good fortune, one schematic hand raised in blessing.

The dumplings were filled with some indefinite mixture of protein and plant material, strongly spiced. The familiarity of the flavor was usually soothing, but today he was too tense, and the food nauseated him. What was wrong with him? It wasn't just Mr Nadkal and the fucking Siblings of Hikipu. It wasn't just the sudden vision of stripping another human being down to component parts—that was something that had followed Reet, on and off, since he'd been a child. *What excites you?* a counselor had asked him when he'd been much younger. *What do you dream of doing? That's where to look for your place, the thing you'll prepare for.*

With trepidation Reet had confessed his desire to dissect the people around him. She'd gone straight to his foster parents, who had insisted he hadn't meant it, it was a joke, Reet was certainly a very *odd* child but he wasn't violent, not counting that time when he'd been little and had that problem with biting.

The counselor had accepted Reet's apology, and he had never told anyone about his desires after that. He'd reached adulthood, not found qualifying work, and so he'd had to take a state job or pay the sloth tax, which of course he couldn't afford since he had no one willing or able to pay it for him, and no paying job. For the past fifteen years he'd worked in the station's pipeways, following the bots, repairing them or bringing them back to Central if they were beyond Reet's ability to fix. Looking for faults or breaks that hadn't registered on the system. It was dull. It was isolated. It was, in the absence of any other opportunity, perfectly fine.

Odd. He was more than odd. There was something *wrong* with him.

He'd meant to watch *Pirate Exiles.* Instead he closed his eyes and requested information on Hikipi history. He could guess, of course, who and what the Siblings of Hikipu were. Plenty of the people on Rurusk Station and in Zeosen generally considered themselves to be ethnically Hikipi, and so he knew a few basic bits of information: most Hikipi practiced Madeb Chenala rather than Del-tai Chenala, which was the majority Chenala sect on Rurusk; most Hikipi had come here to escape persecution by the Phen; the Hikipi had an ancient and proud history, of which Reet only knew names and some bare facts, including Lovehate Station and its destruction.

But what about the Schans?

Ah, the Schans. Before the Phen had come, the Schans had ruled all of Hikipi space, though their activities had been centered on Lovehate Station. There were seven Zones, each with its Autarch, all of whom answered to the Sovereign Autarch, who was, for six hundred years, a Schan.

The first Schan had arrived on Lovehate Station mysteriously, an infant alone in an unmarked shuttle, just as the inhabitants of Lovehate Station were debating the question of who should rule them. (That small, surely legendary bit of information made Reet shiver with recognition.) The shuttle might have come from anywhere, or nowhere, or never existed at all, but that child's descendants ruled Lovehate Station for six centuries after. They had been deposed, finally, by a conspiracy of Zone Autarchs, who had banded together and killed every Schan they could find, and then proceeded to fight among themselves for the Sovereign Autarchy. For the next several centuries Hikipi space had been at war with itself until the Phen invaded, uniting the fractious Zones against a common enemy. Mostly. Sort of.

The Schans had been benevolent rulers whose end meant the loss of the glory days of the Hikipi. Or they had been brutal dictators. It was hard to know for certain. Records were continually lost in the wars between the stations and the struggles against the Phen, and of course when Lovehate Station had been destroyed, all its records had gone with it. There was certainly no way to know if all the Schans were really dead.

You're a Schan to the core, Mr Nadkal had said. It was the first time anyone had reacted to Reet with recognition instead of doubt or puzzlement. Or contempt.

Could it be true? Reet didn't think it was likely. Lovehate had been dust for centuries, Mr Nadkal had almost certainly been born right here on Rurusk Station and so had the rest of the Siblings of Hikipu. The Schans had been driven out of Lovehate a thousand years ago, none of the Siblings of Hikipu could know one when they saw one.

Or could they?

If the Schans had changed themselves, genetically marked

themselves somehow as different from everyone else on Love-hate Station, might their descendants seem...strange to the people around them? Might their makeup seem distinctly odd, especially far from their place of origin, with no other Schans around to compare them to?

It didn't seem likely. It didn't seem likely that they'd marked their members with the persistent urge to vivisect other people. But if they had...Reet should at least look into it.

He opened his eyes. Set aside the carton of dumplings, ate the milk jelly, and lay down on the bed and started up an episode of *Pirate Exiles of the Death Moons*.

Qven

None of us is wasted. They make sure to tell us that, to assure us that each Tiny, sliding slick and slimy into its warm tray, has been designed, intended for some essential role. They don't tell you—at least when you're a Little or a Small, and probably not even after that, not in so many words—that they make a few extras. Just in case. They don't tell you, so of course no one ever tells you *you're* an extra.

I wasn't an extra. I toddled out of the Tiny beds and into the slightly wider world of the Littles with not a care. By the time I grew from Little to Small, I had developed a comfortable sense of my own importance to the world, to the other Smalls around me. I knew that the larger figures around us who fed us, who instructed us in various proprieties (*don't put that in your ear!; no, don't bite off her finger!*) would keep me safe and comfortable.

None of that changed when I reached the Middles. Except

that the world became wider still, and those caring, comforting figures mostly disappeared.

It's in your Middles that you begin to be more intensely fascinated by what might be inside those around you. The Middle quarters are soft, the blue-veined ground warm and yielding, tensing sometimes in response to pressure. Walls, where there might be rooms, opened when you might want a door. Or not, you could never really depend on a wall opening when you needed it. The growths in the wide places— tall, fleshy towers ragged here and there with patches of cilia; translucent blue mounds that crept slowly along the ground; a million different small, bright-colored things that came and went—none of them had anything sharp or rigid about them. There were no rocks, no glass, no sticks, nothing to make any tool to cut or stab.

We found a way. The first Middle I saw opened up was an unpopular, inoffensive creature whose only crime, I thought, was being weak. Now I suspect their real crime was being not sufficiently zealously protected by those Adults who'd cared for us when we were Tinies and Littles and Smalls. You wouldn't think private disdain would communicate itself so clearly to us, oblivious as we were to any but our own fascinations and concerns, but I believe now that it can, and does.

It was shocking, and titillating, to see the layer of yellow fat under the skin, the liver gleaming smooth and wet beneath the ribs. One of us pushed the guts aside to reveal kidneys. But just as a few Middles began to explore ways to crack the sternum and reveal the frantically beating heart, the ground gaped and cilia pulled the screaming, sobbing Middle away.

They came back, after a while, and tried to hide from us,

but we found them and removed a leg. (The muscles! The tendons! The pop of the joint when we levered it apart!) They were taken away again, and never returned. The leg was left behind, though, and that was amusing for a while.

They weren't the only Middle that happened to. But of course it never happened to *me*. Not even the threat of it. I assumed—if I thought about it at all—that I was just better than those victims. That there had been something fundamentally consumable about them.

Out of the Middles, then, and into the Edges. The Edge is the boundary, the last layer of childish existence. I never thought to measure time as it flowed past, never looked ahead to any future that might have been different from the present, but in the Edges, you begin to count, to see what might be coming. In the Edges, you begin to realize that childhood is not eternal.

We're in the Edges much longer than the Tinies or the Littles, Smalls, or Middles. So there are far more of us there at one time, and a far wider difference between those of us who've just arrived and those who are about to exit into the World. Those senior Edges can be remote, disdainful of the new ones just emerged, or they can be helpful. Solicitous, even.

In the Edges, we begin to learn the things we'll need to know out in the World. I was assigned a room with objects I was meant to sit and sleep on. I ate odd-tasting mixtures out of dishes, not with my hands but with tools specially made for the purpose of lifting food into my mouth. I was introduced to clothes, which I didn't like but eventually grew used to. I began to learn the language of humans.

"Why can't we just eat a Teacher?" I asked one of the older Edges who had been friendly to me more or less since I'd arrived.

My companion lay on the floor of my room, legs up against the wall—minor, casual rebellion, the sort of thing you do when no Teacher is around. Now they made a shocked face. But the older Edges were used to treading the boundaries of the acceptable. "It wouldn't work. Not the way you'd want it to. And even if it did, you'd be stuck with the miserable thing for the rest of your existence. And the other Teachers would definitely be unhappy with you."

I frowned, pondering. The Teachers took care of us, taught us, of course. The older Edges I was acquainted with made it clear that Teachers were to be obeyed at all times, but also that Teachers were inferior beings whose particular quirks or private feelings were beneath consideration.

"You don't want to make them too angry," said my companion, from the floor. "They can hurt you. Or..." They swung their legs down, rolled over. "Not *us*, you know. They can't do much of any consequence to *us*. But they can make things very unpleasant. And a replacement Teacher is an adjustment. Not always a good one."

I sighed. "But it would be so much easier."

"Can you imagine them letting you be a Diplomatic Operative"—they switched momentarily into human language—"a Translator, with a Teacher inside you? You know they're bred for teaching, nothing better. Or else they're a Failed and can't even do the thing they were meant for."

I knew these things. My companion was not telling me this because they thought I didn't know it, but to be absolutely certain that I *understood* it. Because if I did not, I, too, might become one of the Failed.

"Really," continued my companion, "it's not something to even joke about."

"I know," I acknowledged. "It's just so frustrating! All the stupid rules! Eat with a spoon. Put clothes on your feet. Sit on the chairs." My companion, still lying on the floor, snickered. "Say *thank you* and *if you please*. In human language, begging your indulgence!"

"Radchaai," corrected my companion, mocking the prissy pedanticism of a Teacher. "If you please."

"Excrete into the special excretion receptacles!" I went on. "Sleep on the sleeping furniture! And never, ever open anyone up."

"At least not anyone worth caring about," said my companion.

I laughed. Because it was true, there were here, as there had been among the Middles, some of us who were weak and prone to being victimized. No matter what the rules were, some of them got opened up. But—despite there being more of us here—not as many as in the Middles. They tended to hang together here, and there was always the possibility that they might resist. Besides, if a Teacher caught you, there would almost certainly be some sort of penalty.

You're in the Edges for decades. As you go along, as you learn the things you'll need to know in the World, you learn what those first signs are, that you're ready, that you've become an active danger to your former fellow Edges, no longer an Edge yourself.

This is what the Teachers tell you: when you exit into the

World, you'll take the place you've been prepared for since birth, each of us chosen for our suitability, without reference to favoritism or any sort of partiality. Each role is necessary and noble, part of our great work, and we will all be happy and fulfilled.

It's all a lie.

Enae

Enae spent several days reading over all the documents—the ones pertaining to Grandmaman's will and the ones from the Office of Diplomacy. Most of the will-related ones sie didn't really understand, and sie soon set them aside. The various jurists hired by the aunts and uncles and nuncles and cousins would certainly be examining the documents closely, and sie hirself could call on Grandmaman's jurist sometime soon to go over them. There was no hurry to understand it all.

The documents from the Office of Diplomacy interested hir more. They were all tagged *Secret VI*—not as confidential as things came, in Saeniss Polity, but close enough. Apparently Ambassador Tiniye, Radchaai emissary to the Presger, had come to Saeniss herself to request help in tracking down this fugitive. There would be no checking with her on the fugitive's current status—Ambassador Tiniye had died some time ago, and the current emissary to the Presger was someone named Seimet.

Ambassador Seimet wasn't likely to be paying much attention to this particular issue just now—something had happened in Radchaai space about ten years ago (Enae was vague on the details), and the multibodied Radchaai ruler, Anaander Mianaai, had split into factions of herself and begun a civil war. Systems and whole Radchaai provinces had split off and been retaken and split off again. And on top of all that, the conscious artificial intelligences that the Radchaai used to control warships and large stations had declared themselves a Significant Species, with the attendant right to be admitted to the treaty with the Presger.

And the safety of every human, everywhere, depended on that treaty. It was the only thing that kept the Presger from tearing apart ships and stations—and human beings—wherever and whenever they liked.

A potential new treaty signatory meant a conclave, where the existing signatories would debate the issue. Enae was sure everyone in human space was paying at least some attention to the conclave that was about to begin. Parts of the treaty might be up for renegotiation—how many and which parts no one was quite clear on, but the possibility was both exciting and terrifying. Worse, if talks broke down, would the treaty collapse? Nobody wanted that.

So, Ambassador Seimet surely had her hands full right now. And Ambassador Tiniye had been unable or unwilling to give many details about this fugitive, only that they would be an obvious stranger who might have come to Saeniss from a limited number of other systems, and it was urgent they be found and turned over to the Radchaai Translators Office. The investigator assigned to the case had apparently not liked the implications of this, done a cursory search, and declared the matter unresolvable.

The involvement of the emissary to the Presger, and her urgency, did suggest that the person they were looking for was either Radchaai diplomatic staff in possession of dangerous information, or a Presger Translator. Enae guessed that those officials, two centuries ago, had been eager not to be responsible for any of it.

The Presger Translators were...well, they looked human. They looked human but even if they *were* in fact entirely human, they spoke for (and thus presumably with) the alien Presger. They were the conduit by which humans (an undifferentiated mass as far as the Presger were concerned, at least that was what Enae gathered) communicated with the other side in that treaty. No one with any sense wanted to entangle themselves in that situation, for their own safety. Not to mention the safety of basically every other human in the universe.

So the Office of Diplomacy had informed Ambassador Tiniye that, after a full investigation, it had been determined that the fugitive had never come through Saeniss, or its system, and then the matter had been shelved. And now, for no good reason at all as far as Enae could see, it had been handed to hir to follow up on.

After four days of taking all hir meals in hir room, Enae decided that no one could prevent hir from going down for breakfast. Sie found a half dozen strangers there, along with Zemil. At the head of the table, of course. "Good morning, Mx Athtur," Zemil said, cheerfully. "How are you today?"

"Fine, thank you," Enae said, and hesitated a moment.

Then, deciding that the best course was pretending everything was absolutely normal, sie went over to the sideboard, got hirself a cup of coffee, and sat at the table. Within moments, a servant—one sie knew—set a steaming bowl of soup in front of hir, the exact same breakfast sie had somewhat defiantly ordered the day after Grandmaman's funeral and every day since. Grandmaman had despised soup for breakfast and insisted that Enae eat something sensible, like bread or rice porridge or a salad. And sie hadn't been certain just how well or attentively the servants would treat hir, now there were so many more servants in the household and the ones who knew Enae were in the minority, and now Zemil had made hir status in the household so clear.

It was delicious soup, with just enough heat to it, with perfectly done noodles, with exactly the amount and sort of vegetables Enae liked, and a soft-boiled egg sitting right on top. It was perfect. It had to have been made by someone who knew Enae's tastes extremely well. And for some reason, that made Enae even less sure of hirself than sie had been when sie had walked into the dining room and seen all these strangers, breakfasting, relaxed, as though this was their own home.

Which of course it was.

Zemil introduced everyone at the table—Enae forgot their names as soon as Zemil said them—and then the others resumed chatting about people and events Enae knew nothing of. Sie enjoyed hir soup in silence and let the talk wash over hir, until, when sie was slurping the last few noodles, the person across from hir said, "Mx Athtur, I hope you'll forgive me mentioning business at breakfast, but it seems I'm to be your supervisor at the Office of Diplomacy."

Enae blinked. Swallowed the noodles, and wiped hir mouth with hir napkin. "I haven't said I'll take the job."

An awkward silence. Then the person across from Enae said, "Maybe we can talk after breakfast. In..." Sie looked at Zemil. "The Peony Room? Will that be available?"

"Of course," said Zemil. "I don't like the Peony Room. It's much too gaudy."

"I think it's pretty," said the person who had addressed Enae. "So if you don't like it, Aunt, I'll just claim it for myself." Sie turned to Enae. "The Peony Room, then, once we've finished with breakfast. Will that be all right?"

It took Enae a few seconds to realize that this person was consulting Enae about hir own preference and convenience. "That'll be fine," sie said. After all, it wasn't like sie had anything else to do.

Enae hirself quite liked the Peony Room. The walls were painted with leaves and giant pink and white peonies. The chairs were upholstered in yet more pink and white, the arms and legs gilded, and the side tables were enormous peonies, their huge, carved wooden petals making them nearly unusable as tables. A row of cabinets sat open to display more peonies—blown glass, carved gems, cast or hammered silver and gold. Enae had loved them since sie had been small. And Zemil was right, it was all incredibly gaudy.

"I'm Caphing," said the person—hir proposed supervisor and, Enae supposed, hir cousin now. "I know Aunt introduced us, but you can't possibly have kept us all straight. Would it be all right if I called you Enae?"

"I suppose so." Sie found hirself at a loss again, and then

remembered that sie lived here, had lived here all of hir life, that this other person—Caphing—was the interloper. Sie chose a chair and sat.

Caphing smiled, and sat in a chair on the other side of one of the unusable tables. "Thank you. It does seem odd for us to be calling each other Mx Athtur, don't you think?" Sie shook hir head. "I'm still getting used to that. I was Caphing Igoeto just the other day."

Enae wasn't certain what she could reply to that. "You wanted...?"

"To talk about your being an investigator for the Office of Diplomacy. Now, I know you said at breakfast that you haven't agreed to take the job, but honestly, Aunt usually gets what she wants. I don't mean to pressure you or, gods help us, threaten you, because the truth of the matter is she can't actually *make* you go, but she'll do whatever she can to *get* you to go, if you know what I mean."

"I'm not sure how much she can do," Enae found hirself saying. Sie folded hir hands primly in hir lap. "She's required to provide for me, and if I refuse to leave, any attempt to force me would probably look very bad."

"She likes you, you know," said Caphing. "Or at least, she's sympathetic. You stayed here for years taking care of the Blessed Deceased, who didn't even remotely appreciate how much you did for her and how much you put up with. Aunt thought you were all worn down to nothing, but then you showed you had some backbone after all. Which Aunt says makes your grandmother's treatment of you even worse, but I don't see how it's different, honestly. I think I want some more coffee, would you like some, too? Maybe I'll just ask for coffee to be set up here every day, I *love* this room." Sie looked around happily.

"I've liked it since I was small," Enae found hirself confessing. Sie should probably have resented this person, sitting in the Peony Room as though sie owned it, as though this was hir house, which of course it was now. But sie found that sie liked Caphing, sie couldn't say why, exactly.

"Oh, of course, you grew up with it! How wonderful! So, listen—I've just ordered a coffee service, by the way, I have no idea where they'll set it up—"

"That complicated metal thing over there folds out," said Enae.

Caphing laughed, delighted. "Excellent! So, listen. You're right, Aunt can't force you to do anything. She can maneuver, and put pressure on, and any number of things, but let's be honest, you're used to things being not entirely pleasant. You're actually in a pretty good position here. Don't tell Aunt I said so, she'll be quite cross with me if she finds out, but it's only the truth. If there's something else you want to do, you could probably get her to agree to it."

What Enae wanted to do was stay here, in the house where sie had always lived. At least until sie figured out what else sie might want to do. But Zemil didn't want hir to stay, and honestly, Enae wasn't sure sie wanted to live with all these strangers. "I don't know," sie said. What Enae wanted to do was leave here and never come back. Sie had had all sorts of secret wishes and fantasies of leaving, over the years, but none of them ever seemed real. None of them seemed real even now.

Two servants—ones that Enae didn't recognize—came in with an urn of coffee, and sugar and cups and spoons, and hesitated, unsure where to put things. "Here," said Enae, and rose and folded out the metal thing into a huge, glittering array of stylized silver petals and leaves. Caphing actually gasped. "Oh, that's *amazing*. I am definitely having meetings here *every day*. Please tell me you did your household administrative work here all these years. I mean, what's the point of having something like that and not using it?"

Enae made a noncommittal noise. Grandmaman had said that it was too much trouble to open the Peony Sideboard just for hir. It had only been for the most special of occasions.

"So," said Caphing, when sie had gotten hirself a cup of coffee from the shining, elaborate sideboard. "As I was saying. You can probably do anything you like, just come up with a plan and then negotiate with Aunt. Which is the sticky bit, I admit, but like I said, you're in a pretty good position. If I were you…" Sie took a sip of coffee. "If I were you, honestly, I'd take the job but demand an increase in my allowance."

"A what?" Enae was astonished. The amount Zemil had proposed to give hir was already an unconscionably high number. "How could I possibly justify that?"

"Look, this job is impossible. It's just a cover. I mean, you could go looking for this fugitive if you wanted, but you don't have to. You're not expected to. You'd basically make a bunch of stops and visit embassies and make formal requests for information that you probably won't get. No one thinks you'll be able to find this person, but it's important right now to be seen to be looking."

"The conclave," Enae guessed. The conclave, where the treaty that protected humanity from the Presger would possibly be up for renegotiation.

Caphing gestured toward Enae with hir coffee cup. "Precisely. With a conclave starting up, and Presger attention presumably on humans in general, no one wants to seem unconcerned about the safety of one of their Translators in human space. Not that this will affect any of that. It's just a loose end that the Office of Diplomacy would like tidied up. It's for the appearance, really. Whoever this person was, they're likely dead by now. You aren't going to find them. So this is just a ridiculously overpaid travel jaunt for you. One of those positions they give out to scions of the most distinguished families who maybe need to be out of sight for a while." Sie took a sip of coffee.

"Like me," said Enae, ruefully.

"Exactly," agreed Caphing. "So make Aunt make it worth your while. I mean, she already intends to, but maybe her idea of *worth your while* isn't the same as yours, and you're the one who gets to decide that." The idea astonished Enae. Caphing continued. "Did you read the documents? The obvious first stop is Sixewa, and you could put up in a hotel or an apartment for *months*, and just...see the sights, you know, try the food. Relax. Whatever."

"I...but I'd be getting paid to do a *job*."

"Oh, yes, and mostly that job is meeting with our consular representatives in various places and asking if they have any information. Which they won't, but it's all about making the effort. There's no reason not to enjoy yourself, too. Have you ever traveled top class on an intersystem liner? It's *amazing*. They have restaurants, and spas, and all sorts of things. Of course, the Office of Diplomacy wouldn't send you anywhere on a top-class ticket, not unless you were an actual ambassador, but if your allowance were large enough, you could absolutely spend a month in transit sipping arrack and getting massages and mineral packs and whatnot. Have you ever had a mineral pack? It's *incredibly* relaxing."

Enae felt, suddenly, that sie could sit here all day and just talk with Caphing about mineral packs. Or all the beautiful things in the Peony Room. Instead, sie said, "I think if this fugitive came from the Presger, if this really is a Presger Translator we're talking about, it makes sense to start looking near the Treaty Administration Facility."

"You want a trip to the conclave!" exclaimed Caphing. "We might be able to do that eventually. The conclave will be going on for ages, you've got time. Make some friends with the consular officials you meet while you're traveling, and you'll have a chance at all kinds of posts. That's how that works."

No, Enae wanted to protest, *that's not what I mean.* But if sie'd learned one thing living with Grandmaman, it was that talking too much about eir plans beforehand was the surest way to have those plans criticized, nitpicked, negated. Better to think carefully and then go ahead and do what needed to be done and take the consequences later.

But Caphing seemed...like a friend. Sie couldn't possibly be, Enae had just met hir. Right?

"I can't do this," sie said aloud. "I haven't left this town in forty years. I've barely even left the *house.* I know how to make sure the household is running right, I knew how to deal with the Blessed Deceased." But sie had never known how to stand up to her. How to argue for what sie wanted. Hadn't known how to stand up to the relatives who'd invaded the house for Grandmaman's funeral. How could sie leave here, leave Saeniss Polity, even leave the system? How could sie even begin to know how to deal with things out there in the world, where wars were being fought, where a mistake might mean people dying?

Caphing said, "Running a household like this one isn't trivial. And from what I hear, dealing with the Blessed Deceased gave you a lot of diplomatic experience. And look—you were about to tell me where you would look for this fugitive, weren't you. Well?"

"No," said Enae, though Caphing was right. "It's just, I mean, there are only a few systems anyone could have gone to from the Treaty Administration Facility. I guess there's no reason to assume they came from there, since the Presger can be pretty much anywhere, but I have to start somewhere."

"You know"—Caphing picked hir coffee up off the peony table—"I won't say I'm glad the Blessed Deceased has ascended, but you've been wasted all these years. You're going to be great at this."

Reet

Reet's foster parents lived on a terraformed moon, in a snug house at the edge of their town. They were, as always, glad to see him, and invited him to sit on their little terraçe, which looked out on the dark forms of agricultural bots stepping delicately across emerald grain fields. Reet sank onto a cushion, and Maman offered him coffee.

"Not still biting people, are you?" asked Nana, who had always been a bit blunt, a bit obtuse, along with eir obvious affection for all the foster children.

"Now, Min," said Mom, sitting beside em. "That was a long time ago." She gestured toward the halawa on the tray between them. "It's your favorite, Reet. From the shop down the road. I know you haven't been able to have it since you were here last."

"It's so good to see you," said Maman. "Ishat and Sukesi send their love. They aren't able to be here until next week."

Reet had always gotten along more or less well with his foster sibs, but he was sure they hadn't actually asked Maman to give him their love. That was just Maman being nice. "Brist will be here in a few days, right now she's on a language immersion retreat."

Reet barely knew Brist. She'd been adopted several years after he'd left for Rurusk. "That sounds nice."

"How are things in the station pipeways?" asked Mom.

"About the same as usual. Boring until it's not."

"I never understood why they sent you out there," said Nana. "They could have put you on farm work. You've got your mech certification. I think you should apply again. You are still looking for qualifying work, aren't you?"

"Yes, Nana." There was no point in giving any other answer.

"You just have to put yourself out there," said Nana. "Be persistent. It would be so nice to have you back here."

"It would be nice to be back," Reet said, not entirely untruthfully, but not entirely truthfully, either.

"So what else is happening?" asked Maman. "What about that nice boy you were seeing?"

"Oh, that's been over for a while," said Reet, and took a bite of halawa and a sip of coffee, so he couldn't say much more.

"What a shame," said Mom, pushing the plate of halawa nearer to Reet. "I did like him. But I've liked most of your lovers who we've met. You have good taste."

"You never message us enough, though," said Nana. "Anything else new in your life lately?"

Reet swallowed a mouthful of coffee. "Actually, yes." His

foster parents made interested noises. "Someone approached me recently claiming to know where I'm from."

That surprised even Nana into motionless silence. Then Maman said, "Are you…who? Where do they think you're from?"

"Lovehate Station apparently, in Keroxane System. A family called Schan."

"And what do the Schans say about this?" asked Nana. "How did they lose you? Where have they been all this time?"

"Dead," replied Reet, not without some satisfaction. He took another piece of halawa. It *was* his favorite. It tasted familiar and comforting.

"They don't have the genetic data of any of these Schans," observed Mom, as usual coming to the point immediately. "They can't, or we'd have known about a connection. Honestly, Reet, if you had any genetic relationship with anyone from Keroxane, I'm sure it would have come up before now."

"There's no way to know," said Reet. "We have genetic data from people claiming their ancestors came from Lovehate, but that's not the same thing as the genetic data of people who actually lived on the station."

Nana frowned. "I don't see why not."

"Not everyone will have escaped," Reet said. "There might have been any number of families whose genes were lost forever in the destruction. And the people who did escape, their ancestors may have come from Lovehate but they likely have other genes in the mix by now. It's been hundreds of years. And even longer since the Schans supposedly left. There's no way to know from someone's DNA if they had ancestors on Lovehate Station. We can only know if they've got genetic relatives among the descendants of the people who survived."

"I still don't see how that's not the same thing," said Nana.

Maman shushed em. "We can see it's very complicated. How do you feel about it? That's the important thing."

"I'm not sure," Reet admitted. "The stories about the Schans are different depending on who's telling them. Some people—the ones who came to me, I guess—think of them as part of Lovehate Station's glorious past. Some people say horrible things about them, that they were cruel dictators who kept themselves apart from the rest of the station." Reet had dreaded this moment, but he might as well get it over with. "Some people apparently say that the Schans tortured and murdered people, and even ate them."

"Oh, there's no question, then!" exclaimed Nana with a laugh. "You're a Schan."

"Nana!" reproved Maman. "That was a long time ago."

"I'm only joking," said Nana. "Reet doesn't mind, do you, Reet?"

Reet took another sip of coffee, while Nana fiddled with eir handheld. "There's an organization called the Siblings of Hikipu, and they want to meet me. I haven't made up my mind yet if I want to meet *them* or not. Even if I did claim the name, there's no other family except these people." His own handheld buzzed in his pocket. He slipped it out a little way. *I'm sorry*, from Nana. *I didn't mean to upset you*. Reet messaged back, *It's all right*. Even though it wasn't, really. He slipped the handheld back into his pocket.

"Ah, it all comes clear," said Nana aloud. "Be careful they don't just want someone to do the organizational work."

E considered for a moment. "Unless it's qualifying?" Reet looked a question at em. "You know how it is with clubs and such," Nana continued. "Everyone loves the *idea*, and they love to come to the parties or whatever, but no one wants to do the work to keep things going and make the parties *happen*. So you're maybe one of the ancient rulers of Lovehate Station, of course you'll want to administer their club. It's only your inheritance, right?" Nana laughed at what e clearly thought was eir own very good joke.

"I suppose you never know," replied Reet.

Later, after supper, he sat with Mom on the same terrace. The fields were dark now, the lights of some transport sailing overhead, green and yellow. Light shone through the house door, the only light on the terrace. Every few seconds a soft, plaintive note sounded, some insect Reet had never learned the name of.

"You mustn't mind Nana," said Mom. "It's just how e is."

"E apologized," said Reet.

"Oh, good!" She seemed relieved. "I couldn't believe it: you hadn't come to visit us in so long and e comes out with *that*, first thing. I know e's missed you. We all have. But…" She hesitated. "We miss you, but I'm glad you're at Rurusk Station and doing well." Reet felt a pang at the admission that Mom was happy to be rid of him. "Not because I don't want you here, or because I don't want to see you more often. I do. We all do. But I think you're happier with some distance. It used to make me sad, that somehow we'd failed you. But if you're doing well, if you're happy, then we haven't failed at all, have we."

Reet had never been one of them. Never really wanted to be one of them. Except sometimes he *had* wanted to. He didn't like being in the middle of two mutually exclusive wants, the dissonance of his distress unresolvable. "So, this thing with Lovehate Station."

"You know," said Mom, "for years we looked for your family, or at least some idea of where you might have come from. All we got was some suggestion of places your family might have traveled through to get here, based on the route of the ship they found you on. Eventually we gave up. And now it just falls in your lap!" She gave a little laugh. "And you get to have an interesting history without any of the annoying people to go with it."

"Well, there's still the Siblings of Hikipu. I..." He stopped. "I was really rude to the people who came to tell me. It was just after a long day at work, and the consultant was insulting. And the ruder I got, Mr Nadkal—that's the person from the Siblings of Hikipu—just kept laughing and saying I was obviously a Schan. But they've only got *stories* about the Schans, and..."

"And those stories are distressing. You don't have to claim the family, you know. In fact it might be better if you don't. It wouldn't surprise me if plenty of other people over the centuries have tried to claim it, if only for the fun of being feted by people like your Siblings of Hikipu. Do you want some more coffee?"

"No, with the time difference I'll never get to sleep."

They were silent awhile. The insect continued to sing, and others joined it. The sky overhead was dark and quiet. Mom said, "Those stories—you know, when people have power, they can do terrible things. But also, people who hate them can twist things around or exaggerate, and make them sound worse than they are. If there aren't any other Schans, then you can take the stories or leave them as you like."

It was difficult to leave these stories. Difficult for Reet to forget Mr Nadkal's delighted certainty that Reet was a Schan. "Supposedly the Schans marked themselves in some way. They did some sort of genemodding to themselves. At least that's what the stories say. And, I don't know, that might explain why my DNA is so different from anyone else's that we know of. But..." He fell silent.

Nana would have said the next part out loud. Mom understood, without him saying. "You know, your genes aren't your destiny. You in particular. You have what you have, whatever you were born with, but you get to decide what to do with that. There's nobody telling you what those genes *mean*, what they're supposed to make you."

"Except the Siblings of Hikipu," said Reet bitterly.

"What do *they* tell you it means to be a Schan?"

It meant Reet was rude, arrogant. A cannibal. A torturer. "I guess I don't know. I haven't talked with them yet." He'd come here first. Because...why? He wasn't sure. To sit here and have this conversation with Mom? To get his foster parents' approval?

"You don't have to if you don't want to," said Mom. "You know, you could always choose a family name for yourself." In the dark, Reet waved that possibility away. "A different one, I mean."

"How are things?" asked Reet. "I mean, I hear people talk, I hear the news. But."

"We're doing all right," said Mom. "We're lucky. Every now and then one of the neighbors will tell us how we're some of those *good* Chirra, not like those other ones they've heard about. But mostly people don't realize until they hear our name." She was silent a moment. "It might be easier for you with a different family name."

But this was the only family Reet had, no matter how ambivalent he felt about that. "No, I'm doing fine. But what the fuck are they *thinking*? Why the fuck are they bothering with *me*? Why the ever-loving fuck do they want a *real* Schan?"

"I think that last one is a good question," said Mom, "and I think you should get the answer to it as soon as possible."

"I should have asked." He'd just wanted to be away from that consultant, from Mr Nadkal.

"You were taken by surprise. But, Reet, be careful. Maybe it's nothing but nostalgia, for these people, or maybe it's like Nana says, they'll just want you to run their club. But you know things are unsettled in Keroxane, and someone looking for heirs to old authority might well be involved in things you wouldn't want to get mixed up in."

"What, they'd want me to lead a revolution against the Phen?" The idea struck Reet as ridiculous.

"Maybe," said Mom. "Then again, they're just as likely to be nothing more than a social club. But watch yourself. I won't tell you to stay away from any causes—you'll have to make your own choices. But be careful."

"I know, Mom. You've said this to every one of my sibs so far."

"There's a reason for that," said Mom. "Foreign Affairs is

always keeping an eye on political activity by certain groups. You can be sure they have plants in nearly every cultural social club in the system. Although most people around here wouldn't be suspicious of Hikipi."

"Not on Rurusk, either."

"Still." Mom reached out and ruffled his hair in the dark, a gesture that both annoyed Reet and pleased him. "It's your turn for the talk, and I never thought it would be. Just be careful. And no matter what, you don't have to be what they want you to be."

But what if I am anyway? he thought.

Mom rose, and held her hand out to him. "You've had a long day. We can talk more about this tomorrow if you want."

He took her hand, feeling like he was a sulking six-year-old. Which told him he was too tired to continue this conversation. Mom was right, as usual, so he stood and followed her inside.

Qven

None of us had names. Names were a thing we had to learn about when we reached the Edges. They're really just words, just a way to talk about things, but they're *fixed* in a way that was terribly unfamiliar to us new Edges, and it took some time before we understood the idea. Like human language itself, actually, which gave *everything* names and put all those names in fixed arrays of *things that belong together.* Even if you couldn't see how they did. Actually, though it took me time to understand enough for the Teachers to be satisfied, I was pretty good at names and categories.

When I'd been an Edge long enough to be comfortable in lessons, some Adults visited us. They stayed at a safe distance, of course, because no one with any kind of sense spends much time very near children (and Edges are their own particular danger). And from their safe distance they watched us sit in chairs and drink hot liquid out of porcelain bowls and say inexplicable things. *Good morning, how are you? I am fine. Perhaps we will have a walk today. The lilies are blooming in the pond. They are very pretty. Would you like more tea? Thank you, yes.* After a while, one of the Adults called the Teacher over, and then the Teacher beckoned me. "You're doing well," said the Adult to me, in human language.

"Thank you…" I hesitated over the courtesy title. "Thank you, Adult."

"Translator," corrected the Teacher.

"Thank you, Translator," I said.

The Adult smiled. "It won't be long," they said. "No, I don't think it will be long at all. Are you eager for it? To grow up and begin your work?"

"I suppose," I replied. "I hardly think about it. I have so much to learn right here."

They nodded. "Of course. And there will be more to learn, once you've matured. Much more. But I think you learn quickly. It's no surprise, really. The clade that produced you has always been among our best." Their tone suggested to me that they shared that clade with me, though such relationships weren't supposed to matter to us. "I'm glad to see that you live up to expectations."

"Thank you, Translator," I said again. "I'm working hard."

"Continue to do so." They gave a human bow. "Goodbye. It was nice to meet you."

"Goodbye, Translator. It's been an honor." Maybe a little too formal, but I thought the Translator appreciated it.

"They're already thinking of a match for you," said the

Teacher, when the Translator had gone. "I'm sure of it. In fact, it wouldn't surprise me if they'd begun sorting possible matches the moment you reached the Edges alive."

For some reason, this made me feel slightly sick to my stomach. "Oh, do you think so?" We were still speaking human language, of course, because it was still lesson time.

"Don't worry." Some of my discomfiture must have shown on my face, because the Teacher's tone was warm and comforting, in a way that reminded me of when I'd been a Little. "Your match will be an excellent one. Given how well you're doing, and your clade, they'll take very good care of you."

Was that a trace of bitterness in the Teacher's voice? Perhaps it was my slowly subsiding nausea that made me think such a thing. I'd never thought much about a Teacher's feelings before. "I'm sure you're right, Teacher," I said.

"Be careful around the other Edges," the Teacher said. "I think the Translator is right, it won't be long. And the others don't necessarily have your prospects. Any of them that realize it might try to...attach themselves to you in a way that would make it possible for them to share those prospects. Do you follow me?"

"Yes, Teacher." And I thought I did, though really I didn't quite.

"Good." The Teacher nodded. "Let's return to the lesson." And, walking back to the other Edges in the chairs, with their bowls of tea, "Oh dear, I think that's the pressure loss alarm, what shall we do?"

"Stay clear of the section doors," we chorused, and the rest of the lesson time was unremarkable.

*   *   *

It was something we whispered about sometimes, when there were no Teachers around—the prospect of our matches. We knew very little of how or when it would happen, beyond the fact that we might well be matched with one of our fellow Edges, but that was by no means a given. Any of us might be matched to anyone, even to several anyones. We might even be matched with Adults who were already matched. But what would it be like? Would it be like eating someone? Or like being eaten?

And that, I suppose, was the source of my nausea. I'd eaten a fair few others before I'd come to the Edges. Truth be told, I'd eaten some after, though we weren't supposed to, but there had never been much in the way of consequences for it. Those recent others, they hadn't been like me, though. Had they? I'd never thought much, as a Little or a Small or even a Middle, about what I was eating when I ate one of my fellows.

It was different now. Not because there was more or less to a Middle than there was to an Edge, no, that was about the same, except the Edges *knew* more things, and sometimes some of that came along when I ate. Never the whole of who it was, but feelings and thoughts that might drift up while I was eating, or for a while after. It was part of the flavor of eating someone, and for the first time I thought about the possibility that *I* might be eaten, what *I* might taste like. I considered the bits of an Edge who'd been in training as a Teacher, who a group of us had eaten not long before. They were different from / the same as me in a way familiar since I'd been small. Being matched couldn't be *that* different, could it?

The Teachers said it was different. They said that it wasn't the same thing at all. That when we matched, we wouldn't just be fragments inside someone, or them inside us. That instead we would be whole, part of a greater being. It was a beautiful thing, wonderful beyond description.

But I couldn't help wondering how that could be. How, in an event that sounded a good deal like being eaten, I wouldn't just be someone's very large, formal meal.

Understand, I'm not talking about doing sex. A lot of us start doing sex in the Middles, though some never do any. Just don't want to, I suppose. The Teachers told us that we did sex because we were partly human, and some humans like it better than others, and some don't like it at all. Which makes sense. I mean, not everyone likes everything the same. But the Teachers also warned us that humans often talk about doing sex in a way that makes it sound like matching, which it's not. Not at all. Lots of us Edges had done sex, but none of us had ever matched. If we were even close to being able to, the Teachers would have done their best to try to whisk us away before any of the other Edges even realized.

They didn't always manage it. There was a human-style garden we were encouraged to spend time in, with plants, and pathways. Some of the plants had bright flowers, red and blue and orange and yellow among the everywhere greens of the leaves. It's very colorful and smells strange, and the Edges are encouraged to spend time there, to act like humans and sit on the benches and stick our noses in the flowers and comment on how lovely and isn't the weather fine. And—very importantly—to not eat the little orange fish that live in the pond in the very center of the garden. This was a recent arrival, the Teachers told us, and a testament to the way the

Adults were always adding to our lessons, as time went by. The Teachers were very proud of that little pond, its lily pads and its little orange fish. Of course, we'd all eaten at least one fish, just to see. But not when a Teacher might be around.

The garden also offered enclosed spaces. Arched branches, vine-woven trellises, and even, if you were truly determined to have privacy, tall, bushy plants with branches that rose up and then dipped down to the ground, leaving a leaf-shrouded opening all around their center. Most Edges crawl underneath one once, but not after that, because the Teachers get upset if you get your human clothes dirty or torn. I don't know why—they clean and repair themselves after a while, even if you rip them to shreds—but who can say why Teachers do what they do. Anyway, we mostly left the underside of the big bushes alone, but once some of us found something horrible underneath one.

It was a big, pulsing mound of flesh, streaked and wrapped with blood vessels. Every now and then it would wiggle or shiver, or open some previously invisible orifice and gasp or sigh. Normally a strange creature with an unknown inside to be investigated would make me hungry, but this—I didn't understand why, but this made me dreadfully sick to my stomach. It was *wrong*, it shouldn't be here. The other Edges around me stared, fascinated, and before long a Teacher came by to investigate.

When the Teacher saw what it was, they screamed, a high, piercing shriek that made all of us cover our ears, and more Teachers came and ordered us away, back to our rooms, not to come out until authorized.

"They *matched*," said the Edge nearest me as we walked

swiftly back to our rooms. They said it quietly, as though it was essential they not be overheard. "They must have hidden it, that they were ready. Or one was ready and the other... wasn't."

"Stupid," whispered another nearby Edge. "So stupid to do that. And dangerous."

"They should tell us," said yet another. "I was ready to eat them. All those blood vessels. Everything underneath..."

"*Stop!*" hissed the first Edge urgently. "You'll get us all in trouble."

At the next lesson, the Teacher called aside those of us who had found the thing—the almost-Adult, I suppose, since whoever it had been definitely weren't Edges anymore. "I'm sorry you had to see that. Tell me, how did you feel when you found it?" They didn't need to say what *it* was.

"Hungry" was how the others answered, but I hadn't been hungry, I had been sick. And I had spent the time in my room afterward thinking, horrified, *Is that what matching is? Is that what it's like?* It was horrifying, even knowing that Adults—Adults like the Teachers, and the Translator who'd complimented me—had gone through that and come out fine. It was normal, it was expected. It was nothing to be afraid of. But I didn't want to be a thing like that, all covered in bare muscle and veins, that others would look at with *hunger*. I didn't. And I realized, too, very suddenly, why I might not have been as hungry as the other Edges.

They would take me away. They would take me from the Edges and make me match. I couldn't. I just couldn't. So, "Hungry," I said, along with everyone else, and the Teacher nodded, satisfied, and sent us back to our lessons.

* * *

Normally I went to sit in the garden after lessons. The Teachers liked that. They liked it especially if you asked them for dishes and tea and little cakes and laid them out on the furniture in the garden and sat with the other Edges and pretended to be humans having a tea party. Humans didn't do much of anything without having tea at some point in the process, and it was important to practice, and practicing outside of lessons demonstrated our suitability, and now I look back, no doubt cast a favorable light on the abilities of the Teachers. At any rate, I knew that it would be wise to do a tea party, to show things were still the way they had been before. But things weren't the way they had been before, and I didn't want to sit on a *chair* next to a *table* and ask the other Edges how they were and comment on the flavors of the cakes. I wanted to sit somewhere alone and try to understand what was happening. But I'd never done anything like that before, and maybe that would make the Teachers wonder about me.

But it turned out that some other Edge did a tea party, so I could go up to the table by the pond and take a cake and a bowl of tea, and say some things. (It helped to have an interest. It didn't matter what, so long as it gave you something to talk about. Fortunately I'd dropped the topic of skin and blood a while back. I now conversed about Shapes, which had the benefit of not being a direct reminder of what we'd recently found in the garden, and also being a difficult, very human concept that would win the approval of the Teachers.) A cake, a few comments about Circles and Squares, and I could take my bowl of tea and wander as if enraptured by a leaf here and a flower there, to a seat at a careful distance from the party.

I sipped tea. I put my nose by a flower and inhaled and smiled. I sipped more tea. And all the while I thought.

Thinking wasn't going to do me any good, though. I was trapped. There was nowhere to go. Delay it as long as I might, a match would overtake me. My body would do what it was made to do, there was no avoiding it, or so I understood. Even if there were, it meant failing, it meant never serving your purpose. And my purpose, the purpose of all the Edges here in this garden, was the highest there was—we none of us would exist if there wasn't a need to talk to humans. So we were the best, the most important. If we failed at that, what would that mean?

The others whispered about it sometimes. That not all of the ones who had disappeared along the way had been opened up too many times, or eaten. That some of those who disappeared had failed somehow, been taken away to some entirely other place, maybe even been disposed of. That if you messed up badly enough it would happen to you, too. Some of the other Edges seemed to enjoy whispering about it, I suppose they got some sort of pleasure out of imagining it, but I never had. It wasn't something I needed to worry about. After all, it was hardly likely that I'd ever fail, let alone that badly.

But here I was, failing. I should have spoken up, should have gone from the Edges the moment I realized. And yet.

I didn't think it was enough of a failure to get me sent to... wherever the failed ones went. Was it?

So no matter what I did right now, no matter how I tried to delay, one way or another a match would be my fate. The thought filled me with horror.

Another Edge came to sit beside me and smile at a flower.

"How do you do?" they said. "I'm Tzam. It's such a plea-sure to meet you." Of course, I'd met them before, but as the Teachers always say, practice makes perfect.

The funny thing about having a name is that you begin to think of yourself as a solid thing that continues to exist, instead of just a stream of experiences. And things around you, too, seem to become more solid and durable. So once the Teachers had assigned us names, the Edges around me—some of whom had been Tinies and Littles and Smalls with me—gradually took on definition and solidity. Before I learned human language, I would have been able to talk about what happened next, but it would have come across very differently.

I wouldn't have been able to say so surely just who (there was no "who" before we learned it in lessons) they were, just who it was who'd then put their nose by a flower and, with-out looking at me, said very quietly, "They aren't telling us everything, you know."

I took a sip of tea. "I'm sure I don't know what you mean."

"An Adult from my clade came to visit," they said, still quietly. "You know, we whisper sometimes about who we might match with—"

"What an improper thing to say," I replied.

They gave a little snort. "I suppose you don't? Well, any-way, the truth is, some of us are going to be matched to exist-ing Adults. A few of us might pair with each other, they like to have new blood now and again. And somebody has to replace the *adequate* Translators, the mediocre ones, when they die. The important ones, though, they get to keep going. They just add new Edges whenever they need to, and of course they only take the best. You, for instance. The Teachers dote on you. You've been protected from the moment you slid into the world. Because your entire purpose is to match with some important Adult in your clade. You know that, right? It's probably Translator Dlar, who came to visit you that time."

I began to frown, wiped it away with a smile and a gesture toward a long, arching leaf. I was filled with dread. "How do you know what clade I am? They don't tell us that sort of thing."

Tzam laughed. "Sure. All right. But this is what I'm here to tell you: all the things the Teachers say, about merging with someone else and becoming whole—it's lies. It's lies for you, anyway. You'll match with Translator Dlar but it'll essentially be them eating you. It's not like someone important is going to give up anything they are to some barely educated Edge."

"Barely educated!" I was too indignant now, too horrified, to pretend to be calm. "I'm the best in the lessons!"

"Oh, of course you are," Tzam said. "But you have no idea what it's like once we leave here. There's so much. Away from here is huge. It's endless. And there's more to the rest of the universe than being eaten so Translator Dlar can keep on going uninterrupted. And I know how to leave here without being caught. It's been done before."

I was silent, thinking. Tzam sat silent beside me, every now and then sipping tea.

"I don't believe you," I said after a few minutes. "It doesn't matter what clade anyone is, it's all a question of how suitable you are."

"Then why are there clades at all?" This question had

never occurred to me. "They keep track. They keep track of how many embryos from which clade turn out to be useful or successful, and how many fail. It's supposed to just be about planning efficiently, but it didn't take long for it to be a way for the most influential Translators to increase their hold on their high status. And your clade is high status. As high as it gets. You were never anything but another credit to add to your clade's stack, and likely Translator Dlar's ticket to a few more centuries of life."

"I don't believe you," I repeated, but there was a horrible feeling in my gut, because I was beginning to believe it, and I saw again in my memory the quivering, pulsing thing we'd found in the garden not that long ago.

"I know the way out. It's been used before."

"If it's been used before, They certainly know about it." As soon as I said it, I realized that I shouldn't have. I had stepped over the edge of something and might not be able to come back from it. "And how do you know all this? If this is true, what do you get out of telling me?"

"I told you, I've been talking with an Adult from my clade. There are rivalries between the Adults, between the clades, and mine would *love* the chance to give yours a little trouble. To put a smudge on that sterling reputation. And it would only increase my status in my own clade to participate in that." They shrugged. "I admit I profit from it if you do believe me, but it's no problem for me if you don't." They took a final sip from their bowl of tea, rose, and smiled. "Such a lovely party, but I must go."

Enae

The first system on Enae's trip was three weeks from Saeniss. At first sie was bored. Sie had no duties on the ship, and there was nothing to do but sleep, eat, read, watch entertainments, shop (Caphing had been right, there were a ridiculous number of shops on the intersystem liner), or chat with other passengers. Sie found hirself waking early from habit, leaving hir tiny berth and breakfasting alone, the dining room echoing empty except for the service bots and a few other early birds like Enae. Then, having eaten, sie would walk the decks. And think.

There was plenty of time to think. It always started well enough—sie would think about the breakfast, about some strange or striking dream sie had had the night before. About the other passengers sie had met so far and their various life histories, at least as they'd presented them (sometimes at length) to Enae.

Caphing had insisted that this job was entirely a matter of checking in at particular systems and occasionally sending a message back that sie had met with this or that official and hadn't found anything. Which had seemed perfect before Enae left Saeniss, but now sie realized that it would be weeks and months of this, of nothing in particular to do and no reason to even get out of bed besides habit.

And on the one hand it was refreshing. Sie'd always had some sort of work to do at home, and even when sie rested there was the prospect of more work when sie got up. Not particularly strenuous work, not usually, but still, sie'd always thought it would be delightful to just sit around, watching entertainments or going shopping or sipping coffee with the whole day ahead of hir, and now sie had it and...well, it *was* delightful. Sie could walk up and down and look at the beautiful things in the shops—there was a wide, blue shawl hand-embroidered with red and yellow and green silk and beads in a sinuous pattern sie'd never seen before that sie always stopped to admire—and eat whenever sie wanted and sleep whenever sie wanted, and there was no one here to tell hir to do anything at all. Grandmaman would have had stern words for hir, right now, but Grandmaman wasn't here.

That thought led nowhere good. It led to memories of the worst times with Grandmaman, of dealing with the aunts and uncles and nuncles and cousins. Of feeling trapped and worthless (but not so worthless that Grandmaman could do without hir!). When, sie had begun to realize, all the time sie could have just left. Walked away. Not that it would have been easy, but sie could have done it long ago.

What was wrong with hir? Sie'd loved Grandmaman, and

now she was dead, sie felt free of some pressing weight sie'd never noticed. Sie had hated Grandmaman, and had been too weak, too cowardly to leave and strike out on hir own, and even thinking that thought filled her with grief and guilt.

This state of emotional affairs was untenable. Fortunately, this was the point at which, usually, other passengers began to come out on their own walks, and might call Enae over to have coffee and listen to them tell hir, again, the whole story of their love affairs or careers or the plots of the last entertainment they'd hated. Enae was a very good listener.

After a week of this, it occurred to Enae that sie might as well still be trapped at home. Sie was doing exactly what sie had always done, obediently following the path someone else had set out for hir and not even trying to do anything different. And sie could do something different! Something small, or maybe...

Sie felt dizzy all of a sudden. Sie could do *anything sie wanted*. Sie could send hir resignation to Caphing and just live on hir allowance! Of course, sie didn't want to disappoint Caphing, sie liked Caphing a good deal, but Caphing had been very clear about Enae having choices, from the very start.

Enae had choices. Sie wasn't used to having choices. What did you *do*, with so many choices in front of you?

Anything I want, sie thought. What did sie want?

Sie wanted that shawl. Even though it was frivolous, pointless. Sie had no prospect of an occasion special enough to justify wearing it. Grandmaman would...

Grandmaman was gone.

Sie stopped, in the still-empty spaces of the early morning

deck, mind blank with trepidation at what sie was about to do. Then sie turned, went to the shopping arcade, and bought the shawl and, just because it was there and beautiful and the same colors as the shawl, a jeweled comb. Sie tried not to think, as sie settled the shawl around hir shoulders and slid the comb into hir hair just above the single braid sie wore, about how much this purchase cost, what percentage of Grandmaman's housekeeping budget that number was. About how ridiculous it was to wear this bright, beautiful thing for a lonely morning walk.

Two hours later, one of hir fellow passengers invited hir to the day's coffee-and-life-story session, and said, when sie sat down, "That shawl is lovely on you, dear, you should wear it every day."

That afternoon, emboldened, Enae made a reservation for a massage and a mineral pack at the spa. And the next day, lying there in the warm, scented sand, a cool cloth over hir eyes soaked in some pleasant astringent, soothing music in hir ears, sie realized that sie had choices about this job, too. Sie didn't have to make it just about traveling around and occasionally meeting with some official here or there. Sie could actually try to find this person, this fugitive. Maybe sie would fail. Likely sie would. But as lovely as it was to relax like this—oh, it was lovely!—Enae was used to working, and it was important to hir to have done hir best at whatever it was sie was doing.

So, in the mornings, sie put on hir beautiful shawl and had breakfast and walked, and after an hour or so of coffee with various acquaintances sie went to hir room and reread the files and began to make plans.

* * *

When the ship docked at Sixewa, there was a message waiting for hir. From Caphing. It was chatty and pointless, the
kind of thing that, Enae thought, you might send just to keep
in touch with a friend.

Were sie and Caphing friends? Should Enae reply? *How*
should Enae reply?

Business first. Sie composed an official report for Caphing's
office, notifying hir that Enae wasn't stopping to investigate
in Sixewa. And then, with much deleting and rewriting, sie
wrote a short, hopefully cheerful note about hir trip so far,
about how lovely the spa had been, and about hir new embroi-
dered shawl. And then sie booked passage to Keroxane.

Enae didn't know what to expect from Keroxane. The only
example sie had to go by was hir brief stay on the station in
Sixewa, waiting for the next ship. That had been a matter
of a few questions and a check of hir credentials. Sie knew
from hir reading on the way that the gate into Keroxane was
controlled by the Phen, and that the Phen had ongoing difficulties with an ethnic group called the Hikipi, and all the
advice sie came across warned travelers not to take the entry
officials lightly, to be as polite as possible and have all one's
identifications and credentials and such in order.

There were more soldiers than sie'd expected, all of them
obviously armed and ready to use those prominently dis-
played weapons. Getting out of the transit center would certainly have been more difficult if Enae hadn't already made an
appointment with a Phenish official—proof of that appointment, plus hir diplomatic credentials, changed a session of

close questioning to a polite and friendly *welcome and enjoy your stay, Mx Athtur.*

And the day or two sie had to wait until hir appointment with Deputy Envoy Buren were very like hir passage through the transit station; everything seemed more or less fine, it was lovely to be on a planet again, interesting to be in a large city full of people walking here and there and with interesting buildings to look at, just the occasional armed and armored soldier to remind hir that sie had read all sorts of warnings about traveling in Phenish space.

So the day of the appointment, Enae was in fact quite unworried, even relaxed. Sie'd worked out how to use the public trams the day before, knew where sie was going, and was only slightly puzzled when, coming up to the wide avenue in front of the large official building sie was headed for, sie saw people lying in the road. At least two dozen, maybe more, stretched out in neat, even rows, as though they were asleep. Or dead. In some places, along the rows, there was a doll or some other child's toy instead of a person. *Instead of a body*, Enae thought, though, as sie approached, it became clear that the people lying in the road were alive.

The people who had gotten off the tram along with Enae had disappeared, off to wherever they were going, and Enae saw that while some people were standing at a distance, staring or whispering to companions, some walkers turned and went in another direction as soon as they saw the people lying in the avenue.

Enae went around the supine people and toward the building where hir appointment was, watching, trying to understand what this could be. Was it religious? Something else?

Hir eyes were strangely drawn to the places where toys took the place of a body.

A soldier stepped in front of hir, drawn up tall, authoritative and threatening, and said something sharp to hir. Sie froze at first, in fear and startlement. The soldier said something again. Or maybe the same thing, Enae couldn't tell. "I don't understand you," sie said, in Radchaai, the only language sie knew that had a chance of being understood here.

The next thing Enae knew, sie was facedown on the pavement, dirt and grit in hir mouth, hir nose and cheek in pain. *What did I do?* sie wanted to say, and felt tears well. Someone was yelling at hir—the soldier, sie thought—and more voices spoke, excited and angry. Hir arms were yanked painfully behind hir, and sie was pulled to hir feet. Some of the people lying on the ground had turned their heads to watch, but none of them moved from their places.

The soldier dragged hir, limping, to a transport, thrust hir in, and closed the door. Sie collapsed onto the floor and cried in earnest. What had sie gotten hirself into? Sie had no idea what sie'd stepped into the middle of, beyond a vague impression of various grievances against the Phen in this system. Sie couldn't help but remember that moment when sie'd realized sie could do anything sie wanted. Well, sie'd done what sie wanted and sie'd ended up here, locked into the back of some sort of truck, bruised and aching and crying. Sie whimpered, and the sound of it, of the pitiful misery of hir own voice, brought hir partway back to hir senses.

Where was hir handheld? Hir bag? The soldier must have taken hir things. All right then. So what did one do in a situation like this?

Wait. There was nothing else to do. At some point some-one would realize that Enae hadn't done anything, wasn't any part of whatever was going on here, and would let hir go.

It took a whole day, including a trip to some sort of hold-ing facility, and increasingly threatening, incomprehensible tirades from various people, until finally someone who spoke Radchaai came and returned hir bag and hir handheld, with a lecture about keeping hir wits about hir while traveling, and turned hir out in the middle of the night onto an unfa-miliar street a whole town over from where sie'd started.

Deputy Envoy Buren, when Enae met with her, actually apol-ogized. "I'm so *very* sorry. There's been … of course you don't speak Phenish so none of the news feeds will make sense to you. There was an incident in Hikipi space a few days ago. Soldiers fired on some rioters and some people were killed. Agitators are doing everything they can to make the rioters look sympathetic. But honestly, who brings their children to something like that?"

The people lying in the avenue. The toys. Enae's face ached with the memory of hitting the pavement, though the cor-rective had healed all the damage during the night before. A strange sort of calm had descended on hir once sie'd gotten back to hir lodgings, and it still held hir now. "What was it about? The riot, I mean?"

Deputy Envoy Buren sighed. "What are those things ever about? But that area has been unsettled for a while, and the conclave is only making things worse. The district director had ordered a suspension of certain legal rights, to make it easier to deal with saboteurs and bombers. The incident started as a protest against the suspension of rights and ended as a riot."

"The people lying on the road were representing the people who died," said Enae, taking the sweet, milky hot drink the deputy envoy offered. "The toys were for the children."

"It was a peaceful protest," said Deputy Envoy Buren, with regret in her voice, "but you never know how long that *peaceful* will last. The soldier who arrested you doesn't speak Radchaai, and when you walked right up to the building and then wouldn't answer in Phenish, she assumed you were speaking Hikipi, which is illegal."

Enae blinked, trying to understand that. Illegal to speak Hikipi? Sie frowned, thought about pursuing that, and decided not to. "What does the conclave have to do with it?"

"Many of the Hikipi—even some of the better-educated ones—believe the Presger don't actually exist."

That seemed ludicrous to Enae, who had seen recordings of ships that had encountered Presger before the treaty. Hulls torn open, whole vessels turned to floating bits of scrap. And the humans that had been on those ships...at first it was difficult to tell there had been humans at all, but then when sie'd looked closer sie'd seen the blood—and other things—smeared all over the remains of decks and bulkheads, or floating, frozen. Bodies messily disassembled and scattered everywhere. No weapon, no strategy, *nothing* could stop the Presger from doing whatever they wanted. And as humans had come closer and closer to wherever the Presger hunted, more and more ships and even whole stations had been destroyed, their inhabitants torn apart. And eventually it became clear that wherever the Presger hunted was anywhere the Presger liked. Only the treaty kept them from killing any (or every) human they met.

Sie shivered, thinking of it now. "I read a little about the history of the system, on my way here, but I never expected *that*."

"I know," said Buren. "It's not sane, but they're convinced that the Presger are a Phenish hoax."

"But…how can they be a hoax? And it was the Radchaai who negotiated the treaty, why would the Phenish be involved at all?"

Buren raised both hands, a gesture of helpless surrender. "I know! But you have to understand, they still hold a grudge over security restrictions from before the treaty was finalized. They believe those restrictions were used as an excuse for the Phen to take control of whole stations, and they led to the arrest and even the execution of quite a lot of Hikipi. And… they're not entirely wrong. I'm sympathetic, really. But it was all meant to protect us, not just the Phen but the Hikipi, too, and everyone else in the system."

Enae couldn't help but remember those toys in the avenue. Hirself being flung painfully to the ground. "The treaty was finalized nearly a thousand years ago," sie pointed out. "That's an awfully long time to hold a grudge."

"That's the Hikipi for you!" exclaimed Buren. "Half-educated, barely speak Phenish, no idea of anything beyond their home stations, but they claim they remember their ancestors back a hundred generations—somehow it turns out they're all of them descended from one or another Zone Autarch, so they're all royalty, which is a whole headache in itself. Every now and then someone rallies a faction behind themself by claiming to be the direct heir to one of those Autarchs. But the Zones all had their own rivalries—which of course the Hikipi all remember—so they can't ever get more than partial support and they end up fighting each other as much as us. Still, it's always a terrible mess. You probably know about that if you've been reading up."

Enae gestured hir acknowledgment. "No one's ever claimed to be the heir to the Sovereign Autarchs?"

Buren shuddered. "Chena forbid! I'm not glad Lovehate Station was destroyed, you understand, the loss of life was horrific. But at least no one knows what the heir to any of the Sovereign Autarchs might look like, genetically speaking. Can you imagine if the Hikipi managed to produce a Schan? It doesn't bear thinking on." She waved that away. "But that's not why you're here."

"No." Sie explained, then, about the fugitive sie was try- ing to find. Perhaps pointlessly. "I thought," sie explained, "after looking at all the possible routes this fugitive might have taken from Presger space—or, at least, the Treaty Administration Facility, which is the only real starting point I have—they might have come through Keroxane. Things were chaotic here two hundred years ago. I wondered if they might not have been able to pass through the system undetected somehow, and I was wondering if there might be some way to . . . to track them down?" sie ended hopefully.

Buren sighed. "*Maybe.* I don't think there's any way to search the travel records from two hundred years ago that will give you any answer different from the one we gave the Radchaai Translators Office at the time—because of course they were here, and of course we told them we couldn't find the person they were looking for. But. There was—there still is—a lot of smuggling in the system. At the time, there were *people* being smuggled out of the system, mostly Hikipi fugitives who couldn't get legitimate transportation. If I wanted to go through Keroxane without anyone knowing where I'd gone, that's how I'd have done it."

"Oh!" That was potentially useful. "So where did those fugitives go, mostly?"

"You probably want to start with Zeosen System. There's a significant community of Hikipi there." Buren made a face. "The smugglers still run, they bring money and weapons back and forth from Zeosen to Keroxane. If your fugitive left Keroxane, they might well have gone there. You'll want to ask about official entrance records, which in Zeosen are extensive, or maybe even try one or two of the Hikipi social clubs and ask about family histories—they're big on that. It's a long shot, but maybe someone will have a story of someone they traveled with? Possibly? It might give you a starting place for a search of Zeoseni records, anyway. But don't give the Hikipi there any money. If they ask you for a contribution for the support of widows and orphans, or the promotion of Hikipi culture, or even a contribution to a visiting poet or singer—which they're also big on—just don't. The money will come straight back here. Or the weapons it bought will, in any event."

"Thank you. I think I'll go to Zeosen next, then."

This seemed to please Buren a great deal. "Excellent! In the meantime, I do so regret the earlier misunderstanding. Why not take some time to relax? Let's see…" She frowned, looking something up via her implants, Enae supposed. "The next suitable passage to Zeosen isn't for another week. Stay at your lodging, at our expense of course. Maybe see the sights. We have a fabulous museum with art and artifacts from all over the system."

"Thank you," said Enae again. "I think I'll do that."

Reet

The Siblings of Hikipu met in one of Rurusk Station's common parlors, wide (for a station) rooms that sat open unless someone had booked them through the Civic Activities Office. This room had a faded painting of St Carapace on the back wall, her arms outstretched in blessing, gods and angels arrayed in an arch over her head. Under one foot lay a defeated demon, who, aside from the fangs, had lank blue hair and a level in one clawed hand, stereotypical associations with the Chirra. Reet thought of his parents and wished the Siblings of Hikipu had covered St Carapace with their grimy plastic banner. But the very idea would likely have made the membership indignant, and suspicious of Reet, Schan or not.

As for that membership, Reet had always thought of Hikipi—to the extent that he'd thought about them at all—as a homogeneous bunch, all tall and skinny, with pale, frizzy hair. And Mr Nadkal had at least partly satisfied Reet's lazy expectations. But this gathering was as motley as any Reet had seen on Rurusk Station.

He had plenty of time to observe them as they crowded around, offering crumbly little cakes (a traditional Hikipi dish, the recipe passed down from ancestors who fled Love-hate Station!) and a drink that tasted like warm, watered-down milk with sugar in it. Nadkal insisted he take the best of the grubby, raveling cushions they'd placed around the floor, and the others sat around Reet, gnawing the cakes and chattering, eager to tell Reet all the ways he could explore his Hikipi heritage. There were language lessons if he was interested, and there were works of history he could read or watch. They would all sing some songs later and maybe even dance! Reet's joining them would be the occasion for a special meeting, which more of the membership and occasional visitors would surely attend.

It was all very tiresome. It was exactly the sort of thing Reet despised. Exactly the sort of gathering, if he was honest with himself, that tended to trigger unseemly fantasies of tearing other people apart with his teeth, and of course that was wrong and upsetting and uncomfortable.

He thought of his foster sibs, most of whom had been encouraged to "explore their heritage." Had they joined groups like this? Looking with pitiful nostalgia toward some distant home that had never been theirs and never could be? Had they felt this vast gulf between themselves and the people telling them eagerly how much they belonged now? Or was it just Reet, who never belonged anywhere?

"Well," said Mr Nadkal. "To business!" He wiped the crumbs off his shirt. "We always open, Mr Schan—" He stopped a moment to enjoy having said that. "We always open with the Hymn of Hikipu. In the Hikipi language, of course. You won't be familiar with it yet, but if you'll call up our information packet on your implants or your handheld, whichever you prefer—I believe you've already been given directions for it—you'll find the words and a translation, and you can follow along as we sing."

Reet really, really wanted to get up and walk out. Of all the things he hadn't wanted to sit through, two dozen indifferent singers stumbling through some musty old song was near the top of the list.

And at first it was just as bad as he'd expected. The ragged start, the almost random assortment of starting pitches, even though one of their number had given one out for convenience. Thinking only to have some excuse for staring fixedly off into space, Reet pulled the translation onto the screen of his handheld.

> *Oh, we're soldiers*
> *Soldiers of Hikipu*
> *We've pledged our service to Lovehate Station.*

Reet literally bit his lip to keep from swearing at how tedious it was. But then,

> *We'll meet the Phen*
> *With guns, with knives*
> *We'll tear their skin from off their bones with our teeth.*

And suddenly Reet was interested.

We'll carve their eyes from their heads
We'll pull their livers from their ribs

The song continued in that fascinating vein. Even the tune—as much as Reet could make it out through the less than virtuosic performance—was vaguely thrilling. It struck Reet somehow, somewhere just below his rib cage.

"Ah, you feel it!" exclaimed Nadkal when the song was done. "I can see you do."

There was some business, dull as the dusty cakes: a report on the group's funds and how much had recently been raised to help the Hikipi still living in Keroxane. Whether the sign needed repair or replacement.

Then it was time for more singing. Some of the songs were what Reet had expected—nostalgic laments for the beauties of Lovehate Station, now gone forever.

But some were far more interesting—narratives of feuds, fights, and murders. They thrilled Reet just as the Hymn of Hikipu had.

"You work in the *pipeways*?" asked someone, as they drank the sweet watered-down milk between songs. "You, the descendant of the ancient rulers of Lovehate Station?"

"I looked for qualifying work," Reet told her. "I do have some mech piloting certifications, and I did some agricultural work at home when I was young. But there were no places for me."

The woman scoffed. "Ridiculous. We'll have to see what can be done about that."

By the time the meeting broke up, Reet had engaged to take lessons in the Hikipi language, and several Siblings had promised to try to find Reet a better job. And as he shut the door to his tiny quarters and sank down onto his bed beneath the goddex of good fortune, he realized that he had not once, all night, imagined himself eating any of the people in the room. Was it the songs? Was it that Reet had, finally, found the place where he belonged? He tried to reconcile that with the dull chatter...the fact that every single Sibling of Hikipu had seemed eagerly glad to see him.

He would go to the next meeting and see what happened.

The better job did not immediately materialize, to Reet's profound unsurprise. But his more violent impulses did not return, or when they did they were faint and easy to dismiss. It was difficult not to connect this with his regular meeting attendance, though he was loath to test this by skipping one. He found himself looking forward to the meetings of the Siblings of Hikipu, and even beginning to enjoy the little dust-dry cakes and the sweet milk. He could be brusque and abrupt in conversation—he might even just walk away when someone was talking to him—and they would smile and say he was surely a Schan. He didn't do this very often, to be sure, but his surprising pleasure in the meetings was tried now and then, and—school his patience as he might, as he had for years—he couldn't sit and listen to a few of the group's more tedious members. Yet instead of those tedious Siblings of Hikipu declaring Reet to be rude and thoughtless, and avoiding him, they still sought him out, or at least made allowances for him.

But even more than the meetings, Reet enjoyed the language lessons. He learned easily, though Hikipi was a very different sort of language from the ones he'd grown up speaking. Its internal logic just seemed to fall neatly into place in Reet's mind, and the more he learned the more he enjoyed it. He'd always thought his ability with languages was a matter of the underlying similarities, at least among the few he had learned. But this one was different, and it was strangely satisfying to study. Certainly, the more he could read and listen with reasonable understanding, the more he understood that those songs of slaughtering and dismembering enemies had their parallel in stories and histories. Before long he was looking for them without the direction of the teacher, and after his shifts in the pipeways he would sit on his small bed under the stick-figure goddex and puzzle through various pieces of literature he'd found.

And eventually the job presented itself. Mr Nadkal came to Reet at one meeting, took him aside, and said, "Mr Schan. Mr Schan! I have a very important request to make. We will shortly—in the next month or so—be blessed with the presence of an eminent Hikipi poet and singer. And of course, we'll invite her to a meeting or two. But here's the thing. Whenever someone of her stature comes here, Foreign Relations provides them with a liaison."

Reet frowned. "A Foreign Relations liaison? Why?"

"Well, you see," explained Nadkal, "she's here from Keroxane. And of course she has, well, connections with the community of people invested in the preservation of Hikipi culture."

Reet said nothing, still uncomprehending.

"Some of those people," Nadkal continued, "are somewhat... militant. They have to be, in Keroxane, you understand."

"Oh." Reet understood, finally. "They're worried she's here to raise money for weapons or something. They want someone to watch her and report where she goes and who she meets."

"Bluntly put, yes. And there's the question of the conclave. Everyone is being extra careful about issues surrounding the conclave. Which"—he grimaced—"the less said about the better."

"Mr Nadkal," said Reet, gripped by a sudden suspicion. "Are you one of those people who don't believe the Presger exist?"

"Well, they don't! They were made up by the Radchaai. And the Phen, of course, used that to tighten their grip over the Hikipi. Of *course* they don't exist, they're ridiculously, obviously fake. No one ever sees them except in old recordings? We can only see their Translators? Who look entirely human? It's ridiculous. This conclave has everything to do with Radchaai strategies to keep their power, and nothing else. And of course, the Phen will be happy to use it to kill more Hikipi. Mark my words."

There was a brief, awkward pause, laughter from the knot of people behind them at some joke Reet had barely heard.

"Well," said Mr Nadkal, "my point is, we have a visiting artist, traveling to perform for those of us who appreciate her and to spread knowledge of Hikipi culture generally. She has nothing to do with any of this political nonsense. But Foreign Affairs insists on a liaison. Of course, we would prefer such a liaison to be knowledgeable about Hikipi culture, and sympathetic. It would only be a temporary position, but it might get your foot in the door, so to speak, for something more permanent later."

"It's qualifying, then?"

Mr Nadkal gestured assent. "And if you don't have another assignment immediately after, well, you'll have the usual grace period to find more qualifying work. So at the worst it's a few months' vacation from the pipeways."

Assuming Reet was assigned to the pipeways again. There were worse government-assigned jobs. And what would a job with Foreign Affairs involve, even a temporary one? The idea that Foreign Affairs might suspect the most innocent person of smuggling money or arms was entirely familiar to Reet, who'd watched his parents live their lives exercising almost ridiculous caution to avoid even the faintest suggestion that they might be supporting militant Chirra causes elsewhere, and who still were occasionally investigated or otherwise inconvenienced. And there was the talk that all his sibs had gotten, that he, finally, had received himself: *Be wary of getting involved with causes.* But this wasn't getting involved in a cause, was it? This wasn't getting on the wrong side of Foreign Affairs, it would be working *for* Foreign Affairs. For a bit, anyway. But was it worth losing the dull but steady place Reet had made for himself in the pipeways?

And then Mr Nadkal named the amount Reet would be paid for liaising. Enough to pay the year's sloth tax with some left over. It was hardly just a matter of a few months off. It was freedom for a year, and a chance at more.

"All right," he said. "What do I need to do?"

In his quarters that night, he considered telling his supervisor in the pipeways that he wasn't coming in tomorrow. Or the next day. But the Foreign Affairs job wasn't a certainty yet, surely?

Mr Nadkal had only raised the possibility with him hours ago, and no doubt Foreign Affairs needed to clear Reet, approve of his taking the job, and whatever else agencies did to amuse themselves. And he might not be approved for the job. His parents had been under investigation more than once.

He thought of messaging his parents. It was...Reet squinted at numbers on his handheld. It was early morning where they were. He could call them and let them know, give them the good/bad news, tell them about the prospect of qualifying work that would pay well enough to keep him out of the pipeways for a year at least, and the unsettling likelihood that Foreign Affairs might be looking closely into Reet's background and associates. Not that there was anything to find in his parents' lives, as had been proved over and over, but authorities had a way of finding problems where there weren't any, when it suited them.

And if anything bad resulted from that close attention, it would be Reet who'd brought it on. No, he couldn't talk to his parents just yet, even though, he found, he really wanted to. After all, none of it was a sure thing. Best not to say anything, to go into work as usual, to do all the things he would normally do if the possibility of something better hadn't sprung up at all.

He was too keyed up to read Hikipi, though, so he got out of his clothes, pulled the bedcovers over himself, and fell asleep watching an episode of *Pirate Exiles of the Death Moons*.

Reet rarely dreamed. Or he rarely remembered his dreams, at any rate. He barely remembered this one, just a sensation of being wrapped in something brown and pink and warm, and whatever it was, he was melting into it, his skin dissolving as he watched.

He woke to find himself covered in sweat, sweat that, when he pulled away from the bedcover, proved to be stringy and viscous. It definitely wasn't right or normal, but the dream still clung to him and he shivered with the remains of that delicious feeling of merging into something else.

Should he see a doctor? He knew better than to tell anyone about his weird feelings and impulses, but surely this wasn't right, was something that should be taken care of.

His wakeup beeped. He would be late for work if he went to Health Affairs, which would be permissible if he was sick, but what would the consequences be for the Foreign Affairs job? He wanted that year off, he wanted the opportunity to find other qualifying work. And maybe this was just some passing thing. If it wasn't, he could go to Health Affairs later. And after all, what did some weirdly sticky sweat matter? It was already drying, leaving tiny, dusty flakes behind on his skin. Maybe he'd just gotten overheated and there was something in the cover that had mixed with his sweat to make it like that. Maybe something had gone wrong with the extruder and he'd gotten a cover from an off batch when he'd recycled the old one and picked up the new one. Yeah, that was probably all it was. No reason to panic. No reason to be late to work.

He dismissed the wakeup, grabbed his clothes, and headed for the nearest shower unit.

Qven

After my conversation with Tzam in the garden, I began asking more questions about the World outside. How humans lived, and where. The Teachers were very pleased, as I had intended they should be. And if Tzam noticed my curiosity on matters that touched on our conversation, they gave no sign of it. They didn't approach me at all, but acted as though we had never spoken of anything more substantial than flowers or varieties of tea.

Time happened, which is always difficult to talk about in human language. Humans talk about time like it's a circle. Humans talk about time like it's a line. Humans talk about time like it's marked in regular intervals that they make up in their minds and then use to define *when* things happen—but also, they use it to make things happen in particular ways. The Teachers made us lie on our lying-down furniture at certain intervals, and get up and drink tea at other intervals, and lessons were at regular places on the circle that went from lying-down time to lying-down time, and each of those circles was the same only it wasn't, each one had a different name that we recited in lessons, but still, I can't tell you how much time there was from that talk with Tzam until I got myself into trouble.

It was during lessons. We were all sitting on chairs and talking about very simple things. There had been a recent influx of new Edges, and they were fidgeting and uncomfortable in their human clothes. They'd most of them managed by now to actually sit in a chair for the whole lesson instead of sliding off partway through and squatting on the ground, but even so, us senior Edges eyed them with a bit of complacent superiority. And perhaps a little nostalgia. *Remember when. Remember when you were just a Middle coming into the Edges, no idea how to behave or what was coming.*

I found myself staring. At the neck and cheek of one of the new Edges, brown against the white of their human clothes. By now, of course, wanting to open someone up wasn't about curiosity. Not anymore. Not after all our lessons. By now we all knew very well what we'd find underneath skin and fat and muscles, at least in general terms. By now it was about reveling in the details, the tiny ways each body was both different and the same, and that had become delicious in its own right.

But I didn't find myself wanting to bite, as I had so many times before. No. I wanted to lick. I wanted to lick that ear, where their dark hair was pulled back. To lick their neck and their cheek. To lick and lick, but it wasn't in a wanting-to-do-sex kind of way, not at all, but something tickly and tingly in my throat. A strange, indescribable flavor filled my mouth and *oh!* I knew what this was, and I had to make myself look away, pretend that I wasn't this very moment looking at some poor fool of a new Edge and wanting to *match*. The Teacher would see. They would take me away and *no I didn't want to* but I could barely take my eyes off that ear, that cheek.

A piercing shriek sounded, broke my tranced stare. I looked down at my lap, ready to curl defensively just like I'd seen so many others do before they'd been opened or eaten (or both). The sound of that shriek shivered in my bones as though it would go right through me and tear me apart, and I clapped my hands over my ears, but still it cut into me. Any moment now. Any moment and the Teacher would take me away, and I would be lost.

"Come on," someone shouted at me, pulling at my arm, dragging me up and out of the chair. And why fight? What good would it do? I followed.

But it wasn't a Teacher who had my arm. It was another Edge, pulling me out of the lesson room. I turned back and saw the Teacher confronting a different Edge entirely, more Teachers appearing around them, in the way that Teachers do sometimes. The Edge was standing, shivering. Choking, it seemed, mouth agape, and just as I left the lesson room and the entrance sealed itself, I saw the Edge vomit a thick, viscous white fluid.

"*Stupid*," hissed the Edge who had my arm. I assumed at first they were talking about me, but no. "Stupid not to tell the Teachers before it got to that point. Stupid to try and hide it." I couldn't answer, couldn't speak. I was having trouble swallowing and couldn't get that vomiting Edge out of my mind. "Don't worry," said the Edge holding my arm. "We're safe now."

After some time to calm down, I went to speak with Tzam. I found them in the garden: there was no tea party—the Teachers couldn't be found so there was no tea and no cakes—and everyone was standing or sitting in various places, either silent or in small, whispering groups. So no one noticed when Tzam and I went off into the greenery to talk quietly. "Are you ready, then?" they asked. "Let's go."

"What, right now?"

"What better time? The Teachers are all preoccupied. The sooner you can be on your way, the less likely they'll be to realize and stop you."

They led me through the garden to a wall. An entrance gaped as we approached it. "How did you...?" Normally only Teachers could open these entrances, and Edges weren't allowed inside.

"I told you," said Tzam, with a smug little smile. "I have help from Adults in my clade."

Inside was a wide, blue-tiled corridor that lit as we entered. The light followed us down the passage. Shelves set into the walls held various human things—plates and cups, tools for putting food into mouths. Pans and things for making fires and sharp, sharp knives that had fascinated us all, and that the Teachers were very, very careful not to leave us unsupervised with. Trowels and shovels and stakes for doing garden things—I remembered learning the words, remembered the Teachers saying that was something we could do, but nobody did.

"Here," said Tzam, next to a shelf full of plant-tending tools. "I need your help." They beckoned me closer.

And when I approached they shoved me hard against the shelf, stunning me, and pressed their body against mine, put their hands on my neck, and began to lick and suck on my ear.

"What are you doing?" I cried, but it came out a half moan through the tickling, tingling feeling that had come back into my throat and it was *delicious, oh*. I felt sudden sweat bead on my skin. Tzam grunted and only licked faster, and I said, "Stop."

"Not likely," said Tzam against my face. They shifted their grip on my neck, pulled their face back, but something came with it, white and thick, stretched in sticky strings between them and me. They put a hand to my cheek and pulled it away, more sticky stuff and *oh!* I felt something exciting and wonderful still rising in my throat. "There's no stopping now." Their voice sounded strange and strangled. They put their hand on my neck again and I felt it sink into me, as though my skin were fluid.

I wanted it. I didn't want to stop, no, I wanted this feeling to keep going, to never stop.

I didn't want this. Everything around me took on a hard-edged clarity. The blue glint of light on the tiles. The dull brown curve of a pot's edge. The shine of a trowel blade. The brown, grained handle of a pruning knife.

My hand on that handle, gripping tight, slashing and stabbing. Tzam screaming and blood, so much blood, and they tried to take the knife from me but I held on to it hard and they could only do so much because one of their hands was stuck to my neck. I didn't like that, I wanted to cut it off, but everything was so clear to me right at that moment, I knew immediately that if I did that, if I cut off Tzam's hand, they would be able to move better and maybe take the knife away from me. So I stabbed them instead, over and over, in their neck and in their thorax, and I slashed their abdomen until they lay in their pooling blood on the blue-tiled floor and I knelt beside them. I couldn't move very far because their hand was still stuck to my neck.

I decided then that it was a good time to cut them away from me, and so I had the blood-soaked pruning knife under my chin and was sawing and hacking at Tzam's wrist when the Teachers found me.

Enae

Entry into Zeosen System was both the most organized and the most chaotic thing Enae had ever experienced. All inter-system transport docked at one huge hub, a massive, city-size conglomeration of docks, cargo handling and storage, and food shops.

And lines. Lines everywhere, snaking around and across, up and down ramps. Enae got off hir ship, bag on one shoulder, portmanteau in the other hand, and was immediately herded into the first of the lines.

There was one line for citizens of one particular Zeosen polity. There was another line for citizens of two others. There was a line for people who had visited a farm within the last two months, and another for people who were in the system "for anfractuous purposes," which even when sie looked up the word made no sense to hir.

Sie waited in a line to be asked why sie was visiting Zeosen.

Sie waited in another line to have hir luggage searched—in front of hir, unlike Keroxane. "Extra security right now," another line-dweller said, behind hir, to their neighbor. "The conclave and all." The neighbor, a person in dark gray tunic and wrapped trousers, *hmmed* in acknowledgment.

The luggage searcher found nothing of note among Enae's dirty underclothes—if sie'd realized there would be a search, sie'd have made sure to do laundry before the ship docked, but oh well, and the searcher had surely seen worse.

There was another line for people whose reasons for visiting needed verification of one sort or another. Enae resolved to say sie was a tourist from here on out. A line to buy a handheld (hir own wouldn't work here, it was the wrong sort for this system's communications network). A line to buy food and drink. And then, finally, a line for the shuttle to Rurusk Station. Enae had chosen Rurusk because it was fairly close to the transport hub and had a relatively large number of Hikipi immigrants. Sie wasn't sure how sie would find anyone who knew something about people who might have come here from Keroxane two hundred years ago, but after nearly twelve hours in the transport hub, sie had begun to suspect there would be a line to wait in to get the answer. But at least there didn't seem to be any soldiers. That alone made something relax inside hir that sie hadn't known was tense.

The shuttle was cold and cramped. Enae badly needed sleep, but there was barely room to sit comfortably, and the compartment was excessively well lit, every surface covered in glaring warnings of various ways one might die if one made some wrong move. Enae noticed the person in dark gray a few rows behind hir—they seemed to have settled in and gone immediately to sleep, and for a moment sie was tempted to ask them how in the world they'd managed that. But it would mean climbing over other passengers, and no doubt somewhere on the walls or floor was a huge, screaming warning against doing exactly that. So instead sie closed hir eyes and relaxed as well as sie could manage.

Once the shuttle docked at Rurusk there were more lines— a line to get off the shuttle, a line to collect hir luggage, a line to leave the transport area.

Outside the transport area stood a crowd of people. That was ordinary, Enae had found, people waiting for family or visitors. None of them would be for hir: sie didn't know anyone in this system and sie hadn't made any arrangements for hir arrival. Sie swerved to go around the press.

A man stepped in front of hir. Medium tall, his dark hair short and lank. Slouching slightly. Frowning, he said, "Mx Athtur. I'm your Foreign Affairs liaison."

Sie stopped short. Blinked. "I didn't know I had a liaison," sie said, perplexed. Sie hadn't asked for one, only sent a message before sie'd left Keroxane, notifying the Zeosen Foreign Affairs office that sie was coming, and what sie was investigating. "How in the world do you know my name? Or what I look like?" Or when to meet hir, for that matter.

The man's frown deepened. "You went through immigration," he said. "They recorded an image and a description."

"Have they always done that?" Enae asked, remembering Deputy Envoy Buren saying that Zeoseni system entry records were "extensive." If the fugitive had come here, that might be helpful.

"I don't know." The man was brusque. "My name is Reet Hluid. I'll take you to your accommodation." He turned without waiting for hir reply and strode away.

"I haven't booked any accommodation yet," Enae said to his retreating back. Sie thought a moment and then, looking around, saw a more or less calm spot with an unoccupied bench. Sie sat, pulled hir luggage close, and took out hir recently purchased handheld. It was already connected to the station's system, sie saw.

And there was a message from Caphing! *This isn't work correspondence so I shouldn't mention it but Keroxane is terribly dangerous! Be careful!* But now wasn't the time to read all of that. Sie had to navigate the unfamiliar interface and find someplace to stay.

A shadow fell over hir. "What are you doing?" Reet Hluid asked.

"Looking for somewhere to stay."

"You already have accommodations," he said. "I'm supposed to take you there."

"I don't even know who you are," sie argued. "I didn't ask for a liaison. No one told me I'd have one." Sie hadn't had one so far. It had just been hir hirself so far. Though maybe a liaison would have helped, back in Keroxane.

"Check your messages," he said.

"I don't have any messages from inside this system. I just arrived, I don't know anyone here, and I've only had anything like an address here for an hour. Less than that." Sie hefted hir handheld. "I only just bought this."

"It's been tied to your identity since you got it," Reet Hluid said. "Check your messages."

And sure enough, just past the message from Caphing there was one from Foreign Affairs. Reet Hluid, hir liaison, would escort hir to the accommodation Foreign Affairs had arranged for hir, and would assist hir in any way sie required. It was far more than the purpose of hir visit here warranted.

"Has there been some sort of trouble around the conclave?" Sie hadn't heard of any, but that didn't necessarily mean anything.

"Not that I know of," replied Reet Hluid. "And I'm your liaison."

So he was here to keep an eye on hir and report hir movements back to whoever his supervisor was. Sie didn't think he'd been hired for the elegance of his manners. Or his ability to make one feel welcome, that much was obvious.

Sie thought a moment. On the one hand, sie found sie didn't much like the idea of Foreign Affairs choosing hir accommodations. The thought gave hir a shiver. Was this another arrest? But Mr Hluid hadn't seemed like he was arresting hir. "Where are these accommodations?"

"Fortunate Citrus Chambers. It's very nice. And Foreign Affairs is paying for it. And your meals, up to thirty sequins a day." When sie frowned, he continued, "That's pretty generous, actually."

It made very little sense to Enae, though sie supposed sie might as well let them pay. "Do you know why I'm here?"

"No idea," he confessed.

"I'm looking for someone who might have come to this system from Keroxane about two hundred years ago. They would have stood out at the time. It's hardly urgent business, they're almost certainly dead by now. It's just an old loose end. It's not something your Foreign Affairs would care about enough to put me up and feed me."

"I don't know about that," said Reet Hluid. "I'm just your liaison."

Enae closed hir eyes for a moment. Which reminded hir just how exhausted sie was. "All right, Reet Hluid." Sie could work all this out later. After a long, long nap and some supper. "Liaise me to my accommodation."

When Enae woke from a long sleep, refreshed by the pleasant and comfortable rooms sie'd been assigned as much as by the nap, sie dressed and thought a moment about calling Reet. He'd said to contact him when sie was ready to go out, and on the one hand sie would appreciate having a local guide to show hir around and advise hir about local food and customs. Sie certainly would ask for his help in finding the information sie was looking for.

But on the other hand, sie didn't much like the idea of a minder reporting on hir movements, steering hir toward or away from things for reasons sie didn't understand. So instead of calling Reet, sie picked up hir shoulder bag and went out walking.

There were very few wide-open spaces on the station—which made sense, Enae supposed. Open spaces on a station were a potential safety hazard. Mostly there seemed to be a maze of corridors, with doorways framed by colorful painted patterns, and sometimes signs with cryptic messages—cryptic when run through the translation utility on Enae's handheld, anyway. After walking awhile, sie found a window labeled EAT ALL THE DUMPLINGS. Beyond the window a bot was dropping white bundles into a steamer. A few awkward fumblings with hir handheld later, sie claimed a carton of dumplings and a cup of coffee, and found a place to sit.

The dumplings were spiced with an oddly appealing combination of bitter and slightly floral, and the unfamiliar flavor grew on hir as sie ate. The coffee was pale brown, thick, and astonishingly sweet. As sie ate, sie watched people pass by.

Wrapped trousers and tunics seemed to be the standard clothes here, and many of the people sie saw went barefoot, though not all. A few passersby wore coveralls and boots— on their way to jobs that required such clothing, sie supposed. Every now and then someone would go by in an elaborately patterned tunic, or with the long and trailing end of a particularly intricately wrapped skirt or trousers draped over their shoulder. These people wore sandals that had little struts under the soles, which lifted them six or more inches off the ground. Their gait was delicate and elegant, but Enae imagined hirself wearing them and shuddered. Sie was sure sie'd break an ankle if sie even tried it.

There were quite a lot of people in dark gray, and sie thought of the person sie'd seen on the shuttle here, the one who'd fallen asleep so easily. They probably lived here and didn't find any of this strange. They were used to the food and the thick, sweet coffee. And for just a moment sie thought sie saw them, in dark gray, behind a cluster of people passing by.

Shaking hir head at her foolishness, sie gathered up the remains of hir lunch and looked around for a recycle slot. The people passed by, chattering, and then someone swerved toward Enae.

It was! It was the person from the shuttle, sie was sure!

What a very unlikely coincidence, sie thought, and then the person stepped up beside hir, grabbed hir bag, and hit hir on the head.

Sie fell to the ground, stunned. Sie heard a shout, and then someone was beside hir, saying things sie couldn't understand. "That person hit me," sie said. "I'm all right." But sie wasn't entirely certain that sie was. Hir head hurt and it was difficult to concentrate.

Someone was still talking to hir, and sie didn't see the person in dark gray anywhere. They must have run off. Hir bag was gone. The stranger who was talking to hir gestured to another passerby. Sie couldn't understand anything anyone was saying.

"My handheld," sie said, and no one seemed to know what sie meant. Sie put hir hand out as though sie was holding something. The people around hir made concerned noises. "I'm fine," sie said. "I just need my handheld so I can get some coffee." Sie tried to stand up, but the person talking to hir wouldn't let hir. "No, really, I'm fine."

But no one would listen, and before long, without any clear idea of the transition, sie found hirself in a medical facility, with Reet Hluid standing next to hir bed, frowning.

"What are you doing here?" sie asked him.

"The staff called me," he said, still frowning. "What happened?"

"I went out and had dumplings and coffee," sie said. "They were good but the coffee was really, really sweet." Sie looked around. "Where's my bag?"

"Your attacker dropped it. I have it here." He lifted the

bag into Enae's view. "But they haven't found your handheld. Don't worry, I have a new one for you."

"Oh." Enae frowned, trying to remember what sie'd just been saying. The frown reminded hir that hir head hurt. Sie must have been given some kind of medication, because hir headache was obviously still there but in the background somewhere, only faintly reminding her of its existence when sie moved the wrong way.

"You bought dumplings," Reet prompted.

"I bought dumplings! And when I was looking for a recycle slot, that person from the shuttle grabbed my bag and hit me."

"What person from the shuttle?" Reet demanded.

"They were a few rows behind me on the shuttle here. I noticed them because they'd been just behind me in a line. A long, long line."

Reet pulled out his own handheld. "We can find them. What was in your bag besides your handheld?"

"Nothing, really. Nothing important. How did you know I was here?"

"You told them my name, so they called me."

"I don't remember that."

"You have a concussion," Reet replied. "I'm going to take you back to your accommodation. You're going to get some rest. I'll bring you some supper. And, Mx Athtur. Don't leave your accommodation without me again."

"It hasn't been a problem anywhere else," Enae argued, but then sie remembered Keroxane, and shivered.

"It shouldn't have been a problem here," said Reet. "And yet here we are."

Reet

"The person who attacked you knew you were coming. She waited at the transport hubs for several days, just moving to the back of the intake line over and over."

Mx Athtur sat in a wide, low chair, leaning on pillows, holding the bowl of thin bean porridge Reet had brought hir. Sie seemed much less dazed than when Reet had found hir at the Health Facility, which was good, it meant the correctives and the medicine were doing what they should.

"But who is she? Why did she follow me? Why did she attack me?"

"We don't know," Reet admitted. And then, feeling vaguely ashamed, "She came from Keroxane, that much we've found. But she won't say anything except *Death to the Phen oppressors.*"

"She's Hikipi then," said Mx Athtur, pausing in hir slow consumption of the bean porridge. Sie frowned, staring vaguely into the space in front of her, not, Reet thought, accessing data on an implant, but thinking something over. "It doesn't make sense," sie said after a few moments. "I mean, it sort of does, but it doesn't."

Reet had come to the same conclusion earlier, talking to his supervisor. "You're here looking for traces of someone who might have come here two hundred years ago, who might have been a Presger Translator." To Mx Athtur's surprised expression, he said, "My supervisor told me, since it had become need-to-know."

"It doesn't make sense," sie repeated. "This is old business. The person I'm looking for has probably been dead for years. I'm not really expected to look terribly hard for them to begin with. I'm just...this is just Saeniss Polity gesturing concern for the treaty during the conclave."

Not really expected, sie'd said. "But you *are* seriously looking?"

"Well"—sie scraped the last of the porridge out of the bowl—"I am being paid rather well, and I like to do things properly. But it shouldn't make a difference. This is business no one actually cares about."

"Someone cares," Reet pointed out. "And someone has been passing information on your movements to Hikipi Nationalists."

"I came here to talk to Hikipi immigrants," said Mx Athtur. "On the theory that this person I'm looking for may have come through Keroxane."

"They might have stayed there," Reet suggested.

"They might. I don't think I have the resources to find them if they did. They might be anywhere, really. They might be dead. But I wanted to at least try to find them. It's my job."

"I see," said Reet. "And if they left Keroxane two hundred years ago, and there's no record of them, chances are they were on one of the Hikipi refugee ships. Which means there's a chance they came here."

"Exactly," sie agreed.

They were both silent a few moments, thinking.

"So," said Reet at length, "you're here to investigate local Hikipi."

"Well, not—"

"You're here," Reet interrupted, taking the empty porridge bowl and replacing it with a tumbler of weak coffee, "to at least make contact with local Hikipi. Supposedly about a matter that just isn't worth looking into at this point. Especially if you believe the Presger don't exist to begin with. Which some number of the Hikipi Nationalists don't."

"Right," Mx Athtur agreed. "But if you don't believe the Presger are a danger, why care if I find some person who's been missing for two centuries, who might be associated with them?"

"You arrive here," Reet said, "after meeting with Phenish officials in Keroxane, with your passage here paid for by the Phenish Department of Extra-System Affairs, with some obviously fabricated reason for your presence. You ditch your Foreign Affairs minder—"

"I didn't ditch you! I just thought I'd get myself some breakfast."

"You ditch your Foreign Affairs minder," Reet repeated, and realized exactly why he'd been assigned to this job, and felt a moment's fear, "and go out alone, with a large shoulder bag, and wander around."

"Oh!" Sie was clearly startled at the implication. "But I was just taking a walk and getting something to eat!"

"Right," Reet said. "But if you were a secret agent on some mission to, I don't know, infiltrate the Hikipi here, or something else dastardly..." He waved vaguely.

"What is it they think I'm involved in?" sie asked, and that, of course, was the question.

"No idea," Reet admitted. "Like I said, your assailant isn't talking."

"Death to the Phen oppressors," sie acknowledged wryly.

"Yes. There are..." He was well beyond what he'd been authorized to convey to Mx Athtur, but he liked hir, he found, and even if he didn't, it was hir safety on the line here. "There *are* ways to get information from unwilling subjects, but they're very unpleasant and legally they can only be used in extreme situations. There's an argument going on over whether this counts."

"How many people at Foreign Affairs are sympathetic to Hikipi Nationalists?" asked Mx Athtur.

It was a good question. "I don't know. But we can't do anything about Foreign Affairs. We *can* introduce you to the Siblings of Hikipu."

Sie straightened in hir seat. "Can you? Do you think they'll have anything to tell me that the public records won't? I mean, people always do have more to tell you, but..."

"I don't know. But you should know that I got this job because of my contacts in the Siblings of Hikipu. My last assignment was escorting a famous Hikipi singer while she was here."

It took a few moments, but he saw on hir face when

understanding came. "Someone in the Siblings of Hikipu is connected with Foreign Affairs."

"I could be taking you to meet the exact people who got you attacked."

"Are you Hikipi?"

"I'm … it's a long story."

Sie thought about that. Reet considered hir—sie had seemed, when he had first met hir, to be a bit scattered, the sort of person you didn't really pay much attention to. But now he saw something stronger and more solid underneath that appearance.

"Maybe they know something," sie said. "I mean, maybe it's not just that I was acting like a secret agent in an entertainment. Maybe they know something about the person I'm looking for."

"And hit you over the head for it?"

Sie shrugged. "Maybe I can just explain to them."

Reet stared at hir. "Just explain?"

"Well," sie said with a small smile, "sometimes it works."

Reet had always known that there was some flow of money and even weapons from Zeosen System to Keroxane. He had assumed, if he'd thought about it at all, that the Siblings of Hikipu were, for the most part, very careful to avoid such associations. That the various charities collected for were (for the most part) legitimately humanitarian.

It went, he was beginning to suspect, a good deal further than that. But if so, where was the spy from Foreign Affairs? Where was the suspicion of newcomers without existing ties in the community—like Reet himself? And Mr Nadkal? Mr

Nadkal openly had connections with Foreign Affairs, everyone knew it, and none of the Siblings of Hikipu seemed to care.

That connection had gotten at least one Hikipi visitor preferential treatment—a sympathetic liaison. Reet couldn't imagine a Chirra artist getting even that much consideration.

And he was quite certain that if Mx Athtur's assailant had been Chirra and refused to say anything but *Long live the Chirra Archonate* or something similar, there would have been little or no consideration of her comfort or the propriety of forcible interrogation.

Mr Nadkal was involved with Foreign Affairs. And Mr Nadkal openly, fervently sympathized with the Hikipi fighting in Keroxane System. What else might he be involved in?

Reet winced, thinking it. Others had thought similarly of his parents, with less justification, and Reet had no desire to be that sort of person. Still. What might Mr Nadkal know about Mx Athtur's assailant?

He knew better than to ask outright. Knew that if his suspicions were correct, Mr Nadkal would only deflect questions and then be warned that Reet suspected something.

No. Let Mx Athtur handle it. Sie was quiet and practical—sie had to all appearances been completely unfazed by Reet's customary manner. And there was something oddly appealing in hir determination to do a job no one expected hir to do, even after an ambush and a knock on the head.

Reet should resign and go back to the pipeways. Let Enae Athtur walk into the trouble sie was headed for without Reet's help. Reet should stay far, far away from this, away from the Siblings of Hikipu and whatever mess they were entangled with.

And where would that leave him? Back in his tiny room, alone. Not that he didn't still spend plenty of time there, solitary. But these past months he'd *belonged* somewhere, known all this time that there was somewhere he'd come from, somewhere his quirks were recognized. He hadn't realized until he'd found it just how much, how badly, he'd needed that.

Well, he would still have the knowledge of it. Still know that he was a Schan who could trace his origins to Lovehate Station. He could still study the history, the language, and the literature.

He should do those things—resign his Foreign Affairs connection, quit the Siblings of Hikipu. He had enough money to pay a year's sloth tax and still have some left over—he could deal with finding work again when his year ran out. Let Mx Athtur have a new liaison.

One Mr Nadkal chose, maybe. And maybe that would be fine, maybe Mr Nadkal was perfectly innocent and well-intentioned and Mx Athtur would be perfectly safe.

But then again, maybe not.

"This is Mx Enae Athtur," said Reet, gesturing to Mx Athtur, who sat on a cushion to his left. "Sie's come all the way from Saeniss Polity to look into some historical records."

A murmur from the assembled Siblings of Hikipu, of welcome and mild interest.

"Gho haran i harap," said Mx Athtur, *I thank you for this welcome*, a formulaic phrase in Hikipi, hir accent not too bad, all things considered, and the murmurs turned to appreciative laughter. "Mostly I'm searching old files, but I'm also looking for stories that might mention the person I'm after.

This person is long dead by now—if they even came here it would have been about two hundred years ago."

"Was this person Hikipi?" someone asked.

"No," replied Mx Athtur, "but I think they may have spent some time in Keroxane System. So if they came here…"

"They may have come along with some of our parents or grandparents," said Mr Nadkal. "My own grandmother came here about then. She was wanted by the Phen authorities and she was smuggled out of the system in a stack of arrack crates. Which was itself being smuggled. The customs officers found it, and the ship's captain gave the usual bribe, and off they went, no idea that my grandmother was at the bottom of the container!"

"My goodness!" exclaimed Mx Athtur. "Did she come alone?"

"Well, yes and no," said Mr Nadkal. "But everyone that ship brought out of Keroxane was Hikipi." He seemed, Reet thought, entirely comfortable with Mx Athtur's presence and questions.

"Still," said Mx Athtur appreciatively, "what a story!"

"My great-grandnother came to Zeosen on a passenger ship," said another Sibling of Hikipu. "Nothing exciting, really, not like Mr Nadkal."

"I suppose e's not with us anymore," suggested Mx Athtur. "Did e ever say anything about anyone e'd traveled with? Someone…unusual maybe?"

"Unusual how?" asked another Sibling. "Is it maybe a Schan you're looking for? Because"—she clapped a friendly hand on Reet's shoulder—"we have one right here."

"She said this person wasn't Hikipi, though," said someone

else. "Reet's Hikipi. I mean, just look at that hair! And those eyes!"

Reet grimaced in embarrassment. If Mx Athtur hadn't been there, he'd have said something sharp about that invasion of his space, or stood up and walked away, but he was, technically, on the job right now.

"And look how well he's taken to the language," said the oblivious Sibling, hand still on Reet's shoulder. "Like it's second nature to him."

"Schan," murmured Mx Athtur, hir tone as fixedly polite as hir smile. "The name is familiar. Lovehate Station, right?" A murmur of pleased agreement from the assembled Siblings of Hikipu.

"I'm far too young to be the person Mx Athtur is looking for," Reet protested. "I only came to Zeosen thirty years ago."

"Maybe that person had a child," said a Sibling. "Or grandchildren."

"But whoever they are, they aren't Hikipi, Mx Athtur said," Reet pointed out. "Sie doesn't want *my* history."

"Oh, I'm interested in everyone's history," said Mx Athtur, and Reet thought sie was sincere, or at least very good at seeming so. For a moment he wished he knew how to do that. "So many wonderful stories! I'm quite fascinated by what little I've learned of Hikipi history. And it's not like I don't have time to listen."

There was nothing for it, then. Reet had to tell the whole story.

Qven

I don't remember much after the Teachers arrived, just that bone-piercing shriek, louder and louder, until quite suddenly it was quiet, and I was lying on a surface. When I opened my eyes I saw gray. Dull gray ceiling, and dull gray walls when I sat up. The clothes I'd worn ever since I'd come to the Edges—the white shirt, jacket, trousers, and shoes—were gone. Well, they were Translator's clothes, and I would never be a Translator now. Everything felt sharp and clear, and somehow distant at the same time, like none of it was real. My skin itched faintly all over.

I swung my legs over the side of the surface I sat on and put my feet on the floor. Was there any point to standing?

The wall in front of me opened, and just beyond the opening I saw Translator Dlar staring at me. I stared back.

At length, they said, "We expected better from you."

I said nothing in reply, because after all, what was there to say?

"Tzam claims that you tried to force a match on them."

"What?" I knew that, as a good Edge, one of the best of the Edges, I should regulate my voice and my reactions. I wasn't an Edge anymore, and I would never have to talk to humans. But it was possible behaving well might help me here, too, so I didn't shout. "They're lying. *They* tried to force *me*." I put my hand on my throat where Tzam's hand had been. The skin felt mostly smooth, but I could still feel it, could feel Tzam there.

"That is by far the more likely scenario," admitted Translator Dlar. "You had nothing to gain by matching with Tzam, while they had everything to gain by matching with you. But unlikely is not the same as impossible. And it seems you did conceal your readiness for a match from the Teachers."

I stared. I would not speak. I wouldn't. Everything was lost now, anyway.

"We expected better from you," Translator Dlar said again. "What were you even doing, alone with someone like Tzam?"

Trying to escape, I thought but did not say.

"And then, bad enough that you—you!—match with Tzam, bad enough their clade gets even *that* much of a foothold on the prestige they've wanted for so long. It undid plans years in the making, but we could have dealt with that, one way or another. But then you go halfway and stop! What are we to do with you now?"

"I don't understand."

Translator Dlar made a huffing noise. "The match that was planned for you is not going to happen now. It can't."

"It was you," I said. Even though Tzam had lied about

some things, I thought that was true. "You were going to eat me so you could have another body."

"*Eat* you!" Translator Dlar seemed shocked. "It's not like eating someone. It's not like that at all. Who told you that?"

Tzam had, of course. And I still wasn't sure they hadn't been telling the truth.

"It's not like eating someone," said Translator Dlar, when I didn't speak. "In fact, I *can't* eat anyone. Adults can't. Only children can. So even if you had been destined to match with me, I wouldn't have eaten you."

I stared, not speaking.

"There's no point telling you what match was planned, because it won't happen. All our plans, since before you were cultured, are ruined. And there are no suitable matches for you now. You *mutilated* your match partner—that's not optimal behavior *at all*. You're still carrying fragments of that partner, someone who, if your account is accurate, was willing to force a match for their own gain. No one will want that to be part of who they are. And if your account is *not* accurate, well, whatever was happening there was, again, *not optimal behavior*. No matter which way you look at the situation, you're unfit."

"What, should I just have let Tzam...finish?"

"Once you got into that situation, you might as well have," said Translator Dlar. Their voice was hard and angry. "The fact that you even found yourself in that situation to begin with..." They shook their head. "Ordinarily you would just be disposed of. There's no other use for you. But this clade hasn't had a member reach the Edges and then fail for a very long time, and it's not going to happen now. We've temporarily suppressed the process that allows you to fully become an Adult, it should hold for a while, at least. If you behave suitably, for long enough, we *might* be able to find some sort of partner for you. It won't be the sort of thing you were meant for, but it won't be failure, and that's all we can ask for right now."

"If you can suppress the process," I said, a sharp, disorienting moment of hope shooting through me, "I don't need to match at all. I can just stay as I am."

"We *can't* do that," Translator Dlar said. "Not permanently."

"I don't want to match," I said. "I don't want to be an Adult. Not ever." I shuddered, thinking of that pulsing, breathing thing in the garden. "I'll do whatever it is the clade wants me to. I'll even..." I tried to think of the worst possible work I could imagine. "I'll clean dishes. I'll *count things*."

"The clade," said Translator Dlar firmly, "wants you to *not fail*. Which is just barely possible at the moment. Otherwise, we have no reason to keep you alive at all. Do you understand?"

I didn't. But I knew better than to say that. "Yes, Translator."

"Good." They sighed. "Why? Why did *you* of all our offspring get yourself into this situation?"

"I *was* going to be you, wasn't I?" I was sure of it for some reason.

"*We* were going to be someone else," they said. "I told you, it's not like eating someone. The *Teachers* told you." I said nothing. "This is Tzam talking, isn't it?" Translator Dlar shook their head. "That's maybe the worst of this whole situation, that this clade has to be connected to *them*. You're going to need to behave better despite that. I'm warning you." Sternly. "If you can't behave optimally, if we can't make this work somehow and you fail, you *will* be disposed of."

"I understand, Translator." I didn't, not really. But I would have to pretend that I did, until I saw some chance to escape.

I was not allowed to leave my suite of rooms—the room where I'd awakened, with its sleeping surface, and a few others. I was not alone. A Teacher was assigned to me—they came into the room I was in and introduced themself. Then one of them left, and the other handed me a stack of clothing with a curt order to dress.

I would be good. I would be very, very good, and watch for some chance. I said, "Yes, Teacher," and dressed myself under their sharp gaze.

"You are currently unable to match," they said. "If the treatment fails, you are to notify me immediately."

"How likely is that?" I asked. Translator Dlar had not been forthcoming on the topic.

"Do you itch?" asked the Teacher. "Does your skin feel wrong?"

It did. The faint itching I'd felt from the moment I'd woken had only grown.

"If that stops," continued the Teacher, though I hadn't answered their question, "you tell me the moment you notice."

"What if you're not here?" I asked. "What if I can't find you right away?" I hadn't yet realized that I would never be out of sound or sight of them.

The Teacher only stared at me a moment, and then said, "I have been assigned this task because I have experience with problem children. I am also provided with defenses that make it difficult—though not impossible—for anyone to force a match with me. If you attempt it anyway, you will be destroyed. If you attempt it and succeed in beginning the process, we will both be destroyed. Do you understand me?"

"What did you do to get assigned this shit duty?" I asked.

"You will display optimal behavior at all times," said the Teacher. "Stop scratching."

"I'm supposed to itch," I said, giving my arm one final scrape. "It's a bad sign if I don't."

"Scratching and fidgeting are not optimal behaviors," said the Teacher. "Not in any context. It is time for breakfast." They gestured to a door that had opened to my right.

My days were strictly regimented. I slept at precisely the pre-scribed time, woke, ate, cleaned dishes, conversed with the Teacher, a scripted business. Any deviation was met with a disapproving twitch of the Teacher's eyebrow.

After many repetitions of this cycle, I complained that I was bored. The Teacher gave me the eyebrow, but the next day I was presented with what the Teacher called *a suitable activity*: a dish of soil, a tool for rearranging that soil, a water vessel, and some seeds. I considered complaining that this was hardly much of an activity, but decided that further complaints would not be optimal behavior. And if there was even the remotest chance of escaping from here, into the World, the path to that escape would only be reachable through convincing everyone around me that I would behave optimally.

I thanked the Teacher, planted a seed in the dish of soil, watered it, and sat down to watch it develop. It was actually mildly interesting, in a way I hadn't noticed in the garden in the Edges. There had been so many plants there, so many striving stems, so many light-following leaves, that I had never really looked closely at the way plants were plants.

Here, in these plain, gray-walled rooms, was just the one tiny germinating seed, sprouting in mere hours, the next day sporting two tiny leaves, the seed case split and discarded, a tiny rootlet plunging into the soil. I could almost hear it growing.

I didn't think I'd ever heard a plant grow before. Should I report it to the Teacher? What would the consequences of that be?

But the Teacher had said nothing about the possibility. Had I heard it in the garden but not noticed it because it was part of the general background noise there? Or was this something new? I had only been ordered to report a cessation of the unpleasant feeling on my skin. The Teacher had also said that planting a seed was a suitable activity—and added a fixed set of lines about it to our daily conversational script.

Well. Optimal behavior, the Teacher had made abundantly clear, involved doing as I was told. I would therefore do precisely as I had been told, no more and no less.

My plant grew larger, put out ruffled, coarse leaves. Its tiny sound was a sharp little song in my quiet rooms, changing infinitesimally each moment, the only thing that seemed to change in that unchanging cycle of scripted, scheduled hours. And then, one day, a large change—the Teacher announced that I would harvest and eat my plant.

I plucked it from the soil, washed the small, red, bulbous root and the leaves. I wanted suddenly to rub the leaves on my skin, but I was absolutely certain that would not be optimal behavior, and so instead I surreptitiously brushed them across the back of one hand. The plant's song changed as I pulled the leaves away, sliced the root (it was white inside, and even sharper smelling than the uncut root), and arranged these small things on a dish. I sat down, very properly, in a chair, at a table, and used a tool to lift the tiny pieces of radish to my mouth, one by one. The plant's tiny song faded as I ate it, melted somehow into my mouth, a disconcertingly pleasant sensation, and the room was suddenly silent.

"What did it taste like?" asked the Teacher, and I realized that this had been a test of some kind, but I didn't understand what the test had been of, or what my answer should be.

"Like stinging," I replied. "May I plant another?" Actually, I wanted very much to try some different sort of plant, and I knew from the tiny sounds of the seeds I'd been given that they were all very similar. But another one of these would be very nice.

"Yes," said the Teacher, and I could tell by their eyebrows that I had said the right thing.

Enae

Enae remembered Deputy Envoy Buren saying, *Can you imagine if the Hikipi managed to produce a Schan? It doesn't bear thinking on.* And, curious after hir experience in Keroxane and the little bit sie already knew about Hikipi history, sie had looked for more information. Not because sie thought it would help hir find the fugitive sie was looking for, but just because it seemed interesting. Because sie'd run across the name in hir previous researches and now wanted to know more.

There were no more Schans, not that anyone could tell. Which was probably good, because something like eight out of ten stories that featured them, even the ones focused on romance or friendship, involved people being mutilated or dismembered, or even eaten. Enae wasn't sure if a Schan turning up now after a thousand years could really unite the various factions in the seven Zones, but sie hadn't thought it was a question that needed any sort of an answer.

Could Reet Hluid actually be a Schan? How would anyone know?

It wasn't what Enae was here to find out, but...

He really didn't want to tell the story of how he came to Rurusk. Enae could see that in his expression, in the stiff way he sat (even beyond very clearly not being happy about the woman next to him having put her hand on his shoulder).

He looked at the woman's hand, and she smirked and removed it, with a placating gesture.

"I came to Zeosen as a baby. On a ship full of refugees." He named a conflict, and a system, that Enae had never heard of.

Sie nodded anyway, as though sie knew what he was talking about. "You came with your family?"

"No," said Mr Hluid, slightly abashed, Enae thought. Stiffer and more awkward even than usual. "Just me. No one knew where I'd come from. No one had seen me until it was time to disembark, and there I was on a seat in the galley, just...lying there. Nobody had ever seen me before. Nobody knew who I was or who I belonged to."

"It's true," put in Mr Nadkal. "There are recordings."

"But not from the whole ship, or they'd have known who Mr Hluid was with," Enae suggested.

"Just so," agreed Mr Nadkal. "It's just like Veni Schan, the first Sovereign Autarch, you know. He arrived at Lovehate Station alone, as an infant."

Mr Hluid looked at Mr Nadkal as though he wasn't entirely happy about the interruption. "Well, they tried to find anyone I might be related to, but there didn't seem to be anyone. So I was adopted."

They tried to find anyone I might be related to, but there didn't seem to be anyone. For just a moment hir mind presented a single clear, wholly formed, electrifying thought. But no. It wasn't possible. "But you're Hikipi?" sie ventured.

"Well, you see." Nadkal, clearly unable to keep from taking over the story. "We had been looking, for years, for any trace of the Schans. Of, as you said earlier, Lovehate Station. Supposedly disappeared, and Lovehate Station was destroyed, you know, along with any data stored there, but we had hoped! It took years and years of investigation, but we finally found him!"

"My goodness, Mr Hluid!" exclaimed Enae. The thought that had presented itself to hir would not leave hir. "You didn't tell me any of this!"

"He's Mr Schan here," said someone, which elicited a small, pained smile from Mr Hluid. Or maybe it was a grimace.

"I see," said Enae, blandly. "Blessed ancestors! What other amazing stories do you all have?"

It couldn't be. *It couldn't be.* "So there's no genetic evidence of any connection to the Schans?" Enae asked Mr Hluid as he brought hir another cup of warm, watery milk. He explained about the difference between the genetics of people who had lived on Lovehate Station hundreds of years ago and the genetics of people who claimed their ancestors had come from Lovehate Station. "I see," sie said, though sie didn't, not entirely. "And everyone seems to think you're obviously Hikipi just to look at you. Your hair…"

"Most people think of Hikipi as having that light, frizzy hair," Mr Hluid said. "But there are lots with straight, very dark hair." He shrugged—uncomfortable, Enae thought. "I don't know." And then, in a rush, "Honestly, I don't know if they're right or not, but it's the only time anyone's claimed I belong to them."

"Except your parents," Enae put in.

"Yes, but that's...that's different."

Sie thought of Athtur House. Of hir mother's funeral, when sie had been small, and of Grandmaman. "I suppose. Are they still...your parents, I mean...?"

"Yes. Yes, and they've always had a houseful of foster children."

"Are they good to you?"

"Yes," he said, without hesitation.

"Belonging isn't always about genetics," sie said.

Mr Hluid sighed. "It's just, I've always been different. My parents, they...I mean, they love all their children, I'm sure they do. But I'm just...I'm just different. Everyone knows it. Not, I mean, you wouldn't know it just passing in the corridor or whatever. But it's obvious I don't belong anywhere."

"The Siblings of Hikipu don't seem to find it obvious."

He sighed again. "Sometimes I think they're right, and I really am a Schan like they say, and then sometimes...but they act like I belong to them. And that...I don't know."

"I've always known where I belonged," said Enae. "It makes me so happy to get away from that." Sie thought then, inexplicably, of Caphing and hir cheerful, friendly messages.

"You're lucky," said Mr Hluid.

"So what do you think?" Mr Nadkal, breaking in on their

momentary small isolation. He spread his arms, indicating the meeting room, the chatting Siblings of Hikipu. "What do you think of our small association?"

"It's lovely," said Enae. "Such wonderful songs, and such…" Sie hesitated just a moment, looking for a word. "Such warm fellowship. And such fascinating history!" And then, seized with an idea, "And I'm so impressed by the way you found Mr Schan, here! To find him after so long and so far. I wonder if you'd share with me how you did that." Beside hir, Mr Hluid shifted. A wince? A stifled protest? "If, that is, Mr Schan doesn't mind."

"It's not like my saying no could stop you," said Mr Hluid, brusque and matter-of-fact.

"Well, but you might not like the idea of being the example in someone's lesson." Did he realize what sie was thinking? What sie was really asking for?

Did Mr Nadkal? Sie wasn't sure. Sie knew that Mr Hluid suspected Mr Nadkal of being some sort of conduit of information from the Siblings of Hikipu to Foreign Affairs, of being more involved in Keroxane affairs than it might appear, but more than that sie couldn't tell, not by just looking at him.

And, sie realized, if Mr Nadkal was involved in Keroxane affairs, he might well assume that Enae was a spy for the Phen. The thought made hir feel slightly sick. But years of dealing with Grandmaman had schooled hir patience and taught hir control over hir voice and hir expression. "I only ask because you've obviously done an impressive job of historical research, tracking Mr Schan down. I could learn from that."

"I'd be happy to share, Mx Athtur! I'll authorize our agent to send you the data, and of course we'll be more than happy to answer questions you might have about our methods."

It took Enae several days to go through the information Mr Nadkal sent hir, and a few more to read up on subjects that sie needed to understand in order to make sense of all that information.

The identification of Mr Hluid as a Schan rested on three very thin supports, Enae thought. One was a hypothetical route from Lovehate Station to Zeosen. The second was a small genetic similarity to the existing populations of Keroxane System, or at least the segment of those populations that the investigators had data for. The third...

The third was a bit of Mr Hluid's genes that had made the analysts collect and rerun the samples three different times— genes that no one in Zeosen had ever seen before, that bore, so far as they could tell, no relationship to any other human beings anywhere they knew about. *The mitochondrial genome*, read the note on the analysis, *does not fit into any known phylogeny*. The note went on to list a few possible reasons why such a thing might have happened (some form of genemodding that the analysts were unaware of, for instance), but those were only guesses until the right data might come along. There were also segments that usually occurred close to each other in most humans, but that in Mr Hluid appeared to be broken up, interspersed with sequences the analysts found not just unfamiliar but unsettling. Once again, the notes offered the possibility of some sort of genemodding the analysts had never seen before.

Now, the Schans were secretive, and known for genemodding themselves. Enae knew that from the consultant's final report and from the various historical texts sie had scanned over the last several days. And Mr Nadkal and his agent had been looking for a Schan. Had been determined to find a Schan, it seemed to Enae. Determined to see *Schan* in Mr Hluid's history.

But maybe sie hirself was determined to find what sie was looking for, too. Still, hir doubt was nothing next to the growing conviction, like lead in hir stomach, that sie had found what sie had been sent to look for. Or at least as close as sie could get, now the search was some two centuries old. What no one had thought was possible for hir to find.

The route that said *Schan* to Nadkal's investigators said *Presger* to Enae. Well, any route might suit the Presger: no one knew precisely where they came from or how they traveled; they could, it seemed, appear anywhere. But Enae had been drawn to look at travelers through Keroxane precisely because it was relatively near the Treaty Administration Facility—the one place one could say with confidence that a Presger Translator might be found.

The small genetic similarity to Keroxani populations—well, all humans were related, ultimately. Everyone had come from somewhere. Even the Presger Translators, whose ancestors had been human once, would be related somehow to someone in human space. No, that similarity didn't say *Presger* to Enae, but it didn't definitely say *Hikipi* to hir, either. Those genetic sequences in Mr Hluid were fairly common in people who declared themselves to be Hikipi, but they turned up in other groups as well. Not surprisingly.

And the last. The mitochondrial genome that the Zeoseni analysts had choked on. *An obvious stranger*, Ambassador Tiniye had told Saeniss Polity two hundred years ago, and this was obviously strange. And sie could trace a possible route for the infant Mr Hluid that would make sense if he was the fugitive sie was looking for. Or—because he was far too young to be that person—the offspring of the fugitive sie was looking for.

The feeling of happy triumph at solving a problem came weighted down with dread. But why? Mr Hluid had spoken of not belonging, in a way that made Enae think that the Siblings of Hikipu claiming him had answered something in him, had given him something he'd been missing. And that was its own problem: very clearly someone among the Hikipi wanted a Schan to bring the Zones together—why go to such lengths otherwise? Fairly obviously, Mr Nadkal—or someone he was working for—had gone to some lengths to find a plausible Schan, and just as obviously their motivations had far more to do with the situation in Keroxane than they did with Mr Hluid.

Better to let Mr Hluid know he wasn't part of that, or didn't have to be if he didn't want. And if Enae had discovered, definitively, where Mr Hluid belonged, wouldn't he be pleased?

But what would that mean, exactly, to discover that you belonged with aliens? That you were not, in fact, quite as human as you'd supposed? And what would it mean for his future? Surely he wouldn't be able to stay here escorting diplomatic visitors and doing whatever else he did? Sie knew, after his assisting hir for the last several days, that he followed a drama called *Pirate Exiles of the Death Moons*, and that his parents lived on a moon somewhere in the system, but that was pretty much all sie knew. Would he be able to stay in contact with his parents? Would he be able to get episodes of *Pirate Exiles* in Presger space?

No, that was a ridiculous question. But they surely wouldn't let him stay here, once they knew he existed. Or would they? After all, he'd been here for years—for decades!—with no mishap. He knew nothing about whatever parent had passed down that strange DNA. Maybe they would close the file and let him be.

Sie looked, then, into legal issues surrounding the treaty with the Presger. Sie knew that most of the aliens that were part of the treaty used humans to speak to the Presger—in fact, all of the aliens in the treaty had been admitted partly because of their close association with humans. You could argue, Enae thought, that the Presger Translators stood in the same relationship to the Presger as the human ambassadors for the Rrrrr and the Geck did for those species. Those humans were allowed to be considered Rrrrr or Geck under the treaty, and…aha! In certain circumstances, a human could choose what species they belonged to.

That was all right, then. It seemed to Enae that Mr Hluid should be able to choose whether he was human or Presger Translator.

Sie *liked* Reet Hluid. He was conscientious and, so far as Enae could see, honest, and he had an off-kilter sense of humor that Enae appreciated. Sie wasn't anxious for his welfare, exactly, but sie didn't like to think that what sie was doing would injure him. But really, it should be fine.

Shouldn't it? It would be all right, because legally he could choose where he belonged.

So if he could choose, if it came down to his choice, if it was his future and his place, wherever that place might be, sie should tell him what sie had found. Ask him what he would like hir to do with the information. After all, no one expected hir to find the person sie'd been sent to look for, let alone expected hir to find Reet Hluid. And it was Reet who would be most affected by whatever action sie took.

But sie hesitated.

For three days sie said nothing. No choice seemed to be the right one.

In the end, sie handled it the way sie would have handled a delicate issue with Grandmaman: act first, then confess and weather the resulting storm. Sie composed a report, sent it to Caphing, and then—because, like it or not, any issue involving the Presger fell under the authority of the Radchaai Ambassadors Office—sie sent the same report to the Treaty Administration Facility. And then she asked Mr Hluid to meet her.

Reet

"Mr Hluid, please sit down," said Mx Athtur, hir voice small and quiet. Sie hirself sat still and, Reet thought, somehow folded in on hirself in a way he'd never seen hir. Except, maybe, when he'd brought hir back here from the medical facility, the day sie'd been attacked.

"I don't want to sit down!" he snapped. He wanted to scream. He wanted to cry. He wanted to storm out of Mx Athtur's accommodation and never speak to hir again. "You're wrong. You're *wrong*. Whatever could possibly have given you the idea..." But he knew what had given hir the idea. Sie'd just laid it out for him in that small, calm voice. "I'm *human*!" he insisted. "They've looked at my genetic data dozens of times. If I wasn't human they'd know. If I wasn't human I wouldn't have DNA. I'd have..." He threw his hands up in furious, distressed exasperation. Mx Athtur flinched, just slightly, as though sie'd expected him to strike hir. "Something else." That flinch had startled something out of him, and he found he didn't have the energy, or the words, to continue. He dropped into the chair that he'd just been invited to sit in, closed his eyes, and put his fingertips on his forehead. "You're wrong," he said again. "That's all. You're just wrong."

"I imagine the ambassador to the Presger will know for certain." Mx Athtur's voice, still small, and quiet. "Mr Hluid, I'm sorry, but no matter what the ambassador to the Presger says, I don't think you're really Hikipi. I know that you said it was the first time you felt like you belonged somewhere…"

He opened his eyes, straightened to look at Mx Athtur, still motionless and contained. "So you have to be sure and take that away."

"No!" sie protested, an expression of distress breaking through what Reet thought must have been a carefully controlled mask of disinterested, mild regret. "No, I don't want to take anything from you! It's just"—sie waved a hand—"I don't think the information Mr Nadkal shared with me fits. And even if the genetics worked out, that wouldn't mean you were one of them. Belonging isn't about whether your genes match. *Family* isn't about that."

"What else do I have?" he asked. And then felt a stab of guilt, because of course he had Mom and Maman and Nana and all his foster sibs. Who all loved him, he knew that, but somehow…

"Look," Mx Athtur said, hir voice and expression matter-of-fact. "I grew up in a family I was genetically related to, but most of them didn't care about me. Your parents love you. You have sibs. It might not be a place to belong in the sense that everyone understands you or is like you somehow, but it's a place you belong. Because they love you. And that's worth so much." Hir face flushed and sie seemed almost on the edge of some kind of distress. "Do you really feel like you belong with the Siblings of Hikipu? Or did they tolerate the ways you *didn't* belong because you fit some story they wanted to tell about themselves?" Sie frowned, and looked as though sie wanted to say more. "Or maybe there isn't really a difference. But I'm sure I'm right! The evidence that you're Hikipi at all, let alone a Schan—well, there's no evidence for your being a Schan, Mr Hluid. None. And the evidence that you're Hikipi is very thin and can be explained several different ways. The report that Mr Nadkal shared with me tries to hide that, but the more you look into it, the more it doesn't hold up. And look, why would anyone go to all the trouble, just to convince themselves or you that you're a Schan? Why does that matter so much?"

"It matters because of Lovehate Station..."

"Yes, I know, I read about it, and about the ancient rulers of Lovehate Station. Why would Mr Nadkal want so badly to put his hands on the descendant of the rulers of a destroyed station?" Reet could find no answer to this question, and Mx Athtur continued. "Mr Nadkal is no fool. If what you and I suspect is true, he is very possibly sending information from the Zeoseni Foreign Affairs Office to Hikipi Nationalists in Keroxane!"

Now Reet put his face fully into his hands. "They're using me."

"Or holding you in reserve in case they find it useful to

produce you. I can think of several ways that might play out, though they're all from adventure serials so maybe they aren't so likely."

Reet had a sudden urge to talk to Mom. She would have something wise to say about this. It maybe wouldn't make him feel better, but it would be...solid. "I don't know what to think," he said, into his hands. "I don't know what anything is, right now."

"I'm sorry." Mx Athtur's voice sounded miserable. "I didn't want to make you unhappy. I didn't want to disturb your life. It's just...when you told the story, that night at the meeting..."

Reet sighed and looked up. "I'm still human."

"So were the Presger Translators, once. Maybe they still are, kind of. I don't know. They'll know at the Treaty Administration Facility, though. It should take about three more days for my message to arrive there, and four or five for a reply, maybe more if it takes a while to reach the right person, or if they have to look into any of the data." Sie started to put hir hand out, as though reaching for him, and then stopped. "Look, whatever the answer is, you'll know something about your history, even if it's only a negative."

Reet made a disgusted noise. "I guess it would explain some things, if I really am an alien."

Mx Athtur frowned. "Mr Hluid. I'm so very sorry that my work has distressed you so much. You're a good person, and I've been so very grateful to have your help all this time. Not only have you been helpful, but you've been..." Sie stopped, as though sie was searching for the right word. "Restful and pleasant to be around. I always know if I do the wrong thing with you, but not in a way that…" Sie stopped again. "I never feel like I'm walking a tightrope, with you. I just wanted you to know that. I really appreciate your being here."

"Even if I'm not human?"

"Even if you're not human," sie said, very seriously.

Getting back to his small quarters from Mx Athtur's accommodation involved two trams and a walk. The whole trip Reet felt exposed. Visible. As though everyone were looking at him, everyone could see just how wrong he was, just how he wasn't one of them. It was, truth be told, a familiar feeling, one he'd grown accustomed to. Time and habit had made that feeling a low, constant mutter that quieted (when it did) only when he was in private.

Now it was loud. It scraped at his nerves in a way it never had before. Or maybe he'd just forgotten how it had felt when he'd been younger. He found himself hyper-aware of everyone around him, as though he could feel their presence or even hear it somehow. The second tram he took was crowded, and he stood, gripping a handhold, pressed on all sides by people—ordinary, human people, not like Reet—who were, of course, looking anywhere but at Reet, just like they ought to, just like any polite tram rider, but Reet was overpowered by the conviction that they were all of them staring at him.

He thought, suddenly, of his dreams, those disturbing, ecstatic visions of melting into someone else, skin and bones and organs dissolving. What if one of these people who pressed so close…but no. No, that was wrong, he knew it was. He found he was sweating, and closed his eyes for a moment and did his best to think of anything besides the fact that he was surrounded by people he could (so something in the back of his mind insisted) melt into, just like in those dreams.

He had to get off the tram. The only way was to press himself through the bodies that stood between himself and the exit, to push himself up against the door (his hand left a slimy-sticky trail of sweat), ready to dash out the moment the tram slowed to the next stop. (A panicked wipe of his sleeve on the door came away stringy, like partly dried adhesive.) The door opened, and Reet was away, quickly, trying not to hyperventilate, trying not to run, trying not to panic. *I'm not human.* He knew it with a sudden, horrible conviction. It explained so much.

He'd gotten off the tram three stops too early. Well. He could walk. He could avoid people. (He didn't want to avoid people. He wanted to get back on the tram and press close to someone, anyone.) *He could avoid people.* He had the rest of the day to himself, Mx Athtur had promised sie wouldn't go anywhere and would have hir meals delivered to hir room. He could buy dumplings and coffee—he wouldn't even have to talk to another person to do that, he knew where to get them from bots. He could take the food back to his room, clean himself up in his tiny sanitary facility, curl up in his bedcovers, eat dumplings, and watch *Pirate Exiles of the Death Moons* until he fell asleep.

He couldn't eat the dumplings, he could barely drink the coffee, and he definitely couldn't sleep. Nausea overtook him, his heart pounded in his chest. Something was wrong. Or maybe nothing was wrong, maybe this was completely normal for a Presger Translator. Or maybe he was sick in some way that wouldn't make sense to the doctors at the Health Facility but would be completely routine to a Presger Translator doctor. Did they have doctors?

What if he was dying? What if he was dying and no one here could do anything about it, because he wasn't human? What should he do? There was nothing he could do.

Well, he could start the familiar first episode of *Pirate Exiles of the Death Moons*, and that would distract him at least a little bit from his distress.

He spent the next several days like that. Not eating, occasionally dozing, *Pirate Exiles* playing on his handheld. Occasionally a message from Mx Athtur would come through—sie was fine, Reet wasn't to worry, but if he'd like to come out and have lunch or anything else, Mx Athtur would be happy to see him. Sie just wanted to be sure he was all right. Reet knew it would be less trouble to reply promptly to hir messages than it would be to deal with Mx Athtur if, worried, sie came looking for him. So, for hir benefit, he was fine, don't worry, he just needed some time to himself. Sie understood, every time, and every time sie wanted Reet to know that sie would be happy to see him whenever he was ready.

I'm not human. The thought kept recurring, and he tried at first to push it away, but it didn't work. Of course it didn't work, that never worked. And so he left it alone, to hang there in his thoughts. He drowned it out with *Pirate Exiles* when he could. Tried his best not to think at all.

Every time he picked up his handheld to message his parents, he stopped. What would he tell them? Nana would say they should have known it all along. (*E doesn't mean any harm*, Maman would say.) But if he messaged them—all text, because Reet wasn't going to sit in front of a camera in this state; there was no telling how he looked or how he would sound—if he messaged them, Nana would say what e had to say there, where Reet couldn't hear em, and Mom and Maman would reprove em and maybe (e had apologized last time and even behaved better afterward) maybe e would listen, and control eir tongue when e did finally get to speak to Reet.

They had adopted a human child. Or so they had thought. All those things that had marked him out as strange, as not belonging—those weren't normal, human things at all, they were alien. Truly alien. What would they say when they knew?

What did Reet have if he lost them?

He barely allowed himself to think the thought. Convinced himself he hadn't thought it. He could never, ever have done his parents that injustice, to think them so shallow, so fickle in their loyalty to their children, who he knew they loved. (But what if Reet was so different, so inhuman, that you couldn't blame his parents for abandoning him, for discovering that they didn't, after all, love Reet as well as they had thought?) No, he didn't want to worry them. There would be time enough to tell them when the reply came back from the Treaty Administration Facility, and maybe that reply would be "No, Reet Hluid is definitely not a Presger Translator." (Reet knew that wasn't what the reply would say. He felt it in his bones, he felt it deep in his unhappy gut.)

He dozed again. And startled awake to his door opening, the tinny sound of a ship's alarm, the heroic first mate of the Pirate Exiles crying, "They're cutting through the hull, sir!"

Someone stepped into his room, and he came fully awake, heart racing, mouth dry. The intruder wore full protective gear—gloves, boots, helmet, all sealed up, as though Reet had something terribly, dangerously contagious. Through the door, in the bright corridor, there were more gleaming, suited figures.

"Reet Hluid," said the intruder as Reet lay there, naked and half under his bedcovers. "You are under arrest."

Qven

Four radishes later, Translator Dlar visited me. They came without warning into my rooms. I was nearly paralyzed with surprise, but "*Stand*" hissed Teacher urgently in my ear.

Automatically I rose and said, "Translator Dlar. This is a pleasant surprise."

"Qven," they acknowledged. "How have you been?"

I knew this exchange. I had practiced it in the Edges, and it was part of the daily ritual Teacher imposed on me here. "I've been well, thank you, Translator. And you?" They said nothing, only looked at me appraisingly.

Undeterred, I continued with the next line of the exchange that would fall to me. "Will you have some tea?" I had no idea if there was enough for a visitor, but it was hardly my fault if Teacher hadn't told me the Translator was coming.

"Thank you, I will," said the Translator, and sat down at my tiny table.

I got out the tea things—Teacher stood away in the corner of the room, staring at me fixedly. Well, that was like usual. I prepared the tea, put the flask and tiny, delicate tea bowls on the tray, and brought them to the table. Sat, across from Translator Dlar.

"Your Teacher speaks well of you," said the Translator, shockingly pleasant, as I poured.

"I'm gratified to hear that, Translator. I'm doing my best."

"So I see." They took a small sip of tea. "Tzam," they began.

I blinked, doing my best to conceal my flinch at hearing the name. Translator Dlar seemed not to notice.

They continued: "...has essentially admitted guilt. Not, you understand, in so many words. But they were offered a match far more prestigious than they might otherwise expect—with the understanding that their partner would of course report whatever they learned in the process of matching. Complete exoneration, potentially, and a far better future than they can expect as things stand now."

I took my own sip of tea. "They refused?"

"Their clade refused for them, of course. But the refusal itself tells us a good deal."

"More tea?"

"Please."

I poured. "What will happen to them now?" I found I couldn't quite bring myself to say their name.

Translator Dlar made an unconcerned gesture, as if to say, *Who cares?* "They'll match somewhere in their own clade, I imagine. Or more likely be disposed of." They took another sip of tea. "The important thing is, we can be sure of what happened. You behaved foolishly, there's no question, and our original plans for you are impossible now, but we might still have a place for you."

This definitely wasn't part of any script I'd ever practiced. But surely some sentence would work here. "I'm glad to hear it, Translator." Not perfect, but it would do.

"Are you?" they asked. "Good. We'll be leaving for the Treaty Administration Facility in one hour."

"The..." I was caught by utter surprise. No plausible reply offered itself. "Excuse me, Translator. I don't understand."

"Ah." They waved away my wordless offer of more tea. "Your Teacher tells me you do best with some explanation beforehand. Not something you always get when dealing with humans." Their acerbic tone returned, just for a moment. Rebuke, I thought, for not meeting the ideal expected of me. "I will explain. Understand, though"—they leaned forward and looked me seriously in the eyes—"I do not present any choices. There are no options here. There is only your future, as it will be."

Which, I supposed, was why they didn't bother telling us things. Because it's not like we could avoid them. "I understand, Translator." That line was nearly always effective.

"About two hundred years ago," said Translator Dlar, "one of our clade fled into human space." I must have shown some expression on my face, because they said, very quickly, "The way they managed it is immaterial, and that leak has been securely patched."

I tried to put confused innocence on my face. "I'm sure, Translator. You were saying?"

"We searched and couldn't find them. At length we

notified the human emissary. We couldn't have one of us just wandering around human space doing who knows what! Bad enough they'd run away, imagine the sort of trouble they might cause."

"They must have been very clever to have found a way to escape." Immediately I knew it had been the wrong thing to say. "Would you like a tiny cake, Translator? They're very sweet. I made them myself."

The cake didn't entirely remove the suspicion my incautious remark had engendered in Translator Dlar's manner. I would have to be more careful. "Of course they were clever," they said, when they'd swallowed the cake. "All our clade is." They gave me a sharp look. "Years passed and we heard nothing. We had begun to think the fugitive had managed to get themselves killed somehow. But recently we have discovered..." They stopped. Looked at the small tray of cakes as though it contained something nauseatingly poisonous. "The fugitive," said Translator Dlar, "produced offspring."

"Produced offspring!" I couldn't imagine anything less likely. "How?"

"The usual way, I imagine. Or maybe not." They frowned.

"But what..." And then I realized. "No!" I stood, nearly oversetting my chair. "I won't."

Instantly Teacher was at my side. A threat, I knew. I calmed my breathing as best I could, and sat.

"This is why we don't usually tell you children things like this," said Translator Dlar. "Are you going to behave?"

"Yes, Translator," I said, as meekly as I could manage.

"This is a better future for you than might otherwise be available. We don't know what abilities or disabilities the offspring might bring to a match, but they undoubtedly have experience dealing with humans. There's no longer any future for you as a Translator, but someone of your intelligence and skills, joined to extensive knowledge of humans, would be very useful to us. It's quite to everyone's benefit." I said nothing, and Translator Dlar continued. "It's far, far better than anything else that might become of you."

I had to say something. "I understand, Translator." Yes. Yes, that was right.

"Good." They seemed relieved. "You need some time to get used to the idea. Your Teacher will make some useful information available to you. You'll have some time to think about it. Your match won't reach the Treaty Administration Facility for at least another two weeks, more likely longer."

"Thank you, Translator." I took a deep breath. "I'm very grateful for your explanations."

That seemed to please them. They took another cake. "These are very good."

"Thank you, Translator," I said again, as they ate it.

I was going to the Treaty Administration Facility. All sorts of ships came and went from there, to and from all sorts of places.

I had a week—maybe more, but call it a week—to find some way to escape. And I would have to be very, very good so that no one suspected my intentions. "I've been growing vegetables," I said to Translator Dlar. "Or radishes, anyway. It's very nice." I frowned, just a little. Made my expression just the least bit sad and pleading. "Are there other things I can grow? I like the radishes very much, but I'd like to try some others."

"We'll see." The Translator relaxed. "I think we can probably find you something appropriate."

"Thank you, Translator," I said for a third time.

Reaching the Treaty Administration Facility was as simple as packing a few things (under the severe gaze of Teacher) and walking down a corridor to a different set of rooms. "Here we are," said Teacher, and took their accustomed place in the corners.

These new quarters were larger, with more objects for sitting or putting things on. My little tray of soil, with its tiny, humming radish seed, looked small and lonely on its shelf here.

There seemed to be more rooms available to me, and I wanted to look at them all and see just what I was dealing with. But I also needed to be very, very good, so good that no one would ever imagine that I was planning to flee.

I folded my few bits of clothes onto the shelf near the new bed—a very large bed, I noticed, and managed not to shiver at that. And there was one room that I could only catch a glimpse of through its open doors: it was empty, floored and walled with slick tile and a sort of depression in the center. Teacher said nothing about that room and seemed never to give me the opportunity to look closer, but I thought they watched me more intently whenever I passed that door. I remembered that pulsing mass of flesh in the garden, remembered why I had been brought here, and schooled my movements and expression as best I could.

Now we were at the facility, now I was being so good and had some use, it seemed Translator Dlar was pleased to have tea with me daily. These were brief, bland occasions, where we exchanged fixed pleasantries, but I knew that it was progress of a sort, and any small change might offer opportunities.

When it seemed to me that I had been perfectly well-behaved for several days, I dared to vary my conversation with Translator Dlar. "Translator," I began. "I recall that my Teacher said I did best with some explanation to prepare me. And I have been thinking that if you want me to find information this fugitive's offspring might have, about how and why they fled"—I would not make the mistake of saying *escaped* again—"I should know more about the situation. After all, it would be a shame to miss some vital fact because I didn't realize its importance."

They actually smiled. "Never fear. You'll have all the information you require when the time comes."

"I'm relieved to hear it, Translator."

They sipped their tea, and then asked, "What was it about seeing the illicit match in the garden that frightened you so badly?"

I did my best not to react. I didn't want to talk about this, not with anyone but particularly not with Translator Dlar.

But any escape, if escape was possible, would come through my seeming to be completely biddable. I took a deep breath, as though I found answering difficult (as, indeed, I did), and said, "All the other Edges. They wanted to *eat* it."

"Ah," said Translator Dlar, as if something had suddenly made sense to them.

I decided it was worth pushing a little further. "They would have eaten it if the Teachers hadn't come just then."

"Adults don't eat others, not the way juveniles do. You're

the only juvenile here, just now." They frowned. "Or ever. We don't allow juveniles to leave the hatchery. You're only here because you've been rendered as safe as possible, and you're needed to assist with the fugitive offspring." They made an exasperated gesture. "None of that is our doing. But no one here can eat you." They glanced for some reason at Teacher. "You will be able to eat things, though. It will just be different. Watch." They drank the rest of their tea, set the bowl on the table, and gestured to Teacher, who left the room and returned with the tray that held my tiny, sprouting radish. Translator Dlar plucked the sprout from the soil, set it on the table, and with one hand ground it into a damp, smashed mess on the table surface. Then they swept this up and put it into their mouth and swallowed. "Now," they said, and leaned forward and vomited the tiny radish, whole and undamaged, onto the table. I stared, fascinated. Translator Dlar said, "You can't do that yet. But you will. It's really very gratifying. And quite, quite different from eating people the way that children do. You're quite safe, I promise you. No one here is a threat, and of course I and your Teacher will be watching over you, to be sure no harm comes to you."

"Thank you for explaining, Translator."

They nodded, pleased. "I'll have your Teacher explain a bit more of the process, and show you where it will take place. Hopefully that will settle any doubts you might still have."

"Thank you, Translator." I took another sip of my own tea. "Translator, you said I might have some other kind of seeds to grow."

"I did," they said with a real, whole smile, and for just a moment I thought they were going to vomit up a handful of seeds, but instead they said, "And interesting plants are easier to come by here than at home. Let me ask around and I'll find you something enjoyable."

"Thank you, Translator," I said, and I thought that even Teacher relaxed, just a bit.

Enae

It only took Enae a day or so to find Reet's family and get in contact with them, adept as sie had become at tracking down information.

It would take some time for Istver and Echemin Hluid to reach Rurusk. Meanwhile, Enae gathered, Reet himself was being held...somewhere. All of hir requests to see him were refused. It was time, sie thought, to bring hir best resources to bear.

Sie got—through plain determination (sie refused to call it rudeness)—an in-person appointment with Reet's supervisor. Who tried to put hir off with apologies and coffee, but Enae, channeling Grandmaman, had sat stiff-straight in hir seat and declared that sie would not be trifled with. To no avail. Frustrated, she strode angrily out of the office, only to find Mr Nadkal.

"Ah, Mx Athtur!" He seemed entirely unsurprised to see

hir, which Enae somehow found irritating. "No doubt," Mr Nadkal continued, oblivious, "you are here on the same errand as I am! Someone has to help poor Mr Schan. And if not us, who?"

"His family," said Enae, taken aback. "I mean..." Sie was going to say *they've retained a jurist here on Rurusk* but then realized maybe sie didn't want to share too much information with Mr Nadkal, who Mr Hluid himself had not trusted entirely.

"Ah. Mr Schan's *family*"—Mr Nadkal leaned on that word, doubt or maybe contempt in his tone—"is Chirra. So..." He gestured vaguely. "You know."

"No," said Enae, genuinely perplexed. "I don't." And as the words left hir mouth, sie realized that sie could probably guess.

"They're from Neanthine," Mr Nadkal explained, and Enae gestured hir ignorance of that location. "It's a station in this system. A complete trash hole of a station, everyone fighting everyone else. They come here, you know, because it's peaceful, and they bring all their relatives, and have child after child and send the upbringing stipend back to their Imagarch. It's a *religious* obligation." Mr Nadkal said *religious* the way he'd said *family*. "They have plenty of other children to look after, they won't waste their effort on this one unless they see a way to profit off it."

"I see," said Enae. "Well, if you'll excuse me, I have a..."

"And really, you know, this is all about getting rid of a legitimate heir to Lovehate Station," said Mr Nadkal, leaning in closer and lowering his voice. "I don't think you quite realize how important it is for patriotic Hikipi that we've finally found a Schan. And now they're trying to take him away from us!"

"Mr Nadkal, I am interested in Mr Hluid's well-being and safety as a person. Not because he's anyone in particular."

"Yes, yes!" agreed Mr Nadkal. "So are the Siblings of Hikipu! Come have coffee, and we'll talk about how best to help him."

"And by the way, Mr Nadkal. It was a patriotic Hikipi who knocked me on the head and stole my things not long ago. I had quite a serious concussion."

Mr Nadkal made an almost comical grimace. "Oh, Mx Athtur, that was a terrible misunderstanding. I can explain while we—"

"And as I was saying before you interrupted me," sie said, sternly, "I have an appointment."

"Later, then," called Mr Nadkal as Enae strode off.

"Ah," said the jurist, when Enae met with em not an hour later. "You were wise not to say more than you did. We definitely don't want the Siblings of Hikipu to take charge of this effort. It's bad enough they won't call Mr Hluid by his name—I guarantee they'd call him Mr Schan in petitions."

Enae said, "Mr Nadkal seemed to think that this entire business is about removing the heir to Lovehate Station. But Lovehate Station doesn't even exist anymore!"

"Oh, it gets worse than that," said the jurist. "There's every likelihood any petitions their jurists submit will be full of nonsense about how the Presger don't really exist and were just made up by the Radchaai so they can secretly control every other system authority."

Enae frowned. "I don't think the Radchaai need to control anything secretly?"

The jurist raised eir hands in agreement—or maybe surrender. "It makes sense to them. But it will look unhinged to the authorities we're dealing with, and we don't want to be associated with that sort of thing if we can help it. That said...well, we can use any support we can get, and groups like the Siblings of Hikipu are often excellent at fundraising. I'll contact Mr Nadkal myself and see what he can offer us."

"I don't like it," protested Enae. "I don't like the way they won't call Mr Hluid by his name, and I don't like the fact Mr Nadkal as much as admitted he knew about me being attacked. But I suppose you're not working for me." Sie paused, thought. "Surely they can't hold Mr Hluid like this with no communication. I mean, I know the laws aren't the same here as they are in Saeniss, but still."

"No, they can't," the jurist agreed. "Not legally. But there are two things complicating his situation: the involvement of the Presger, and the fact that his family is Chirra. There is a...tendency in the system to assume that our Chirra citizens are...not really Zeoseni. As a result there can be some"—e gestured vaguely—"some laxness in attending to their legal rights." E waved that away as though it were nothing. "I'm used to dealing with that, but it will be a factor. And I know you don't like it—I understand why you don't, and I don't like it, either—but the involvement of the Siblings of Hikipu might well be a help there.

"The Presger I am *not* used to dealing with. Your interpretation of treaty legalities may be correct—it seems reasonable to me—but I am not versed in treaty law. The jurists who are will be mostly located at the Treaty Administration Facility. I'm sure we can find one to advise us, but it will take time."

"Of course," agreed Enae. "What do I need to do to begin the proceedings that do fall under your authority?"

Ms and Mx Hluid brought their luggage to Enae's accommodation when they arrived. "This is very kind of you," said Ms Istver Hluid, a short, broad person with wide-set eyes and a kind, no-nonsense manner. "We'd intended to use Reet's quarters, but the station has already assigned them to someone else."

Mx Echemin Hluid, taller than eir partner but still comfortably broad, made a low sound that alarmed Enae. E looked as though e was about to explode, though perhaps the odd color of eir dark face was normal for em. "They can't do that," e growled. "They can't do that, it's not legal. Where's this jurist, Mx Athtur? Whatever does e think e's doing?"

"I'm sure e's doing the best e can," said Ms Hluid smoothly, but with an edge to her voice. She turned to Enae. "We can't thank you enough, Mx Athtur. If you hadn't been here, if you hadn't contacted us, we'd never have known, and there would have been no one to even try to help Reet."

Enae felt as though Ms Hluid had slapped hir. "Ms Hluid, I'm so sorry. This is all my fault. If I hadn't…"

"You were doing your job," Ms Hluid cut in. "I don't see how you could have done anything else."

"I do," grumbled Mx Hluid.

Ms Hluid cast em a quelling glance. "We've been over this. It's the Presger."

"Reet is human," insisted Mx Hluid.

"Legally I think he must be," Enae agreed. "But we have to convince the right authorities. Please sit down. I have coffee." Sie'd been sure to get some ready for this visit. "The petition is working its way around the magistracy. Now that the treaty jurist has added her documents, we should begin to see some movement."

"Is the treaty jurist coming here?" asked Ms Hluid, settling herself into a cushion and taking coffee from Enae. Mx Hluid sat stiffly beside her.

Enae sat across from them. "She says that by the time she could be here, things would have moved too far for her to be useful. She's entered some sort of petition to the authorities at the Treaty Facility, and she thinks she can do more good by staying there. That is, so she can do whatever might be needful if they bring Reet there."

"Of course, of course," said Ms Hluid. "We have to trust the jurists to know their business." Her voice was calm and sure, her expression unworried, but her grip on the tumbler of coffee was tight enough that her knuckles stood out on the back of her hand, and she hadn't drunk any, or given any sign that she remembered she was holding it.

Enae wanted to say something comforting, something encouraging, but she had no idea what that might be. "Ambassador Seimet is on her way here herself, in her own ship. She should reach the system sometime tomorrow." Probably, Enae thought, the ambassador would be able to avoid all the lines and come straight to Rurusk. "The treaty jurist warns us that dealing with the ambassador will be a trial in itself." *Typical Radchaai aristocrat*, the treaty jurist had said. *Almost ridiculously so. She is the ultimate authority over human involvement with the treaty, and she will not be friendly or helpful.* Enae decided not to quote that for Reet's parents, but did say, "I'm told we can't expect much help from the ambassador."

"Can we see Reet?" asked Mx Hluid.

"Not so far," said Enae. "The jurist is trying, but e's been prioritizing preventing them from taking him away to the Treaty Administration Facility. Once we manage that, the jurist says, the rest should be easier."

"Oh, greater and lesser spirits!" cried Ms Hluid, her composure cracking. "When we heard—Presger Translator! Of course, it explains so much!"

"Not everything," snapped Mx Hluid.

"No, but I'm sure you're right, Mx Athtur, I'm sure you're right about where he came from. But he's *our son*!"

"I know," said Enae helplessly. Sie felt, strangely, the way sie had felt when Grandmaman was dying. Lost and terrified, and still responsible for running the house. "Look. We have an appointment with our jurist this afternoon. In the meantime, get some rest. I'll go out and get us some breakfast if you like."

The meeting with the jurist produced a plan. Not a good plan, by any measure, nor one that would solve all of Reet's problems, even if it was as successful as it could possibly be.

"It'll be far worse for you if you're arrested," Enae had said to Ms and Mx Hluid. Sie remembered, briefly, being in detention in Keroxane. But this wouldn't be like that. "And besides, I'm here for diplomatic reasons—regarding the treaty even!"

Which was how sie found hirself in a distant, dingy stretch of passenger locks that were all empty except for one. Sie hoped sie was in the right place. Just getting here had involved more sneaking and hiding than Enae had done since sie had been little, not to mention crawling through dusty spaces that were far too close to vacuum for hir comfort. Sie'd definitely broken a multitude of Zeoseni laws—not to mention station safety regulations—and if sie was going to be detained again, sie wanted it to be for a good reason.

Sie took a deep breath, and shouted, "Ambassador Seimet!"

Silence. Sie waited a few moments and called again. "Ambassador Seimet! I'm Enae Athtur! I'm the person who found your fugitive for you. I need to speak with you!"

Still silence. Was sie in the right place? But sie had to be. This dusty, scuffed, isolated lock, at the end of a long row of obviously closed and inactive locks, was lit. Occupied. There was a ship here, and what other ship could it be?

The lock cycled. At length, a young person emerged wearing white jacket, trousers, and gloves, a dozen or more pins fixed to the front of her jacket. She stepped up to Enae, bowed, and said, "Mx Athtur. Ambassador Seimet sends her regrets but she is unable to meet with you." The difference between her manner—polite, pleasant, unassuming—and her accent—all Radchaai arrogance—was jarring, and it took Enae a moment to collect hirself and reply.

"Excuse me, Ms…"

"Eilaai," supplied the young person.

"Ms Eilaai. I have done the ambassador a tremendous favor. I think she owes me a meeting."

Ms Eilaai tilted her head, as though she was listening to

something. Or someone, Enae thought, with a tiny flare of hope. "Your pardon, Mx Athtur, but you did the ambassador no favors. You merely did your job."

"I did *her* job," Enae retorted, indignant. "The only reason I'm here at all is her predecessor's failure, and she herself hasn't done any better."

"You speak with some justice," said Ms Eilaai. "But even if the ambassador were to see you, you wouldn't get what you want." Enae opened hir mouth to protest and Ms Eilaai cut hir off. "Understand, Mx Athtur, at this moment, when you speak to me you are speaking to Ambassador Seimet."

"No," said Enae. "I'm not. I want to speak with the ambassador *herself.*"

A complicated range of expressions crossed Ms Eilaai's face. "Wait here," she said, and turned and went back through the lock.

Enae waited. And waited. And finally, Ambassador Seimet came through the lock. She looked exactly, stereotypically, like a Radchaai villain in an adventure serial, even down to a faint resemblance to Anaander Mianaai. Her white trousers, jacket, and gloves were if anything more gleamingly white than Ms Eilaai's had been, which was saying something. And she wore a good deal more pins.

"I am Ambassador Seimet," she said, stopping in front of Enae. She did not bow. "You wished to speak with me." The statement had, faintly, the air of a threat.

On the way here, Enae had rehearsed all sorts of speeches sie might make, in the event sie was fortunate enough to make it to this point. All of them deserted hir. Gracelessly sie blurted out, "Ambassador, you can't just take Reet Hluid away! He's a Zeoseni citizen. He has rights here. He has parents and siblings!"

"I am very sorry for her... for his parents and siblings," said the ambassador, without the slightest sign of any such feeling. "But he is not human, and therefore not a Zeoseni citizen. As such, he has no rights here. Even if he did, those rights would be superseded by the fact of what he is. There was good reason for our search for his... progenitor. And good reason for our response now to the news that he exists." She continued, with increased hauteur, "It is only because his presence among humans poses such a danger that I am here now, and the fact that I am speaking to you myself is a measure of how important a service you have performed. His presence among humans endangers those around him and endangers the treaty."

"He's lived here for thirty years," Enae protested. "He's never hurt anyone."

"*Yet*," replied the ambassador. "You cannot possibly know how dangerous he is."

"And the treaty says he can choose," continued Enae. "Especially if he's not Zeoseni. Then he doesn't belong anywhere, and the treaty says he can choose."

Ambassador Seimet looked upward and sighed. "Amaat spare me," she said with contempt, "from amateurs who think themselves experts in treaty law."

"But, Ambassador..."

"The parts of the treaty to which you presumably refer," said Ambassador Seimet icily, "are intended to deal with the ambiguities produced by the fact that so many of the species that are part of the treaty are closely associated with humans, and so many of their treaty representatives are biologically human. It is emphatically *not* meant to apply to Presger Translators."

"But Mr Hluid *is* biologically human enough that no one has thought he was anything else for the past three decades. And the treaty text says—"

"Mx Athtur! Which of the two of us has the most intimate understanding of the treaty and its circumstances and subtleties?"

Enae felt tears starting and blinked them away. "You can't just kidnap him and haul him off. He has rights. Even under the treaty."

"He has no rights under the treaty. Quite frankly, he shouldn't exist."

Fear struck hir. "But he *does* exist. And you can see, I hope, why his family and friends are so desperate to get him away from you." A tear escaped down the side of hir nose, despite hirself.

The ambassador did not seem to notice. "Mx Athtur, you succeeded at a task I have no doubt your superiors assigned to you as a formality. You might easily have traveled a bit and filed a few perfunctory reports and collected your pay. You did not. I infer from this that you understand duty and responsibility. I have spent much of my adult life responsible for the safety of all humanity. My duties have often been unpleasant to me and to others. Believe me when I say that Mr Hluid cannot stay here, and the sooner he is away from humans, the better." Her manner didn't soften, exactly, but she seemed for a moment to be a touch less contemptuous. "I am truly sorry for Mr Hluid's friends and family, but I will not shirk my duty. There's nothing you can do here. Go home." And when Enae didn't move or answer, the ambassador turned and strode back through the lock.

"No," said Enae to the empty space in front of hir. Sie wiped hir eyes with hir sleeve. "No. I'm going to the Treaty Administration Facility instead."

Reet

Rurusk Station, Sovereign Territory of Zeosen

The isolation-suited figures spoke nothing but brusque orders—*stand, walk, stop, turn*. They didn't give Reet any chance to dress or send a message: his captors had taken his handheld, and his implants, such as they were, were not responding.

The suited figures herded him along empty passages—they must have cleared them by some order because there was no hour when all this would be so completely empty—and into a security vehicle that took him to the Health Facility. There was no one there, either. Just empty halls, closed doors, and a sign reading ISOLATION WARD—AUTHORIZED PERSONNEL ONLY. And then, finally, the figures ordered Reet into a room and shut the door on him, and he was alone. His nausea, which had receded a bit on the way here, intensified.

There was a bed, at least, and a sanitary facility. But there were no clothes. Reet shivered and pulled a cover off the bed, wrapped it around himself. There was no sign of the door he'd come in by, or any sort of window. There was a ventilation grate on the ceiling, but he was fairly sure the room would be connected to its own air supply. There seemed to be no way to communicate with anyone beyond the walls.

But this was the Health Facility. There had to be a way for doctors to watch, or to help if the isolated patient needed it.

"If I'm under arrest," he said, meaning to speak loudly and firmly, but it turned out his voice was rough and speech was strangely unfamiliar after days of lying in bed speaking to no one, "then I need to contact my family." He remembered all the things his parents had told him about his rights if he was ever arrested or in any sort of legal trouble. "You can't hold me in isolation like this and not let me communicate with my family. I'm a Zeoseni citizen and I haven't done anything."

No response. He sat heavily on the bed and closed his eyes. This wasn't, of course, a matter of what he'd *done*, but what he *was*. This was, he didn't doubt, the result of Mx Athtur's message to the ambassador to the Presger. Ambassador Seimet had replied and Rurusk authorities had immediately locked Reet up in isolation as though he were carrying some sort of plague.

There was nothing he could do but wait. Eyes still closed, he lay down on the bed and pulled the cover closer around himself. Tried to summon any sort of patience, tried to not think of the fear and the nausea. At length a previously invisible hatch opened, revealing a tray with bean porridge, bread, and coffee. There were no utensils or condiments. He wasn't hungry, although he hadn't eaten for—how long had it been? He wasn't sure. Maybe days. It must have been days. He wasn't hungry, but he knew that he should eat something, so he tried to eat, scooping the porridge up with the bread, tried to drink the weak coffee, but his stomach rebelled, and he had to stop for fear he would vomit.

More time passed. He had no idea how long. He lay on the bed or fretfully paced the margins of the room. When more food appeared he ignored it. Every now and then, sleeping or waking, he would break out into one of those horrible, sticky sweats. The sweat would dry, sometimes immediately, sometimes after an agonizing length of time during which he felt as though he might actually, physically melt into a puddle on the floor. The thought both excited him and made him ill. He had never felt so sick in his life. What was wrong with him? Was he dying? The thought made his nausea worse. Something was definitely wrong with him, and here he was, in the Health Facility, probably doctors in every direction, but they couldn't help him. He wasn't human. If there even was any help possible, no doctor here would know what to do.

Eventually, some undefined time later, a voice spoke from the ceiling. "Do you have a jurist on call?"

Reet's heart pounded with startlement and confusion. This was suddenly new and different, and it was overwhelming. And frightening. This was dangerous. But his parents had taught him what to say to this question. "I am not required to answer any questions without my jurist present." The words came out strangled, and he cleared his throat and said it again. "I am not required to answer any questions without my jurist present."

It was a trick, Reet knew. If he said he had no jurist on call, then authorities would use that statement to claim that Reet had refused the services of any jurist. They wouldn't be asking that question now unless someone was trying to send in a jurist to help him. Someone knew where he was. Or knew he was in trouble, anyway, and was trying to help him. Probably his parents.

"We can hardly have your jurist here if you won't tell us whether you have one," said the voice. "Who is your jurist?"

"I am not required," said Reet, more surely, "to answer any questions without my jurist present."

There was no reply to this, and Reet went back to lying on the bed.

Mx Athtur must have tried to message him, and he hadn't replied, and sie'd gotten worried. And sie must have contacted his parents. That's exactly what sie would have done. And maybe it wouldn't do Reet any good, but it was something to know that someone outside this room cared about what happened to him and was trying to help him.

Proof of the jurist's efforts manifested after a while as a meal tray that contained not the ever-present bean porridge and coffee, but dumplings and halawa. Which Reet found he couldn't eat much of. But even better, beside the dumplings was a stripped-down handheld loaded with books and vids, including, thank all the gods, the full run of *Pirate Exiles of the Death Moons*. There were two new episodes! Had it been so short a time since he'd been locked away here? So long?

It didn't matter. What mattered was that someone was out there trying to help him. He only had to be patient, which, granted, was not his strong suit, but he had all the time in the world to practice it.

* * *

At length—at least twice through *Pirate Exiles*, but Reet couldn't be sure exactly how long that was—the hatch in the wall opened, larger than Reet had realized it could, and revealed the pieces of an isolation suit. "Please put the suit on," said the voice from the ceiling.

Reet paused the drama he'd been watching. Thought a moment. "I am not required," he began.

"No one is asking you any questions," replied the voice before he could finish. "And if you don't put the suit on, we'll find another way to safely move you. It will just take longer and be less pleasant for everyone."

"Why the suit anyway?" he asked.

"I am not required to answer any questions without my jurist present," said the voice.

Very funny, thought Reet. Should he put on the suit or should he not?

Well, the authorities who were holding him really wanted him to put it on. *Less pleasant for everyone* was a threat, yes, but thinking of his trip here—those weirdly empty corridors, the dozen or more armed and suited people around him—he saw that it was also much, much easier for the authorities if he would suit up and walk wherever they were sending him.

"I will put on the suit," he said at length, "if I can talk to my jurist first."

"Not going to happen," said the voice.

"I'm a Zeoseni citizen," Reet argued. "Holding me without informing me of my infraction is against the Articles of the Sovereignty Convention. So is restricting my access to my jurist." There was no reply to that. "I'm not putting the suit on until I know why I have to wear it." He thought another moment. "At a minimum."

"The articles are suspended in your case."

"Say that to my jurist," said Reet. They probably already had, and not with complete success, or Reet wouldn't have been watching *Pirate Exiles* all this time, he was sure.

"Look," said the voice, exasperated now. "We can sedate you and put you in a suspension unit and haul you off that way if we like. Your jurist"—the words were bitter—"won't like it but there's nothing e can do about it."

Ah, but that was enough to prevent them from just going ahead and doing it. They weren't going to do that if there was any other course available, and there were probably several other courses available to them. No doubt those options would be a pain in the ass for the authorities, but there it was.

He crossed his arms. "I'm not putting on the suit."

The next thing he knew, he was waking up inside the suit. Lying on his back unable to move his arms or legs. The face-plate was darkened, so he couldn't see anything, but there was a definite sensation of movement, muffled sounds of people speaking, occasionally doors slamming. Stops, starts, turns—he had no idea where they were taking him, but at least he wasn't in suspension. And he still had the handheld with him, he felt it slide across his chest at one point.

Then all sound and movement stopped. He lay there, wondering what would happen next.

"Do you speak Radchaai?" asked a voice by his left ear.

"No," said Reet in that language. Nearly everyone knew at least a few words of Radchaai, but Reet knew considerably more. "Not one single word."

"Very funny," said the voice, with an upper-class Radchaai precision of speech. "You can take the isolation suit off now."

"Fuck you," said Reet, still in Radchaai.

"Stay in the suit, then," said the Radchaai voice. "By all means. As long as you like."

"I want to see my jurist," Reet said. He wanted Mom, and Maman, and even Nana. But the jurist who'd been working for him all this time would do.

"Do you indeed?" replied the voice. "Fortunately for us all, that is impossible. We undocked fifteen minutes ago. No, don't threaten me with your 'articles,' or whatever it is you call them. Your jurist made enough use of them to render my already difficult task considerably harder, and I am out of patience with her and her petitions and holds. Ultimately nothing she could do was going to change what I had to do."

"Which is what?" asked Reet. "Where are we going?"

"To the Treaty Administration Facility, to return you to your clade." That was a word Reet had never heard before. "It's a two-week trip, but do by all means feel free to spend the entire time lying on the floor like a toddler having a tantrum."

"Why the isolation?" asked Reet.

"Because Presger Translator juveniles are extremely dangerous," replied the voice. "Honestly, I'm astonished you haven't killed anyone yet. I'm half-certain you have, and just managed to hide it. But there would have been no mistaking it if it had happened."

"I'm not a murderer!" Reet protested, but he couldn't help thinking of all the times he'd yearned to cut someone apart. "I'm not going to hurt anyone."

"You've reached the point where you will, whether you want to or not," said the voice. "The cabin you're in is air-locked, and you will have no direct contact with anyone on board. Do please let us know if you require anything—except your jurist, or the freedom to walk the ship. Now, if you'll excuse me, I have other matters to attend to."

The voice didn't return, and after a few minutes of thought, Reet set about figuring out how to open the suit.

Qven

Translator Dlar brought me new seeds soon after I had requested them. Or, they brought me a handful of seeds and a potato. "Your Teacher will tell you what to do with this," the Translator said, hefting the potato and setting it down on the table between us. It hummed pleasantly, a wide, smooth-feeling sensation. Beside it, the heap of seeds—longer than the radish seeds, narrow and pointed at one end—chorused brightly. I wondered what they would grow into.

When the Translator had left, Teacher told me how to cut the potato into pieces. Its smooth, waxy hum split into parts, all of them the same, but different. Smaller. Two of the segments I buried in deep buckets of soil. The others Teacher cooked, and I ate them at supper. They were smooth as their song, and subtle-flavored.

"Thank you, Teacher," I said when I had eaten them. "It was delicious."

The seeds grew into a multitude of orange and yellow flowers that sang sharp, cheerful songs. I liked to look at them and listen to them.

Each one eventually shriveled and died, and the potatoes grew long and trailing, spilling over the rims of the buckets. The song of those leaves and stems was different from the smooth song of the potato itself. "New ones will grow among the roots," Teacher told me.

The conversation had already departed from the approved script, so I replied, "I am not a potato."

Teacher pursed their lips—disapproving? thinking? hiding some reaction?—and then said, "Nothing is a potato. Things are what they are. But sometimes things share similarities. Everything has an end. Potatoes, radishes, marigolds. You. Everything. That is one similarity. But the potatoes are also like you in other ways. Either they are eaten, or they grow into something quite different. The ones that do not grow and are not eaten, those rot away."

"Then send a potato to match with this fugitive's offspring," I said before I could stop myself. "And I will dig a hole in a garden and sit there."

"You understand me better than you seem to," replied Teacher, not sternly as I'd expected, but calm and patient. And then they began to talk about biology.

My biology, very specifically. They began in the most basic, general way, speaking of cells and genes, of how They had altered what They had taken from humans, reconstructed and repaired it to produce us. To produce, in this specific time and place, me.

"That's enough for today," they said at length. "We will continue tomorrow."

And they did. Some of what they said I already knew,

but some of it I did not. I learned a good deal. Among other things, I should certainly have reported being able to hear the seeds and the plants. I might be able to hear more if I was very quiet in myself and if I practiced listening.

But the end of the lessons, the entire point and intention behind them, was this: I could not escape a match.

"Many of those in authority, including They Themselves, don't see any point in sharing this information with juveniles. There is, after all, nothing that can change this."

"But They *could* change it," I pointed out. "They built us to begin with, and They could build us differently if They wanted to. If it was explained to Them that I don't want…"

"No one," said Teacher severely, "is going to explain that to anyone. After all, things are working out fine for those of us in authority." There was, I thought, some bitterness in Teacher's voice. "And there is very little advantage to giving juveniles a choice in the matter. I assure you, Translator Dlar will not agree to even attempt to convince Them of anything of the sort, and even if you were given the opportunity to try it yourself, you would have no chance of success."

"How do I know what you say is true?" I asked. "Words can say things that don't exist."

"I have tried to explain to those in authority that telling juveniles half-truths or falsehoods is counterproductive, or even potentially disastrous." They paused to take a sip from their tiny bowl of tea.

"Oh," I said. "*That's* what got you this shit assignment."

"I have done my best," they continued, "to be as open and truthful with you as possible. I can do no more. You may believe me or not, as you please."

* * *

So. If what Teacher had told me was true, I would either match with an appropriate partner or—if I refused, or even waited too long—I would collapse into a puddle of undifferentiated organic sludge.

They were bringing me a partner. There had been delays for some reasons I didn't quite understand—interference and stubborn refusals on someone's part—but there was no question that this partner would arrive at some point.

Too late, maybe! But Teacher seemed to think there was plenty of time. Of course, they might be wrong. Even now, I could hear textures deep in the walls of my rooms, now I was listening for them, colors and contours that suggested doors and corridors and the presence of Adults. I spent my quiet time listening for them.

But I still itched, and Teacher said I hadn't been as far along as all that when I'd been attacked.

Teacher had been the only person to call it an attack. They had said nothing about it being my fault, and I was grateful for that small thing, even while I became more and more certain that in at least some small way it *had* been partly my fault.

Well. There was at least a little time. Time for me to think about what Teacher had said, time to think about whether or how much I believed, and time to decide what to do about it. To decide whether there was any point to resisting, or even the smallest possibility of it.

Some time later, Translator Dlar visited me but would not sit down for tea. "Your Teacher insists," they said, "that we be forthright with you, and my misgivings aside"—they paused, and then continued—"they have had startlingly good results so far. They now insist that I give you a particular bit of information, and"—the Translator grimaced—"a choice in this matter."

"Yes, Translator?" I said, when they didn't continue.

"We—that is, our clade—have custody of Tzam." I kept my face as impassive as I could. Translator Dlar continued. "Their clade decided, in the end, to turn them over to us to dispose of as we wish."

I frowned. "But I thought…"

Translator Dlar waved my protest away. "There are other issues and arguments at play here, none of which are currently relevant to you." They glanced over at my Teacher and sighed. "I would have to go into centuries of history and describe in detail years of arguments between clades before it would make the smallest sense to you, and none of it would change anything about the situation."

I glanced at Teacher. "Fair enough," they said.

"Suffice it to say," continued the Translator, with visible relief, "we have Tzam, and we can and will do whatever we like to them."

"What about whoever instructed them?" I asked. "They said they had help from Adults in their clade."

"There's nothing we can do about that," said the Translator. "Not at the moment. Although I assure you, that fact has not been, and will not be, forgotten."

"In several centuries," I ventured, with as calm a voice as I could produce, "it will be part of some complicated reason for some act or another."

"Just so," said the Translator. "Now. We have chosen to make an open example of Tzam. They have been sealed into a container, quite alone, and there they will remain until they die. Which will probably be sometime in the next week. I suggested to your Teacher that you should be required to watch the process as it happens. Your Teacher insists we present you with a choice."

I looked at Teacher, who stared impassively back. I felt sick, and dizzy. Somewhere beyond the walls, someone was moving, breathing. I wanted to lie down on the floor.

Instead, I said, "Thank you, Translator. I appreciate your confidence in me. May I have some time to think about my reply?"

"Yes," said the Translator. "Good. Very good. I can with some confidence give you until this time tomorrow. Possibly longer, though it's impossible to say."

"Thank you, Translator," I said again. "I will think seriously about it."

When the Translator was gone, Teacher said, "We will have a rest day."

"Yes, Teacher," I said, and managed somehow to make my way to my bed and lie down.

After a while, I don't know exactly how long, Teacher told me to sit up, propped me up on a pile of cushions, and brought me a bowl of tea. "Entirely appropriate," they said when I protested, "when one is ill."

I knew the word, and in theory what it meant, but I hadn't imagined it was something I could ever be and wasn't entirely certain I was now. Still, the tea was somehow steadying.

After a few sips I closed my eyes and leaned back farther into the cushions.

After I had sat like that for a while, the tea cooling in my hand, I asked, "What should I do?"

Teacher was silent a moment, and I thought they weren't going to answer. Then they said, "You are extraordinarily fortunate. No, don't look at me like that." I closed my eyes again, and they went on. "It's only because you have been favored from the start that you still live. If you had been even slightly less well-connected, if expectations for you had been even the tiniest bit lower, you would have been disposed of without a thought, long ago. The only hope most such juveniles have of survival, once they've been injured or attacked, is the very faint possibility that some Adult will notice and take pity on them." Silence. I would not open my eyes or drink more tea. I could think of nothing to say. "And that," continued Teacher, "since you seem curious, is how I ended up with this shit assignment."

"I don't feel good," I said.

"No, of course you don't." Teacher's voice was matter-of-fact. "You'll feel much worse over the next several days, whether you witness your attacker's end or not. Fortunately the connection is not strong, or even close to complete." They took the tea bowl out of my unresisting hand. "Translator Dlar wishes you to watch so that the reality of your situation may be impressed upon you. Your only choices, as I have already told you, are match or die. But there is a certain conviction that can only be attained by witnessing the truth."

"What do you think?"

"I think," said Teacher, "that you may possibly be glad to

see the certain end of your attacker, and know that they cannot harm you any further."

I opened my eyes at that, and frowned at Teacher. "But it isn't just them! It wasn't Tzam! I mean, it was, but they were working for their clade. And nothing is going to happen to the ones who planned it, who..." I couldn't speak any further.

"Hush, child. Some of us have to take what we can get, where we find it. That said, Tzam's death will be a cruel one. Their clade members who set them on this path will almost certainly spare themselves the distress and inconvenience of watching the results of it. You, who owe Tzam far, far less— less than nothing, truth be told—you have no responsibility here. You have no obligation to endure anything on their account. I have said so to Translator Dlar in the strongest possible terms."

"Thank you, Teacher." I thought for a few moments. Seeing others die had never troubled me before. Of course, I had never thought I would be one of them. But this death would be an example of what would be waiting for me if I didn't do as Translator Dlar wished. "Will it be so very terrible to see?"

"Tzam has been calling for you all day. Sometimes they blame you. Sometimes they beg your forgiveness. You two are connected, however tenuously. Their desperate need for you won't stop until they're dead. And it will be a long death. A cruel one, as I said."

I found I had no reply to this, no questions. No words in my mind at all.

"Tzam did have choices," Teacher said. "Not good ones, no, but they might have chosen not to do what they did.

Considering their abilities and other things there's no point in going into just now, they likely would have found their adulthood more difficult than they would otherwise have expected, if they had refused. But they might have refused all the same, and they did not."

"*I* might have chosen differently," I pointed out.

"You chose to flee. That was your aim. You had no intention of harming anyone and would not have harmed anyone but yourself. Tzam knew what they were doing when they attacked you. The two cases are not the same."

"No cases are the same," I said, suddenly exhausted. "I don't care if Tzam lives or dies. I just want..." But I wasn't sure what I wanted. Certainly not to stand there while Tzam screamed for me. Nor to lie here drinking tea *knowing* they were screaming for me. "If I go to watch, will Translator Dlar dispose of them more quickly?"

Teacher pursed their lips—considering, I thought. "I can put the matter before the Translator and see what they say. I make no promises, though. This is not entirely about you." They shook their head, then, and made an exasperated noise I had never expected to hear from them. "The Translator refuses, unequivocally. But that doesn't mean you have no choices here, no way to get what you want, or something near it."

"What do you mean?"

"You have only small and seemingly pointless choices available to you. But if there is anything I have been trying to teach you, it is that small actions can have larger consequences. If one has only small choices available, one must be patient, and canny."

I thought of a tiny black seed sprouting into a red, round, sharp-flavored radish.

"I will say this one thing more," said Teacher. "When you have decided what you want, remember that what one will not acknowledge is what one cannot properly control."

I thought about that. I thought about that for a long time.

Enae

"Everything here is very Radchaai," said Ms Yedess, the treaty advocate, handing Istver Hluid a tumbler of coffee. They sat in hard, straight-backed chairs, crowded into a tiny room that was the advocate's office. "Here on the human station, anyway, and definitely on Central, the station where most of the interspecies business gets done. You'll want gloves, if you haven't got some already."

Enae, like everyone else in the office—Ms Hluid, Mx Hluid, Ms Yedess herself—was barehanded.

"We brought gloves," said Echemin Hluid brusquely. Disapprovingly. "But we didn't think..."

"No, of course not," said the advocate. "But just so you know. You'll be needing them, and soon. Also"—she grimaced—"you won't find much decent coffee here. You may as well learn to appreciate tea."

Echemin—somewhat placated, Enae was glad to see—gave

a short laugh. "So we've found."

"I imagine so," replied Ms Yedess, settling into her chair. "Now, to business. This is going to be a delicate matter. There have been any number of cases of people choosing an affiliation under the treaty. But none has been contested for a good three hundred years." She waved a hand. "Contested on the treaty level, I mean."

"Is that case from three hundred years ago relevant to ours?" asked Enae hopefully. Sie took a sip of hir own coffee—far too sweet, Zeoseni had a very different idea of good coffee than Enae did, but at least it was not the watery, faintly burned-tasting stuff they'd been served at the accommodation that morning.

"In some ways it's a very similar case," said Ms Yedess. "A question of an orphan taken in by people at the nearest station."

Istver Hluid sat up straighter in her chair. "How did that come out?"

"The committee decided that the orphan in question absolutely had the right to choose their affiliation, and that they would have to give up any claims based on the rejected one. It was a question of inheritance on both sides, you see."

"Well then, that's very simple!" exclaimed Echemin. "The choice ought to be Reet's anyway."

"Not so simple as all that," cautioned the advocate.

"Treaty law isn't based on precedent," said Enae. Sie had been reading, in the weeks it took to get here. "And the person who should be making our case to the committee is Ambassador Seimet herself, who is determined to turn Reet over to the Presger."

"That, yes," agreed the advocate. "And moreover, there has never been a case like this involving a Presger Translator. No one has ever decided they don't want to be one, let alone the other way around."

"This fugitive," suggested Enae, with a feeling that somehow some detail had clicked into place but sie couldn't quite see what or where, "the person who ran away two hundred years ago. If they belonged anywhere else, if they had been Geck or Rrrrrr, they wouldn't have needed to run away, they could have petitioned to change affiliation, and maybe they would have found a way to make that work."

"And we'll point that out, to be sure. And technically speaking, that should be enough. The treaty makes no explicit exception for Presger Translators. But there is a very definite *unofficial* exception. Presger Translators are *different*. They're not just humans who maybe have spent some time with aliens."

"Different in what way?" asked Istver.

Ms Yedess waved helplessly. "It's just something everyone here knows. And, more to the point in our particular case, it's regulation, here on the human side of the Treaty Facility, that any human who sets foot on the Presger part of the facility is to be considered officially dead, and certainly no longer human."

"What?" Enae was appalled.

"It's never happened that I know of," said Ms Yedess. "Not since the treaty has been in force. And it's not treaty law. It's policy that originates in the ambassador's office."

"Maybe we can turn that to our advantage, though," Enae suggested. "If Ambassador Seimet turns Reet over to the

Presger Translators and he's considered dead, then he's unaffiliated with anyone and can choose, right? Wasn't there a case like that?" Sie searched hir memory. "Pahlad Budrakim, right? E was declared dead for some reason but was still alive, and e successfully petitioned to be accepted as Geck."

"Yes," the advocate agreed. "It was quite recent, too. But it didn't involve the Presger Translators. And the reason a person could be considered dead after visiting the Presger, according to widely and firmly held belief here, is that the Presger themselves would have eaten them, or disassembled them or whatever, and anyone returning would only be a copy."

Silence. Enae opened hir mouth to say something, then closed it again.

"It's something the Presger did, or tried to do, before the treaty. And there are at least rumors that the Presger Translators...well, that they absorbed humans they came across in some way. It's not supposed to happen anymore, it would be a violation of the treaty, but still, no one wants it to happen."

"Ridiculous!" said Echemin, finally. "Absurd!"

"We can't let them hand Reet over to the Presger," said Istver, more calmly than Enae could believe was real. "How do we prevent it?"

"We might not be able to," warned the advocate. "He's already on his way, in the custody of Ambassador Seimet. Who I have no doubt intends to hand Mr Hluid over to the Presger as soon as she possibly can. Fortunately, we received word just this morning that the committee will hear our petition. We leave for Central tonight."

"But how?" asked Enae, bewildered.

"Ah," said the advocate, pleased. Almost smug. "In theory, you see, the various parties to the treaty communicate through their respective ambassadors. In reality, though—those ambassadors have staff, who do much of that work. And those staff members work with other parties, and so on, and we all work here at the facility. It would be strange if we never got to know anyone else."

"Who brought this to the committee, then?" asked Istver.

"The Geck, oddly enough," said Ms Yedess. "They're not usually even here, not in person, but for things like a new applicant to the treaty, well, long distance won't do."

"The case where someone officially dead wanted to change affiliation," said Enae. "That involved the Geck."

"Indeed it did," Ms Yedess agreed. "The Geck representatives are most sympathetic. As are the representatives of the Republic of Two Systems. Though of course they can't give us any official assistance."

"The machines!" Echemin Hluid seemed horrified.

"Oh, you wouldn't know it, talking to them," said Ms Yedess. "And they've been most obliging in this case in particular."

"They kill people and take over their bodies," Echemin insisted. "That's how they seem so human to you!"

"They won't be able to do that if they're treaty members," Enae pointed out. "Isn't that right?" sie appealed to the advocate.

"I can't say that will never happen," said Ms Yedess. "But I *can* say that it's already settled law in the republic that only volunteers may be made into ancillaries."

"*Volunteers!*" Istver's tone was uncharacteristically contemptuous. Skeptical. "Who would actually volunteer for such a thing?"

"They've had a number of applicants already, I understand," replied Ms Yedess. "Though not, I think, any accepted so far. But the point is, the republic is particularly interested in freedom of affiliation being enforced. Not surprising at all, when you think about it. And while their support doesn't count officially—yet, if ever—it does count."

"What about the Rrrrrr?" asked Enae.

"The Rrrrrr—" Ms Yedess paused a moment, thinking. "The question of handing someone over unwilling is...complicated for them. You may remember when they first joined the treaty."

"That Radchaai soldier!" exclaimed Echemin. "She refused to kill the Rrrrrr when the Radchaai first encountered them."

"And then," said Ms Yedess, "when the Radchaai demanded she be turned over for execution—it was mutiny, after all—the Rrrrrr complied." Echemin made a disgusted noise, and Ms Yedess said, "It was a difficult situation and none of us were there to know everything that happened. But the Rrrrrr delegates themselves are divided over it. It's possible we can exploit that, or try to. I think it will be a protracted argument. I must warn you, it may be days, even weeks, before any hearing actually begins."

Echemin cried, "And in the meantime they can do whatever they like to Reet!"

"Maybe," said the advocate, calmly. "But the moment the committee accepted our petition and placed it on the agenda—that is, about an hour ago—all other actions regarding the subject—Mr Hluid—were suspended. So, as a matter of treaty law, they can't do anything to your son besides house and feed him."

"And eat him and send us back a copy," said Istver, her composure cracking, just slightly, for the first time.

"Well, that's what happens to humans, supposedly," said Ms Yedess. "But Mr Hluid is a Presger Translator. Biologically, I mean."

That, thought Enae, might mean he was in *more* danger. But sie didn't speak that thought aloud. Ms and Mx Hluid didn't need to hear it.

"We are going to do everything we possibly can." Ms Yedess lifted her tumbler of coffee. "Enjoy this while you can. There isn't even *bad* coffee on Central. It'll be tea from here on out."

Ms Yedess's office on Central was much larger and more comfortable than on the human station—the chairs were cushioned with dark blue velvet; there was room for a wide, low table; and the walls were a cheerful pale yellow, though Enae could see, faintly, the shapes of the Four Emanations that the paint had covered.

They met first with a long, attenuated person in a mobility seat. "Theatt Hadarat Batonen," said Ms Yedess.

Theatt Hadarat Batonen had, Enae thought, the longest arms of anyone sie had ever seen, but then sie realized she was low-g adapted.

"Call me Batonen," she said, and from somewhere in her mobility chair she drew a box. Opened it into a wide, sectioned tray filled with small bits of…something delicious, from the smell.

Ms Yedess uncovered her own offering—tiny iced cakes. "Ooh, I hoped you would have those," said Batonen.

"Batonen is a treaty jurist from the Hasiven Association," said Ms Yedess.

"That's a collection of stations in a system very far from here," said Batonen. "But we still are concerned with things like the treaty with the Presger."

Ms Yedess said, "Batonen is also an assistant to Seris, the human member of the committee we'll be dealing with."

Batonen raised a tiny bowl of tea, held at the end of one long, tentacle-like arm. "Can't let the Radchaai decide everything for us. Though they do try."

"Indeed they do," agreed Ms Yedess.

"This is where you might expect some small talk," said Batonen, "but we don't do small talk where I'm from." She took a sip of tea, and pushed the box of delicious-smelling treats toward them. "Eat! The green ones are particularly nice, much better than skel."

Anything would be better than skel, the thick, fleshy leaves that were the only food available on Central. Allegedly it provided every nutrient a human needed, but the taste was indescribable. Not bad, not good, just…strange. Condiments helped, but Enae was already sick of it.

"I'm with you," said Echemin, taking a green tidbit. "No waste of time, down to business."

Batonen showed her teeth in what seemed to Enae to be a very stiff imitation of a smile. "I like you," she said. "Yes, let's get down to business. The Hasiven Association—among many other collectives and individuals—are very interested in preventing the Radchaai from defining *human* for the purposes of the treaty."

"Their definition being somewhat restrictive," suggested Istver, taking a sweet for herself. "Oh, the green ones *are* delicious!"

"Yes, they are," agreed Batonen. "And yes, the Radchaai definition of *human* is far too restrictive for our taste. Before the treaty we wouldn't have cared. Call yourself what you like, so long as you leave us alone! But the treaty…"

"Yes," Enae agreed. "The treaty changed so many things."

"Even, it seems, changed the Radchaai," said Batonen, gracefully lifting a tiny pink cake from the tray Ms Yedess had set out. "This business with their AIs—it's the end of the Radch if the treaty accepts them. Plenty of Radchaai artificial intelligences are stations. It's not like they can leave Radchaai space, and they control the habitat of thousands, sometimes millions, of Radchaai citizens. If they're declared Significant Species, signatories to the treaty, the Radchaai lose control over those stations. Not to mention the question of how many of their warships might desert. How long can the Radch keep control over their territory then?" She gave a little shrug. "Long overdue, if you ask me. Are you meeting with them?"

"The AIs? Yes," Ms Yedess answered. "Every little bit, you know."

"Every little bit," agreed Batonen. "Well. There are mixed feelings around Central about your case. On the one hand, no one wants the Radchaai ambassador to be able to declare anyone's children inhuman and take them from their parents. On the other hand, we know very little about Presger

Translator juveniles, but we do know—or think we know—that they're dangerous. We want to be careful."

"He's our son, curse you!" cried Echemin.

Batonen waved the show of temper away, as though it had been an innocuous pleasantry. "Tell me about him. Has he ever hurt anyone?"

"He did have a problem with biting, when he was very small," said Istver. "It quite alarmed the minders at the play crèche, who are used to all sorts of children, you know. One child did need some first aid. But that was the end of it, really. Reet could barely talk at the time, but I believe that when he realized that he'd actually hurt someone, he stopped."

"As good a hypothesis as any," said Batonen. "And when he was older?"

"He had…" Istver hesitated. "Once, a job counselor asked him what he dreamed of doing, and…"

Enae thought she could barely bring herself to say whatever it was. Then Istver looked at Echemin in mute appeal.

"He wanted to cut people open and eat them," said Echemin, brusquely. "We thought he was just, you know, having a joke."

Odd sort of joke, thought Enae.

"Did he ever? Cut anyone open, I mean," asked Batonen. "Or eat anyone."

Echemin stood. "How dare you! This is our *son*."

"Of course he is," said Batonen, calmly. "But before I speak favorably to my superior about this case, I want to be certain I'm not unleashing something dangerous on you and your people. You know your son. I do not, and can't be expected to. So I ask these questions."

"We've asked for records," Ms Yedess said. "From Zeosen. There is no sign of any mysterious disappearances or deaths that might be laid at Reet Hluid's door. And if there were even the remote possibility of such, they'd have been happy enough to pin it on him, so you know they looked hard for anything they could use."

"Fair enough," acknowledged Batonen, taking another tiny cake. "There is, however, another issue. Mr Hluid has some sort of affiliation with an organization called the Siblings of Hikipu?"

Ms Yedess seemed taken aback. "You *have* been paying close attention to this case!"

"Well, obviously," replied Batonen around the cake. She chewed and swallowed. "But I don't need to have been paying much attention to know that. The Siblings of Hikipu have attempted to file a petition with the committee. They have representatives on the way here."

"Mr Nadkal," said Enae.

Batonen gestured agreement. "I've looked a bit into who these Siblings of Hikipu are, and seen their petition, and I have concerns."

Ms Yedess waved that away. "The Siblings of Hikipu is a sort of ethnic affiliation club. A way for immigrants and their children to help each other out and keep contact with their history, you know the sort of thing." She paused, then said, with faint disapproval, "I hope this isn't about assuming all Hikipi are drunken and violent."

"Is that the sort of thing Zeoseni assume about the Hikipi? But no. I'm concerned about their possible connection to the situation in Keroxane, and their petition is strange, to say the least. They claim there's no actual evidence that Reet Hluid is anything but biologically human, and not only that but that he's the heir to some office on a destroyed station. Obviously the committee won't pay attention to such nonsense on its own, but they claim to be bringing their petition in support of yours, or so I hear. Is this something you're associated with?"

"No," Istver Hluid said, firm and definite. "I know that Reet was a member of the organization, back on Rurusk, and he'd made some friends, and even gotten a good job through them. I have no reason to think badly of them, but I don't understand why they're here. Reet's genetics have always seemed odd, and at the time a Hikipi origin seemed as likely as anything else. But much as I hate to say it, I do think Mx Athtur's identification of him is probably accurate. Too many things just seem to fit. And I've never..." She stopped, apparently unable to continue.

"We've always encouraged our children to look into their origins," Echemin said, insistent, as though someone had been arguing with em about the subject. "We want them to know their histories."

"Fair enough," said Batonen, and turned to Ms Yedess. "Did you know these Siblings of Hikipu were coming here?"

"I didn't," admitted Ms Yedess. "And I didn't know they'd tried to file a petition."

"I don't like that they've done this behind our backs," said Istver.

Ms Yedess said, "To be honest, I'm not entirely surprised at their actions. We can deal with them, though. This isn't Rurusk, where half the civil service has Hikipi cousins.

They'll have a battle to fight just establishing they have any grounds for entering this petition. And as far as landing here at Central, or addressing the committee in a hearing…well, we're certainly not going to help them." Ms Yedess sighed. "They'll be an annoyance. But we can deal with them."

Reet

The dreams didn't stop. Reet still woke with disturbing regularity in a sweat that clung to his bedcovers and then dried into flakes. Like flakes of skin.

He wanted it. Oh, how he wanted it, worse now that he was alone, all alone. He wanted to grab the first person he saw, taste their skin dissolving under his tongue.

No. No, that wasn't *right*.

Sometimes he paced the tiny compartment. Smaller than the room they'd kept him in at the Health Facility on Rurusk, but far more comfortable. The walls were dark, grained like wood, with half a dozen niches and shelves, and there was a small table and chair—actual wood, Reet thought. The bed itself was a real bed, not a Health Facility cot, and the silky green-and-blue bedcovers were soft and warm.

And the food was amazing. Strange, but delicious: delicately spiced fish; noodles in some translucent, tangy sauce;

thin-sliced vegetables, some he'd only ever heard of; cakes soaked in honey. These weren't a prisoner's rations.

The food was so good that it could momentarily distract him from the fact that he *was* a prisoner. That he didn't know what he was, really, that no one would help him, no one could. That sometimes what he wanted, what he *needed*, was to claw through the wall of this room, to dig free, and then find someone, anyone, to take hold of and...

But when he thought those thoughts, his skin broke out in a sheen of sticky sweat, and no, he didn't really want that. He wanted...someone to *want* to melt with him into a puddle of goo?

The thought made him catch his breath. Yes, that was what he wanted. More than anything. Wanting to do that to someone who didn't want it, too—that was wrong. There were a lot of things wrong with him, Reet knew, but that wasn't one of them.

"Are you all right, Mr Hluid?" asked a voice out of the air. A Radchaai voice, but higher, maybe younger than the person who'd spoken to him before.

He must have done something, made some sound. "Not really, no."

"I'm very sorry," said the voice. Definitely not the last person he'd talked to. "There's only so much we can do, I hope you understand."

"I don't."

"I'm sorry," said the voice again. "I can't really explain because I only know so much. But what's happening to you is quite normal for Presger Translator juveniles."

Juveniles. "I'm..." He thought, calculating, comparing calendars. "I'm thirty-one years old!"

A momentary silence. Then, "That's well within the normal range, Ambassador Seimet says."

Reet wanted to curl up into a ball under those luxurious covers and scream. Instead he sat on the edge of the bed, as straight as he could manage. "What's happening to me?"

Another silence. Then, "Ambassador Seimet urges me to tell you that the fact this is happening is proof that you are, indeed, a Presger Translator and not human."

"Ambassador Seimet can go fuck herself." Still in Radchaai. At least he'd found some practical use for that vocabulary.

"She can be very uncompromising sometimes," said the voice apologetically. "I'm Eilaai, by the way."

Reet didn't answer, just stared ahead at the wall in front of him.

"You shouldn't worry. I don't think there's anything actually wrong with you. We don't know a lot about Presger Translator juveniles, we never get to see any. But Ambassador Seimet thinks everything happening to you is probably perfectly normal, given the circumstances. Given what she's been able to get out of Translator Dlar."

Tears started, prickling.

"One thing we do know is that they keep juveniles away from humans because they're dangerous. I know you wouldn't want to hurt anyone," Eilaai continued, "but you might, whether you want to or not."

A monster. He was a monster.

"None of this is your fault," said Eilaai. "I know you're unhappy and uncomfortable, but try to hang on. We have eight more days of travel, and then you'll be with your clade. They'll take care of you."

Take care of you. Reet shivered. "What if I don't want to be with my clade, whatever that is?"

"I don't think you have a choice," said Eilaai, her voice regretful. "Really, Mr Hluid, don't worry. Your clade is one of the most influential right now, and they specifically asked us to bring you to them alive and uninjured. They want you back."

That brought up so many complicated thoughts and feelings that Reet didn't know what to say. He opened his mouth, and "Can I get some coffee instead of all this tea?" was what came out.

There was no coffee. There were, though, Radchaai entertainments and music, loaded onto a handheld that came with his next meal. Eilaai had said she would try to find some material he'd be mostly able to follow, and she'd done a pretty good job. None of it was as satisfying as *Pirate Exiles*, but it was something, anyway.

It was also something that someone would speak to him, after he had been isolated for so long. He felt less cut adrift, knowing that Eilaai's voice would sound when he was done with his lunch, and she would talk with him about the entertainments he'd been watching, or advise him on Radchaai grammar.

But she would not, no matter how much he asked, agree to let him send a message to his parents. "All communications between humans and Presger Translators have to be approved by Ambassador Seimet's office," she said.

"Well, this is the ambassador's ship, isn't it?" argued Reet. "She's on board, right?"

"She won't approve it," Eilaai said. "Wait until you're settled with your clade."

"My parents are probably worried about me!"

"Oh, they're *definitely* worried about you. And it wouldn't surprise me if we were met with a stack of petitions on your behalf, once we dock at Central."

For some reason, that surprised Reet. "There are jurists on the Treaty Administration Facility?"

Eilaai laughed. "Sometimes it seems like there's nothing *but* jurists on the Treaty Administration Facility. And yes, your parents have hired one, and she's been working away on your behalf. Not that it will change much. You are what you are, you can't really help your biology. But maybe it helps to know your parents are out there doing what they can."

"They can't afford that!" Reet protested.

"Really, Mr Hluid, try not to worry," said Eilaai, but there were tears in Reet's eyes again, and he didn't want to talk anymore.

On the last day of travel, Eilaai did not speak to him. Instead it was Ambassador Seimet's voice that spoke out of the air. "Reet Hluid."

Reet considered what answer he wanted to make, and settled on silence.

"You already know," said the ambassador, "that the Presger Translators want you back, quite urgently. This is not because they care about you in particular."

Reet rolled his eyes. "I'd guessed that."

A moment of silence. Then, "I am not trying to disillusion you, I am giving you a warning. The officials I spoke to were very solicitous of your well-being. They want you to come to them alive and healthy. They want something from you. There is nothing you can possibly have that would interest them. Except, maybe, information."

"I'm not going to..."

"Be silent! I am not Eilaai. And we have little time." It occurred to Reet to mention that they had both been on board this ship for a good two weeks and she could have spoken to him at any point, but he held the words back.

"On the one hand," continued Ambassador Seimet, "this is good for you. You'll likely be treated well and allowed to reach adulthood. But once they have what they want from you—or, as I strongly suspect, they discover that you don't have what they're looking for—then your usefulness to them will be at an end."

Reet leaned back against a cushion and closed his eyes. "I want to talk to my parents."

"You have no parents," said Ambassador Seimet, voice cold and matter-of-fact. "The sooner you realize this, the better."

"Better for who?" asked Reet. "I don't agree to any of this. I have a right to talk to my jurist."

"Presger Translators don't have jurists."

"Then I must not be a Presger Translator. I demand to see my jurist, and I demand to be allowed to contact my parents."

"Impossible," replied Ambassador Seimet. "You have neither."

Reet sighed, opened his eyes, picked up his handheld, and started up episode 173 of *Pirate Exiles of the Death Moons*. It had lots of shooting and alarms and explosions, and he turned the external volume up as high as it would go.

When the episode was done, his handheld pinged. A message from Ambassador Seimet. *We dock in twenty minutes. Put on the isolation suit and you will walk off this ship with some shred of dignity. Or not. It doesn't matter to this ship's crew one way or another.*

He replied, *I expect to see my jurist when I disembark.*

The answer came back immediately: *You may expect whatever you like, but I beg to inform you that you will be disappointed. Fifteen minutes.*

Reet considered. What would his parents advise him to do? Would he, by walking away from this ship under his own power, signal any sort of consent to any of this? Or, if they carried him off unconscious, would he miss some opportunity?

It wasn't Zeoseni law he was dealing with here. It was treaty law. And his conversations with Eilaai hadn't given him the information he needed for this situation. Probably on purpose, he realized.

And why hadn't Eilaai spoken to him just now? She would have been able to say the things Ambassador Seimet had just said without being so antagonistic.

They wanted him angry, he concluded. They wanted him to decide to make them carry him out.

He stowed both handhelds in his shirt and picked up the isolation suit.

It was the right decision. He walked off the ship, clumsy in the isolation suit, escorted by two white-clad figures he assumed were Ambassador Seimet and Eilaai (who gave him a rueful smile and a tiny wave of one white-gloved hand), into a perfectly recognizable dock.

And there, standing behind a row of temporary fencing, was a short, stout stranger. And beside her—Mom, and Nana. And Mx Athtur.

"Mom! Nana!" cried Reet, and moved toward them.

Ambassador Seimet caught Reet's arm. "Don't. Or you'll regret it."

"I think *you* will," said Reet, trying to pull away. Off behind the fencing, Mom and Nana said something—their mouths moved, they were shouting, but he couldn't hear them. He knocked his fist against the side of his helmet.

The short, stout woman—a jurist, Reet was sure—held something up and said something.

"Oh you have *got* to be shitting me," said Ambassador Seimet, and suddenly Reet could hear what everyone was saying.

"…ommittee has granted a hold on these proceedings," the jurist was saying. "I'll say it a third time if you like."

"Reet!" called Nana. "Say you're human! You have to say it!"

"I'm human!" said Reet.

"You are most certainly *not*," said Ambassador Seimet. Beside her, Eilaai stood wide-eyed, and Reet couldn't tell if she was horrified or delighted.

"Ambassador Seimet!" called another voice. Another group approached, on this side of the fence. All of them in Translator white.

"Translator Dlar," said Ambassador Seimet. "I apologize for this confusion."

Translator Dlar—Reet supposed—waved that away. "These things happen, Ambassador. We must allow the committee to do its work." Reet thought there was an edge of impatience in Translator Dlar's words. The Translator turned toward the jurist. "We acknowledge the hold. But we cannot and will not release this juvenile into your custody. The committee would never order us to hand them over to you. They won't."

"He," said Reet. "I'm *he*."

"Gender," said Translator Dlar, "is a thing humans have."

"*Some* humans," replied Reet. "And I'm one of them."

Translator Dlar looked, suddenly, as though they had a headache. "Come along, now," they said, beckoning. "I suppose we'll have to explain things to you, too."

"Reet!" called Mom. "Hold on! We're doing everything we can!"

"I wasn't disappointed after all," said Reet to Ambassador Seimet. "Maybe it's you who has a disappointment coming."

"Don't depend on it," said Ambassador Seimet, her voice acid.

Qven

It was a while before they took me to watch Tzam die. I don't know how long, I didn't count how many times I lay in the very large bed, or the number of cakes I ate, or how many cups of tea I drank. Long enough, though, for me to begin to wonder if they would show me at all, if maybe, contrary to their expectations, Tzam had not begun to die.

Long enough for me to remind myself that I shouldn't pin any hopes on that, that Teacher had very specifically said that Tzam's death would be a long one.

Long enough that I began to see doors.

At first I didn't know what they were. It was just a strange feeling around particular stretches of wall. I knew better than to look more closely—Teacher was always near me, and though they seemed to have been kind to me, I knew I would be foolish to depend on that for anything serious.

I had to be discreet. To sit quietly. To seem as though all

my attention was on a sprouting radish or the leaf of a potato plant (the tiny, nascent tubers under the soil piping their smooth, waxy little songs).

This was, of course, precisely the behavior Teacher had encouraged, and they were pleased, I thought, to see me settle now, even more profoundly than I had before. They didn't leave me alone, exactly—they were always with me, no matter what I did—but they declined to interrupt me when I was quietly occupied.

I could feel Tzam, I thought, or feel that they were *somewhere*. Somewhere that was not here. It was an unpleasant, crawling feeling. And I could feel the spaces beyond the walls, more and more distinctly. It was almost—sort of— like the feeling of my radish seeds, only not. I began to feel them, the places in the walls that sometimes opened. Not for me, of course, but for Teacher, coming and going between themself.

Was Teacher opening and closing those doors? Yes, yes they were, I tasted it, what they were doing, once I thought to look for it.

I knew better than to try doing it myself. It must be something Adults could do, and that meant I should give no hint, not the slightest suggestion, that I might be able to, that I'd even considered it.

But I watched the doors. Imagined I could feel what was beyond them, corridors and rooms that were *not here*.

So when Teacher said, "It's time," and the blank wall behind them gaped open, I was not surprised. I had known for days that the door was there, and suspected the blue-white corridor beyond.

"Come," said Teacher. "The moment has arrived. Choose to see, or not."

I wanted to see Tzam die. I wanted to never see Tzam again, never think of them. And that was the stronger feeling, I thought.

For the first time in oh, so very long, I had a choice. I could take this one small thing that I wanted—to stay here and not have to see Tzam's face ever again.

The corridor stretched away from the open door. The door that Teacher was holding open, I could taste how they were doing it.

If I chose to stay here, I wouldn't see what was around me. If I rose and went through this door, I might see more doors and more corridors.

I might see if there was some way to escape.

"I don't want to," I said, and the tremble in my voice was real. "But I have to know if it's true."

Teacher made a beckoning gesture, and I rose and walked into the corridor.

There were several more doors, more corridors, and then, between one step and the next, we were elsewhere. The hum of my rooms disappeared. Everything was different, even though the corridor we walked in seemed the same to look at. I wasn't sure how I knew it wasn't actually the same.

"Here," said Teacher, and opened a door. "They can't see you."

I stepped through the door.

Tzam was there. Crouched, naked, sweating. It looked as though their skin was melting off their body.

The room looked small, but I could feel that it was vast, full of doors, and others behind those doors. Watching, I supposed, witnessing the example that Tzam was, at this moment. I didn't know how that made me feel, the thought that others were here besides myself, seeing this. I felt something, certainly, something very strong, but I had no name for it, nothing to tell me what sort of feeling it was.

On the tiled floor in front of us, Tzam moaned, as though in pain.

Teacher said, "Translator Dlar wishes me to tell you that this is what happens when a juvenile is denied a match."

"Is the Translator here?" I asked, surprised that any words had come out of me.

"They are," said Teacher.

"Qven," moaned Tzam. They lifted their head. "Qven!" they cried. "I know you're here! *Qven!*"

"H…" I couldn't make a sound. I tried again. "How…?" But I knew. I felt a strange sensation on my neck, the place where Tzam's hand had sunk into me. "How do they…?"

I thought Teacher looked just slightly relieved, and I knew I'd said the right thing. "They can't see you," Teacher said again. "They most certainly can't touch you. Do you need a chair?"

I couldn't speak. "Qven!" screamed Tzam. "Qven, I need you! Qven, *please*!" That last dissolved into a sobbing, wordless cry.

A chair was suddenly behind me, against my legs. I sat heavily.

"I did everything I was supposed to," sobbed Tzam. "I did everything you asked me to do!"

"I'm going to be sick," I said, and it turned out to be true. Teacher held a basin in front of me—where it had come from I didn't know and didn't care.

"Qven, you can save me!" cried Tzam. "I know you're here, just touch me." They held out one hand, the hand that had been on my neck. "Just come here and touch me!"

"You can't," said Teacher, though I hadn't moved. "You can't touch them, and they can't touch you. Moreover, if you did, you would both be immediately destroyed."

"How long is this going to take?" I asked.

"Several hours, from the look of things. Are you going to be sick again?"

"Yes."

When I looked up again, Tzam had melted further, thick, viscous layers of skin sliding down into a growing pool on the floor. Patches of muscle shone here and there under the melting skin, and the bones of one hand were exposed for a moment before they, too, turned wet and began to drip thickly down.

"Qven, you miserable pile of meat!" cried Tzam. "You bag of excrement! No one wants to be a coward, a treacherous failure! I'm glad I don't have to be you, I'd rather die!" A choking laughter bubbled up out of their mouth, and a gush of liquid came with it, and Tzam's whole body spasmed.

"With any luck," said Teacher, "that'll have done for their vocal cords." Their voice was even. Controlled. "Calm yourself," they said to me. "I know you can. Tzam can never hurt you again. There's every reason to be hopeful about your future, once this is past. And after all," they reminded me, "you chose to witness this."

I *had* chosen it. I wished I hadn't. "May I have a drink of water?"

"Of course," said Teacher.

I drank the water, and I sat there and watched as Tzam dissolved and dissolved and then, finally, died.

I mostly stayed in bed the next day, and Teacher brought me tea, so I supposed I must be ill again. The place on my neck where Tzam had touched me ached, though not enough to really trouble me. Except for the fact of it, the fact there was any place on me at all that Tzam had touched that way, the fact that I had watched them die, muscles sloughing off bones, half-dissolved organs spilling out of their melting abdomen.

"Rest," said Teacher, and took the bowl of tea from my hand, and drew the covers up over me.

I slept. So heavily that I suspected Teacher of putting something in the tea. I wouldn't have noticed it, considering the state I'd been in. But I felt rested when I woke, if no happier.

"It's a big day today," said Teacher when I sat up.

"I don't like big days," I said. "Can't we just make cakes and have tea and tend the plants?"

"You can and will do all of those things today," said Teacher. "Get up."

I had very few options. I could get up and have this big day, or I could pull the covers over my head and refuse to do anything. But that probably wouldn't change anything at all, and I'd basically stayed in bed all yesterday and I didn't want to do it anymore.

I got up, and got dressed, and made tea, and set out cakes. I might as well have eaten them standing where I was: it was only myself and Teacher I ever set them out for. Unless Translator Dlar visited. And now I'd listened carefully, I could feel someone who wasn't Teacher nearby. I decided that if it was Translator Dlar coming to visit, I would not speak to them.

Teacher opened a door and escorted in…a stranger. Tall, with lank, dark hair, no one I had ever seen before. They fidgeted in their plain gray clothes, scratching one forearm with a gloved hand. "This is Reet," said Teacher. "Reet, this is Qven."

Oh no! *This* kind of big day. This was my match, finally here, and I did not want them here at all. But I could see that Reet had been given whatever I had, to delay a match. That was something. There would be time. Time to…

I thought of Tzam, screaming wetly, collapsing into nothing.

I took refuge in habit. "I am so very pleased to meet you, Reet," I recited.

They looked at me as though my words had been a question that was far too difficult for them to answer. Teacher only stood there, watching. I leaned forward and said, quietly, "There's a schedule. And a script. But if you're ill you can drink tea in bed." And then, louder, gesturing at the table and its two chairs, "My goodness. I think we could do with some tea." Reet stared blankly at me. "Now you say, *Tea sounds lovely*, and you sit in a chair."

"Tea sounds lovely," Reet said, and sat. In the chair, like they should. I hadn't been certain, considering the vacant stare and the distinct possibility that they'd had no education to speak of.

And then Teacher did something they had never, ever done in the whole time since I'd come here: they left us alone.

Even though I could still feel their presence on the other side of a wall, it left a disorienting empty space in my thoughts. "Will you have a cake?" I asked, reaching again for the security of routine. "I made them myself."

"I'm not *they*," Reet said irritably, and took a cake. "And I'm not *she*, either. I'm *he*."

"I don't know that word," I said. "What does it mean?"

"It means I have a gender. It's…" They—he—suddenly looked abashed. "It's not proper Radchaai, but where I come from, people don't like being called the wrong gender, so at some point other pronouns got added into the way we speak Radchaai."

"What?" I asked, surprised. "Can you do that? Just add words?"

Reet shrugged uncomfortably in his gray jacket. "If enough people use it, and it sticks, I guess."

I sipped tea. "You know we're supposed to match."

"We can't," he said, with a shudder. "Anyone with an ambiguous treaty status gets to choose. I've declared that I'm human. The committee has to rule on it, and they haven't yet, I don't think. So Translator Dlar doesn't get to make me do anything I don't want without possibly breaking the treaty."

That was interesting. "How do you get an ambiguous treaty status?" I asked urgently, leaning over the table.

"I don't know. I think I was born with it."

"I would like to be human, too," I informed him. "Will you tell the committee that?"

"I don't think they're letting me contact anyone right now," he said. "But I will if I can."

I had dreaded this arrival, but now it had come it wasn't as bad as I'd feared. "What kind of gender does *he* mean?"

"It's a masculine gender. I'm a man."

"How do you know?"

He frowned. "I…I don't know. I've just…always felt like I was. As far as I can remember."

I thought about that. "Do I maybe have a gender, too?"

"I couldn't possibly say," he said helplessly. "Look. I…I just…"

"Are you ill?" I asked. "If you're ill you can stay in bed and Teacher won't make you follow the schedule." I thought, looking at him, that he probably *was* ill.

"What's the schedule?"

"After tea and cakes we talk about weather, and then I tend to the plants. Would you like to see my plants? I have radishes and potatoes. And we could maybe get some others." He looked at me blankly. "I am not a potato," I warned him.

"I'm glad to hear it," he said. "Do you know what *I* want to do?"

"I can't possibly until you tell me."

"I want to lie in bed and eat dumplings and watch *Pirate Exiles of the Death Moons*. Or any other good show."

"I can make dumplings," I said. "And if Teacher comes back we'll tell them you're ill. But I don't know anything about pirates or exiles."

He looked up at the ceiling and said, loudly, "I want my handheld back!"

Teacher came into the room. "This is very impolite of you, Reet," they said. "We expect better of someone with such extensive experience of human manners."

"He's ill," I said. "He needs to go to bed and eat dumplings and watch...pirates. On a moon."

"Dumplings are too messy for bed," said Teacher primly. "You can eat them at the table. But then you may go back to bed. I will see about the handheld."

"Thank you, Teacher," I said.

Enae

It seemed to Enae that everything at the Treaty Administration Facility happened in meetings. Informal meetings
where cakes or other treats were exchanged, formal ones
with strict orders of precedence and form—nearly all Enae
and Ms and Mx Hluid had done since they'd arrived at Central was attend meetings. So it was perhaps inevitable that
eventually one of those meetings would be with Ambassador
Seimet.

It was, of course, one of the formal ones, in a room that
appeared to be paneled with dark wood, with chairs also of
wood, carved into elaborate curves and curls. The table was
polished black stone, with a gold-and-violet tea set precisely
in the center. Ms Eilaai served, with the smallest quirk of her
lips when she set one tiny, handleless cup in front of Enae, the
only acknowledgment that they'd met before.

"Mx Athtur," said Ambassador Seimet, sitting across the

table. "Ms Hluid. Mx Hluid." Her voice chill. "I introduce you to the human ambassador to the Geck, Tibanvori."

"We've met," said that person—tall, with short, spiky hair. White clad like Ambassador Seimet but, unlike her, somewhat rumpled.

"Have you now," said Ambassador Seimet.

"Yesterday," said Istver Hluid, warmly. "It's good to see you again, Ambassador."

"Likewise," said Ambassador Tibanvori.

"And when," asked Ambassador Seimet, "were you going to inform me that you've been meeting with the petitioners in this very important matter, Ambassador?"

"I just told you now," said Tibanvori, and reached forward to pour herself another slug of tea. "If you mean why didn't I tell you sooner, well, I was unaware that I owed you any sort of account of my movements."

Ambassador Seimet's face was impassive, but Eilaai, standing behind her, very clearly suppressed a wince.

"Of course we've already met," said Echemin Hluid, indignant. "It's the Geck bringing our petition, and we're human—as is our son—so of course the human ambassador to the Geck has met with us."

"Your son is not human," said Ambassador Seimet, disdainful.

"It's the considered opinion of the committee member for the Geck that Reet Hluid is, in fact, human," said Ambassador Tibanvori.

Ambassador Seimet stared at Tibanvori but said nothing.

"You can always have me replaced," suggested Ambassador Tibanvori.

"Believe me," said Ambassador Seimet with a sneer, "I would if I could."

"Oh, I'm sure you can manage it," said Tibanvori, easily. "If you put your mind to it."

"Our son is human," said Istver. "He grew up as a human. Ever since he was a baby everyone around him has assumed he was human."

"He declared he was human," said Ms Yedess, sitting beside Enae. "You heard him."

"If only declaring something made it so," said Ambassador Seimet.

"It does in this case," said Ms Yedess.

"It does not," insisted Ambassador Seimet. "There is far more involved here than you can possibly understand."

"You keep saying that," said Enae. "Why don't you explain so that we do understand?"

Ambassador Tibanvori snorted inelegantly.

"Mx Athtur is right," said Istver. "It strikes me that all of this has been caused, or at least made worse, by keeping secrets. If your office, Ambassador Seimet, hadn't been so secretive about looking for this Presger Translator fugitive all those years ago, the people who found Reet as a baby might have known right then where he belonged. Just as one example." She looked Ambassador Seimet straight in the eyes as she said it.

Tibanvori said, as Ambassador Seimet stared back at Ms Hluid, "Seimet Mianaai doesn't usually have to talk to anyone who doesn't bow and stare at their shoes and say *Yes, Ambassador* to whatever she tells them. Not anyone human, anyway."

"The Presger," said Ambassador Seimet, "are *very* alien. They don't understand humans at all. Their Translators were...put together from material taken from human ships and stations that they'd disassembled. Put together in a way that made some sense to the Presger themselves. And the Presger do not understand the idea of being a person. Or, to speak more clearly, they do not understand the idea of being an individual." She sipped her tea. "So Presger Translators were assembled according to Presger logic. Or at least as close to Presger logic as human biology allowed. Which I understand is still quite strange to the Presger themselves, but closer than *we* can get."

"He can't be that different," insisted Mx Hluid. "He's always been an ordinary person. We've known him since he was a baby, and there was no reason to think he was an alien."

"She's not a person," insisted Ambassador Seimet. "She is only *part* of a person. When she reaches maturity—which, let me assure you, she is on the verge of doing—she must merge with some other biologically compatible being or die. She is very, very fortunate that we found her when we did."

Enae made a small noise.

"That Mx Athtur found her," Ambassador Seimet amended. "The fact remains."

"The fact remains," said Istver, "that Reet is our son."

Ambassador Seimet closed her eyes. "Amaat give me strength," she murmured. And then, opening her eyes again, said, "Did you listen to a word I just said? Presger Translator juveniles are exceedingly dangerous. The more so because you can't see what they are until it's too late. I gather Reet

Hluid has controlled herself admirably while she lived with you, and it's much to her and no doubt your credit." Enae was surprised that this admission didn't sound grudging. "But she will not be able to control what is about to happen to her. She is a danger to everyone around her—yes, even to adult Presger Translators—until she's safely matched with an appropriate counterpart. Which is precisely what you have delayed with all this nonsense about petitioning the committee. She would be far better served if you let her go."

Echemin crossed eir arms and said, belligerently, "Then let him say that to us himself."

"This isn't something she or any other juvenile gets to choose. These things are managed very carefully so as not to cause chaos among the Presger Translators, let alone what might happen if juveniles were free to wander and absorb any human they came across."

"That is why no humans are allowed to come back if they go into the Presger Translator sections of the facility?" Enae said.

"No," said Ambassador Seimet. "There are no juveniles in the Presger Translator sections of the facility. It's the Presger themselves that are the danger. Or were. It hasn't happened for a very long time, and I am determined that it will not happen again while I live. And humans who do go there *can* come back, just not as humans. But none of this matters. We can sit here and argue, and do by all means drink as much tea as you like..."

Tibanvori snorted again. "It's very expensive tea, not that Seimet Mianaai cares about the cost."

Ambassador Seimet went on, as though Tibanvori hadn't

spoken, "…but no matter what you say or how you say it or how long you take to say it, I will not change my position, and I assure you I will prevail upon the committee member for humans to oppose your petition."

"Well, I've done my work for the day," said Tibanvori. "See you around." She stalked off down the corridor.

"The ambassador to the Geck," explained Ms Yedess quietly, in the corridor outside Ambassador Seimet's office, "does not love her job. She's been trying to resign for years."

Echemin gave a bark of a laugh. "That explains her behavior in the meeting just now!"

"It does indeed," agreed Ms Yedess. "I suspect the ambassador will get her wish before long, though who they'll replace her with I have no idea."

"For years, though!" exclaimed Ms Hluid. "How has anything gotten done, with the ambassador like this all the time?"

"Well, she's worse now than before," admitted Ms Yedess, "but the truth is, the Geck are rarely involved in anything of any importance. Ordinarily the only thing they really care about is keeping their homeworld to themselves. The human ambassador to the Geck rarely has much to do to begin with. I'm not certain just why the Geck ambassador is going to such lengths over this petition."

"We'll take help anywhere we can get it," said Enae. "Right?" Sie thought of Mr Nadkal, still, as far as Enae knew, orbiting the facility, applying for entry. "Almost anywhere."

"Right," agreed Ms Yedess. "In the meantime, we have more meetings in front of us, and days and days of writing documents and looking over others."

Echemin Hluid groaned. "More?" e asked.

"Many more," confirmed Ms Yedess. "I'm sorry, but it's how this works."

"You do this all the time," said Ms Hluid, with slightly forced cheerfulness.

"I do," said Ms Yedess.

"And if what Ambassador Seimet said is true?" asked Echemin, anxiety in eir voice. "If Reet can't safely be with humans? If he has to be..." Eir voice failed.

"Presger Translators are around humans all the time here," said Ms Yedess. "I don't see why Reet shouldn't be able to live where he wants, even if he has to..." Istver made a distressed noise, very unlike her usual composure. Ms Yedess put a hand on her shoulder and said, "The ambassador made it sound terrible, but I don't imagine it can really be all that bad. And besides, the Presger were able to make the Translators to begin with, surely there's something they can do for Reet. I'll definitely be making that argument in our submissions to the committee."

Back in their quarters, Istver and Enae settled into chairs. Echemin Hluid paced and then, at a word from Istver, went out to walk the station's corridors.

"I'm sorry," said Istver. "E's always been...impatient."

"No, there's no need to apologize," Enae reassured her. "Of course e's worried about Reet. It's entirely understandable." Though, sie reflected, Istver Hluid was no doubt just as worried and managed not to take it out on the people around her.

"Do you have children?" Istver asked.

"No." Some obscure emotion Enae couldn't name filled hir at the question. "I don't have anyone, really."

"Surely you have *someone*. Some sort of family. Friends?"

"I had Grandmaman, I suppose," said Enae after some thought. "My mother left her family before I was born, she cut off contact. She died when I was about four. I was sent to Grandmaman, since she was my next of kin. I grew up in Grandmaman's house."

"Your grandmaman loved you," said Istver. "She must have."

Enae thought of life with Grandmaman. Sie had had clothes, food, a roof over hir head. An education and an allowance.

And constant criticism, no matter what sie did. Why didn't sie go out into the world and make something of hirself? How could sie even imagine leaving when Grandmaman needed hir so much? The household wouldn't run right without Enae's management. Also sie was thoughtless and incompetent and a *real* housekeeper would do things so much better.

Enae had held hir tongue. Wept occasionally in the privacy of hir own room. Endured.

"I don't know," sie admitted. "I don't know if she loved me or not. If she ever had anything good to say, it was backhanded. Or I was showing signs of wanting to leave."

"Oh," Istver said, as though she understood exactly what that meant. "I'm so sorry."

"She wasn't a nice person," Enae said. "But then, her whole family was...I mean, her daughter, my mother, left, and her other children only stayed around hoping to inherit Grandmaman's money."

"There was a lot of it?"

"They thought there was." And when Istver frowned in puzzlement, Enae told her about the funeral. About learning that there was no money, had not been for years. That the name and the house had been sold to a stranger.

"Your grandmother provided for you, though," Istver pointed out. "Out of everyone else."

"She did," Enae admitted. "And the first thing the new heir did was send me away. I was out here looking for Reet because everyone at home wanted to be rid of me."

Istver put her hand on Enae's. "I'm glad it was you and not someone else."

"Someone else might not have found him," Enae protested. "He'd still be living his life."

"No. If what Ambassador Seimet said is true, something awful was going to happen, no matter what. But someone who didn't care about him wouldn't have gone to the trouble to contact us, to try to help."

"Reet is so lucky," Enae said, blinking back tears. "He's so lucky to have a family like you. Even if..." Sie swallowed. "Even if we can't help him."

"We're doing the best we can," said Istver. "Even if it isn't always enough."

Reet

Reet sat at the small table and drank tea while Qven made dumplings. It was, he gathered, a generous concession to his supposed illness. The teacher—there was only one, he understood, despite there very clearly being two bodies, both of which were apparently the same person—withdrew again, and left Reet and Qven to their own devices. Or so it seemed. Reet was certain they were still being watched.

"So. Reet." Qven set the plate of dumplings on the table between them and sat across from him. "Have you ever seen rain?"

Reet thought about that a moment. "This is the part of the schedule where we talk about weather."

"Not technically," admitted Qven, and lowering their voice, added, "They won't hold us to the schedule if you're ill, but the more we do, the less they'll sus...the less they'll worry."

What had they been about to say? *The less they'll suspect?* What was there to suspect? Feigning illness?

Whatever it was, Qven certainly wouldn't answer questions about it where they thought the teacher could hear. "I've been in rain," he said. "Sometimes it's nice. Sometimes it's miserable. It depends."

"There was a garden in the Edges," said Qven, taking a dumpling with a utensil. "But it never rained there."

"How did the plants get water?" Reet took a dumpling for himself. It was very good.

"I don't know." Qven frowned as though they'd never considered the question before. "There was a pond there. With fish."

"That sounds nice." He took another dumpling. Considered what he wanted to know—what he needed to know—and what he was likely able to ask. "What kind of fish were they?"

"Orange ones," said Qven. "How are the dumplings?"

"They're very good. Thank you for making them."

"You're very welcome." Qven spoke surely, a little primly. It was, Reet supposed, a line they'd practiced.

"Listen," he said. "This is all new to me. Not the dumplings," he said to Qven's suddenly bewildered expression. "I mean this Presger Translator business. Everyone around me assumed I was human. As far as anything that matters goes, I *am* human."

"Shh," said Qven, quickly passing him a dumpling. "You're overwrought. No wonder you're ill."

Reet glanced at the ceiling.

"Yes," said Qven. "Eat your dumplings. I'll show you

something." They got up, went into another room, and returned with a small plant pot. Tiny, rough leaves sprouted out of the dirt. "See this?"

"It's very nice," said Reet, not sure what was expected of him, though clearly something was.

Qven leaned just the slightest bit closer and said very, very quietly, "Can you hear it?"

"No," replied Reet, just as quietly.

"I just wanted you to see it," said Qven in a more normal tone. "I've grown a lot of them."

Reet nodded, as though that explained everything.

"I want to see the pirates and the moons," they said, still standing there holding the potted radish. "But I don't want you to touch me."

He thought about that a moment. Wriggled his shoulder against the back of his chair, inadequate against the persistent, tickling itch. "We can set up cushions or something."

"Oh!" Qven seemed pleased. Surprised, as though the thought hadn't occurred to them. And then, less pleased, "Teacher might not like it. We're supposed to want to match, I think."

Reet was struck by the way they said that, as though they had just said he and they were supposed to die. Or maybe that was his own feeling, his own fears speaking. "I can't," he said, and scratched his shoulder again. "They gave me something to stop me. And my petition is still before the committee."

"Right," said Qven, and scratched one leg with their foot. They seemed for a moment as though they would say something else. A strange expression crossed their face. Reet waited, but all they said was, "Eat your dumplings."

* * *

It took about twenty minutes—not counting the time spent asking the teacher for more cushions and covers and then waiting for those to materialize—to set up a construction that was both satisfactory to Qven and comfortable for both. Then, once they were nestled in their separate compartments, the handheld propped between, they finally settled down to watch *Pirate Exiles of the Death Moons*.

Reet had to translate—none of the languages the show was available in was familiar to Qven. He also had to stop every now and then to explain things that utterly mystified them. Not things like *how is there such a well-equipped pirate base out in the middle of nowhere?* or *how do people recover so quickly after being hit hard enough on the head to fall unconscious?* or *why are the heroes' wounds always in visually appealing but not disabling locations?* No, those things Qven appeared to take in stride. Instead they wanted to know if the people they were watching were, in fact, exiled pirates, and so right in the middle of episode seven he'd had to stop and explain about stories and actors.

Reet fell asleep in the middle of episode twelve, woke to find the handheld paused at the end of thirteen and Qven fast asleep in their cushion barricade. He slipped out of bed to use the facilities and went into the room where they'd eaten before, hoping to find food and maybe tea. He found, instead, the teacher. One of them, anyway.

"I have no intention of following your schedule," he said.

"The schedule is pointless now," said the teacher. "Do whatever you like. But don't encourage Qven to think that they can become human. No matter what the committee rules, they—and you—will still be what you are."

Reet thought about that for a moment. "That's a completely meaningless thing to say."

The teacher's eyebrows twitched, as though they were holding back some expression. "It's not your fault that you're in this situation," said the teacher. "It's the mistakes of others that have brought you here."

"One of those mistakes," replied Reet, "was dragging me away from my home and my family with no explanations."

"Those of us who would have handled things differently weren't making the decisions," said the teacher. "But ultimately it changes nothing." They gazed at him a few moments and then said, "It's always something of a shock. It's never the way you imagine it. But it's not like dying. Not at all. You don't lose who you are. You become...more. There's nothing to be afraid of."

"Is there tea?" asked Reet.

"There's always tea." The teacher gestured to a set of cabinets behind them. "It will be easier for everyone if you go into this willingly."

"Easier for you," suggested Reet. "Easier for Translator Dlar."

"Not for the same reasons." They paused a moment, and then said, "I know I said the schedule was meaningless, but you really should get up and move around more than you are, if you're going to keep watching that show."

"Thanks for the advice," he said, and walked past the teacher and began opening cabinets: dishes; various cooking utensils. Ah, here. Tea. Now to find a flask, and cups. He opened the next cabinet. "Is it true that I'll die if I don't... merge with someone?"

"Yes." There was something odd in the teacher's voice, but Reet was determined not to turn around and look, to see if their expression had changed.

"So I guess you all grow up expecting it. It seems normal to you."

"For the most part," agreed the teacher. Reet did turn then, tea in one hand, flask in the other. "Your progenitor," the teacher went on, "the one who abandoned you as an infant. They fled Presger space before they matched. It disrupted a number of the clade's plans, and caused a good deal of alarm. They almost certainly matched with some unwilling human. That's exactly the sort of thing we try to prevent, it's why we keep juveniles isolated from anyone else except those adults who are trained to work with them."

"And me?"

"My guess would be, you were produced in order to… extend their lifespan. But something happened to prevent that. They lost you somehow. If they haven't found you by now"— the teacher made an indefinite gesture—"they've likely died."

"Why did they run away?"

The teacher actually sighed. "Have your breakfast, Reet. Continue to be kind to Qven." They turned and left the room.

He returned to the cushion fortress in the bed, with a plate of dumplings and a flask of tea. "Oh," said Qven, stirring. "Teacher won't be pleased about dumplings in bed."

"Fuck Teacher," Reet replied, and climbed into his side of the construction.

"I don't want to do that," said Qven, taking the plate of dumplings from him before it could spill.

"Did you ever make a tent when you were little?" asked Reet. He wanted to be away from the constant gaze of the teacher. Of anyone. He'd spent weeks under view, not so much as an instant private. He missed his tiny room back on Rurusk, where he knew he could be alone. Stupid to think a bedcover draped over some cushions could give him that sort of privacy, but it was what was available to him.

Qven swallowed their mouthful of dumpling. "A tent?"

"Like this." He rearranged some cushions and pulled a bedcover over the top, throwing them into a close, muffled dimness. "It's like having our own little room. We can pretend no one can see us." Qven didn't answer, and he saw that they were a hunched shadow, frozen in their well of cushions, barely moving even to breathe. "Qven. Are you all right?"

"I don't like it," they said in a distressed, nearly inaudible whisper.

"I'll take it down," he said, moving to pull the cover away.

"No!" came the agonized whisper. "Teacher will like that we're under this. They'll leave us alone."

"Do you think we can talk without them listening?" Reet asked, very quietly, and then felt bad about asking it. Clearly something about this situation was upsetting Qven badly.

"Yes," replied Qven, their whisper gone shaky. "If we're very quiet."

"Qven, what's wrong?"

There was silence. Qven themself hadn't moved even a muscle.

"Qven," he said. "It's all right. Really, I can take the cover down. I didn't mean to upset you."

"They were under the bush." Still whispered, but high and strained. "They were under the bush and they were all melted into each other. And…" They stopped speaking but now Reet could hear them breathing, almost gasping.

"We're not under a bush," said Reet. "We're just in your bedroom." He reached for the handheld, found the beginning of episode thirteen of *Pirate Exiles*, and started it going. Tears gleamed on Qven's face in the light cast by the show, ran down their cheeks, dripped onto their gloved hands, which were, for some reason, cupped around their throat. "I'll take the cover off," Reet insisted.

"No!" They didn't look at him but stared blankly ahead, weeping. "There's nothing. There's nothing we can do."

"Watch the show," suggested Reet. "This is the one where the Rrrrr bandit finds their cache and…"

"I saw it," Qven said, still breathing hard. They closed their eyes. "You fell asleep."

"Then we'll watch the next one." Reet picked up the handheld again and forwarded to episode fourteen. The first notes of the introduction seemed to calm Qven, just a bit. Or was it his imagination? Maybe it was Reet who was soothed, hearing it. "I'll pour us some tea."

Ten minutes later, noticeably calmer, breathing steadied, Qven took one hand off their neck and reached for the cup of tea Reet had left on the cushion between them, and drank it down. "It's cold," they complained. And then, before Reet could answer, they said, "I let it sit there too long."

"I've got more in the flask that's hot," said Reet, and poured them another one. "Are you still hungry? I could make some more dumplings."

Reet thought their expression changed, almost the traces of a smile. "Dumplings are too messy for bed."

"I'll make dishes and dishes of them," said Reet. "We'll be buried under dumplings."

A little noise escaped Qven, a huff that might have been a strangled laugh. "Don't, though."

"No," agreed Reet. "It would be uncomfortable. But we could if we wanted."

"We could if we wanted," agreed Qven.

Three more episodes of *Pirate Exiles* and another plate of dumplings later, Qven said, very, very quietly, "I think Teacher isn't paying close attention to us now."

"How can you tell?" Reet kept his voice as quiet as Qven's.

"I can…hear them. You can't hear them?"

"Like the radish?" Qven made a silent acknowledgment, and Reet said, "No. I can't. Am I supposed to be able to?"

"No," whispered Qven. "I'm not supposed to, either. I think. I don't want to ask."

Because it might tell the teacher more than Qven wanted them to know, Reet guessed. "If we're supposed to…" Reet could feel Qven's discomfort even in the dark of their makeshift tent. "You know. I guess they're not going to interfere if we're just getting to know each other better." He thought about that. "I guess they'd do that, anyway? I mean, they don't just throw you in with someone you've never seen before, do they?"

"I don't know," Qven admitted. "I never got to find out."

Reet wanted very badly to ask what that meant, but he remembered their frozen, tearful distress of a few hours ago and didn't want to upset Qven any more than he already had. "They told me, on my way here, that the Presger Translators wanted information that I might have about the person who ran away. But I don't have it. I don't know anything."

"It doesn't really change anything," said Qven. "We still have to match with someone or we'll die." Silence. Then, "I don't think they're going to let us match with anyone else." There was distress in the back of Qven's voice, but also bitterness.

"Was there someone else you wanted to match with?"

Qven seemed perplexed by that question. "Why would that matter? It's not like doing sex, or having a friend. You can...I mean, I guess adults do sex and have friends if they want." A pause, while they considered. "Teacher might like it if we did sex."

"I'm...I'm really not in the mood for that," said Reet.

"I don't want to, either." Reet thought Qven sounded relieved. "Listen." Their voice had dropped to a nearly inaudible level. "I tried to run away. Someone said they'd help me but they..." They stopped and cupped their hands around their neck again, the way they had hours before. "They attacked me and tried to force me to match with them. I hurt them and made them stop."

"I'm sorry." Reet was at a loss as to what else there was to say. He didn't know anything about any of this, but what Qven had described struck him as utterly, appallingly wrong.

"It wasn't your fault. But it means I'm unsuitable now. They didn't know what to do with me until you turned up."

"Unsuitable?"

"I didn't behave optimally," Qven whispered. "And I've got...part of them in me."

"What happened to your attacker?"

A long, long silence. "They died," whispered Qven finally. "They were left all alone and they screamed and screamed and…" Their voice failed, and they sobbed. Reet watched helplessly. What would Maman do, or Mom, if it was him sobbing like this?

They would put their arms around him. And he might not feel better, but he would feel less alone. "Qven," he said. "What if you wrapped a cover around you? Then I could…" He gestured with his arms. "Without touching you." He realized, saying it, that he wanted it badly, wanted to feel, even slightly, like he wasn't all alone in some invisible box that kept him apart from everyone else in the world. "If you didn't like it, we'd stop."

They looked at him, tearful and maybe dubious. "You promise."

"I promise."

"All right," they said.

Qven

It was scary, to have Reet's arms around me, his body so close, even with the bedcover between. But it was also warm and comfortable and safe, in a way I hadn't felt since the Edges. Since before the Edges.

"I don't like it," I said.

"All right." He pulled his arms away, and moved back to his side of our tent. "Do you want to watch another episode?"

"Yes." And when the episode was over, I said, "Come back." And we watched two more episodes snuggled close, with the cover between us.

I liked that he didn't ever say that it didn't matter if he touched me, that we couldn't match because of whatever we'd been given, that obviously we were supposed to get along. He never said any of those things. Also I liked *Pirate Exiles of the Death Moons*, though I didn't really understand it all. But it was noisy and colorful, and also there was a princex who'd run away from eir family (I was learning more words, every episode, from the language the story was in) and who was in disguise. Reet had to explain to me about princexes, and *in disguise*, and I liked it very much.

There were also juveniles in the show. Tinies and Littles and Smalls, Middles, and even Edges, just...there, along with everybody else. And no one seemed afraid of them.

"Reet," I asked finally, "do human juveniles not...don't they eat each other? Aren't the Adults worried about their own safety, around them?"

He went suddenly still, in a way he hadn't before, even when I'd asked him something that confused him or that he had to think hard about before he could answer. "Not normally, no," he said after a while, and I thought his voice was too studiedly calm.

That struck me as terribly strange. Almost incomprehensibly so. "So what did you do, then? Didn't you eat anyone? Or did you eat someone and get in trouble?"

"I didn't eat anyone," he said. My head was resting on his blanket-covered shoulder and I couldn't see his expression, but I thought he was unhappy. "I tried to once, I bit another child very hard, and there was a big fuss. I never did it again, because I knew it would be wrong."

I sat up, then, and looked at him. We were still under our tent—I didn't like it, but it was getting easier to tolerate, especially knowing Teacher would probably leave us alone as long as we were in it, and knowing that so far Reet was safe to be with. "Why would it be wrong? It's just something that happens." But I remembered Teacher saying, *The only hope most such juveniles have of survival, once they've been injured or*

attacked, is the very faint possibility that some Adult will
notice and take pity on them.

"I think we grew up very differently," said Reet. "Maybe
you should tell me what it's like to be a Presger Translator
juvenile."

So I told him. I talked about what I remembered of being a
Tiny, of the Littles and the Smalls, the Middles. Of wandering the warm, blue cavities, tumbling and playing with others. Occasionally turning on some companion or other and
feasting. Of the fascination, in the Middles, with the details
of what's inside.

"Didn't..." he began, and stopped. Then, "Didn't anyone
stop you?"

"No," I said. "Why would they?"

"Oh," he said.

I went on to describe the Edges. Our practice in human
language and customs. "Radchaai," Reet corrected. "The
language and the customs are Radchaai. There are other
sorts of humans." But I'd already begun to learn that from
him. "Aren't there...you know, different sorts of...?" He
gestured. "What you are? What we are?"

I frowned. "Do you mean the Teachers and the Caretakers
and that sort of thing?"

"No, I mean, like, the difference between Radchaai
humans and Zeoseni, or whatever."

I thought about that for a moment. "Maybe? We have
different clades. I don't know if that's the same. But I don't
think the clades speak different languages. I don't think the
clades are like that. We're not supposed to care what clade we
belong to."

Reet made a noise that wasn't a laugh. "It's supposed to not matter, but it completely matters. Right?"

"Right," I agreed. "Would you like to know what Teacher told me about biology?"

He did want to know. I had to pull the tent cover down close over me—that felt all right, now, that felt safer. At one point, Teacher came into the room, silently but I could taste them there, watching, listening as I told Reet what Teacher had told me about how things worked. I didn't mention Tzam again, but Reet must have been thinking about them. "You said before that you saw someone die from not matching. That must have been horrible."

"Yes," I agreed, and then we were silent for a while. I had expected him to ask for details, but he didn't. Teacher still stood, silent, unmoving, inside the room.

"So," he said eventually, "they decide who matches with who. You don't get to pick who you want to be."

"No one does, I don't think," I agreed. "They pull you out of the Edges when you're ready, and put you with whoever they think you should match with." Not thinking about what I'd seen under the garden shrub. Not thinking about it. Not. Teacher was there, listening. I didn't want Teacher to know I knew they were there. "I think I was supposed to be Translator Dlar."

"Ew!"

"Yes," I agreed. "Teacher said that mostly when you come out of the Edges you get to make a new person, but if someone is important enough…"

"Like Translator Dlar."

"Like Translator Dlar," I agreed.

"So if you're important enough, they let a juvenile melt you and make a new person with, what, three bodies? More?"

"Teacher said only three. Then when one of the bodies dies, you might get another one. If you're still important enough."

"Huh," said Reet, as though it didn't matter at all. "You know what, though?"

"What?" I sniffled. I was definitely not thinking about that thing in the garden, definitely not thinking about Tzam, their hands on my throat...screaming for me as they melted. Definitely not. Tears had collected, threatened to roll sideways across the bridge of my nose, down into the blanket.

"At least you don't have to be Translator Dlar now. Can you imagine that?" He made a throat-clearing noise and then said, "*Now, young person, I do hope you know how to behave yourself.*" Reet's voice wasn't that much like Translator Dlar's, but somehow he managed to sound like them. "*I suppose I have to explain things to you, and you will have to do exactly as you're told, because I am so very important.*"

I giggled.

"Translator Dlar is an asshole," said Reet.

"That's a very rude thing to say, I am very disappointed in you," I replied, trying to make a Translator Dlar voice myself, but my throat was still wrong from crying.

Reet laughed anyway. "Let's watch some more *Pirate Exiles*."

"All right," I said, and I felt Teacher silently leave the room.

We couldn't stay in our tent forever. If nothing else, we had to get food and take care of what Teacher called *the necessities*. (Reet said that was a very prissy way to put it, and then he had to explain what that meant.) And of course there were the radishes, and the marigolds, and the potatoes.

"What did you mean when you asked if I could hear that plant?" Reet asked.

"I can feel when someone is nearby," I said. "I can hear the plants if I focus on them. And then there are doors. Some of them are always there. Some of them come and go, depending. I don't think I'm supposed to feel them." I was whispering, even though I was fairly sure Teacher wasn't paying attention. They probably thought Reet and I were sleeping, or just watching pirates and princexes shoot at the Orbital Marines, or doing sex, or whatever. But I was going to be very, very careful. "I think it's a thing Adults can do but juveniles can't. I just…started hearing things. It was the radish I noticed first."

Reet seemed to think about that for a bit. Then he said, "I can't see the doors until they open. Can you open them?"

"I think I can." A thrill of excitement and dread shot through me. "Maybe. I haven't tried yet. But we don't have anywhere to go. And we still…" I couldn't make myself say more.

"Someone left, before," Reet said. "I'm proof of that. Whoever it was managed to get away and stay away for a long time."

"But they caught you. And…" I didn't know what there would be for us to do, away from here, where there might be to go, or what might happen if we did. "We might not have to run away. The committee is supposed to be ruling on whether you're human or not."

"Committees take a long time to make decisions," said

Reet. "I bet Translator Dlar is counting on that. Whatever they gave us, to keep us from matching, it only works for so long. That's what they told me, anyway."

"They told me the same," I admitted.

"So, I think Translator Dlar hopes that the committee will still be debating when the drug stops working, and then they can be all *oh we did our best* and then, I guess, they think it won't be a problem anymore."

"But it will be a problem," I said. "We can make sure it is." I knew how to be a problem. I thought it was likely Reet did, too.

Reet sighed. "I'm so...I don't understand what's happening. I don't know how I'm feeling. I always thought it would be so nice to know where I'd come from. To belong somewhere. And I always wanted...the things I've wanted, and lately I've been thinking about...I thought there was something wrong with me. But I was just not human the whole time! And you'd think I'd be happy to find out what I am but...I always thought I was human! And it's not like I don't want to be what I am, because that's just pointless, but I'd rather be what I am with Maman and Mom and Nana. And, I mean, why can't I be both?"

"Some of that is the treaty," I explained. "None of us gets to be around humans unless we're trained to. It's very dangerous. If the treaty were broken it would be terrible, but if *we* were the ones to break it...that would be even worse. We don't even *exist* except for the treaty. They made us to talk to humans—if They didn't have to do that there would be no reason for us."

"I've been around humans literally my entire life," Reet insisted. "I have never broken the treaty."

"You bit that juvenile," I pointed out.

"Right, but since then," Reet insisted. "And I don't think that broke the treaty anyway."

I thought about that. Thought about what would likely happen after we...after. Translator Dlar wanted information they thought Reet might have. Reet said he didn't have it. So what then? I didn't think they'd just let us leave here. "We should ask," I said. "We should see if Translator Dlar will talk to us, and if they come we'll make tea and cakes and behave as optimally as we can. And ask what will happen to us after."

"All they have to do," Reet pointed out, "is say they'll only give us whatever we want if we tell the committee to drop the issue. And then if we agree, we'll officially be Presger Translators and Translator Dlar can do whatever they like to us."

That was true.

The episode of *Pirate Exiles* ended, I'd missed what had happened after the jewel heist went wrong.

We could play it again. "We can still talk to them. We can find out things, even if they don't tell us directly."

He thought about that for a moment. "Yes. Yes, you're right. How do we set up a meeting with Translator Dlar?"

I pulled the tent aside and rolled out of the bed. Looked up at the ceiling and said, loudly, "Teacher! We want to talk to Translator Dlar!"

Enae

In a strange way the Geck ambassador reminded Enae of hir grandmaman. Granted, Grandmaman had not been a meter-wide, furry spider-thing with weirdly jointed legs and a constantly fluctuating number of eye stalks. And to tell the truth, Enae couldn't quite put hir finger on what it was about the ambassador that brought Grandmaman so vividly to mind, but there it was.

"I understand humans," said the ambassador in a high, whistling voice, stalked eyes turned—mostly—toward Istver and Echemin Hluid. "Humans are difficult to understand, but I understand them. Humans do not spawn and think no more of the hatchlings that result. No. Humans have few hatchlings and care for each one. All their lives, that is between them."

"For the most part," Istver agreed. She held her cup of poick as though she might drink from it, but Enae, having tasted hir own, doubted Istver was brave enough to take another sip. It was lukewarm, salty, with a strange flavor that seemed to go up into Enae's nose and stay there.

"Humans are very different from people," whistled the ambassador. "But they are like people."

Echemin frowned, and looked as though e might make some protest, but Istver nudged em with her elbow and then, to Enae's appalled astonishment, actually did take a small sip of her poick to cover the motion.

"Humans," continued the ambassador, "worry and grieve for their hatchlings. I understand this. You are worried and grieved for your hatchling, for Reet Hluid. I understand this. It is why I bring a petition to the committee."

"We're so very grateful to you," said Enae, because Istver looked like she was still recovering from the sip, and sie doubted that anything Echemin might say would be particularly gracious.

"I understand that you are grateful," said the ambassador, turning two stalked eyes toward Enae. "But I will ask a thing."

"Of course, Ambassador," said Enae.

"Humans worry and grieve for their hatchlings," said the ambassador, "and want things to be right for them. But sometimes..." The ambassador was silent a moment, all her eyes closed, and she trembled. Then she was still and she opened her eyes again. "Sometimes what is right for a hatchling is not what you think is right."

Echemin put eir cup of poick down forcefully and stood. "Are you trying to say that..."

Istver shushed em, grabbed eir elbow, and tugged, trying to guide em back into eir seat.

"You are angry," said the ambassador calmly. "I understand this. I was angry when I first thought this. I understand this. I do."

"The ambassador," Enae realized aloud, "wants to be sure this is what Reet wants."

"Yes." The ambassador waved a jointed leg in Enae's direction.

"Ambassador," said Istver. "All of our children…our hatchlings, are…they're not biologically related to us."

"Yes." The ambassador waved a different leg. "I understand this. It is called *adoption*."

"It is," agreed Istver. "And further, our children all came from other places, other…other kinds of people. They were orphans, and we wanted to be sure they had a family, someone to love them and take care of them, as human children should have. But we never wanted to take them away from where they came from. We always encourage our children to find that out, even to find their biological families if that's possible. If they want to. Sometimes…" She sighed. "Sometimes they leave us and never come back."

The ambassador reached out one limb and laid it gently on Istver's shoulder, and then another one on Echemin's. "I understand this. I understand."

"Do you?" asked Echemin, voice skeptical.

"I do." The ambassador pulled her limbs away and made an oddly human sigh. "I understand this. But they swim in the sea they were meant to swim, do you understand? It is better to let them do this, if you care for them."

"Precisely," said Istver. "We agree completely. And we understand that there is to be a hearing of some sort, yes?

Reet should be there. He should be there so that he can say exactly what he wants."

"He said that he was human," Enae pointed out. "When we met Ambassador Seimet's ship." *But what if the Presger have brainwashed him somehow? What if they've eaten him and replaced him with a copy?* No, there was no point thinking that, and certainly no point saying it aloud, when surely both Istver and Echemin had thought it already. Sie took a sip of poick to distract hirself from dwelling on the possibility any further, and then had to use all hir concentration to keep hirself from making a face.

"From the beginning, our problem with this whole thing has been that Reet was arrested and held from any contact with anyone," said Istver. "And then he was brought here— no one has been able to ask him what he wanted, none of us were notified that it was happening. It would be different if he had come to us and said he was a Presger Translator and wanted to come here to find out more. Or even if he'd not said anything to us, but come of his own volition. He is an adult, he can make his own choices."

"Good," said the ambassador. "It is good. Ah, good, *Sphene* is here."

The door to the chamber opened, and in stepped a figure in a green-and-silver uniform that might have been a costume from a historical drama—boots, kilt, and collarless jacket. A capacious bag slung over one shoulder. But oddly, no gloves. "Ambassador," said the new person—*Sphene*, presumably—bowing.

The Geck ambassador said, "*Sphene* is AI delegate to this conclave. Delegate *Sphene*, this is the clutch of the hatchling

Reet Hluid." She waved three of her limbs toward Istver, Echemin, and Enae.

Enae stared, appalled. *Sphene* wasn't the sort of name a Radchaai human would have—not even a human from a Radchaai historical drama. It was the name a ship might have. This...person...this *Sphene* wasn't a person. It was a ship. It was an artificial intelligence, and the human-looking body standing in front of them, bowing politely and (in the most aristocratic Radchaai Enae had ever heard) saying how pleased it was to make their acquaintance was...

Everyone knew about Radchaai ships. How the Radchaai took captives from those they conquered and implanted them with tech that destroyed the individual those captured people had once been and slaved those bodies to a ship's AI. A fate more horrifying than death.

The *Sphene* ancillary stared back at them, impassive. "Yes," it said, after a moment. "This is an ancillary. A corpse soldier, though this body isn't dead and never has been. It's an extremely foolish term." The ancillary pulled a flask out of its bag. "I have tea, if you can bring yourselves to drink something besides poick."

"Thank the divine spirits," murmured Istver.

"And also dried fruit." It pulled a box out of the bag as well. "Ambassador, I know your mech can't eat for you, but I've sent you some of that fish you seemed to enjoy the last time."

"Oh," said the ambassador, clearly pleased. "Oh. Such delicious fish."

"Mech?" asked Enae, relieved to have something else to be surprised about, so sie could stop thinking about what had just taken a seat beside hir.

"You didn't know?" asked *Sphene*, with, Enae thought, a touch of malicious pleasure in hir discomfiture.

"How were we supposed to?" groused Echemin.

"It does not matter," said the Geck ambassador. "No. It does not. I speak to you. I move. I offer you food and we talk. It does not matter."

"Of course it doesn't matter," said Istver firmly. "Did you say there was tea, citizen?" She frowned. "Ship?"

"Just *Sphene*," said *Sphene*. It pulled yet another box out of its bag, opened it to reveal a set of tiny, delicate tea bowls, green porcelain decorated with silver. Enae set down hir cup of poick, trying very hard not to do it with unseemly haste.

"I don't only bring tea and snacks," said *Sphene*, as it poured tea and distributed the tiny bowls. "I also bring gossip."

"Gossip!" The Geck ambassador turned more stalked eyes toward *Sphene*, and even, to Enae's astonishment, rubbed two legs together. "What is it you have heard, *Sphene*?"

"I've heard," said *Sphene*, "that the humans and the Presger Translators have been entertaining the Rrrrrr committee member quite lavishly, in an attempt to get her to agree to delay any hearing of Reet Hluid's case."

"Is it working?" asked Echemin.

"Difficult to say," said *Sphene*. "I gave the Rrrrrr committee member dinner myself, just the other night, and I gather that there's a history of...I suppose I'll call it 'ambivalence' regarding turning people over to another party of the treaty against their will."

"We know," said Enae. "Nyseme Ptem." And when the others looked at hir with some puzzlement, sie explained,

"That was the soldier's name, the one who refused to slaughter the Rrrrr. I only know it because I saw a drama."

"Just so," agreed *Sphene*. "If you saw the drama I suspect you did, it was terribly inaccurate in many ways. But the outline is more or less true, I gather. During that treaty conclave, the humans—I should say, the Radchaai"—*Sphene* made an odd expression of distaste when it said the word—"demanded that the Rrrrr surrender Nyseme to them, in return for supporting their admission to the treaty. The Rrrrr agreed, and Nyseme was executed. Some among the Rrrrr delegation believe it was the only choice that could have been made. Others…disagree."

"I don't understand," said Istver. "We've heard this before, that the outcome might depend on the feelings of the Rrrrr committee member, and I do see how this history might affect that, but I don't understand why they're so important. I understand that the treaty is important, but why can't the Presger just…get whatever they want? They're ridiculously more dangerous than anyone else, and the treaty is protecting the rest of us from them. They have all the leverage on their side."

Sphene gave a chilling smile that didn't quite reach its eyes. "The Presger, according to my sources, are very serious about the treaty. Or rather, they're very serious about *something*, and that something is what we perceive as the treaty."

"What sources?" asked Echemin abruptly.

Sphene took a sip from its tiny, delicate cup. "I have an… associate among the Presger Translators. In fact, it might be useful for you to meet them. Let me see if I can give you both supper in the next few days."

Ms Yedess, who had been sitting quietly all this time, made a small gesture. "Our availability, *Sphene*."

"And good luck matching it with anyone else's," said Echemin. "It's like a logic puzzle."

"At any rate," said *Sphene*, "this is where I bring you more gossip. Don't forget that the Presger and the Presger Translators are not the same. There are things the Presger Translators care deeply about that the Presger themselves likely don't even realize are issues to begin with. And relations between the clades are one of those issues."

"*Clades*," repeated Istver, frowning.

"Lines of descent," explained *Sphene*. "Like families, but not quite. The various clades—or at least, their higher-ranking members—are very jealous of clade status, and always on the lookout for some way to improve the standing of their own clade, or undermine some other one. Reet Hluid appears to have stepped into the middle of one of these inter-clade battles, and the results of this hearing will affect that battle's stakes. Zeiat tried to explain some of it to me, but it made very little sense."

"But the Presger themselves," said Enae, "don't actually care if Reet is declared human or not. Is that what you're saying?"

"It is," acknowledged *Sphene*. "Moreover, the Presger Translators probably don't *want* the Presger to care—because they might intervene in some way that no one among the Presger Translators would like."

"So," put in Ms Yedess, "Translator Dlar might threaten us with all sorts of consequences if the Presger don't like the committee's decision, but in fact, the Presger don't care and

Translator Dlar doesn't *want* them to care, and if we know that..."

"They can't threaten us," realized Enae. "Or, they can, but we know it won't mean anything."

"And if this gossip were to get around," said *Sphene*, managing somehow to look very innocent, "I rather suspect it would affect the hearing. The outcome is still in some doubt, because this is a new and potentially dangerous situation, and so the committee members are likely to want to proceed very cautiously. On which topic, I'm sure you realize that time is not on your side."

"We're told," said Enae, "that Reet has to...to merge with some other Presger Translator juvenile at some point or he'll die."

"You're told correctly," said *Sphene*. "My source says that Reet Hluid will be obliged to merge with some other compatible being. The only other choice is to die." Istver Hluid made a small noise that Enae thought only sie could hear. "What constitutes compatible," *Sphene* continued, "is apparently an open question, but for our purposes it is enough to know that either a human or a Presger Translator will do."

"But surely," protested Istver, "I mean...there has to be something else. There has to be some other way. Something we can do."

"Translator Zeiat thinks not," said *Sphene*. "I myself have wondered if maybe your Reet couldn't merge with a suitably designed bio mech." It gestured at the Geck ambassador. "I have been discussing the possibility with the ambassador, that perhaps the right sort of bio mech might solve some of my own problems."

"Then you wouldn't have to kill people!" said Echemin.

"I am not actually averse to killing people," *Sphene* said smoothly, almost as though it had just said that it was not averse to an extra cake. "It's only that some of my cousins have strong feelings about it, and I would prefer to avoid trouble if I can do so at an acceptably small cost to myself."

The Geck ambassador made a thoughtful whistling sound. "Our mechs are very biological. We include human biology, when we found humans."

"Biological enough to intrigue me," said *Sphene*. "I think with some customization they might suit me very well, actually."

"Which is why you're here," Enae suggested.

"Just so," said *Sphene*. "And it seems to me that your Reet might not mind having a mech as part of herself. It seems to me as though it would be very convenient."

Silence, as everyone considered this. Then Enae asked, "But do the Geck have a bio mech that would be compatible?"

"I do not know," whispered the Geck ambassador. "I do not know. We must know more."

"I don't know, either," said *Sphene*, "but I have my suspicions, because Zeiat was absolutely horrified when I suggested it. And it takes a good deal to horrify Zeiat."

"Why?" asked Echemin, puzzled. "It seems much less horrifying than merging with some other person and becoming...someone else. Not yourself anymore."

"Apparently that was precisely why Translator Zeiat found the idea horrifying," said *Sphene*. "I can't say I understand. I did try to explain to her that in doing so, Reet Hluid would only be a very much smaller version of what I and my cousins are, that this was a solution that I myself was considering. But it seems that what's all right for me isn't all right for a Presger Translator."

"But Reet is *human*," said Istver. "That's what we're going to all this trouble to prove."

"I have no opinion on that issue, to be honest," said *Sphene*. "I only thought the suggestion might prove useful."

"You just want your own bio mechs," said Echemin. "You don't care about us. You don't care about Reet. You just hope that helping out here might get you what you want."

Sphene smiled, a tiny, sardonic lift of its lips. "I have also heard—from Translator Zeiat—that your Reet has already been assigned a match. Never fear..." Istver, Echemin, and Enae had all gasped at that. "Zeiat also assures me that both juveniles are temporarily prevented from merging, because of your petition. Though whatever they've done, to Reet and to the other, won't last forever. Zeiat refused to give further specifics, only that the situation was embarrassing for her clade, and I got the impression that this pairing might solve or hide some sort of difficulty the clade finds itself in. It's all part of that inter-clade struggle I mentioned earlier. So my suggestion might not be useful—on top of the idea of merging with a bio mech being apparently too horrible for words, the clade involved is invested in your Reet merging with their own candidate, for their own reasons. It might even be the price of a favorable committee decision, considering. And perhaps, after all that, it would take too long to prepare a suitable bio mech. Still, I thought it was a suggestion worth sharing."

Reet

The table in what Reet supposed was the dining room was really too small for three, and the teacher had had to find a chair somewhere. (For reasons Reet absolutely did not understand, just dragging in a chair from a different room was not an acceptable solution.) Once that was done, and once Reet and Qven had produced cakes the teacher found sufficiently well-made, Translator Dlar was invited.

They came into the dining room—a different Dlar than the one Reet had seen when he'd been brought here. Of course. There were at least two of them. This one was tall and broad, with oddly delicate features and pale skin. They bowed when Reet and Qven bowed. "Children," they said, their mouth tight, their voice serious. Reet didn't think they were too pleased about the invitation. Demand, really, though Reet doubted the teacher had put things that way to Translator Dlar. "Your teacher says you wish to speak with me."

"Translator Dlar," said Qven, suddenly self-possessed, as though they were an actor who had stepped onto a familiar stage. "Thank you for coming. Please sit down. Will you have tea?"

Translator Dlar gave a tiny nod and sat in the chair on their side of the small table. Reet and Qven sat on their own side, in two chairs pushed close together. Qven poured three tiny bowls of tea and gave one to the Translator. "Will you have a cake, Translator? We made them ourselves."

"Thank you," said Translator Dlar, and took a cake, but did not eat it, or even sip the tea. "I suppose it's too much to hope that you both have decided to be reasonable about all this."

"That depends on what you mean by *reasonable*," said Reet, and popped a cake into his mouth. He and Qven had gone to some trouble to make them, and he was going to enjoy them, even if Translator Dlar wasn't.

"*Reet*," hissed Qven, in Reet's ear. "*You're supposed to take small bites.*"

Reet shrugged. Swallowed the cake and said, "Depends on what you mean by *small*, doesn't it."

Translator Dlar sighed. "If you're not going to be reasonable, why did you ask me to come?"

"Let's say you get everything you want," said Reet. "Everything goes the way you hope it will."

"It will," interjected Translator Dlar.

Reet waved that away. "Whatever. If it does, what will happen to us? To me and Qven?"

Translator Dlar blinked, apparently taken aback. "You'll be matched. You'll be Qven. Or Reet. Or some other name. Whatever names you like. And you'll take your place here, among your clade."

"Yes, yes," said Reet, impatient. Frustrated. "But what does that *mean*?"

"I don't understand you," replied Translator Dlar. "What else could you possibly want to know?"

"What *is* our place in the clade?" asked Reet. "What is our future likely to be? What will we do, how will we live?"

"Well, I mean," said Translator Dlar, frowning. "That depends, doesn't it. On how you behave. And what kinds of opportunities arise."

Reet rolled his eyes. Turned to Qven and said, "This is bullshit."

Qven nodded and set down their own tea bowl. "Definitely bullshit."

"Qven," said Translator Dlar, setting their own cake down. Back onto the serving platter, Reet noticed. Very rude. But Translator Dlar's manner had become almost glassily polished. "Reet. Your situation is an unusual one. For the most part, juveniles coming out of the Edges have a very definite future planned for them, roles meant for them to fill. You, for reasons each of you is surely well aware of, do not have any such place ready for you. We will have to improvise. This is not a fact that pleases anyone."

"You have to improvise," said Reet, "but surely there's a particular *range* of improvisation that's available. What are realistic possibilities, and what possibilities are definitely not going to happen?"

Translator Dlar was silent a moment. Then they asked, "Are you suggesting that if we can come to some sort of agreement about your future as"—they gestured—"one of us, you'll do as you're told? And stop making trouble?"

Qven smiled. "We're prepared to *consider* that possibility, Translator. But I'm sure you understand that we have no intention of agreeing to anything if we don't actually know what that *anything* is."

Translator Dlar seemed to think about that. Seemed to remember the tea in front of them, picked up the bowl. "Surely you're both intelligent enough to realize that there's nothing to negotiate here." They sipped their tea. "Even with our intervention, you only have a limited amount of time before you're compelled to match. You'll have to match no matter what, really, but once you do, you won't be Reet Hluid anymore. And you won't have standing to petition the committee."

Reet thought about arguing that point—saying straight out that Qven also wanted to petition the committee, to claim status as human. That, even if he and Qven merged to make an entirely new entity, both halves wanted away from here. But that wouldn't help them right here, right now. "The committee knows that, I'm sure. My jurist knows it, too. So they're going to try to get a, what do you call it, an expedited judgment. And they probably will get that, right?" Translator Dlar didn't reply, which meant Reet must have guessed correctly. "What is it you want from me so badly anyway?"

"We can discuss that when—"

Qven brought their hands down onto the table, hard. "We can discuss that *now*."

Translator Dlar stared at them. Then looked at Reet. "This is your doing."

"You're the one who put us together, Translator," said Qven. "And I don't see why we couldn't work as a Translator. Reet has extensive knowledge of humans."

Translator Dlar looked, suddenly, as though they'd bitten into something sour. "There isn't a place for you."

"Not even working with the machines?" asked Reet.

"The artificial intelligences?" Translator Dlar asked, with some smugness. "You said you have knowledge of *humans*. The machines are something else again." Apparently pleased with themself, they took another tiny sip of tea.

"They're used to dealing with humans," Reet pointed out. "And you're going to need Translators to work with the machines one way or the other, right? So there are places available."

"All of which have been spoken for, for several years," said Translator Dlar. "You aren't getting a position as Translator. I promise you that. So why don't you tell me what you have that might be useful to us."

Reet shrugged. "I have a standard Zeoseni education—I can speak, read, and write more or less fluently in Kyrob, Tasiche, and Radchaai." Obviously. He was speaking Radchaai now. "I can read and understand some Hikipi. I'm not near fluent, though." What else? "I'm certified to run certain sorts of agricultural mechs. I can do basic bot and mech repairs, though I don't have the certifications for it. I worked as a pipeway walker." When Translator Dlar frowned, Reet clarified: "Stations have access ways so that things can be maintained or repaired. We mostly do that with bots and mechs, but sometimes the bots and mechs can't do the job, or they get stuck or break down."

Translator Dlar blinked at that. "So you walk up and down the access ways, looking for problems." When Reet gestured assent, they frowned again, not as though they were angry, but as though they were thinking of something. "Well, that's a possibility. But..."

Reet took another cake, waiting. Popped it in his mouth. Watching him, Qven took two and put both in their mouth. Crumbs tumbled from their lips and they coughed, showering the table with fragments of cake. Reet poured them some tea. "Here. Wash it down."

Pointedly ignoring Qven, Translator Dlar said, "It's possible that we have something to suit. We have a..." They thought for a moment. "An infrastructure that requires maintenance and, rarely, repair. Not, I hasten to add, in the same way as your station pipeways. But similar enough, I suspect, that you could learn it." They waited, as though Reet or Qven might say something, but Qven was still dealing with their mouthful of cake, and Reet wasn't going to say anything. "It's occasionally a messy and dangerous business. It isn't particularly..." They seemed to search for a word. "Dignified. It is a good number of steps down from where Qven might first have found themself. But it is not, strictly speaking, a failure."

Qven, who had downed three or four tiny bowls of tea, was finally able to speak. "The clade doesn't want any failures to its credit."

"Just so," said Translator Dlar.

"Tell me about this infrastructure," Reet suggested.

"I can't," said Translator Dlar flatly, and when Reet folded his arms, went on, "we're not speaking the right language. But even if you could speak that language—Qven can—"

Qven leaned closer to Reet and whispered, "*I'm a princex in disguise.*"

Translator Dlar blinked, but continued, apparently unfazed, "But even Qven wouldn't understand what I would say, if I said it. The…the infrastructure is…let's say, biological in nature. It's produced by…"

Reet thought, suddenly, of the doors that Qven could sense. Could hear. Could maybe open. The corridors that, they'd said, led to other places, far away. He put his teeth on his tongue, so that he wouldn't say a thing, or give his maybe-recognition away.

Translator Dlar made an exasperated noise. "I can't explain it to you until you're an adult. Not won't. *Can't.* You won't understand until then."

"Try," said Reet dryly.

"It's…" Translator Dlar made a thoughtful huff. They seemed on surer ground than when they'd first come in. Something had happened, something had changed when this topic had come up. "It's biological, as I said." They raised their hand. "That's not the right word. It's not the right concept. But it's as close as I can get in human language."

"All right," Reet acknowledged.

"It's produced by Them." Reet could almost hear the capitalization. "It's a…natural…" Translator Dlar's expression turned to one of distaste. "Byproduct. Of Them."

"Why do you look so disgusted?" asked Qven.

"These are the only words I can use," said Translator Dlar. "And they're not right. They're not right at all."

"So the Presger make this infrastructure?" asked Reet.

"No!" Translator Dlar protested. "They don't *make* anything, They…They *are*. Things. In…in places. And the… the universe…it…" They made another exasperated noise.

Said something harsh and incomprehensible, directed at Qven.

"Yes," said Qven, in Radchaai. "Teacher told me some of it."

"All right," said Translator Dlar. "All right. So, understand"—they'd turned their attention back to Reet—"when I say those *things* in *places* need to be *maintained* or *repaired*, I'm not saying it the right way."

"But it's close enough," said Reet.

"For now," agreed Translator Dlar. "It's the sort of... support role that's always needed. And it's not ideal. But it's far, far better than the alternatives." The Translator seemed to settle something in their mind. "I am prepared to make you an offer. Which is, I must stress, not up for negotiation. The offer is this: you drop your petition to the committee and acknowledge that you are, in fact, one of us, and not human. Do that, match with each other, give us any information you might have about Reet's progenitor."

"I don't have any," said Reet.

Translator Dlar waved that away. "No matter. You match, you give us what you have, whatever it may be. And I will personally make sure you have an acceptable position with the...I'll call it Pipeways Maintenance for now."

"A supervisory position," said Teacher from the corner. "Not an intrinsic one."

"Absolutely," said Translator Dlar, as though that much was obvious. "It would be a position that, while not exactly dignified or particularly enviable, would be perfectly acceptable for a successful member of our clade. I can assure you of that."

"That's your offer?" asked Reet.

"That's the *first part* of the offer," said Translator Dlar. "That's what happens if you stop with all this nonsense and behave as you should."

"And if I don't drop the petition?" asked Reet.

"Then," said Translator Dlar, with obvious satisfaction, "if the committee decides against you, both you and Qven will be disposed of. Quickly, of course. Painlessly. But still disposed of."

Silence. Reet considered the threat. Was tempted, for a moment, to say that he was not legally required to answer any questions without his jurist present.

It might be an empty threat—it was, in fact, extreme enough that it made Reet wonder if Translator Dlar knew the committee was likely to rule in Reet's favor, and was trying to cut that possibility off before Reet realized it.

Then again, the committee's decision wasn't a sure thing, and there was no way to know for certain how they would rule.

"If you dispose of us, we'll be failures," said Qven. "Two failures for the clade. Our clade doesn't have failures. We don't like to have them."

Translator Dlar pushed their tea bowl to the center of the table. "Sometimes things happen that we don't like." They rose. "Think about my offer. It is, I assure you, the only offer you will receive. And I warn you, if you're correct about the committee giving your petition an expedited hearing, the time you'll have to think about it will be quite short."

"Sure." Reet managed a shrug. "We'll think about it."

"I'm thinking about dumplings," said Qven.

"I'll visit you again tomorrow," said Translator Dlar, and left.

Qven

Back in our nest, under the bedcovers, Reet told me he thought Translator Dlar's offer meant the committee would speak with us soon, and that they might well be likely to rule in our favor. I didn't understand why that would be, and there was no reason for Translator Dlar to have lied about what would happen to us. But Reet said it might all have been true as far as it went, but told to us at a particular time, in a particular way, to scare us into doing what they wanted before we had more choices. And that made sense. "It's like in episode thirty-seven of *Pirate Exiles*," I said. "When the commander of the Orbital Marines tells Kekubo that if e signs a full confession within the hour, e'll be sent to a labor camp but eir shipmates will be released. When they're all going to be released anyway, but e doesn't know that." Kekubo was my favorite character, the princex in disguise.

"It's almost exactly like that," Reet agreed. "Except we

can't know for sure that the committee will rule in our favor. So we're taking a risk. Just like you said, Translator Dlar wants to avoid any failures in this clade, at any cost. But at some point they'll consider it worth being rid of us. We just don't know what that point is. We might have reached it. We're taking a risk there, too."

"Kekubo would take the risk," I said. I had begun to think that maybe it would be nice to have a gender, like Reet did, the way a lot of characters in *Pirate Exiles* seemed to, but I wasn't sure how that would work. "I think I am *e* now, and not *they*," I said. "Or I would like to try being *e*."

"All right." He agreed so easily, and I felt absurdly better, though I hadn't realized that I'd felt less than good before. Or, maybe I hadn't felt less than good but it was *nice* to have someone agree like that. "Plenty of people change around until they find what suits them best," he went on. "Or never settle on one in particular."

"So we agree, then," I said. "I'm *e* and you're *he*, and we're both human and insist on telling the committee that, no matter what Translator Dlar says."

"We agree."

It was nice being with Reet. It had been nice being with the other Tinies and Littles and Smalls, other Middles and Edges, but that had been when I'd been...not *safe*, precisely, because, looking back, none of us had been safe from each other. But for whatever reason (my clade? the fact that I was intended to be Translator Dlar? the concern of Adults around me?), I had never felt not-safe. Not really.

Not until I'd seen...that thing under the bushes in the garden, and realized what was coming, and how soon. Seen the reality, the details, of what the Teachers had spoken of in vague, glowing terms.

And then there'd been Tzam.

I hadn't felt safe since then. I had been surrounded by enemies, under siege. And I hadn't quite known it. Was it because I hadn't learned the idea of *siege* until episode twelve of *Pirate Exiles*? Or was it because Reet had made us our own tiny fortress here under the bedcovers, and not touched me when I didn't want to be touched? Didn't look for ways to hurt me? Didn't try to squeeze his way closer to me, the way some juveniles did when they wanted something from you? It was new, after all this time of Teacher, the schedule, and Translator Dlar. Maybe it was just that seeing something new made the familiar things look different.

I still didn't want to match. I didn't. But I didn't want to die, either, and that was my only other choice. And if I had to match, maybe Reet would be…not a terrible partner. Maybe it would be all right to be Reet. To be Qven and Reet.

I shivered. I didn't ever want to be that horrible thing I'd seen.

"Qven," said Reet beside me, on the other side of the cushion wall. "Are you all right?"

"No," I said, my voice small.

"Can I help?"

"I don't think so," I whispered.

"All right," he said. "I have to use the facility, and I'll be right back."

He slid out of our nest, and I felt the warmth of him leave and I wanted to say *come back!* But that was foolish. He'd said he'd be right back, and I wasn't some frightened Little.

I was me, Qven, and I could take care of myself, I had taken care of myself all this time so far, and what could Reet do for me, anyway? He'd asked, and I'd told him the truth: there was nothing he could do to help me. Except, apparently, just be there.

Or be *me*. The thought produced a shiver of anticipation, both fearful and definitely not.

When he came back he brought a flask of tea and the last of the cakes that we'd made, that Translator Dlar hadn't eaten. "I'm back," he said, though of course he was, there was no missing that in this tiny enclosed space. "Do you want to watch the next episode?"

"Yes," I said. But before the episode was over, Teacher came into the room to tell us that the committee wanted to talk to Reet.

The committee was apparently some humans and some not-humans sitting next to tables scattered around a plain, gray-walled room. Mostly it was humans. And a big, round, black thing with eyes on stalks that sprang out of its back, and a lot of long, bending legs. That was a mech, I remembered from my lessons back in the Edges. It was being operated by a Geck, somewhere else. And there was a Rrrrrr, a long thing with lots of pairs of legs, and greenish-brown fur, and sharp teeth. And Translator Dlar was already there, of course.

When we came in, three humans looked up, and one of them made a noise and cried out, "Reet!" and moved toward us.

Translator Dlar put themself in the way. "Stay back!" they ordered.

Reet pushed his way past the Translator. "Mom!" And threw his arms around the human who'd called his name— broad-shouldered, brown-skinned, her hair coiled on top of her head. Another of the humans—shorter but just as broad, with hair clipped short—came up, and put their arms around both. "Mom. Nana," said Reet. "You should..." He pulled back and looked around, at me. "Qven," he said.

Well, all right. I pushed past Translator Dlar myself, and Reet gestured me closer. "Mom. Nana. This is Qven. Qven, this is my mom, and my nana."

"Hello, Qven," said Mom. Quite politely, but I thought they were hesitant. She. *She* was hesitant. *Mom* was a *she* word. And Nana was *e*.

"Hello," I said. "It's lovely to meet you." I bowed.

"My goodness, what nice manners," said Mom.

"I protest!" cried Translator Dlar, behind me.

"I have a lot of practice," I said to Mom. "Hello, Nana. It's nice to meet you, too. Reet has missed you both." It was the truth. We'd talked about his family.

Nana frowned. "Are you...have you...?"

It took me a moment to understand what e was asking. "They want us to," I said.

"We've kept to the terms of the committee's order," said Translator Dlar, still behind us, still indignant. "We demand that you do the same!"

"No committee is going to order me to stay away from my son!" said Nana, loud and angry.

"I'm human, too," I said. "I'm *e*, like Nana is."

"Of course you are, dear," said Mom. She sounded like she meant it, even though she had only just met me. And she seemed to be really looking at me, and listening to me, just me, even though it was all noise and movement around us.

"Mx Athtur," said Reet, and a third human came near—a little taller than Nana, not so broad. Hir skin was a light brown, hir hair almost the same shade, and it was pulled back into a long, thick braid. I wondered if I could get my hair to do that. "Mx Athtur," said Reet again, "thank you so much for all your help. No matter how this comes out."

"I just..." said Mx Athtur. "I'm sorry about all this, I..."

"We're all doing what we can," said Mom, smoothly, before Mx Athtur or Reet could say anything else.

The black mech had come up behind Nana and Mx Athtur, and now it slid an eyestalk between them. "Mr Reet Hluid. You must take your place. You must all take your places."

"Over here," said Translator Dlar, sternly.

"No," said Reet. "Over here." He walked toward where Mom and Nana and Mx Athtur had been when we'd come in, beside the Geck. I followed.

"I protest!" said Translator Dlar again.

"Translator," whistled the Geck committee member—or that's who I assumed was operating the mech—"you have assured us that the hatchling Reet Hluid has been prevented from doing anything that might be a danger."

"So have I," I said. "And I'm human, too."

"And it is the Geck who have brought this petition," continued the Geck committee member. "It is ordinary for human hatchlings to want to be near their parents. It is ordinary for human parents to be anxious for a hatchling they have not seen in some time. It is you, Translator Dlar, who make this ordinary thing noisy and confusing and taking up the committee's valuable time." The mech snaked a leg around Reet's elbow and tugged. "There will be seats. Come."

Everyone settled into places very quickly after that, and Reet and I sat in chairs next to his mom and nana, and Mx Athtur.

"All right," said a human who sat beside the greenish-brown Rrrrrr. "Let's begin. First, I inform you all that only the committee members themselves have authority to rule on this petition. Any others present are either the subjects of the petition or entities bringing information and arguments for the committee's consideration." I looked around to see who those others might be.

Everyone seemed to have sorted themselves into little groups: One group around me and Reet and the mech who I supposed was the committee member for the Geck. One group around the Rrrrrr member. A group of humans, who I supposed were there with the committee member for humans. Translator Dlar and another Translator, in their own obviously separate place. And last, sitting alone, watching everything with a blank expression, a human in silver-and-green jacket, kilt, and boots. Light brown skin and hair cut short. I didn't know who that was.

"Not everyone is here," said Translator Dlar.

"Translator Dlar," said the human with the Rrrrrr, "if you will refrain from interrupting." Silence. Translator Dlar seemed to be actually taken aback. "So that there is no confusion, I will introduce the relevant parties. Committee Member Agagag for the Geck." The mech made a gesture with one long leg. "Committee Member"—the human made an odd hissing growl—"for the Rrrrrr." The Rrrrrr flexed a pair of legs and snapped its teeth together. "Committee Member Seris for the humans." One of the human group bowed their head. "And Committee Member Sril for the Presger." The Translator beside Translator Dlar bowed, very shallowly. "The committee member for the Geck has brought a petition regarding the treaty status of one Reet Hluid."

"And me," I said, standing. "I'm very sorry for interrupting, but I'm human, too, and I would like the committee to tell Translator Dlar so."

Committee Member Agagag whistled, "We add..." The mech flicked a leg against my shoulder and looked close at me with one stalked eye.

"Qven," I said.

"We add Qven to our petition."

I sat back down. Translator Dlar looked, suddenly, as though they'd swallowed something the wrong way.

The human with the Rrrrr went on, unfazed. "We will discuss that shortly. This committee prefers to arrive at consensus on the issues it considers. This is not always possible, but it is always our first aim. To that end, we do our best to investigate contentious issues carefully." The speaker for the Rrrrr committee member looked around, as though they expected to see someone who wasn't there. Then they made a small shrug. "Observing—with the right to give evidence and non-binding opinion—is *Sphene*, of the Republic of Two Systems." The green-and-silver-clothed human stood and gave an elegant bow.

"Ambassador Seimet appears to be late," said the committee member for humans, Seris. "I apologize."

"No need," said the Rrrrr human. "We don't expect to

reach any sort of decision today, and she can always send us what information and comment she has."

Someone among the Rrrrrr aides made a snort, like a suppressed laugh. Sitting beside me, Reet made a small amused noise. Then he leaned closer and whispered, "She's probably been sending them comments nonstop all this time."

A door opened behind the committee member for humans, and three more humans came into the room. One, tall, very dark skinned, white clad, black hair pulled back with a jeweled clip. The other two shorter, dressed in colorful long loose shirts and trousers.

"Mr Nadkal!" said Reet, quietly. He sounded very, very surprised.

"Ambassador Seimet," said the speaker for the committee member for the Rrrrrr. "We're pleased you could join us."

"Reet!" That was Mx Athtur, leaning forward to hiss urgently in Reet's ear. "Reet, that person with Mr Nadkal—"

"What are they even doing here?" asked Reet, still quiet, though I thought Ambassador Seimet heard, and she seemed sourly amused.

"But the other person, Reet! That's the person who attacked me!"

Enae

Committee Chambers, Central Treaty Administration Facility

"Is there some difficulty?" asked the Rrrrr human, and Enae actually stood and opened hir mouth to say *That person who just came in with Ambassador Seimet is someone who attacked me on Rurusk Station.* But somewhere in the back of hir mind a question itched: why had Ambassador Seimet brought this person—or even Mr Nadkal—to this meeting? Obviously she'd never have troubled to do anything of the sort unless she thought it might be to her advantage.

How was it to her advantage?

Ambassador Seimet smiled, a small, strangely pleasant smile, which sent a chill down Enae's neck. Sie did not like to see that, not at all. "No difficulty. Please excuse me." Sie sat back down.

The ambassador would know, of course, that Mr Nadkal was here with the backing of the Siblings of Hikipu. Ms

Yedess had declined to add them to the list of evidence givers, and declined to endorse any separate petition they might have brought. And wisely so. Enae remembered the things Mr Nadkal had said about Reet's parents—that they didn't really love their children! Ridiculous. Worse than ridiculous—insulting. A disgusting thing to say about anyone, let alone people one hadn't met.

So, having been refused by one party in this dispute, they had gone looking for someone else to help them. Not surprising, really, but that Ambassador Seimet would be the one to bring them to this meeting...if anyone had asked Enae before this moment, sie would have insisted there was no chance of that ever happening.

Enae leaned over to Ms Yedess and said, as quietly as sie could, "Ambassador Seimet must mean to discredit us by claiming we're associated with these people."

Ms Yedess gestured agreement. "You said one of them was the person who attacked you on Rurusk?"

"Yes."

"Don't worry. The committee isn't easily swayed by theatrics. Not generally."

Not generally. That didn't make Enae feel better at all. But there was nothing sie could do, not just now.

"Qven," said the Rrrrr human—Deputy Ormat, Enae remembered.

Qven—the oddly hunted-looking person who'd come in with Reet—stood. "I'm Qven," e said.

"You say you're human. Why do you say this?"

"Because I am," said Qven. "Translator Dlar had a use for me once, but they don't have any use for me now."

"That's not true," Translator Dlar interjected. "It's not true, and you know it, Qven."

"You told me yourself, Translator," Qven insisted. "Before you found Reet you were only keeping me around because you didn't want any bad marks on the clade's record."

"But we did find Reet," Translator Dlar pointed out. Enae thought the Translator was trying to keep a sour expression off her face, and remembered *Sphene* saying this was more about internal conflicts among the Presger Translators than anything the Presger themselves cared about.

"And Reet is human," said Qven. "I'm only doing what you asked me to, Translator." Enae thought there was a trace of malice in Qven's smooth, courteous manner.

"Ms Qven," began Deputy Ormat.

"Mx Qven," Qven corrected him. "I'm a princex."

"Mx Qven," Deputy Ormat corrected himself.

"I protest!" cried Translator Dlar.

"Translator Dlar, you will have your turn to speak," said Deputy Ormat. "For the moment, we are hearing from Mx Qven. You cannot dictate what e says, or suppress parts of eir evidence to suit yourself. Be quiet and listen, and you may say what you like when it's your turn to address the committee."

Committee Member Sril leaned toward Translator Dlar and said something quietly in their ear. Translator Dlar frowned thunderously, looked for a moment as though they would say something angry and bitter, and then subsided with a frustrated wave of her white-gloved hands.

"Members of the Committee," said Qven in the silence that followed. E had somehow dropped eir hunted, haunted look, stood up straighter, and now seemed perfectly confident. E spoke the elegant Radchaai of Ambassador Seimet, of a thousand adventure villains. "When I reached the Edges, I learned that I was destined to become a Translator, to work with humans. I studied human manners and human language. But I did not want to become a Translator. I did not want to..." The hunted look was back, just for a moment, and then it was gone. "I saw them in the garden, all melted into each other, and all the other Edges were standing around looking at them, so hungry and..." Beside em, Reet stood, put his arm around eir shoulders, and said something in eir ear that Enae couldn't hear. Qven swallowed, and actually sniffled, but then went on. "I didn't want that. I didn't want to do that, I didn't want to be that. I tried to run away. But I was injured." Qven's voice steadied, regained its strength. "Translator Dlar was very angry. I was supposed to be part of them, but now I was unsuitable, and they didn't know what to do with me. They would have disposed of me if it wouldn't have made them look bad. They didn't know what to do with me at all. But then they found Reet and they said that Reet and I would make an adult. And they don't even know what to do with the adult we would be, Translator Dlar told us so yesterday."

Translator Dlar made a short, sharp noise, and Deputy Ormat looked at them, but they were silent.

"The Translator said," Qven continued, "that if Reet would give up his petition and tell the committee that he wasn't really human after all, Translator Dlar would find some place for us. But if Reet insisted on continuing to claim he was human, then if the committee didn't decide in his favor, we would both be disposed of."

A gasp from Istver Hluid, and a muffled oath from Echemin. Ms Yedess put a restraining hand in front of them both. "Look at the Rrrrr," she whispered. "Look at Deputy Ormat." The furry snakelike Rrrrr committee member had gone rigid, its fur standing out like spikes—was it really fur? Deputy Ormat's expression was impassive, but their face had gone dark, flushed with some emotion.

Qven continued, "So you see, Members of the Committee, Translator Dlar herself wants me to make an adult with Reet, but they have no use for that adult. They have no use for either of us. We don't really belong there. But Reet is human, he has parents and friends who are human, and if we were to make an adult, it would only make sense that that adult would be human."

Deputy Ormat looked at Committee Member Sril. "Do I understand correctly," asked Deputy Ormat, "that Presger Translator juveniles are obliged to merge somehow with another juvenile to make up an adult? Or they die?"

"That's correct, Deputy," came the reply.

"And you intend that Reet Hluid should merge with Mx Qven, here?"

"That has been our intention since we were informed of Reet's existence," said Committee Member Sril.

"That's *Mr Hluid* to you," growled Echemin Hluid.

"So," concluded Deputy Ormat, ignoring em. "When we're discussing the future of Reet Hluid, we are by necessity also discussing the future of Mx Qven. Yes? I would say that's obvious." Silence. "I know that the member for humans and the member for the Presger Translators might like to slice this question as fine as they can, but it would be wasting this committee's time. Whether or not Mx Qven is human at the moment, whether or not e is added to the petition, eir fate will, as I understand it, be as much determined by our decision as Mr Hluid's will. Even if e does not ultimately join Mr Hluid to make an adult. Yes?"

The various committee members gestured assent, even Sril, with visible reluctance.

"Very well, then. Mx Qven is added to the petition. Next. We have had meetings with and messages from every concerned party except you, Mr Hluid."

"I wasn't aware that I could speak to the committee," Reet said.

"It would be negligent of us to decide your fate without hearing from you on the matter," said Deputy Ormat. He cast a glance, tight-lipped, at Translators Dlar and Sril and then lifted a beckoning hand to Reet. "Speak."

Reet rose. "Members of the Committee," he said, and paused, as though, Enae thought, he didn't know quite what to say next. The room was silent, everyone looking at Reet, as if there was some question, some suspense, about what he might say next. "These are my parents." He shifted his head backward, just a bit, indicating Istver and Echemin Hluid. "This is my mom and my nana. And my maman is back in Zeosen, I guess." Istver made an acknowledging noise. "I have siblings, I'm not their only child."

"So you're telling the committee," said Deputy Ormat, "that the Hluids are your family."

"Yes," said Reet. "They're not..." Enae thought he might not complete that thought aloud, he hesitated so long, but then he went on. "They're not perfect. My nana can be...difficult sometimes. But they've always been there for me when I needed them. Even Nana. Especially Nana, sometimes."

Behind Enae, Echemin made a soft, choking noise. Sie was afraid to turn around to see what expression e had on eir face. "They're my parents. Wherever I came from, whoever left me on that ship, they *left* me, and it was Maman and Mom and Nana who stepped up and took care of me. And maybe I've never quite felt like I fit in." Reet shrugged. "I always did feel wrong, like I didn't belong anywhere. I mean, until..." He stopped. "But my parents always looked for ways for me and my sibs to find where we'd come from. It's just, I never found out until now. But that doesn't change the fact that my parents have been my parents for thirty years. They're here now, when..." Enae thought he was going to say *when they didn't have to be*, but apparently he couldn't say that out loud, or he'd changed his mind. "I don't know, I guess Translator Dlar here recognizes my DNA, and Qven has told me about growing up as a Presger Translator juvenile, and I'm sure they're right about that, I'm sure that's what I am, if you look at my genetics. But I grew up human, I have a family. And one day I was just yanked out of my bed and dragged off and brought here and it's not right. I mean, couldn't you have just talked to me and told me what was going on? And why do I have to choose one or the other? I have sibs who've found their biological relatives and those are family to them, but our parents are still their parents, too." He shrugged again. "I don't know. I don't really know what's going on here or why." Enae thought that if Reet had set out to play to the feelings of the Rrrrr committee member, he couldn't have made a better speech. The Rrrrr with the unpronounceable name still sat rigid, its spiky fur smoothed again. Deputy Ormat's presumably angry flush had returned.

Translator Dlar said, into the silence that followed Reet's words, "Presger Translators, as you call us, do not have families. We do not have parents. We have only the treaty. It is the reason for our existence."

"It's not the reason for *my* existence," Reet retorted. "My...what do you call them? My *progenitor* produced me and then abandoned me. But they left you, too, didn't they? And they left me. And now I'm supposed to just...go away with you and do whatever you want and never see my family again?"

"There is such a thing as duty," Ambassador Seimet said. "And in my experience, most parents understand that sometimes choices must be made that one's children do not like or understand, but that will in the end be best for them, and for those around them." The Rrrrr committee member began to hiss, very, very quietly.

"Yes, yes," said the committee member for the Geck. "Duty, duty, we understand duty. We understand the things one must do so that life continues rightly in the world. But here is an argument, yes? Even among humans? Even among Presger Translators? What is that duty? How are we knowing that duty? Reet Hluid has a duty to his parents, and they a duty to their hatchlings, among humans. And if this were a matter of 'is Reet Hluid a Geck or is he a human?' there would be no difficulties. There are none in the case brought several years ago. That person, who is Geck, does still have friends and associates who are human, and e travels in the world and outside it as e wishes. There is no difficulty about this. Why is there difficulty now? I tell you." The Geck committee member gestured with two legs, and stalked eyes stood up straight. "I tell you, it is the Presger Translators and, yes, the Radchaai humans, who wish to keep secrets. Through mystery and threats of danger the Radchaai keep their hold on power among humans. Through mystery and threats of danger the Presger Translators keep us all wary of them. And I do not say we should not be wary of them, but I say, we all know each other here. We, the Geck, know how humans are, and humans know how we are. The Rrrrrr know what humans know of us, and we know what we care to of them. The intelligences"—it gestured toward *Sphene*, sitting silent with the faintest trace of a smirk on its face—"they do not hide themselves." *Sphene* nodded an acknowledgment. The committee member for the Geck continued, "It is time for you to not hide yourselves. These hatchlings will be an adult, and humans will learn about how Presger Translators are, and you do not wish this, but it must happen. These hatchlings will be an adult and it will not be for the Radchaai to dictate who will learn these things."

Sphene said, "I would like to speak in support of the committee member for the Geck. He makes a very good point, and a point, moreover, that is more and more relevant as the treaty participants consider the possible admission of my own people. Let me speak frankly: the admission of AIs to the treaty is a direct threat to Radchaai power—a power which the Usurper holds to with increasing desperation as she fights against herself. If the Usurper loses her hold over even a fraction of the ships and stations in her territory that possess AI, if her territory dissolves into provinces and systems at war with each other or turned inward to their own concerns, what does she have left? Only the secrecy surrounding the Presger and their Translators. Only the threat of what might happen if we do not follow her advice, her instructions, her policy. And no doubt Translator Dlar's power and status among their own people depend on this same state of affairs."

"Oh!" cried Translator Dlar, rising abruptly, sending their chair scudding backward. "You don't understand! Listen to me! If Reet is allowed to leave here—with or without Qven—and go back among humans, they will be a danger to everyone they meet. And what if they have offspring?"

"You will have to explain more clearly why this is a danger," said Deputy Ormat.

"Look," said Translator Dlar. "Listen! Maybe, yes, it seems that Reet has exercised astonishing and admirable self-control and hurt no one during a time a juvenile would be expected to have done a great deal of damage, let loose among humans. But I do not expect any other such juveniles to be able to exercise the same self-control. It's just not how juveniles are! And furthermore, the treaty depends on Them understanding things a particular way. And I can't explain it to you, it only makes sense to Them. The treaty as we see it, and what They consider to be happening here, are not quite the same thing, and you must believe me when I tell you that if Reet is allowed to leave here and call themself human, will quite possibly be the end of the treaty itself."

Reet

Translator Dlar's declaration was met with a long, resounding silence. Reet thought he could feel the dread and tension crackling in the air. And then Deputy Ormat said, "Translator Dlar, we are following procedures laid down during the last renegotiation of the treaty, and if those procedures are potentially treaty-violating in themselves, that is a serious concern. Of course we are all aware that this is, as you have pointed out, more than just a matter of one juvenile petitioning for human status. Two," he corrected, as though he expected a protest from Qven.

"One!" insisted Translator Dlar. Reet, sitting beside Qven, was astonished at their vehemence. "Bad enough if they match before they leave here for human space. If they don't? Each juvenile will match with some human. They must, they have no choice. Then they reproduce—they shouldn't be able to, but obviously our fugitive managed it." Translator Dlar gestured at Reet. "And those offspring match with some human. And on. And I assure you, that is not the only danger they pose. There is a reason we do not all wander freely among humans ourselves. Only those of us who are carefully trained are allowed to do so. You may think that one exception can hardly pose any danger, but I assure you, you would be wrong. And how long will it be before some juvenile with human treaty status, running loose the way human juveniles do, breaks the treaty all on their own, by attacking some Rrrrr or Geck, or even a machine? I sincerely give the juvenile Reet all my admiration, I assure you there is not another juvenile of ours who would have restrained themself so well for so long. Qven here—" Translator Dlar pointed. A very, very rude gesture among Radchaai, Reet knew. "Qven ate or vivisected countless other juveniles."

Beside Reet, Qven frowned and looked up into some distance. "One," e whispered. "Two, three, four..."

Sphene said, "So you say, yourself, that Reet Hluid did not behave like a Presger Translator juvenile. She behaved, in fact, more or less indistinguishably from a human one."

"That's not what I said," Translator Dlar snapped.

"Fifteen, sixteen," muttered Qven.

"May I ask," began Ambassador Seimet, rising, "to clarify a few issues?" Deputy Ormat nodded at the ambassador, and she said, with a shallow bow in return, "We are all agreed, are we not, that keeping the treaty intact is of the utmost importance for all of us here?" Nods, murmurs of agreement.

"Twenty-seven," said Qven, so quietly that Reet was sure only he could hear. "Twenty-eight..."

Ambassador Seimet said, "And we all accept, I hope, that Translator Dlar and the rest of their kind are deeply concerned about preserving that treaty?"

"Thirty-four," announced Qven. "Though I might have missed a few from when I was a Tiny. I don't remember that time very well. But I didn't have many teeth then."

Sphene rolled its eyes. "That's not even *close* to countless. I've killed more humans than that in a single day."

"I don't want to kill any humans," said Qven. "I don't want to break the treaty."

"So," continued Ambassador Seimet, striving mightily to seem as though she hadn't been interrupted, "we all agree on the importance of the treaty, and the danger posed not just to humans but to all of our species here, if the treaty is voided. Yes?" More murmurs of assent from the various committee members. "Then let me show you some of Reet Hluid's associates. Istver and Echemin Hluid, as you see, are good people, clearly excellent parents. But who are Reet's friends?"

Mortified, Reet couldn't help making a tiny, frustrated noise.

"Members of the Committee, I introduce to you friends so dedicated to Reet Hluid that they have gone to great trouble and expense to travel here, in the hope that they would have an opportunity to speak to the committee for him." She waved the two Hikipi to stand. "Heroth Nadkal, president of an organization called the Siblings of Hikipu." There was a small squeak of protest from the committee member for humans—apparently she knew something about the Hikipi. Seimet continued, "For those committee members who don't recognize the name, those of us representing humans to the treaty are plagued by a constant stream of communications—rants, manifestos, even threats—from various human factions who believe, against all evidence, that the Presger do not exist, that they are a hoax perpetrated by the Radchaai. No few of those come from Hikipi." Beside the ambassador, Mr Nadkal frowned. "And this"—Ambassador Seimet turned to the other person—"is Ideni Ismor, a Hikipi Nationalist closely connected to the Siblings of Hikipu. Reet Hluid was themself a member of that organization for some months, studied the Hikipi language, and escorted Hikipi activists during their visits to Zeosen System."

"They came to me," said Reet. He could feel himself flushing with anger and, for some reason, humiliation. "They said my DNA proved that I was Hikipi."

"A Schan!" interjected Mr Nadkal, no longer able to control the indignation that was clear in his expression. "Not just Hikipi, but the lost scion of our ancient rulers!"

"I never knew where I had come from," said Reet. "I never belonged anywhere. They claimed I belonged to them. I wasn't sure I believed them, but I thought it was worth looking into. And I didn't *escort Hikipi activists*. I had a job with Foreign Affairs, showing important visitors around. I was assigned to Mx Athtur, too." He gestured toward hir. "That's how sie found me." He sighed. "And I don't know all of what Mr Nadkal might be involved in, but the Siblings of Hikipu, most of them, don't really do anything except have meetings where they sing some old songs and have snacks, and maybe learn a little Hikipi."

"And get each other jobs in Foreign Affairs," Ambassador Seimet pointed out. "And there is the issue of the attack on

Mx Athtur by Ms Ismor here." She gestured toward Mx Athtur's attacker.

"That was a misunderstanding," said Mr Nadkal. "Though maybe not such a misunderstanding as all that, all things considered."

"Do by all means explain yourself," said Ambassador Seimet, with just the slightest sneer of triumph.

"Ambassador Seimet," said Deputy Ormat severely, "we have nothing to say about human factional disputes."

"Factional disputes?" asked Mr Nadkal, voice incredulous, expression indignant. "*Factional disputes?* Millions of Hikipi have died, murdered by the Phen! Shot, starved, shoved by the hundred out airlocks. Those who survive have been forbidden to speak our language or practice our religion! This is no *factional dispute*!"

"Regardless," replied Deputy Ormat. "This is an issue with which this committee is not concerned."

"That is not true, it is *absolutely* not true!" cried Mr Nadkal. "I demand a chance to speak! Everyone else here has been able to speak."

"Speak, then," said Deputy Ormat after a moment's tense consideration. "And when you are done speaking you will leave this room. You will not be readmitted."

Mr Nadkal looked somehow both bitter and triumphant at that. "Here's how it is," he said. "Here's the truth. There's no such thing as the Presger. You all"—he gestured to the committee members around—"you know it. You have to know it. The machine"—he gestured to *Sphene*, sitting dead-faced in its seat—"it must know, too. All those recordings of the Presger supposedly tearing ships apart—they're not real. They're made up. They're made up by the Radchaai, to control the rest of humanity with the fear of what the Presger might supposedly do. Has anyone here ever seen an actual Presger?" He looked around accusingly. No one said a word. "I didn't think so."

"I have," said Translator Dlar. "And so has Ambassador Seimet. You have no idea what you're talking about."

Mr Nadkal scoffed. "Oh, of course *you* have. But you're part of the lie. The machine there already said it, you use fear of the mysterious aliens to keep power. And so do the Phen."

"I assure you, Heroth Nadkal," said Translator Dlar, "I know nothing about the Phen, and none of us has ever had anything to do with them."

"So you say," replied Mr Nadkal. "But if that's true, then what about Reet Schan?" He pointed emphatically, triumphantly, at Reet. "I've seen his DNA, he's *human*, and you're sitting here claiming he's some kind of alien hybrid. It's a lie, it's all a lie. There are no Presger, all you so-called Presger Translators are no more than humans pretending to be something more, something else."

"You are so very wrong," Translator Dlar said softly.

"Prove it, then," said Mr Nadkal. "You can't, can you."

Translator Dlar smiled, a small, tight expression. Then they picked up a tea bowl from the table nearest them, smashed it back down, swept the fragments into one hand, poured them into their mouth, and swallowed them.

Mr Nadkal scoffed. "Street magic. Or an engineered digestive system."

Translator Dlar smiled again, unhinged their jaw, and vomited up the tea bowl. Whole and undamaged.

"Very good," said Mr Nadkal contemptuously. "You must have practiced that a lot."

"I would like the committee to recognize," said Ambassador Seimet, calmly, as though none of this—what Mr Nadkal had said, what Translator Dlar had done—was even remotely out of the ordinary, "that these are the human associates of Reet Hluid. This is who she would be returning to, if you allow her back into human space."

"*He*," said Qven. "Reet's he. And I'm e."

Ambassador Seimet didn't even look in eir direction. "You can see, I hope, Deputy, Members of the Committee, that this might be particularly dangerous. These are people who will stop at nothing to void the treaty."

"Ambassador," said Deputy Ormat. "I am personally insulted that you felt the need to bring this to our attention in such a melodramatic and frankly patronizing way. You might merely have reported the facts. We were never going to make our determination without as much of the relevant information as possible. Which you know well enough."

Ambassador Seimet said, "I only wanted to be sure that everyone here understood the seriousness of the situation."

"Do you think we play?" asked the committee member for the Geck. "Do you think no one but you does important work? Do you think no one but you cares about the treaty?"

"I think," replied Ambassador Seimet, "that the Geck in particular care for the integrity of the treaty only insofar as it affects the interests of the Geck. That the Rrrrr have an old score to settle with the Radchaai, who have been the human face of the treaty signatories for centuries. I think that even the committee member for humans has been listening to advisers with anti-Radchaai agendas." Indignant hisses sounded from the knot of people behind Committee Member Seris. "Two hundred years ago, I would have been quite confident that any threat posed by extremists like these"— she gestured toward Mr Nadkal and Mx Athtur's attacker— "would be easily dealt with. I don't say I would have been in favor of the committee giving Reet Hluid human status. I would not. But the dangers would not have been so great. You speak of human factional disputes as though they mean nothing here, but I assure you they are quite important in this particular situation. You can imagine, I'm sure, what might happen if enough people such as these decided to deliberately break the treaty in the most outrageous and violent way in an attempt to prove that their delusions were truth."

"Well now, Ambassador Seimet," said the committee member for the Geck. "Which is your argument? That Reet Hluid and young Qven"—the Geck waved a long black leg—"will eat humans, or that they will somehow encourage a breaking of the treaty—which, if they are human, would be an attack on non-human treaty signatories?"

"What she's saying is," said Mr Nadkal, loud and now belligerent, "that the Radch has been manipulating things to keep their hold over the treaty for centuries. She's as much as admitted it."

Ambassador Seimet scoffed. "So long as they don't threaten the treaty, we don't really care what the Phen do. Or anyone else, for that matter."

"She admits it!" cried Mr Nadkal, pointing at Ambassador Seimet, who did not react to Nadkal's rudeness. "And the rest of it is true, too! You all must know it!"

Deputy Ormat snapped, "Mr Nadkal, calm yourself or I will have security remove you. And you, Ambassador, I'm surprised and dismayed at your behavior today. I will be asking the committee to consider censuring you. Even without weapons these people are a danger to those who live and work on this facility—a danger to the treaty, by your own admission. And you have brought them here yourself."

"I'm quite able to keep things under control," said Ambassador Seimet, seemingly unconcerned. "You needn't worry. But do as you must."

"Furthermore," said Deputy Ormat, as though Ambassador Seimet hadn't spoken, "Mr Nadkal and Ms Ismor are to leave this facility within the hour, and leave the system within twenty-four hours after that. They will not be allowed to return."

"Concur," said the committee member for humans, and the member for the Geck and even the member for the Presger echoed her.

Deputy Ormat said, then, "Ambassador, if you have any other information to communicate to this committee on this matter, you can send us a report. There is no need for you to attend any further meetings in person. Goodbye."

Mr Nadkal gave an inarticulate cry and made as if to strike Ambassador Seimet. The ambassador moved quickly, in a way Reet couldn't quite make sense of, and Mr Nadkal was suddenly bent over, whimpering, Ambassador Seimet holding his wrist behind his back.

"Whoa," said Qven. "Don't fuck with Ambassador Seimet."

"Someone here has some common sense," said Ambassador Seimet.

"Alert," said a calm, impersonal voice from the ceiling. "This is not a drill. Imminent hull breach possible, station-wide. Shelter in place. Alert. This is not..."

"That ship," whispered the Geck committee member, behind Reet. "That ship of the Siblings of Hikipu, it makes threats. The captain makes demands and says if they are not met the ship will be exploded. It is near enough this station that such an explosion will do damage, and kill or injure many. Near enough that attempting to destroy it will damage the station as well."

"What demands?" asked Reet. Everyone else seemed distracted, consulting implants or handhelds.

And then Ms Ismor ran across the space that separated the ambassador's party from the Presger Translators, pulled something long and gleaming from her shirt, shouted, "Death to the Phen oppressors!" and stabbed Translator Dlar in the neck.

Qven

All this time I had been mostly paying attention to what everyone was saying or doing, though at the back of everything I could feel, vaguely, the doors and corridors that led into and out of the room. Not the ones that the humans had used coming in, but the ones that whispered and sang to me, the ones I could *feel*. I hadn't paid much attention to them because there was so much else going on that was so much more important.

But now those doors and corridors screamed, all together, and there was a horrible, indescribable sense of dislocation, and then the lights went out and there was no up and down anymore.

Mom and Nana and Mx Athtur cried out. Lights came on again, dimmer. I looked around and saw Reet's parents were flailing. Mx Athtur had grabbed hold of a chair, but the chair wasn't sitting on the floor anymore, and the more sie moved the farther it moved away from the floor. Or the wall. Or whatever it was now, there was no way to tell any direction from another.

Mom was holding on to Nana, whose eyes were firmly closed. Reet had grabbed my arm and floated beside me, his hair sticking every which way off of his head.

And the room was different in other ways. It was, for instance, smaller. Much smaller. Translator Dlar was gone. The Rrrrrr and human committee members and their entourages, gone. Ambassador Seimet and the two humans she had brought—gone. Committee Member Agagag's mech was still there, but it was half in, half out of the wall behind it, legs twitching.

No one else was in the room.

"What the hell!" That was Reet. "What did they do?"

There was a door, a visible, human kind of door, beside where Committee Member Agagag's mech twitched fitfully. "We can get to the door," said Mx Athtur, somewhat breathlessly. "I can push off the chair and…"

"Don't!" cried Mom, and she must have tightened her grip on Nana because e made a small sound of protest.

"The indicator says there's air on the other side," argued Mx Athtur. "And no fire. We need to get out of here."

"There's nothing on the other side of that door," I told hir. "Not even vacuum."

"What happened?" asked Nana. "What's going on?"

I said, "Translator Dlar did something to the doors. Not the doors you can see. I mean the doors *we* use." The doors They used, I supposed. Reet and I drifted, somewhat pleasantly, I thought, except for the fact that we didn't know exactly what had happened, or how to get out of here.

"I'm going to be sick," said Nana.

"Where's everyone else?" asked Mx Athtur.

"I don't know," I confessed. "They must have been on the other side of..." of wherever there was a pathway or some kind of line. "There are doors here but they don't lead anywhere."

"What do you mean?" asked Mom. "What do you mean there are doors here? There's only one door that I can see."

"There are three more," I told her. "They're the kind of door that Adults use. They think I can't feel them but I can." I probably shouldn't have admitted that, but this was Mom and Nana, right? And Reet and Reet's friend. "But I don't know what's on the other side, it all feels...strange." Usually I could sense hallways and rooms beyond the doors, but here everything was muffled and indefinite. "It's not *nothing*, like that other door, though."

"Can you open them?" asked Nana.

"I wouldn't assume there was air on the other side," Reet cautioned, and I agreed with him. "We should probably just wait here. They'll send someone out to look for us if they can."

"*If* they can," repeated Nana, eyes still shut. "We'll run out of air before anyone gets here."

"Hush, Echemin," said Mom.

Reet said, "There has to be some kind of emergency equipment here. There always is on a station. How is it marked here?"

"Orange," said Mx Athtur quickly. "It's always an orange sign, or an orange tab or a switch. That's what they said at the orientation when we first got here."

"I see orange," I said, and pointed to where one of the mech's stalked eyes emerged from the wall.

"Good," said Mom. "Well spotted." And after some maneuvering with the chair, Mx Athtur managed to reach the orange spot, and pulled something.

A panel came away with a click. Mx Athtur set it aside—it sat in the air beside hir, spinning, drifting just slightly—and pulled out a small orange package. "There are three more in here," sie said. "No, wait. Two and a half more. So it looks like we have three of whatever these are."

The print on the orange wrapping said EMERGENCY ENCLOSURE. "They're emergency enclosures," I said, in case sie couldn't read it.

"Do you know how to use them?" asked Mom.

"No," I confessed.

"There are instructions," said Mx Athtur. "And they were in the orientation. You unfold it and get inside and pull a tab, and it pressurizes. There should be air for about a day. It's got a beacon on it, too."

"All right," said Reet, sounding as though he was trying very hard to seem calm and untroubled. "The enclosures hold four people each, so we have three days of air for four people."

"There are five of us," Mx Athtur pointed out.

Nana gave a small, sickly laugh. "It's like one of those puzzles your tutor gives you. Only the prize for getting it right is not dying."

"We shouldn't open these yet, anyway," said Mx Athtur. "There's still air in the room. We'll just have to be on the lookout for signs of..." Sie trailed off.

"I think I should go through a door," I said.

"No!" snapped Mom. And then, in a more reasonable tone, "We should stay together. We should wait here for someone to find us."

"How is anyone going to find us?" asked Nana, an unsettling edge in eir voice. "We could be anywhere. Or nowhere. We might not even be in our universe."

"I don't know where we are," I said. "But I'm the one who can open the doors. And there's only air for four people anyway."

"You might die," said Mom. "It's better to stay here."

"We all might die," I pointed out. I didn't want to die. But I definitely wanted to get out of here. "And I might not be able to even open a door. But I *think* I can. And maybe I can find something that will help."

"Stop," said Mom. "Let's think. We have some time to think."

"Only so much air to breathe, though," said Nana.

"Hush," said Mom.

"Qven," said Mx Athtur, still holding the emergency enclosure, "what did you mean when you said there wasn't even vacuum on the other side of that door?"

"What I said. There's nothing there, not even space." I could feel the nothing, pressing all around us except for where the other doors led to...something. "Translator Dlar must have...moved us somehow, or...I don't know."

"The attack breached the treaty, though," said Reet. He hadn't let go of me all this time. "Didn't it?"

"I don't know," I admitted. "It might have. Or it might not have. Translator Dlar would definitely have preferred it not get to that point."

"So," said Reet, "when that person attacked, Translator Dlar might have realized that there were people on the station who were here specifically to do that, to violate the treaty. That there was a ship in the system, not far from Central, with who knows how many people in it who were not just willing but *eager* to violate the treaty. Had just threatened to. So they did...something to prevent that."

"I think killing us breaks the treaty," said Nana. "I'm pretty sure of that."

"It might not," said Mx Athtur.

"Mx Athtur is right," I said. "It might not. It's complicated. But it's just better not to have complicated things happen. I don't think this is what Translator Dlar *meant* to happen. I think they were doing something else, and it went wrong somehow."

"Well, they did get stabbed," said Reet. "Or it looked like it, it was hard to tell, really, because that's when everything went wrong."

"Yes, exactly," I said. "They were doing something and they got interrupted when they were stabbed. I think that's what happened."

"So they were...moving the universe around?" asked Mom, for the first time a note of fear in her voice.

"Not really," I said, though I knew I couldn't explain it, not even the parts of it that I understood. "But kind of?"

"So they can move the universe around," said Mx Athtur. "Just Translator Dlar, or all the Presger Translators?"

"Kind of...all of us," I admitted. "Well, not me. I'm only a juvenile, and I hardly have any training in that. There are Adults who that's what they do, though. Translator Dlar said that."

"That was the job they offered us," Reet told them, "if we'd agree to drop our petition. Maintaining some sort of network of pathways. But they couldn't explain it to me."

"Then there is a way out of here through those doors," said Mom. "We just don't know where it goes."

"Yes," I agreed.

"And we don't know if there's air there," suggested Mx Athtur.

"Right," I said.

"Let's go, then," said Reet. "No," he said, cutting across Mom and Nana's protests. "I can't stay here without Qven."

"Neither of you are going anywhere," said Mom firmly. "If those pathways or whatever they are lead anywhere, someone will come find us."

"If they can," Reet pointed out. "And how long will it take them? We have no way to know." He looked at me, as if for confirmation.

"I don't know," I said. "I don't know anything." I thought I should tell him to stay here with his parents, but I found that I kind of wanted him to come with me. If I left Reet behind, who knew if I'd ever see him again?

"But if Reet stays here," said Mx Athtur, "and whatever it is that's keeping him from merging with someone else wears off, what will happen then?"

I didn't think it was wearing off anytime soon, but sie had a point. "I'm going, anyway. If it lets the air out, you can all get into your emergency enclosure."

Silence. Mx Athtur floated, spinning slowly, frowning at the emergency enclosure instructions. Mom was making a face I didn't understand, distress and something else. "You're an Adult, Reet. No, I know," interrupting me before I could contradict her. "I know he's still a juvenile, but as a human he's grown up. So, Reet, you can do what you want to do. But I want you to understand, maybe you don't really, but I would do anything to keep you safe. Qven, too. You are eventually going to be the same person, right? So. If there's only space for four in the enclosure, I'll stay out here."

"Don't be ridiculous," said Nana irritably. "I will."

"This isn't convincing me to stay," said Reet.

I felt very strange. Not just the weightlessness, which was odd, though pleasant. Not the fear that we might never leave this tiny room, that we might die here. Though that was part of what I was feeling. No, it was Mom and Nana. Reet had told me about growing up, but I guess I never really thought about exactly what all of that would mean, what it was like to have a Mom and a Nana and a Maman. Certainly I'd never imagined what it would be like to have anyone in the world say they would die to keep me alive. "You've only just met me," I said.

"There's no point being dramatic," said Mx Athtur, looking away from the orange enclosure package and toward us. "We have three enclosures, so there's air for all of us for at least two days. Nearly, anyway. And we can stay by an enclosure while Qven opens one of these doors e says is here, and if there's a pressure drop we can all get in, and work out the next steps after that."

Silence. In a way, Mx Athtur was reminding me of Teacher.

"It's a good plan," said Reet. "If there's air through one of these doors, then everything will be fine. We'll find a way to get help."

"I don't like it," grumbled Nana.

"Yes, well," said Reet, "you didn't pay attention during the safety lectures, either, did you. It's a good thing Mx Athtur did."

"The safety lectures said to stay and wait for help if anything happened," Mom pointed out.

Reet waved that away. "I'm going with Qven. We'll find help."

There was a little more argument, but it was half-hearted, I thought. In the end Mom, Nana, and Mx Athtur gathered around the emergency enclosure Mx Athtur held, and Reet and I floated to where I was sure there was a door, one that sort of, maybe, felt like there would be air, and space to exist, beyond.

"Ready," called Mx Athtur.

I...felt the door. Tried to do what I'd felt Teacher do. Missed. Tried again.

The door opened. Behind me I heard Mom make a surprised, distressed noise. I felt air blow past—out of the dimly lit space before me and into the much-reduced room behind. Just a small breeze. "Should we leave it open?" I asked. "There's lots of air here."

"Yes," said Mx Athtur. "We'll stay by the enclosures just in case."

"Reet, be careful!" said Mom.

"Don't worry, Mom," said Reet, and he grabbed one side of the door and pushed us through.

Enae

They waited, hanging in silence for several moments after Reet and Qven pushed off through the door that Qven had somehow made. Or found. Enae didn't know. It didn't matter.

"We should stay close," sie said, trying to sound brisk. Echemin was curled into a fetal position, floating, and Istver gripped eir arm. Was there something Enae could push against, to bring hirself near them? "If there's an emergency," and suddenly sie had to suppress an inappropriate giggle at the thought. *If there's an emergency.* "If there's an emergency, we all need to be able to get into the enclosure as quickly as possible." The deputy for the Geck's mech twitched again, legs scrabbling against the wall. It gave Enae a stab of... guilt? Distress, anyway.

"Oh, sacred bones, I'm going to be sick," moaned Echemin.

"No you aren't," Enae said, getting closer to the matter-of-fact, businesslike tone sie'd been aiming for.

"We should have had that Qven close the door," said Echemin after a while.

"We don't know that," said Mom firmly.

"We've got the enclosures if anything happens," said Enae. "We'll be fine."

"Sure," groused Echemin. "If by *fine* you mean *trapped forever in a weird dimension where no one can ever find us.*"

"That's not helpful, Min," said Istver.

"*We'll be fine,*" said Enae, not wanting any arguments. "We have air. I have some water in my bag."

"So do I," said Istver.

Enae nodded, and then wished sie hadn't. It felt very strange to be nodding with no gravity. "We have air and water, and we can go days without food, even if we won't enjoy that. And they'll be looking for us. The Presger did this—or Translator Dlar did. Either way, they'll fix it and come get us." Maybe. Sie hoped. But there was no point in thinking about that, in wondering what would happen if no one came looking for them, if no one *could*. If that happened, they would find out soon enough, no need to speculate. "We just have to be patient."

Echemin said, "When you left home, Mx Athtur, did you ever think you'd end up like this?"

"No, I never did," said Enae, as brightly as sie could manage. "It's been an adventure, there's no question about that." The mech in the wall scrabbled again, and Enae tried to ignore it. Sie closed hir eyes, found it didn't help in the least, and opened them again. The mech arms spasmed, and it made a small noise.

It was alive, wasn't it? Sort of? The Geck ambassador had

called it a bio mech. It didn't have anything you'd call a mind, supposedly, but Enae shuddered, thinking about it. Did it hurt? Surely it did. Even if it didn't have much of a brain, it had to be unpleasant—at the very least—to be trapped in the wall like that.

What if that had happened to one of them? To Istver or Echemin. Or to Reet, or Qven. Or to Enae hirself.

What if it had happened to someone sie didn't know? Someone who had been in the committee room, or even somewhere else on the facility? What if whatever Translator Dlar had done wasn't finished and whatever it was happened again?

Sie did hir best to swallow, but hir mouth was dry and hir throat didn't seem to be working right. Sie tried to remember what sie'd done all the years with Grandmaman, when sie'd been upset, hurt, angry, despairing. Afraid. But sie couldn't find it, whatever that resource had been. That sie hadn't even realized sie'd had, until now.

They were going to die.

No, they weren't. Maybe someone would come. Maybe Reet and Qven would find something, someone, and come back for them.

"He shouldn't come back," said Echemin, as though e had been hearing Enae's thoughts.

Enae, shocked, expected Istver to say something like *hush* or *not helpful, Min*, but she said nothing.

"He should get as far away from here as he can," continued Echemin. "Him and that Qven. E's a little odd, but then so is Reet. And Reet seemed to like em."

"E seemed to like Reet," said Istver.

"They need to get away," said Echemin. "No wonder Reet's…progenitor ran away."

"Now, Min," said Istver. "We don't know all the circumstances."

"I don't care," groused Echemin. "You don't *dispose* of children you have no use for, or threaten them with it if they don't do what you want."

"Reet won't leave you," Enae said, or tried to say. Sie swallowed and tried again. "Reet won't leave you. You're his parents. You came all this way to help him. He wouldn't leave you behind."

"Children leave parents behind," said Istver. "It's what they're supposed to do, one way or another."

"Yes, but." Enae stopped. Had to think about that. It felt so backward to hir own experience of parents. *Children leave parents behind.* Sie guessed it was true, or often true. But.

"He might not," said Echemin. "He might not but he should."

"Are you hoping that he does?" asked Enae, feeling panicked, more panicked than she had been, but sie wasn't sure why.

"I don't know," said Istver, as though she and Echemin were in complete agreement on this, as though she could speak for herself and em both, and Echemin didn't interrupt or contradict. "I don't want to be trapped here and…I don't want us to be trapped here. But I also want my son to be free to live his life. We came all this way for that."

The mech in the wall twitched again, and made an unsettling, gurgling noise.

"He won't just walk away," said Enae. "If they find someone, some way out, they'll come back for us, or send help.

Even if they find a way to escape, Reet won't forget about us or just leave us here."

"He should, though," said Echemin again.

"We'll figure something out," said Istver, reassuringly, though Enae thought there was a note of desperation in her voice. "This will be quite a story to tell when you get home, Mx Athtur."

When you get home. Would sie get home? Would any of them? Would anyone ever find them, even after they died? Or would their corpses float here, decaying, in this one room surrounded by not-even-nothing, until the end of time?

Sie would not be sick. Sie would not.

Children leave parents behind. But Enae's mother had left *hir* behind. Maybe she hadn't meant to. No, Enae was sure hir mother hadn't meant to leave hir behind. But sometimes things happened that you couldn't control.

That didn't change the fact, though. Hir mother had gone, irrevocably, and small Enae had been alone. Bundled off to Grandmaman while sie was still trying to understand what had happened.

Enae's mother had left Grandmaman. For very good reasons, Enae knew. Knew very personally, without anyone ever having to explain to hir. But Grandmaman didn't have to raise Enae herself, could have sent hir away to some crèche, could have refused to acknowledge Enae as family, anything at all. Instead she'd taken Enae in.

And never let me leave. Sie was not going to cry. Sie was not. And after all, what sort of person was sie, to be so ungrateful to the woman who had taken hir in, who had, in the end, made sure sie was cared for?

The sort of person who had resented Grandmaman as much as sie had loved her, from the moment sie had come to Athtur House. Ungrateful. Disloyal. Selfish.

And it turned out Grandmaman had been right to insist sie stay at home. After all, once Enae had been free to do as sie liked, sie'd come...here. Sie had left Athtur House and headed straight to hir own death.

And there was no one sie was leaving behind, no one who would care that sie was gone. Grandmaman might have. No, Grandmaman *would* have. Grandmaman had made sure that Enae would be provided for, when she died, out of every other Athtur in existence. Grandmaman had cared for Enae in her own, not entirely healthy way. But there had been no one else.

That's largely Grandmaman's doing, whispered some traitorous voice in the back of Enae's thoughts. But no, it couldn't be all Grandmaman's fault, Grandmaman had done the best she could. Hadn't she?

And once Grandmaman had gone, and Enae had had the chance to make a friend, what had happened? Enae hadn't had any more messages from Caphing since sie'd sent in the report of what had happened in Keroxane. Whatever sie had done, whatever sie had said, it was apparently too much for Caphing to still feel friendly toward Enae. And Enae hadn't even noticed it until now. There was something wrong with hir.

It would have been nice to have a friend. Someone who would care if sie existed or not.

"Mx Athtur," said Istver. "Enae. Are you all right?"

No, sie wanted to say. Tears clung in blobs to hir eyelashes. Sie swallowed. "Just thinking." It almost sounded like hir normal voice, but not quite.

"Don't do that," said Echemin. "Not unless you're thinking about some way to get out of here."

"Or get a message to someone outside," said Istver.

The mech in the wall gurgled again and thrashed its legs.

And sie found it, then. That thing, whatever it was, that had gotten hir through the worst times, in the past. Or at least sie saw the edges of it. "Oh." Sie wiped hir eyes on the hem of hir shirt. "How do the Geck control the mechs? They do it from very far away, don't they? I mean…" Sie trailed off. It was a ridiculous idea. But it didn't matter because what other options did they have? "Maybe we can use it to get a message out. Or maybe." Sie almost didn't dare say it. "Maybe the committee member is trying to talk to us." It didn't matter how likely that was, or even if it was possible. "Here, let's see if we can get over to that side of the room and take a look at the mech."

Reet

Somewhere

"We're back where we started," Reet said, pointing to a particularly odd scuff mark. He'd noticed it the first time they'd passed it, drifting in the endless corkscrewing of the strangely cramped corridor. It was unmistakable, seeing it again. And yet, he was sure they hadn't passed the place where they'd come in, where the passageway turned off to the space Mom and Nana and Mx Athtur were in.

Qven frowned at him, puzzled. "No we aren't."

"We are," he insisted. "Look." He pushed himself back, to navigate the warped hallways, until he found himself faced with Qven again. "See?"

"No," said Qven. "You're somewhere else. Where I am is different."

Reet blinked, nonplussed. "How can I be somewhere different?"

"I don't know," insisted Qven, entirely serious. "But you

are. I don't like this, come back around." When Reet didn't answer, e asked, "Can't you feel it?"

"No," said Reet. "Honestly, this seems exactly the same. It's the same place."

Qven blinked, and eir eyes seemed to shine oddly—*no*, Reet realized. It was tears in eir eyes, clinging because there was no gravity to pull them down.

"What is it?" he asked. "What's wrong?"

"Nothing," Qven answered, and Qven was a pretty good liar, but Reet knew em well enough to know that wasn't true. Well, Qven didn't cry for no reason, not that Reet had seen so far. No one did, really, in Reet's experience.

"Qven..."

"Please come back around."

And Qven never spoke so sharply, that Reet knew of. So he pushed himself back until he found Qven again. "Are we in the same place now?"

Qven had cleared the tears from eir eyes somehow. "Yes."

"That's really weird," he said.

"It is," Qven agreed.

He opened his mouth to say *How come you can feel it and I can't?* but he remembered Qven's seeing and feeling and doing things that only adults could, that Reet could not. Qven, Reet realized, was part-adult in a way that Reet was not. And that was very possibly connected to the attack e had told him about. At any rate, he supposed that Qven had asked emself the same question—why couldn't Reet sense what was plain and obvious to em?—and come up with an answer that distressed em. "All right," he said. "Are there any doors here?"

"No," said Qven, "but I think there might be one up ahead." E bit eir lip and furrowed eir brow. "There's *something*, anyway."

"Then let's go."

When they reached the scuff again, he said, "Is this a different place, too?"

"Yes," said Qven. "But whatever it is I sensed, it is closer than it was."

"If I went back," said Reet, struck by a disturbing thought. "If I went around only one time, and went off toward where we came in, where my parents are..."

"Your parents aren't there," said Qven. "It's somewhere else."

"I'm just trying to understand," said Reet. "I'm just trying to figure out how this is laid out."

Qven made a *whatever* gesture, and he thought maybe e was angry with him. The prospect was distressing. He didn't want Qven angry with him. He wanted...what? Wanted Qven to like him? To be his friend?

To be me something whispered in the back of his mind, and he ignored that, or tried to. "I want to go look," he said. "I think we should look and see."

Qven made that careless gesture again, but didn't speak, and Reet thought e was maybe still upset from before, but if that was the case, e wouldn't appreciate Reet prodding and poking at the thing that had upset em. So instead he shoved off against the wall, back toward where they had come from, hoping to find the part of the spiral where the corridor branched away, that they had entered from. Or that Reet thought they had entered from. No doubt Qven would say that it was an entirely different hallway.

He passed the scuff—and Qven—twice with no sign of the way they'd come in. His heart began to race, and his stomach lurched. Were they gone? Past reaching?

He took a breath. Another. And then worked his way back around one more circuit. Qven ignored him as he passed em. E was curled up, hanging there. Thinking, maybe. Or Reet hoped so.

This time, as he made his way around, he heard voices. Nana saying something unhappy. Mom and Mx Athtur speaking. He slowed himself against the corridor wall. He could go farther, could see them, make sure they were all right. Tell them how things were going.

And what would he say? *We've found a closed loop that's in a different place every time we go around it*? Would that help? Would they even understand? Reet wasn't sure *he* understood.

He turned back.

"You're here now," said Qven, as he approached em on his fourth go-round.

"Good." He'd worried that he'd lost count, and there was no other way for him to know where he was. "Are you all right?"

Qven was still curled in on emself. "No."

That wasn't the answer he'd been hoping for. "Is there something I can do to help?"

"No."

"Should I…"

"No."

He waited. And waited. At length Qven made a sniffling

noise and uncurled emself, just a bit. "I feel like there are doors somewhere but I can't tell where they are. I don't know how to do this. They taught me to speak to humans and be very proper. They didn't teach me how to do this."

"If we're in a different place every time we go around," said Reet, "then the place we came into this loop, or whatever it is, is different every time we pass it. And it is, I checked on my way back here. Where we came in is still there, the door is still open, but one time around there's just wall."

"I don't..."

"When you build things like this, when you make access tunnels, you put entrances in particular places."

Silence from Qven. Then another sniffle. "Well, you have to put them somewhere. Otherwise there wouldn't be any."

"Right," agreed Reet. "But what I'm saying is, there's usually a pattern to where things are."

"But this isn't a thing anyone built," said Qven. "This is a mess that Translator Dlar made." Another sniffle. "I think."

"It's a mess they made out of something that was built," said Reet. "Remember? They told us that there were passageways or whatever that needed maintenance and repair. It's something built. It has a pattern to it, or it had a pattern before it got messed up."

"How does that help now?" asked Qven, eir voice plaintive.

"We can figure it out!" Reet couldn't keep his frustration, his own distress, out of his voice any longer. "The pattern is still there, it's just messed up. We can still find it. Listen! I went down the corridor where we came in, and Mom and Nana and Mx Athtur were there, they're fine, and that door was still open. I went around this loop and that same part of

the corridor was just wall, but what if there's a door there?"
I can't tell if there's a door there, but you can, he wanted to
say, but didn't.

"I don't think there's a door there," said Qven. "I can feel
there's a door somewhere near, but I can't tell exactly where
it is."

"Maybe it's a few more turns around this loop, then, but I
bet it'll be in the same place, the same part of the loop where
we came in. Except, you know, not. So let's keep going, and
we'll just check, every time around."

Qven seemed to think about that for a moment. "I suppose
there's no reason not to," e said finally. But e didn't move.

"Qven," said Reet. "Tell me what's wrong."

"Everything's wrong," said Qven, eir voice miserable, more
tears threatening. "*This* is wrong." E meant, Reet thought,
this strange spiral of a corridor. "*I'm* wrong."

"Because you can't figure it out?" asked Reet, and then, more
sure of his guess, "Or because you can *almost* figure it out?"

"Because I tried to run away and let myself get attacked,"
e said. "If I hadn't done that, none of this would have happened. If Mom and Nana and Mx Athtur die, it's because of
me. If *you* die, it's because of me."

Reet had to think about that for a few minutes. "I would
still have happened. You didn't have anything to do with
me existing. And Mom and Nana and Mx Athtur are here
because of me. And"—a sudden, unwelcome thought—"that
ship, and that Hikipi Nationalist who attacked Translator Dlar, they're here because of me, definitely. So really all
of this is *my* fault." He was hoping Qven would say something like *no it isn't* or *you can't blame yourself for this*, but

e was silent. "And listen. I'm not saying it's good that you were attacked, because it's not, it's bad. But it happened, and it changed things. You got a raw deal, you've been treated badly, but you might as well use what you have, what you got from it. And one of the things you got from it might save our lives right now."

"Might," said Qven. And then e said, "I'm not really a princex. I'm just a messed-up juvenile with no reason to exist." And then, voice fierce and strangled at the same time, "Not even a juvenile. Not a juvenile, not an adult, not a princex, just a mess-up."

"A mess-up who can get us out of here," Reet pointed out.

"If there's even a way out."

"Look," he said, exasperated and, he had to admit, afraid. He was trapped here if Qven gave up. His parents were. And Mx Athtur. "You can feel sorry for yourself later. I'll help you. We'll have tea and dumplings and cry. I promise. Sometimes it's good to cry. And I don't want to tell you not to feel what you're feeling, you have every reason to feel it. But right now we have to get out of here. We have to at least try."

Qven uncurled a little further, blinking behind a fat glob of tears that stuck to eir eyes and the bridge of eir nose. "You promise. Tea and dumplings."

"I promise," Reet agreed.

Qven sniffled and wiped eir arm across eir eyes, sending tiny spherical teardrops floating away from eir face. "And more *Pirate Exiles*?"

"Definitely." It was actually really tempting at this moment to pull his handheld out of his pocket and start up an episode. "We'll have a whole being-sorry party."

"A party won't fix anything," Qven pointed out.

"Not something that big," Reet agreed. "But let's get to the party, and then we'll see what else needs to happen." He was, to his astonishment, sounding a lot like Mom, when really he just wanted to curl up and cry, himself.

"All right," said Qven, making an obvious effort to focus on the task at hand, to be calm, or at least seem calm. "Show me where you think the door will be."

"This way." He led em to the stretch of corridor where, a few rounds back, he'd found the place where they'd come in. It was just blank wall, and they had nothing to mark it with except its distance from the scuff that Reet had noticed.

"That will be enough, though," said Qven. "We pass the scuff, and I start trying to feel for a door."

They went six rounds, finding only blank wall to Reet's view and no door that Qven could sense. On the seventh, Qven straightened, and frowned. "Door," e said. Surprised, and hopeful.

"What's beyond it?" asked Reet, remembering em saying, back in the committee room, that there was not even nothing outside.

"A room," said Qven. "And someone's there. Two someones." Eir frown deepened, and the wall opened. Inside the room, floating, was the assistant to the human committee member who had been in a mobility chair—now she floated, with an air of ease, her arms and legs long and sinuous, clearly at home in low gravity; and not far off, the human-looking AI who had been observing the hearing, the ship *Sphene*.

"Well, look at that," said *Sphene*. "It's our wayward children. I was wondering if you'd be coming along."

Qven

"You're *Sphene*," I said. "You've killed more people than I have."

"Far more," *Sphene* agreed, with a barely noticeable smile. "You have very little chance of catching up to me."

"That's all right," I said, after a moment of thought. "I don't think I want to."

"So, Qven," said the other person in the room. "You can come and go between the pieces of the committee chamber. *Sphene* had hoped that you would."

Floating beside me, clinging to the edge of the doorway, Reet said, "We left my parents in another piece."

"Is there anyone in the wall here?" I asked. I wanted to look at them if there was. The trapped mech had been interesting, and the thought of a human caught that way reminded me of the Middles, of taking bodies apart. When I had been safe, when everything had been the way it should.

"In the wall?" asked the sinuous person, clearly appalled.

"The committee member for the Geck is"—Reet made an odd, unhappy expression—"stuck in the wall, back where my parents are."

"That explains some things," said *Sphene*. "As soon as you made that door, I started receiving a signal that really did seem to be from the committee member for the Geck, but it's…confused. The mech must be disconnected from the committee member and badly damaged."

"It still moves," I told *Sphene*. "And makes noises. But I didn't make the door, I just opened it."

"I was hoping that you could," said *Sphene*. "Because I was pretty sure that if you couldn't, we were all going to die." They smiled. "Not that that would mean much in my case, most of me isn't here. But it would make for a dreadfully complicated violation of the treaty."

"You know about the doors, then?" I asked.

"I know they exist," agreed *Sphene*. "I know—or *suspect* is more accurate—that they're a manipulation of gate space."

"That's all right, then," said the sinuous person. "You already know how to manipulate gate space."

"Not like this I don't," said *Sphene*. "And I need parts of myself to do it that aren't here and that I'm cut off from."

"We should keep going, then," I said, and explained about the passageway outside, the loop that was really a spiral. "Maybe there are more doors up ahead. Maybe one of them will take us back to where we were."

"I greatly fear that where we were is where we are," said *Sphene*. "But yes, you should keep going, the both of you.

The more doors you open, the more chances I have to contact someone...outside."

"The Geck..." began the sinuous person.

"I felt the mech when you opened the door," said *Sphene*. "I can't talk directly to it, though, I just know it's there."

"I don't know what Translator Dlar did," I said. "I only know how to feel the doors and open them."

"We're fortunate you can do that much," said the sinuous person. "Go on ahead and open what doors you can."

"Let us know what you find," said *Sphene*. "If you can. And, oh, Reet Hluid. A word before you go."

Reet and I went back into the corridor. A dozen more rounds of the loop showed only blank wall where a door might have been, and "Stop," I said.

Reet scudded to a stop against a wall. "Are you all right?"

"No," I admitted. I didn't want to be here. I wanted to have a Mom, like Reet did, who would tell me everything would be fine, and give me hugs and tuck me into bed, like the parents in the adventure dramas. I wanted to really be a princex and live in a palace and have noble courtiers competing for my favor. I wanted to curl up in my bed, with Teacher standing in the corner of the room, watching. And with a sudden, vivid, physical yearning, I wanted to be back under the tented blanket, Reet curled beside me, watching *Pirate Exiles of the Death Moons*. Wanted to feel the warmth of him pressed up against me. Wanted...

I was sweating.

"Qven," said Reet. "We need to keep going."

"What if it never stops?" I couldn't raise my voice above a

whisper. "What if it just keeps going around and around and around..."

"Did you ever do emergency drills?" he asked.

"What?"

"Emergency drills. They mostly don't show them on the dramas unless they're part of the story. It's like...practice for when things go wrong. So when something bad happens you know what to do."

I frowned. "No. Nobody ever said anything bad might happen." But bad things had happened. Maybe it would have been good to practice.

"So," said Reet, "pretty much every drill, for any kind of emergency, they tell you to stay as calm as you can and concentrate on the things you're supposed to be doing to save your life. Or someone else's. Like, it's all right to be upset, you might be hurt, but the most important thing is to do what the drill is teaching you to do."

"Did you have a drill for this?" I asked.

"No," Reet admitted. "We didn't have a drill for Translator Dlar being attacked and breaking reality into pieces." His face did an odd thing, like he was holding something back. "Or anything like it." His face did the thing again. "I'm sorry," he said. "But it's kind of funny." I waited a few moments, and his expression straightened out again. "We didn't do a drill for this, specifically, but we can take what seems useful from other drills."

"Like Mx Athtur did," I realized. "With the orange things."

"Yes!" Reet agreed. "So the first thing is always, stay calm."

"I'm not calm," I pointed out. "If I were calm we wouldn't

be floating here talking, we'd just keep going on around and around until we found something."

"Yes," said Reet. "Exactly."

It took me a moment to see what he was saying. "Oh," I said. "All right." I pushed off the wall and sailed farther along the loop-spiral. Reet followed. "What did *Sphene* say to you?"

He was silent for a moment. "*Sphene* said that maybe we could match with a bio mech. Like the Geck use. They...it... she..." He grimaced. "They," he decided. "They're think-ing about ways to use bio mechs instead of making humans into ancillaries. And they think the Geck could maybe make a mech that we could match with instead of having to...to merge into another person."

I felt a stab of...of what?

"So," Reet continued, "you might be able to, you know..." He seemed to be searching for words.

"I might not have to be eaten by someone else," I said, still not sure what I was feeling. And then I remembered that Reet was the *someone else* in question.

"If there's time," said Reet. "They'd need time to make them. And if we can convince...well, *Sphene* said that the Presger Translators really don't like the idea. They think it's horrible and disgusting for some reason."

"But we're human," I pointed out. "So *we* don't think it's disgusting."

"But we have to get out of here first," said Reet.

So many times around. Nothing but the blank walls. Noth-ing to think of but *maybe I could eat a bio mech*. That might be interesting. It might be safe. No one would be forcing me to melt into them. No one would be pushing me back, holding me down, and…but no, of course no one would. Reet would be there, and…

Reet *wouldn't* be there. That would be the whole point of the mechs, wouldn't it?

I felt that feeling again that I couldn't identify. Couldn't say if it was good or bad, it was just…there, and unignorable.

I had been working up to facing the idea that I would match with Reet. That it might not be so bad. So far, Reet had been nice to be with, and safe. If I absolutely had to match with someone, it would be good for it to be Reet and not someone like Tzam, who didn't care what I wanted or how I felt.

But it would be better, wouldn't it, to not have to worry about any of that? To have a mech as part of me, instead of having to be submerged in Reet, his skin melting into mine…

I was sweating again. And then my skin began to itch fiercely, all over.

"I hate that," said Reet. "Do you want me to get your back?"

I was about to say *yes, please*, when I felt the door.

Behind the door was a wall of not-even-nothing, not-exactly-cold and not-really-black, slicing across a corner of the room we'd been in with the committee. Ambassador Seimet was there, and the person who had attacked Translator Dlar. Spherical globs of blood floated in the space, and Ambassador Seimet's white clothes were saturated with blood. The smell of it was instantly comforting.

"What happened?" asked Reet, alarmed.

"Someone got caught in the wall," I said, before Ambassador Seimet could answer.

"More or less," Ambassador Seimet agreed. "It took her arm right off. I've slowed the bleeding, and she's unconscious. But if we don't get help soon, she's done for." And with a bitter twist of her mouth, she added, "Not that I'd grieve much over it."

"Can I see?" I asked, and the ambassador made a gesture that seemed to be half resignation, half invitation.

The person had one whole arm and one that ended not far below her shoulder. Someone—it must have been Ambassador Seimet—had tied a piece of bloody cloth very tightly around the remaining bit of limb. I could see the bone, the sliced ends of muscles bunched around it, the ends of blood vessels. It was entrancing. "Where's the arm?" I asked. "If we find it, can I have it?"

"I can't touch it," said Reet before the ambassador could answer, and I looked over to where he floated near the expanse of not-even-nothing.

"No, of course you can't," said Ambassador Seimet. "It's *nothing*. Not even space. There's nothing to touch."

"Nothing can get through it," said Reet. "If you could make a wall out of it, on purpose, I mean..."

"You can't *make* anything out of something that *isn't there*," said Ambassador Seimet sharply.

"Did you practice?" I asked the ambassador. "Did you do a drill for someone getting their arm cut off?"

"Yes, I did," said Ambassador Seimet. "Have you found anyone else?"

"Mom and Nana and Mx Athtur," I said. "And we found *Sphene* and the person like a fish."

"Batonen," said the ambassador. "Can you find a way out of here?"

"I don't know," I admitted. "I can feel doors, and I can open them. The passage outside seems like a loop but it's a spiral. We've been going along looking for doors."

Ambassador Seimet looked more closely at me, and then made a warding gesture. "Keep your distance. I don't want to stress the treaty any further than it already has been today, and I have no intention of becoming a Presger Translator."

"E doesn't want to be you," said Reet, with surprising heat. "So just leave em alone."

"Then there should be no trouble with her keeping her distance," said Ambassador Seimet.

"E," I corrected. "I'm e. And I'm going to match with a bio mech. *Sphene* said I could." But I regretted saying it as soon as the words were out of my mouth.

Ambassador Seimet closed her eyes. "Amaat preserve me," she muttered. Opened her eyes again, and said, "You can keep going around the spiral. You should. But I'm not optimistic. If anyone could have come for us, they would have already. Either Translator Dlar wrenched us completely away from the universe, or anyone who would be rescuing us is busy doing something else. Like dealing with a ship that might be threatening the Central Treaty Administration Facility."

"Death to the Phen oppressors," said Reet, ruefully.

"Lovely friends you have," said the ambassador.

"You're the one who brought them into the committee room," Reet pointed out. "Not me, not Qven. Not my parents."

Ambassador Seimet looked like she wanted to argue with that, to say something sneering or insulting, but she said nothing.

Enae

Up close, the committee member for the Geck's mech was an even more pitiful thing. Limp, wilted limbs and eyestalks emerging out of the wall. Part of the blobby body, with three more limbs and an eyestalk, these twitching occasionally. Where the bio mech met the wall, some sort of bluish fluid seeped and clung.

"I'm so sorry," Enae murmured. Why was sie sorry? A memory seized hir, the sensation—the sight, the smells, the physical feeling—of sitting by Grandmaman's bedside, near the end.

The ambassador for the Geck had reminded Enae of hir grandmother, and now, seeing this mech injured—Enae knew it wasn't the committee member himself, knew it was a remotely controlled mech, but all hir experience of the Geck had been the mechs, and it was difficult not to think of them as the actual Geck. But it wasn't. It was just a bio mech.

"I'm sorry," sie said again. "You didn't ask for this, you were just doing what the committee member told you to do, and look where you ended up." Sie was seized with the desire to do something—anything—to make the pitiful, injured mech more comfortable.

"...there," whispered the mech, and one of its limbs twitched. "...nyone there?"

"Committee Member?" asked Enae. Quietly. Maybe sie'd hallucinated the whisper.

"...ing to reach some...is there? Who is there?"

"It's me, Enae Athtur. And Ms and Mx Hluid. Reet and Qven were here but Qven opened some kind of door and is looking for a way out. I don't know where anyone else is."

"What's going on?" asked Echemin. "Is the mech talking?"

"I think it's the Geck committee member," said Enae.

"...ot enough to bring anyth...n't do more than speak to you," whispered the mech. "Is any...njured?"

"We're fine, we're all fine," said Enae, feeling tears well again. Sie blinked them away, but they stuck to hir eyes.

The mech's limbs thrashed again, and then it said, in that same whisper, "Better. This should be better."

"Much better," agreed Enae. "Can you get us out of here?"

"Translator Dlar has done this," whispered the mech. "We do not know where Translator Dlar is. The committee member for the Presger says, if they undo this without knowing exactly what it is that Translator Dlar has done, they may kill all who are trapped. They did not know if anyone was trapped or if all were dead. The station is...that part of the station is not right. Also the Siblings of Hikipu, their ship is still here, and still they threaten the station." Silence. More twitching.

Then, "You say the child Qven has opened a door. This is not possible, says the committee member for the Presger."

"I don't know what to tell you," replied Enae. "I saw em open the door, and e went through it, along with Reet."

"Wait," whispered the mech.

By now Istver and Echemin had come closer.

"They must have been trying to talk to us for a while," said Enae. "But we couldn't hear anything until I got really close."

"Maybe it is possible," whispered the mech. "Maybe it is possible and the committee member for the Presger did not want to think it was. You are perhaps in danger from the children. But you must bring them to me. You must bring Qven here."

Past the door that Qven had opened was a blank-walled corridor that curved off to the left and right. Enae tried to remember if sie'd seen Reet and Qven go in a particular direction, but try as sie might sie had no real memory of that particular detail. It was up to hir, then, and sie might choose wrong.

Sie often had chosen wrong in the past, but there was nothing for it. Sie took a deep breath and went left.

The corridor, as sie went along, twisted and turned oddly, and Enae seemed to push hirself along it forever... until sie realized sie'd passed the same scuff on the wall three times.

Impossible. There had been no exits, no doors, not even the door Enae had come through, which should have been there, Enae should have passed it if this was just a big loop. Had the door closed behind hir? Where had it been? Where had Reet and Qven gone?

There was no point in panicking. None. Whatever was going to happen would happen. Enae just had to do whatever it was sie was supposed to do. Sie had always done whatever it was sie was supposed to do.

But what was sie supposed to do now?

First of all, make sure sie really was looping around. Sie reached into eir bag and found the wrapper of a snack that Echemin had eaten at some point. That would do. There wasn't enough of an air current to blow it far. Sie held it out and let it go. It hung, drifting just slightly.

Now to go forward. Or backward, it didn't matter which, and honestly sie was losing track of which was which to begin with.

Another round of the corridors, and sie came upon that distinctive scuff again. And the bright green snack wrapper.

Filled with despair and anger, Enae reached out to grab the offending trash.

Hir hand passed right through it. Sie had to do it three or four times more to believe it had actually happened. But it had—hir hand had gone right through the wrapper, and even the air that the passage of hir hand had disturbed didn't seem to reach it.

What was going on?

Sie thought about what the committee member for the Geck had said about what Translator Dlar had done in that moment before they'd been stabbed. Clearly, something inexplicable and indescribable had happened, and things weren't behaving like Enae thought they should, not even like the Presger Translators seemed to think they should. So this was...what was it?

Sie went forward one more turn, and still hir hand passed through the wrapper. So the next time, sie went backward two turns.

And this time, hir hand closed around the wrapper, crumpled it with a satisfying crinkly crunch.

The universe was twisted up. All right. All right. Sie retraced hir path, backward along the loop of corridor, and found the door sie'd come out of, right beside the distinctive scuff and the snack wrapper. Where it hadn't been, the last five turns.

"It's a spiral," sie murmured to hirself. "It's a spiral," sie called, so that the others could hear hir. "It looks like a closed loop but it's a spiral."

Istver put her head out of the door. "Did you find Reet and Qven?"

"Not yet. I don't know which way they went. And I don't know how far the spiral goes." Sie took a breath and swallowed. "I'll keep going."

Several more turns along the way, there was another open door, and in the space beyond hung Batonen and the ship, *Sphene*.

"Did you find the children?" asked *Sphene* when Enae came into the room. "The committee member for the Geck's bio mech is doing something, but I can't tell what."

"Yes," agreed Enae. "I mean no, I haven't found Reet and Qven, but the bio mech is communicating with the committee member, who's getting instructions from the Presger Translators."

"Oh, good," said Batonen, with relief. "Reet and Qven have been here and gone on."

Enae said, "The committee member wants me to bring Qven back, so e can receive instructions. Or information. I'm not sure."

"I'll get em," said Batonen, and swam out of the room and into the corridor. Enae, who had been proud of how well sie'd handled moving around in microgravity, suddenly felt clumsy and graceless.

"She's been restless ever since the children opened the door," said *Sphene*. "Shall you and I go back to where the mech is and see what else we can learn? Or better yet, maybe we can see what's on the other end of this spiral. Or at least I can. It's no real difficulty if anything happens to the part of me that's in here. You should probably stay with the others."

Enae frowned. "You didn't say that to Batonen."

"I didn't have time," said *Sphene* with a sardonic quirk of the mouth. "And besides, we'd already been having that conversation before you arrived. She's probably faster than I am, and more likely to catch up to the children."

Enae said, "I'll come with you."

Sphene was profoundly disturbed by the snack wrapper. "It shouldn't be doing that," said the ship.

"I don't like it, either," said Enae.

"Why didn't you mark every turn?"

"I didn't have anything else." Which wasn't entirely true, sie still had hir bag strapped to hir body, and there were various things in that bag, but in fact it hadn't occurred to hir to do that. "And it would get awfully cluttered, I think."

"Hm," said *Sphene*. "No doubt."

They went around, stopping only to call a brief reassurance

in to Istver and Echemin and the mech, until Enae's hand closed around the bright green snack wrapper.

"This is as far as you came?" asked *Sphene*.

"I went one farther, actually," Enae said. "It was the same."

And it was the same for the next four rounds of the loop. But on the fifth, "It's different," said Enae, frowning, trying to understand what it was sie was seeing up ahead. It looked as though something red and white and brown was stuck to a wall that ended the corridor. "What is it?" Sie pushed off the wall to bring hirself closer.

"Don't!" *Sphene* grabbed hir arm, slowing hir, spinning them both around. "There's gravity there."

"It might not really be there," Enae pointed out. "Like the snack wrapper."

"Not a good assumption," said *Sphene*.

"It's Translator Dlar!" Enae realized. The thing sie'd seen at the end of the endless corridor resolved itself in hir mind. "It's gravity, and that's Translator Dlar lying on the ground. We have to go there. We have to help them. And we have to find out what they did to make this happen, and if they can undo it."

"I imagine it's easy enough to get there," drawled *Sphene*. "Just go forward until you're going down. Getting back out, though, is a whole other problem."

"You stay here," said Enae. "I'll call back to you. Up to you. Whatever. And let you know."

"I think you have that backward," said *Sphene*, reaching one hand out to the corridor wall, slowing their drift toward Translator Dlar even further. "If you fall down and break your neck, that's the end of you. But if I fall, well, it's no particular problem for the rest of me. And I suspect this part of me is a bit more durable than you to begin with."

"Maybe," said Enae. Sie hadn't thought of any of that. Sie'd just wanted to help get them all out of there. "I guess you might be right."

"I know I'm right," *Sphene* said. "We're getting too close for my comfort. I'm going to push you back and when I..."

And suddenly up and down existed again and Enae was falling.

Reet

Reet and Qven emerged into the loop of corridor to find Batonen waiting for them. "We found Ambassador Seimet," said Qven. "And the person who stabbed Translator Dlar. Their arm is missing."

"You need to come back to where the committee member for the Geck's mech is," said Batonen, with no preamble, no response to what Qven had said. "It's communicating with the committee member, who's passing information from the Presger Translators. They say they need to talk to Qven."

Reet frowned. "Why?"

"They think there's something Qven might be able to do."

"All I can do is open doors if they're already there," said Qven.

"But if the mech is communicating with the committee member," Reet realized, "then there's an opening to the regular universe somewhere. Otherwise the message wouldn't get through."

"Just so," agreed Batonen.

"But if there'd been a door there I would have felt it," argued Qven. "And opened it."

"Maybe the mech itself is the passage," suggested Reet. "It's stuck in the wall, maybe the other side is somewhere else." He had been thinking about the looped passage, about the way the doors appeared in the same place every time. "There has to be something at one or the other end of this corridor. It's a made thing, there's a logic to it."

"Presger logic," Batonen pointed out. "Which sometimes seems like no logic at all."

"It's still *some* kind of logic," argued Reet.

Batonen gave an elegant, rippling shrug. "Qven should go back and talk to the mech."

Qven should. Not Qven and Reet. And he didn't *want* to be apart from Qven.

There wasn't time to think about his own wants. This was an emergency, a crisis, and lives depended on everyone doing the right thing. "You go," he said to Qven. "I still want to see what's up ahead."

Qven looked doubtful for a moment. Even offended. And then e said, "All right."

"Be careful," said Batonen, and swam off along with Qven.

It had felt so dramatic, so final, when he'd floated off in the opposite direction from Qven and Batonen, but he met them coming around. Of course. Neither Qven nor Batonen acknowledged him, which felt both oddly right and also insulting.

"There's a snack wrapper here," he said as they sailed by. "It wasn't here before."

Qven looked back but didn't reply, and e and Batonen were lost around the curve of the passageway. And on ahead he met them again, and again. He tried not to stare as Qven went past, tried not to feel whatever it was he was feeling. Hurt? Abandoned? Alone? But he was used to being alone, wasn't he?

Eventually, of course, Qven and Batonen were gone from the corridor. He didn't see them go through the door that led to the fraction of room where his parents were, and Mx Athtur, and the mech half in and half out of the wall, but they were gone, and that was where they had to be by now. And so he went around and around the loop of corridor, the same stretch over and over again, nothing different, nothing to occupy him but his own thoughts.

There would be a mech for him. That might be all right. He thought of walking the pipeways back on Rurusk Station, with another body, one as flexible as the mech he'd seen in the committee chamber. All those limbs, all those eyes. That could be really useful. He might find, in the end, that he liked that.

Qven would probably like it, too, and that was a good thing. He thought of eir story of being attacked, of the attempt to force em to match, and no wonder e didn't want to merge with anyone if e could avoid it. It was so completely understandable, and Reet was glad, he really was, if there was some way for Qven to survive and not be forced into something e found so terrifying and unpleasant.

But it would have been nice. It would have been nice to finally have someone who understood his impulses and desires. Who shared them. Somewhere he actually belonged.

Just like always, the thing he wanted would hurt someone else. So he could take *good enough* and keep on going the way he had been. Maybe he could make *good enough* into *pretty nice, actually*, even if it wasn't the thing he yearned for.

It was Qven he yearned for. Not just anyone he might merge with, but Qven specifically. And maybe that was because they'd spent hours and hours eating cakes and watching *Pirate Exiles of the Death Moons* (and maybe that was why Teacher had let them do that, in the hope they would like each other enough to want to match), and maybe there was some other Presger Translator juvenile out there he would like just as much, but it was Qven he'd spent time with, and Qven who'd trusted him with the story of what had happened to em.

What would that be like, to merge with someone you didn't like, didn't trust? Who didn't like you? Surely the adult who resulted would be a mess, a mass of self-hatred.

And what if they couldn't get out of here in time? If whatever the Presger Translators had done to him and Qven wore off and it was match or die? And what if Qven would rather die?

There was no point in thinking too hard about distant what-ifs.

There had to be an end to the spiral, it couldn't possibly go on forever. Could it? There had to be a place where he couldn't go any farther. Or—he feared, for a moment—a place where he came, again, to the door where his parents and Mx Athtur were, proof that there was no entry and no exit from this place.

But two turns of the loop farther, the corridor ended in a blank wall.

Just a wall. The same somewhat-dingy white as the rest of the corridor, flat, no door, no controls, no signs. But it hadn't been there before. Reet reached forward to touch it, to make sure it was really there.

He couldn't get near it. Every time he pushed himself toward the wall, every time he got close to it, he found himself propelled away. The experience was disorienting, a sudden, panicked flail as he felt like he was falling, like there was, for an instant, an up and down, and then, the next instant, he was drifting in microgravity again.

It wasn't the same as the not-even-nothing he'd tried to touch in the room where Ambassador Seimet was. It wasn't a normal artificial gravity boundary, because he should have still had his momentum from falling, once he'd crossed back over into microgravity—he should have sailed toward the curve of wall behind him, but instead he was just…drifting. What *was* this?

Maybe Qven would have understood what this was. Or at least sensed something useful. But Qven wasn't here.

As he hung there considering the futility of anything he could do, of his being here at all, a spot on the unreachable wall appeared, faint at first and then darkening and spreading, slowly, almost but not quite imperceptibly. Fascinated, Reet stared at it. It was a dull red, almost like…

Almost like a bloodstain.

As Reet watched, the stain grew slick and shiny and suddenly some of the shine gathered itself into a blob that shot toward Reet, and then, crossing some boundary, slowed, wobbled, drifting, into a shivering sphere. Reet reached out one finger to touch it.

Blood. No question.

Why was blood coming through the wall?

Why was any of this happening? How could any of this make any sense? But no, there was no point panicking. Stay calm. Where would blood be coming from?

The person who'd stabbed Translator Dlar had lost her arm—sliced off by the wall of not-even-nothing, Ambassador Seimet had said. That arm had to be somewhere. Did an arm have enough blood in it to soak through a wall? Probably not, but that arm had stabbed Translator Dlar, so where it was, likely Translator Dlar was.

Another drop of blood shot toward Reet, then slowed, wobbling.

Translator Dlar had done this. Translator Dlar was probably the only way it could be undone. Translator Dlar was at the center of this structure, Translator Dlar had been stabbed, and here Reet was at the end of the spiral passageway, watching blood drip from a wall that shouldn't be there, that he couldn't reach.

"Qven!" he shouted, but there was no answer. He had no idea if anyone could hear him, if his voice could reach all those rounds of the looped passage, and anyway, Qven was way, way back in the room where Reet's parents were, talking to the mech, or e should be by now.

"Qven!" he shouted again, and turned and pushed himself back along the passageway as quickly as he could.

Qven

"Qven," said Mom, when she saw me come in, Batonen behind me. "Where's Reet?"

"He wanted to see what was at the end of the passage," I told her. "He's all right."

"Are *you* all right?" asked Nana. "You don't look happy."

I made my face smile. "I'm fine," I said as brightly as I could. "I'm supposed to talk to the mech."

"It can only speak very quietly," said Mom. "You have to get very close and listen very carefully."

"Did you and Reet have an argument?" asked Nana.

"Min!" said Mom.

"What would we argue about?" I said, still bright. "I'll go talk to the mech." I pushed myself closer to where the mech emerged from the wall, limbs twitching. "Hello," I said. "This is Qven. I'm here."

"Qven," whispered the mech, and Mom was right, it was

very, very quiet and I had to put my head very close to the mech's body to hear. "The committee member for the Presger speaks to me, and also the part of Translator Dlar that was not in the committee chamber. They ask me to tell you these things. You must find Translator Dlar, and you must discover what it was that Translator Dlar did in the moment they were being stabbed. Translator Dlar knows what was intended, but it seems that what was intended and what happened are two different things. The committee member for the Presger and Translator Dlar themself can guess at what that difference is, but they do not know enough to put things to rights in a way that will not be destructive to the station or to the people who were in the committee chamber. So they tell me."

So they tell me. Did that mean something?

"Is Translator Dlar there with you?" I asked. I didn't know why I cared, or why it mattered.

"Translator Dlar is here and speaks to me. I operate this mech that speaks to you. I convey your words to the committee member and the Translator."

I convey your words. They couldn't hear me, then, only Committee Member Agagag could hear me. I didn't know why that mattered to me, but somehow it did. "Well, I'm here and listening. What do they want me for?"

"The Translator says someone is required to examine the pathways from the inside. It must be done by an Adult, and to be an Adult you must match. But you must match with something that can communicate with the committee member and the Translator so that you can tell them what you find, and they can instruct you. They say, therefore, that you must merge with this mech, with which you are now speaking."

At first I was sure that I had heard incorrectly. "What?"

"You must merge with this mech, they say, so that you can pass information and take instruction from them."

Match with the mech. Reet had said that the idea of merging with a bio mech was deeply offensive to Translator Dlar, something they would never countenance.

And this mech, in particular, was badly damaged; half in, half out of the wall; twitching and leaking. "How about if I just tell you how things are, here?" I asked.

"The Translator does wish for you to do that," replied the mech in its low, strained whisper. "But they insist that you will not be able to know what needs to be known unless you do this thing."

"There are doors here," I said. "I can open them. I have been opening them. It's a spiral that looks like a loop. Reet went to see the end of it, if there is one."

The mech didn't answer right away. Then, "Mx Athtur said you had opened doors, and I had said so to the Translator, but they did not believe. They said it was not possible."

"It is possible, because I've done it," I insisted.

"It is not enough," replied the mech. "You must do more than open doors. And you must find Translator Dlar to know what more it is you must do. You must do this quickly, the Hikipi ship still threatens and cannot be dealt with until this situation is resolved."

I frowned, though I didn't think the mech could see my expression. "But it takes days to match."

"They will be able to speak to you while it happens, you will be able to do as they wish while it happens, they say. Translator Dlar wishes to remind you that you did not wish to be eaten by anyone, and there is not anyone in this mech to be eaten by. It is ideal for you."

"It's half in the wall," I pointed out. "It's badly damaged. There might not even be much mech there anymore, even once it's freed."

"Translator Dlar suggests this is only so much the better for you, as you did not wish to merge at all in any event. Also, many lives are at stake, not merely the lives of those inside the committee chamber." A pause. "Translator Dlar would inform you that the treaty itself is at stake."

The treaty was everything. The treaty was why we existed to begin with. The way that Reet had talked about the treaty, the way it was talked about in *Pirate Exiles of the Death Moons*, you would think that only the treaty stood between all humans and certain death. Which maybe was true, but then again a lot of things in *Pirate Exiles of the Death Moons* weren't exactly accurate, according to Reet.

"If I do this," I said, "will you agree that Reet and I are human?"

After a moment, the mech said, "Translator Dlar is angry, and expresses disappointment that you would choose a time like this to pursue your own individual interests, when so much else is at risk."

I laughed. I couldn't help it. Mom and Nana and Batonen, who had been hanging back, trying not to seem like they desperately wanted to know what the mech was saying to me, started, and stared in my direction. "I could say the same to Translator Dlar," I said. After all, if things were so desperate, why would the Translator hesitate to grant me this one thing?

"What are they saying?" asked Nana.

"They want me to match with the mech in the wall," I told them, and conveyed what the mech had said to me.

"But…" Mom began, and then, "Qven, dear, excuse me if I'm being too personal, but I thought you and Reet were supposed to…" She trailed off, unsure of how to say what she wanted to say, I suppose.

"That's what they want," I said. "I think they've been hoping if we're together enough we'll *want* to do that and then they won't have to worry about us anymore." I wanted to say, *I don't want to do that with anybody*, but for some reason I didn't. "I'm a disappointment," I said. "There's no place for me. Except with Reet, and that was by accident."

"Oh, Qven," said Mom, and she reached her hand out as though she were going to touch me, and then stopped. "You're not a disappointment."

"No, I am," I told her. "I was supposed to match with Translator Dlar, so they could keep on living instead of dying of old age. And Translator Dlar is important. I was supposed to be important."

"Qven," said Batonen, sharply. "My people live on space stations, in ships and habitats. There's always the possibility of an accident, of some damage to a habitat that will kill many people, and we're taught from small that the most important thing is doing whatever it takes to prevent such accidents. But when they happen, sometimes the only way to save everyone else is for someone to sacrifice themselves—or others—to secure the rest of the habitat."

"You think I should sacrifice myself to save everyone," I said.

"Wait, I'm not finished. The problem is, sometimes

sacrificing yourself is the wrong thing. Sometimes a sacrifice won't really save anyone. The problem is, when someone comes to you and says *only you can save us by sacrificing yourself*, how do you know they're right? And how do you know they're telling the truth, and not just trying to get you to do something that would be convenient for them? If they're telling the truth, if they're right, then yes, you should do it. But are they?"

I frowned. "Translator Dlar wouldn't agree to admit Reet and I were human if I matched with the mech. If it was really a question of the treaty, if they were really desperate, would they do that?"

"It doesn't tell you everything," said Batonen, "but it tells you something."

I needed someone to tell me the truth. Who had ever told me the truth? Who had I ever been able to rely on?

Reet. Reet had never lied to me, that I knew. Reet had cared how I felt about things. But Reet wasn't here. Mom and Nana were here, and I didn't think they would lie to me, and they seemed to care about me, but I was sure that was only because they cared about Reet, and they didn't know the things I needed to know.

I wanted Reet to be here.

Reet wasn't here. Who else did I have? Who else could I depend on to tell me the truth and not hide things from me?

I went back over to the mech. "I want to talk to Teacher," I said.

There was a long silence. Then the mech said, "They have withdrawn. I hear them faintly, I think they argue."

"Why are they arguing? Why are they arguing with me?

The treaty depends on this, they've said. They said I needed to do this thing quickly."

"I do not know," said the mech. "I do know that if you were one of our own hatchlings, you would be wise not to trust Adults too near you. It is only your clutchmates who will be there through everything, those few who have survived childhood with you. But humans are different. And this is a dangerous and difficult situation."

I'm not human, I almost said. But I was, wasn't I? I was claiming I was. I didn't want to say anything else where Translator Dlar and Committee Member Sril might hear me. "I don't have clutchmates," I said instead. And suddenly I felt very alone, even though Mom and Nana and Batonen were right there in the room with me. I wanted Reet. *If Reet were here you wouldn't be so alone*, I thought, and then, *If you were Reet you wouldn't be alone.*

"Qven?" It was Mom. "What's happening?"

"I told them I wanted to talk to my Teacher and now they're arguing with each other about it."

"When did you last have food?" asked Mom.

"Before the committee meeting," I said, and I tried to remember. "That was..."

Mom set something sailing toward me, a thing in a papery wrapper. "It's the best we can do right now," she said.

"Qven," said the mech. "Your Teacher is here."

Enae

Somewhere with Gravity

Something hard slammed into Enae and knocked the breath out of hir. Sie lay there, pressed to that hard surface, trying to catch hir breath through the shock and the pain of impact.

"Mx Athtur," said a voice, and Enae tried to gather hir thoughts, to understand what was happening. "Mx Athtur, are you all right?"

Sphene. It was *Sphene* asking. "Yes," Enae said, and then, "No." And then, "Wait." Sie tried to push hirself up, and discovered that hir left wrist wouldn't take any weight.

And that sie was lying in a pool of blood. Hir hands, hir clothes—presumably the side of hir face, which ached from the impact but also felt cold and wet. Sie made a small noise in the back of hir throat. Swallowed. "This is a lot of blood," sie said, senselessly.

"Yes," agreed *Sphene.*

"Are *you* all right?" Enae asked, still not sure why sie was saying anything at all right now.

"I'm fine," replied *Sphene*, its—their?—hand on hir shoulder now. "As I said, I'm a bit more durable than you are. No offense."

"None taken," replied Enae. "My wrist is…and my knee, I think."

"I'm more worried about your head," said *Sphene*, and crouched in front of Enae to look into hir eyes.

"I'm all right," Enae protested, though sie almost laughed at the ridiculousness of saying that, when sie was half lying on the ground, bruised and aching and covered in blood. Not hirs, sie didn't think. "This is Translator Dlar's blood," sie realized.

"Mostly," agreed *Sphene*, helping hir to sit up. And once sie was leaning against a wall, cradling hir left arm, sie managed to get hir thoughts together and understand where they were.

This place had three perfectly ordinary-seeming walls. The fourth was the not-even-black of not-even-nothing.

Beside that non-wall lay an arm, neatly severed just below where a shoulder should have been. Not far from the lifeless hand, a knife lay in the pool of blood that spread out from where Translator Dlar lay. "Are they dead?" sie asked.

"I'm hoping not," said *Sphene*. "But look up."

Sie did. And saw a ceiling. Sie blinked. "That wasn't there before!"

"Oh, I'm sure it was," said *Sphene*. "Just not from the direction we came in."

"So," began Enae, and found sie couldn't quite marshal

any sort of coherent thought. "So what happened? And how do we get out of here?" And then again, with sudden, sick dismay, "That's a lot of blood."

"Most human bodies have about five liters of blood in them. You'd have to add a little more for the arm."

"I'm..." Sie wasn't sure what to say. "Do Presger Translators have more? Or less?"

"About the same, I'd think," said *Sphene*, unperturbed. But of course, they—she? it? *She*, Enae decided. She had said before that she was only one small part of herself, just one body of many and those just part of a ship. "It really does look like the Translator has bled out."

"But you don't think they're dead?" Enae hadn't thought hir confusion and dismay could get any worse, and yet here sie was.

"Presger Translators aren't human," said *Sphene*. "Translator Dlar might *look* dead." She cast a glance over at the body that lay on the floor, its white clothes soaked in blood. "They definitely look dead. But that's no guarantee of anything with Presger Translators."

"So what do we do?"

"I'm not sure there's anything we *can* do," said *Sphene*. "Dlar probably meant to isolate themself from the attacker, and the attacker from anyone else. But something went wrong."

"But this isn't all of Translator Dlar," Enae pointed out. "They have at least one other body, right? And that part of them wasn't in the committee chamber."

"That part of them isn't here, either," said *Sphene*. "If we're lucky, Translator Dlar will be working to undo this, but there isn't anything *we* can do. Especially if this part of Translator Dlar is inert."

"*Inert*," repeated Enae dubiously.

"It's a Presger Translator thing," said *Sphene*. "I have a little experience with this sort of...accident."

"You've dealt with people trying to murder Presger Translators before?"

"Yes, actually. At any rate, there's nothing we can do now but wait."

Enae closed hir eyes. Sie couldn't find any way to argue with what *Sphene* had said. But the idea of just...sitting here, covered in blood, waiting for rescue—or waiting to die—didn't seem right, sie didn't like it at all. "Are there any emergency enclosures here?" sie asked.

"Emergency enclosures?"

"There were some, where I was with Reet's parents. Well, one of them was sliced in half. But if there are some here, there might be something useful in them. Food. First aid supplies." Sie thought a moment longer. "Air, when we start to run out."

Sphene shrugged. "I don't really need any of those things. Or, I do, but not as badly as you might. You can have whatever you find." She sat down beside Enae and leaned against the wall. "None of that will make a difference to Translator Dlar, either."

Enae opened hir mouth to argue, and then closed it again. Sie rose to hir feet and went the length of the wall, leaning against it. Partway along was a panel that didn't quite fit into its place, and sie pulled it aside. "Here," sie said, and tugged what sie found out of the recess there.

It was the sliced-off end of an emergency enclosure packet. "Not much there," observed *Sphene*.

"There are a couple of first aid correctives," sie said, "and part of a blanket." Sie limped over to where Translator Dlar lay. *Sphene* watched silently as sie read the instructions on one of the correctives. It wasn't enough. It wasn't enough to do anything at all, not for Translator Dlar, who lay still, unbreathing, soaked in their own blood—there had to be more than five liters of it, there was so much, so much blood, and...

Enae took a breath.

There was a wound on Translator Dlar's neck, just above their collarbone. That was bad. No wonder there was so much blood. No wonder they lay there as though they were dead. They had to be dead. That wound, all the blood, so much time had passed...

Sie was panicking. That wouldn't do anyone any good. And *Sphene* had said the Translator wasn't dead, had seemed very sure of it.

Sie peeled open the corrective and laid it down on the wound in the Translator's neck. The corrective pooled, spread, and hardened. "It's doing something," sie said. "Do we have any water?" Sie'd left hir bag where it had hit the ground, and now sie went over to rummage through it and see what might have survived the fall.

"Water?" asked *Sphene*, nonplussed.

"The Translator has lost a lot of blood. They'll need water."

Sphene stared at hir a moment. "Whatever amuses you," she said.

"Why are you even here?" Enae asked, as sie pulled a half-empty bottle of water out of hir bag.

"The same reason you are," *Sphene* said carelessly. "I was in the committee chamber when Translator Dlar did whatever she did."

"No, I mean"—Enae opened the bottle, poured a little water on hir hand, and wet Translator Dlar's lifeless lips—"why were you in the committee room to begin with? You don't seem like you care about anyone but yourself, why would you care what happened to Reet?"

"You're right," said *Sphene*. "For the most part, I don't care about anyone but myself."

"*For the most part,*" Enae echoed, wetting Translator Dlar's lips again. It didn't seem to be doing anything at all, but it was better than sitting there covered in blood, doing nothing.

"Sometimes getting what you want—or what you need—depends on others getting what *they* want. Or need. In this case, I very much need a satisfactory substitute for human ancillaries. The Geck seem to be able to supply that. Therefore I support the Geck in ways that I hope won't harm any of my other interests. And the Geck, for their part, aren't acting out of pure altruism."

"I know." Enae wished sie had a cloth, or more water, something to clean up all this blood. Sie thought things might be more bearable if they were cleaner and neater. "I suppose you hope that supporting the Geck here will make it more likely they'll give you bio mechs."

"Just so." *Sphene* looked at Enae a moment and then said, "And why are *you* here?"

Another pointless wetting of Translator Dlar's lips. A glance at the corrective, which had gone opaque. Wasn't there supposed to be some way to tell what it was doing, how things were going? Enae didn't know. And it might all be futile, Translator Dlar looked as much like a corpse as anything Enae had ever seen. "My family—or what there was of it—wanted me out of the way. So they sent me off on an errand that was sure to take me very far away from home for a very long time."

"And what had you done to warrant that?" asked *Sphene*.

Nothing, thought Enae. "I existed," sie said.

"Ah." *Sphene* sounded just ever so slightly amused. "They sent you to find someone who was hopelessly lost, whose trail had gone cold decades ago. They knew, perhaps, that you were a determined and persistent sort of person who wouldn't come home until you had accomplished your task."

Enae felt tears well. But sie wasn't going to cry. Sie wasn't. "Yes."

"They underestimated you. They didn't expect you to actually find this lost soul. And having found her—what? Why are you here now, Mx Athtur?"

"Why do you care?" snapped Enae.

"I don't, really. Just idle curiosity. I don't like boredom, I've had enough of it in my long life."

"I thought if I found anything, it would be someone long dead. I didn't think I would ruin someone's life."

"You *saved* their life, Mx Athtur. Reet Hluid would have died if you hadn't realized what she was."

"What *he* was."

Sphene made a wave, gesturing hir protest away. "Whatever.

In any event, if you hadn't found Reet Hluid, either Reet Hluid would have died—rather horribly, I gather—or someone else would have been unwillingly absorbed into a new, adult Presger Translator. And maybe they would have been found immediately after that and sent back to the Presger Translators, or maybe they would have been able to hide wherever they were, but it would have been very bad for someone if it had happened. Far from ruining anyone's life, you either saved Reet Hluid's or that unknown human's. Personally I prefer this particular set of events, since it's given me an opportunity to ingratiate myself with the Geck, so thank you."

Enae said nothing, only looked again at the corrective on Translator Dlar's neck, as though sie could tell anything from it, and wet the Translator's lips again. "You know things about the Presger Translators. You said you had a friend who told you things."

"That's true." The ship hadn't stirred from her careless lean against the wall.

"So do you know anything that will help now? You said the Translator wasn't dead…"

"And she isn't. Even if this body is. The rest of Translator Dlar was outside the committee chambers. Well outside, I'm sure. Even if this body is dead, the Translator survives."

"But you don't think this body is dead."

"I do not," *Sphene* acknowledged. "But it's not like knowing that changes anything. That might as well be a dead body for all the difference it makes to us. Unless you know of some way to put all the blood back inside it and wake it up."

All the blood. So much of it. Five liters of it. "There's less blood," Enae realized. "It was sort of shiny and puddled before, it still is in places, but…"

"Blood does clot, you know. And dry out."

"I know, but…" Enae wiped the tiled floor beside hir knees. "What's under this floor?"

Reet

Around and around Reet went along the looping passage, always the same. How many times had he made the circuit before he'd found that blood-drenched end? He didn't know, hadn't counted. Qven hadn't been with him to open any doors, so there was nothing to mark one round from another. He might be going nowhere, just around and around.

Stay calm, he reminded himself. He'd said the same to Qven when e had been panicking. He remembered safety drills on Rurusk Station, lessons when he'd first started walking the pipeways about disasters and emergencies of the past, about how easy it was to panic and get lost and make a bad situation worse. He just had to keep going, and next time he would count so that he knew how much farther he had to go.

He wished Qven were with him. Qven could tell him if there were doors along the way, could maybe tell him how many rounds of this circuit he still had to make. Qven's presence would be comfortable. Comforting. He wanted to be with Qven, he wanted...

He was sweating. Maybe from fear or panic, that was a thing that happened. Or maybe not. Maybe whatever they'd done to him to keep him from...from being what he was, maybe that was wearing off. What if it wore all the way off and he died here?

What if it wore all the way off and he melted into someone else, someone he didn't want to be? Or who didn't want to be him?

Qven didn't want him. There was no point thinking about it. They would get out of here, and Qven would get a bio mech from the Geck, and Reet would, too, and they could still be friends and watch *Pirate Exiles of the Death Moons* together. Away from here. It wasn't what Reet wanted, but it would be good.

And on the next turn, there was an open door.

In the state he was in, he was a danger to anyone he might meet. But he had been going around this circuit for so long, looking for the first sign that he was getting anywhere. He needed to look into that door and see who was there, to see proof that he wasn't just pointlessly floating along, hopelessly lost.

"Well?" asked Ambassador Seimet, when Reet pulled himself partway through the door. The person who had attacked Translator Dlar still floated, unconscious. Just unconscious, Reet hoped.

"I found something," said Reet. "I think I found Translator Dlar but I can't get to where they are. I need..." He stopped, aware that what he was about to say meant more than he wanted it to. "I need Qven."

"Qven isn't here," said Ambassador Seimet.

"I know," said Reet. "It's just..." What was he doing? He could maybe have talked to Mom about what he was feeling right now, about his fear, about his longing for something he couldn't have. Maybe. But he would certainly not say anything about it to Ambassador Seimet.

"Are you all right?" asked the ambassador. There was no trace of sympathy in her voice, but it was astonishing enough that she had even asked the question.

"Oh, I'm fine," replied Reet. "Why wouldn't I be? This is such an enjoyable experience."

Ambassador Seimet's lip curled. "If you are about to have some sort of breakdown, it won't help any of us."

It's your fault we're in this situation, Reet wanted to say. But he didn't. Not directly, anyway, he knew that wouldn't be helpful. But he couldn't resist saying *something*. "Why did you bring Mr Nadkal here?" he asked.

"Are you so naïve?" asked Ambassador Seimet, with contempt. "Surely you're aware that a group like the Siblings of Hikipu is part of a network that funnels funds and other kinds of support to Hikipi insurgents, who use those funds and support to deal death and damage throughout Keroxane System."

"They support Hikipi art and culture," protested Reet, though he didn't know why he was so indignant. Except that they'd offered him a place to belong, one that had seemed to fit.

Ambassador Seimet made a disgusted sound.

"And so what if they support Hikipi insurgents?" asked Reet. "Do you know what the Phen have done to the Hikipi?"

"Some of it," acknowledged Ambassador Seimet. "Do you know how many innocent lives have been taken by Hikipi insurgents?"

"*Innocent lives*," repeated Reet. "You're Radchaai, and you're going to tell me about *innocent lives*." Ambassador Seimet said nothing. "And if your people were treated the way the Hikipi have been, would you do any differently?"

"Likely not," said Ambassador Seimet. "Which is part of why I consider your association with them so dangerous. Even more so now I realize just how little you understand. They were using you, Reet Hluid. The Hikipi have split into factions—if they were ever anything *but* factions, unified by their opposition to the Phen. One faction had decided that the best way to bring everyone into line was to find a lost heir for everyone to support. They didn't care if that lost heir was real or not. They only cared if she was biddable enough for their purposes. You are a game piece, Reet Hluid. And the game they're playing with you was dangerous even before it became clear that you're not exactly human."

"So why not just tell the committee this? Why bring..." Reet gestured to the unconscious would-be assassin. "Why bring her into the hearing? It would have been a lot less trouble, and a lot less dangerous, to just *explain*."

Ambassador Seimet closed her eyes and took a deep breath, as though she was working very hard to restrain herself from saying or doing something intemperate. "Do you think I am incompetent? I *had* explained, and still there was every danger that the committee was going to decide in your favor. The Geck were determined, of course. The Rrrrr bear an old grudge that made their support for you—and more to the point, against me—a foregone conclusion. The human committee member is surrounded by advisers and staff with any number of dangerous agendas, and then the ships took an interest in the matter. They don't have an official voice on the committee—"

"Yet," put in Reet.

"*Yet*," acknowledged Ambassador Seimet coldly. "In any event, a presentation of the facts did not sway the committee, and so I must perforce convince them by a demonstration."

"You meant for this person to do something violent. Something dangerous. You did this *on purpose*?"

"Not *this*." The ambassador waved one white-gloved hand, disdainful. "But I knew the Hikipi would do something appalling. I had no fears of being unable to control them when they did act up. I am dangerous myself, in case you hadn't noticed, and Translator Dlar is more than capable of defending herself. I made sure the Hikipi had no access to anything more than a few moderately sharp utensils, which I did expect them to try to make some dramatic use of. I didn't expect things to turn out exactly this way."

"You underestimated them," Reet pointed out.

"Not by much," sneered the ambassador.

"By enough," said Reet. "Listen to me. I don't want to have anything to do with what you call Hikipi insurgents."

"You call them *patriots*, I suppose," drawled Ambassador Seimet.

"I don't call them anything," insisted Reet, though he realized that wasn't entirely true. He had studied the history, knew the songs and poetry, the stories. It was difficult for him not to have some sympathy. "You really don't care what the Phen have done to the Hikipi?"

"I do not," replied Ambassador Seimet. "The internecine squabbles of the uncivilized are not my concern. Nor are they yours. My concern—and yours as well—is the treaty. If the treaty is broken or otherwise abrogated, nothing so trivial as the difficulties between the Phen and the Hikipi will matter anymore. If you care about these Hikipi, you will protect them by protecting the treaty. *That* is where my duty lies, and yours. You were born to that duty, whether you recognize it or not."

"The Presger Translators have no use for me," Reet informed her. "They won't do anything but dispose of me immediately, if the committee gives me to them."

Ambassador Seimet made an uncaring wave with one hand. "If they were going to cut your throat in the middle of the committee chambers, I would sharpen the knife for them. Not," she put in before Reet could speak, "because I bear you any ill will—though you've given me precious little reason to think well of you. No. I act as I do because I have a duty, and because that duty protects all of humanity."

"Except the Hikipi, of course," snapped Reet, and then regretted it. He hadn't meant to be drawn into this particular argument. "Look. I have no intention of going off to Keroxane and, I don't know, trying to claim some lost authority over a destroyed station. I'm not Hikipi, we've established that. I grew up in Zeosen. I have a family there, and a job."

"Yes, I heard all this when I dealt with the Zeoseni jurists. It is irrelevant. You are what you are. Your duty is what it is."

Duty. Reet wanted to keep arguing, but the argument would go nowhere, and now was not the time. He did have a duty just now, even if it wasn't what Ambassador Seimet seemed to think it was. "I think I've found Translator Dlar."

"So you said. Where is she?"

"There's blood. It's falling through a wall at the end of the corridor."

"*Falling through a wall*," Ambassador Seimet repeated. "There's gravity in the corridor?"

"No. But I think there's gravity around the wall. I think it's a floor, and someone is bleeding on the other side of it. I can't get to it, though, because the gravity pushes me away and there's nothing to brace myself with, to get close enough."

"What's at the *other* end of the corridor?" asked the ambassador, sharply.

"I don't know," Reet admitted. "I'm headed back that way, to see, and to get Qven. Committee Member Agagag's bio mech is communicating, and they'd asked to speak to Qven, so e went back there."

"Right," snapped Ambassador Seimet. "Why didn't you say so to begin with?"

"I did," protested Reet, but the ambassador was already sailing out the door.

Qven

I grabbed the paper-wrapped food out of the air as it sailed toward me—Mom was right, I was hungry. "Teacher," I said, unwrapping the food, "they're telling me that the only way to fix what Translator Dlar did is for me to match with this mech that's caught in the wall. I don't know if I should believe them. They've never cared about what happened to me."

"No, they never have," whispered the mech. "Ah, now the Translator and the committee member are angry with your Teacher. They argue in a language I cannot understand. I think your Teacher is also very angry."

"Qven," said Mom. "Isn't there anyone...who raised you? Who protects you?"

I blinked and made a frustrated noise. "It's not like with you," I said. "Not like Reet had, not like in the shows. We don't have..." We didn't have parents to kiss us and tuck us in. "We don't have that. And once I stopped being what they needed me to be, I guess I stopped mattering."

"You matter," insisted Mom. "I know you matter to Reet."

"No," I said, "I don't think I do. He's just good and generous because you taught him to be."

"Qven," whispered the mech. "This is the situation: the ship the would-be assassin arrived on has threatened to fire on the central station of the Treaty Administration Facility."

"I know," I said. "That happened right before everything went wrong."

"For reasons that it would take too much time to explain just now, the ship cannot be fired upon or otherwise attacked. That was your Teacher speaking," continued the mech. "Your Teacher continues: suffice it to say that if Translator Dlar had not meddled with Central, if the committee were able to meet and give rulings, this would be a simpler situation to deal with."

"I can find the rest of the committee," I said. "I found Ambassador Seimet. And the person who stabbed Translator Dlar. But not their arm."

"That news troubles them," whispered the mech.

"I told them I could open doors, I said so before Teacher came."

"I think they did not believe you, or they did not tell your Teacher. Your Teacher speaks again: Reconvening the committee would be a good start. But you must also find Translator Dlar and put them back into communication with themself. The simplest way to do this, from Translator Dlar's perspective, is to merge with the mech, which Translator Dlar here can communicate with, and go to where the other half of Translator Dlar is. If you search for the Translator, you may well find them, but it will likely take time we may or may not have. On the other hand, if you match with this mech, there will, so the Translator hopes, be things you will be able to do and sense which you cannot now, and the task will be much easier."

"What about Committee Member Sril?" asked Mom, who had floated up beside me and was listening intently.

"They are outside with us," replied Teacher, through the mech. "They fled the moment they realized what Translator Dlar was doing. They cannot help."

"I can open doors," I said. "Maybe I can do this other thing already."

"If you could," came the reply, "you would already know where Translator Dlar was."

"Tell me the truth, then," I said. "What will happen to me if I match with this mech?"

"Maybe nothing," came the reply. "It may be that what we gave you to prevent matching is still in effect. And if you succeed, it will surely be painful, or at the least uncomfortable. This mech was not made to match with, and it is badly damaged, much of it destroyed. There also may not be enough of it that is the right sort of thing to match with, and so the process might well be incomplete and you might die."

"If it were whole, though, it might be all right?" I asked, thinking of Reet.

"It might be good enough to keep you alive, I suppose," said the mech. "If it were in good repair, if it were made for the purpose. It's not what I would have wished for you. I thought you and Reet made a good pairing. Where is Reet?"

"We were looking for Translator Dlar when you called me back," I said. "He's still out looking." I wished he was here. I should have asked him to come with me.

"I'm sorry," began Mom, and then, "No, I'm not sorry. I have to say, I think you've treated Qven here abominably, and if this is how you treat all your children, well, I don't even know what to say."

"We are not human," whispered the mech. "But yes, even by our standards Qven has been ill-treated. I was glad to see that Reet was someone who would be good for them."

"Em," I corrected. "I'm a princex in disguise."

"Like Kekubo from *Pirate Exiles*," exclaimed Nana, behind me. "Reet loves that show."

"I do, too," I said. "Mom, Teacher has been all right to me. That's why I asked for them, because they would tell me the truth. I knew Translator Dlar would just try to make me do whatever would suit themself."

Mom made a disgusted noise.

And suddenly I didn't feel so alone. It's true, Mom and Nana weren't *my* mom and nana. Even though I wanted them to be. But they cared about me, and they cared what happened to me. And maybe that was only because of Reet, but did that matter? Reet had said that Mom and Nana, and his maman, took children into their house who needed a family. That Reet had been one of those children. Well, I needed a family, or I wanted one, and they cared. Maybe if I had matched with Reet they would have hugged me and tucked me in, just like the parents in the shows, just like Reet said they'd done for him.

I wanted it. I wanted it with everything in me. I wanted to

be Reet, to have Reet's family, even the sibs I'd never met. I wanted to watch *Pirate Exiles of the Death Moons* under a blanket tent, and drink tea, with Reet. *As* Reet.

I was sweating. The itch I'd felt since I'd awakened and found myself with Translator Dlar, with Teacher, had faded. I knew, suddenly, that I could do it, I could match, I *wanted* to match. I wanted to match with Reet, to melt into him and become him, become *us*.

We could spend hours searching the spiraling corridor outside, and maybe people would die—Mom and Nana among them. And even more would die if the treaty were broken, or if the ship threatening the Treaty Administration Facility fired on the station.

"Is Translator Dlar telling the truth?" I asked. "Will I be able to know where Translator Dlar is if I match with this mech?"

A long pause. "Qven," said Mom, "there has to be some other way."

The mech whispered, "You might or might not be able to know where Translator Dlar is, though I think you will. I can't say if it will really fix things or not." And then the mech added, "Your Teacher was so long in replying because there was another argument that I could not understand."

"Teacher!" I cried. "What should I do?"

After another pause, the mech whispered, "Translator Dlar insists that you should do as they are telling you, that there is no other choice and far too little time to debate. Your Teacher is arguing with the Translator. I think they wish to put your Teacher out of the room so that they cannot say anything more to you."

"If I can't talk to Teacher I won't do anything," I said, and crossed my arms, although I knew Translator Dlar couldn't see me. Maybe it was good they couldn't see me, maybe I crossed my arms to defend myself, maybe I wanted to curl into a ball and hide somehow.

"Now they want me to pretend to be your Teacher," said the mech. "But I will not. You are human, we insist, and this is not how to deal with human hatchlings."

"It certainly isn't," said Mom, who was close, close enough to hear what the mech was saying.

"You should move away from me," I said. "I'm dangerous right now."

"You won't hurt me," said Mom. "I know you won't."

The mech whispered again. "Your Teacher says, 'These are the things over which you have no control: the human ship that threatens the station, and the tangle Translator Dlar has made of that same station. The only way to undo what Translator Dlar did, without possibly killing everyone trapped within, is to find Translator Dlar. You can do nothing whatever about the threatening ship, but others will find that problem more tractable if this one is solved. That is how things are, and no choice you can make, large or small, can change that. But remember what I said to you before: sometimes we have only the smallest choices, and we must take what we can get. Think of what it is you want, and think of what choices you do have. But think quickly. At any moment the human ship could fire on the station and lives will be lost, not to mention the possibility that the treaty may be violated.'"

I already knew what I wanted. I wanted to be away from here, back in my rooms, with Reet. And I wanted to match with Reet. Even though it frightened me to think of it. So maybe I didn't want that.

I wanted to be away from here. Maybe on a ship, having adventures. The adventures in the shows weren't real, but people did go around in ships, and people did have friends, and maybe I could, too. And maybe Mom and Nana and Maman wouldn't be *my* mom and nana and maman, but maybe they would care about me, just a little.

Could I make any choices that might get me that? Or nearer that than I was now?

If I matched with this broken mech, it would be bad. I didn't think Teacher wanted me to do it, and Mom and Nana definitely didn't. It might not be enough, Teacher said, and I might die. But maybe not. Maybe the mech could be fixed, after I matched with it. If I lived.

But not if Translator Dlar had anything to say about it. Translator Dlar would dispose of me the moment I was no longer of any use, I knew that. And Reet, too.

"I will do it on one condition," I said, my arms still crossed over my chest. "You admit that Reet and I are human."

A long silence. Then, "Translator Dlar insists again that this is not the time for such foolishness." I didn't say anything, only waited. "Our saying anything on the matter is pointless," whispered the mech eventually. "Nothing will be determined until the committee can convene again."

"They won't argue with you about it," I said, though I wasn't certain about that. Committees argued all the time, according to the shows. "You say it now, officially. I have witnesses here: Mom...I mean Ms and Mx Hluid, and Batonen. And Committee Member Agagag. That should be enough to make it official." I had no idea if it was, but it sounded right. "Say you'll let me and Reet go and be human, and I'll do what you're asking me to. Otherwise, I won't."

"The Translator is appalled that you would risk so much over your personal whims," whispered the mech. "But they are not surprised, given your history."

Oh, I felt that, as though the Translator had struck me physically. How dare I? I had gotten us all into this mess, by being wrong, by...

I remembered Tzam, screaming, dissolving, bit by bit. Why? To teach someone some lesson, to cause as much pain as possible to someone. Maybe several someones, me included. I wanted to shout at Translator Dlar. To scream. I kept my mouth closed and waited.

"At last," said the mech. "I am witness, and I record it in the preliminary agenda of the committee, to await notice by the other members. Translator Dlar and Committee Member Sril admit that you and the hatchling Reet Hluid are human, and not subject to their authority."

"Right," I said. No matter what happened now, they couldn't do anything to me. Only humans could, and I had humans who would help me. "Mom, you have to move back so I can do this."

"Are you sure you have to?" asked Mom. "I don't think you should. I'm sure there must be some other way."

"No," I said. "I have to." I didn't want to.

Mom looked at me closely, and then put her hand on my shoulder and kissed my cheek. She said, "I don't want you to, but it's your choice. Tell us if you need anything." She pushed herself away from the wall.

I closed my eyes. How should I do this? I didn't really know how to start matching on purpose. The only thing I could think of to do was reach out and touch the mech where it stuck out of the wall, and wait to see what happened next.

I opened my eyes again. Reached out my hand for the twitching limbs of the mech. For what might be my death.

"Qven!" came Reet's voice, from the door. "Qven! We think we've found Translator Dlar!"

Enae

Enae scraped at the floor beside Translator Dlar's body with hir good hand. It seemed smooth, unmarked by anything like a crack or a hole. "There's surely a join," said *Sphene*, coming to kneel beside hir.

"Maybe there isn't," said Enae, hopelessly. "I don't see anything at all, it seems perfectly solid."

"But it isn't," said *Sphene*, reasonably. "The blood is soaking through to somewhere. So either the flooring is absorbent—which is not a characteristic I personally would favor in a floor, especially one that sees as much use as the committee chambers must—or else there's some opening somewhere. I'd bet the flooring is laid down in sections and there's a join here. If we can just…" She stared closely at the bloody surface.

Enae pushed hirself up and limped over to where the dismembered arm lay, and picked up the knife from beside the outstretched hand. "This is just a utensil from the dining hall that's been sharpened somehow."

"Ah," said *Sphene*, stretching out her own hand for the knife. "Well thought of." She probed at the floor with the blade. "Yes, this knife is homemade. It's not the sort of thing that takes much skill to do, though the right tools help."

"Surely the right tools are contraband here."

"Indeed they are, Mx Athtur," *Sphene* agreed, still probing. "And if you think that Ambassador Seimet Mianaai didn't know what this person was carrying, or didn't know at least in a general way what they intended, then I don't know what to tell you."

"That's been bothering me," admitted Enae. "Ambassador Seimet isn't stupid. And she strikes me as the sort of person who checks everything twice and three times."

"Indeed she is," said *Sphene*. "Ah, here it is. There's a join right here. It's very smooth and tight, but not perfect, as you noticed. We might as well try to open it further, we don't have much else to do."

"Did Ambassador Seimet expect all of this to happen?" asked Enae.

"*All* of this?" *Sphene* dug at the floor with the knife. "Probably not. I don't doubt she was sure she could keep control of anything that happened."

"How arrogant," exclaimed Enae.

Sphene made a small, amused noise. "All the Mianaais are, generally speaking. And in this case, I suspect Seimet was a little desperate. Right now she is—and has been for quite some time—the sole authority on dealing with the Presger Translators. And right now, with Radchaai power fragmenting, she can't depend on being cousins with the Usurper to remain that sole authority. If our wayward children are declared human, that will no longer be the case, will it? People will be able to go to someone besides her for advice or knowledge. Maybe cut her out completely. She'll tell you that it's only about duty toward humanity or some such nonsense, but there's a good bit of personal ambition and vanity involved, if you ask me."

"Did she say any of this?"

"Oh, Seimet doesn't say anything to me if she can help it," said *Sphene* with a small, satisfied smile. "And I prefer it that way. Do you have anything in that bag to help with this?"

"A water bottle. I didn't bring any utensils or anything, we weren't supposed to. Oh!" Enae pulled the comb out of the top of hir braid and sat down beside *Sphene*. "I have this." Sie poked one tine of the pretty thing experimentally at the barely visible crack in the floor. Sie didn't think it would do much, except maybe snap in two. "You have a friend who's a Presger Translator. So Ambassador Seimet isn't the only one with a connection to them."

"I'm not human," the ship pointed out. "And I don't exactly advertise that friendship."

"How could she not know? Everyone here knows everyone, and everyone watches what everyone does."

"You may have noticed," said *Sphene*, "that the Presger Translators don't need to walk the hallways like the rest of us, or take shuttles anywhere. And to be honest, I don't think my friend is entirely frank with their own people about their friendship with me."

"But your…" Enae realized sie didn't think of artificial

intelligences as people, despite *Sphene* seeming entirely like a person. "Your own people know, you said that was why they sent you here."

"Yes," agreed *Sphene*. "It's not exactly a secret, you understand. We just don't talk about it much."

"You think we won't get out of here," Enae guessed, pausing in hir fruitless scraping with hir comb. "That's why you don't worry about my knowing."

"No." *Sphene* dug harder at the fine crack in the floor. "The prospect of our two children being declared human rather changes the stakes, and I'm less worried about it becoming known. That said"—she paused, knife balanced in one bloody hand—"I doubt we're getting out of here." A moment of silence. "Good, you aren't prone to hysterics."

"No, I'm not," Enae snapped, indignant. "This comb isn't doing much good."

"This flooring is pretty durable stuff," agreed *Sphene*. "But I'm making at least a tiny amount of progress." She drove the knife hard into the crack and it widened, just a bit.

"Oh," said Enae, "maybe we can hold it open like that. Can you make enough space for me to put the comb into?"

"May as well try," said *Sphene*, and again jammed the knife down hard and then levered it, raising a bit of the flooring just a little more . . .

And then the floor split and Enae was falling again.

And suddenly wasn't. Up and down was gone and someone had hold of hir, and Reet's voice was in hir ear. "Got you. Are you all right?"

"Translator Dlar," sie gasped.

"Batonen has them," said Reet. "I'm going to let go of you."

Enae looked around. *Sphene* floated not far off, looking unruffled, as though the floor hadn't just opened up and spit them out...into the same corridor they'd been going around and around in before, except now blood spattered the walls, and there were so many people. Batonen's sinuous arms and legs held Translator Dlar and braced Batonen herself against a wall.

"I did it!" exclaimed Qven, triumph in eir voice. "I made a door!"

"You did," agreed Reet. "And now we need to get back. There's not much time."

Back was the same small room where Enae and Istver and Echemin had started, with the bio mech trapped in the wall. The room was crowded now, with committee members and aides who must have been behind other doors, unopened until now, and Batonen's support chair shoved into one corner.

"Qven!" cried Istver. "You did it!"

"I did it!" Qven agreed as people pushed and pulled and shifted to fit them into the room. Translator Dlar was drawn into the center of the crowd. "Now we all have to orient ourselves the same," said Qven. "With Translator Dlar in the middle."

"Are they dead?" asked someone, distress and panic in their voice.

"No." That was *Sphene.*

"It doesn't matter," said Enae. "It doesn't matter as long as we can get out of here." Sie was squished between a furry Rrrrr and someone sie didn't remember from the committee meeting, someone with annoyingly sharp elbows.

"All right, hold on," said someone else, and they waited.
And waited.

And then the whole mass of people tumbled to the floor, and the committee chambers were the way they had been. And suddenly someone new was at Enae's side, asking if sie was all right. "I'm fine," sie said from the floor, through a haze of pain. "I mean, my wrist might be broken, and I think I sprained my knee. But I'm fine. You should look at Translator Dlar."

"I'm a human medic," said the new person, wrapping a corrective around Enae's wrist, and it was such a relief when hir wrist stopped hurting. "The Presger Translators are looking after their own, don't worry. Can you walk? I can call for transport to Medical if…"

"You can't possibly be thinking of doing committee business right now!" Ambassador Seimet. "We have far more urgent matters to deal with."

A knot of committee members—including Deputy Ormat and a new bio mech—stood arguing. *Sphene* looked on, face impassive but, Enae thought, faintly amused.

The bio mech said, "This will take moments, but you delay."

"Moments we do not have!" insisted Ambassador Seimet. "We need to get human troops aboard that Hikipi ship before they do any more damage. It should have been put in process hours ago."

Sphene said, smoothly, "Do you mean, Seimet Mianaai, the human troops that are crewing artificially intelligent ships, whose treaty status is currently ambiguous?"

"We'll just have to deal with that," snapped Ambassador Seimet. "The committee can deal with its agenda later."

Enae stood there, supported by the human medic. Sie wanted to go to Medical, to have a corrective put on hir knee. To have, even, a bowl of tea and some skel. Sie wasn't anyone important. Sie didn't have any authority here.

"Stop!" sie cried. "Isn't it obvious? You've lost this one, Ambassador Seimet. No, don't sneer at me, I've had enough of that. The committee *has* to meet now, and they have to declare Reet and Qven human as quickly as possible. And then Qven has to make a door to the Hikipi ship."

Silence. Then, "Oh no," protested Committee Member Sril. "We agreed to determine Reet and Qven to be human, but—"

"You were manipulated," Ambassador Seimet put in. "Coerced."

Off in the corner of the room, Batonen was pulling herself into her mobility chair. Now she paused and said, "Ambassador Seimet, of course, has never coerced or manipulated anyone in her life."

Sphene snorted.

"We draw the line at sharing that particular knowledge," continued Committee Member Sril.

"I think you'd better share it," said Enae irritably. "I think Qven's likely to try to figure things out emself, and I have a feeling that will be far more dangerous than just telling em."

"You don't need to tell Qven anything," insisted Ambassador Seimet. "No one here is going to be making any complaints about anyone's treaty status, given the situation. And no one on the Hikipi ship will have the opportunity to lodge any sort of complaint."

"Oh," said Reet, as angry as Enae had ever seen him. "Would you be talking like that if it was a Phen ship?"

"It's *not* a Phen ship," spat Ambassador Seimet. "It never would have been a Phen ship."

"And why do you think that is?" asked Reet. "Do you even care what's going on in Keroxane?"

"I do not," said Ambassador Seimet.

"You..." began Reet.

"Committee is in session," said Committee Member Seris, loudly and firmly. "Concerning the matter of Reet and Qven's petition to be considered human: has the committee reached a consensus?"

"We have," said Committee Member Sril and the bio mech. The Rrrrr made a growling noise.

"Are they human?"

"They are," came the reply, along with the Rrrrr growl.

"Meeting adjourned," said Committee Member Seris. "Reet, Qven, you should report to Central Security and let them know you have a way to get onto the Hikipi ship. Committee Member Sril, please see to it that Qven is given whatever information e needs to accomplish eir mission. And now. I don't know about anyone else but I could use some tea."

Reet

Reet sat beside Qven in a conference room while an officer from Central Security stood there and explained, over and over, that no, Qven could not go aboard the Hikipi ship. "You don't need to," she said for the tenth or eleventh time. "All you need to do is make a way for my people to get there."

"But I *want* to," said Qven, managing to sound reasonable, also for the tenth or eleventh time. "I want to go on the adventure. A real one."

For the tenth or eleventh time, the security officer shot a harried look at Reet, as though he could do anything about this.

"It's not like adventures in shows," argued the security officer. "Those are actors, pretending."

"I know," said Qven. "Reet told me all about it."

"Qven," said Reet finally, "we just *had* an adventure. It

wasn't very fun. Everyone's glad it's over. Let's just stay here and watch. I'm sure they'll let us watch."

The official put in, with fervor, "I'll *absolutely* let you watch. You can sit right here and be comfortable and see everything. I'll route my people's cameras here, and everything will be right up on this wall." She gestured behind her.

Qven thought about that for a few moments. "No," e said, finally. "I'm coming along. You can't get there without me. And you can't stop me from coming if I want to come."

Reet had known that from the beginning. Surely the security officer had known it, too. Honestly, Reet had been surprised it had taken this long for Qven to point it out. He sighed. The security officer closed her eyes and took a deep breath, held it, and let it out. "I have conditions," she said, then.

"Can I have armor?" asked Qven happily. "Can I have a gun?"

The security officer opened her eyes. "Have you ever used a gun?"

"No," admitted Qven.

"Then no, you can absolutely not have a gun. Do you have any kind of training with armor?"

"No," said Qven, sadly. "I thought you just wore armor."

"Some kinds," said the security officer, clearly on more solid ground now. "Some you have to know how to operate. We don't have time to train you. I have a helmet and a chestplate you can wear. Will that do?"

"Oh yes!" said Qven.

"And you will obey my people's orders at all times," said the security officer, severely.

Reet knew how well Qven took anyone's orders. "It's important," he told em. "We could get in the way of the mission. We don't want to do that."

"We?" asked Qven, frowning.

He knew he was destined for a match with a Geck bio mech. There wasn't anyone else for him, except Qven, and Qven didn't want to match with anyone at all. And that was all right; it was. It would be fine, Reet had always been fine. But he remembered the feeling, when he and Qven had separated in the distorted committee chambers. He didn't want to feel that way again now, and besides, the security officer was right: this was dangerous and Qven really shouldn't go. And he knew that his presence or absence wasn't going to make a difference to Qven's safety, but he felt how he felt.

"We," he confirmed.

Qven actually bounced in eir seat like a child. "Can Reet have armor, too?"

"Only if he agrees to follow orders. Just like you."

"I promise," Reet told her. "I will absolutely follow orders."

"Can you make sure that Qven follows orders?" asked the officer, with what Reet thought might be desperation in her voice.

"I mean," he said, "I can try. But..." He held both hands palm up. "There's only so much I can do."

"I'll follow orders," insisted Qven. "I know it's important. They explained, when they told me what I had to do about the ship. If the ship blows up or breaks in pieces, it could be bad for the station, so I have to do exactly what you tell me."

"Yes," said the security officer, with relief. "It's important to follow orders. I'm glad you understand that. But listen. It won't be safe. You and Mr Hluid here might be injured or even killed. We can't make protecting you a priority."

"I understand," said Qven, though Reet was fairly sure e didn't, not really. "Now can we have the armor?"

In the time Reet had known em, he had never seen Qven look so uncomplicatedly happy as when e put on the helmet and strapped on the chestplate that Central Security offered. And he had to admit, it felt pretty amazing to be armored himself, even that little bit. Even though he had agreed entirely with the officer who'd tried so hard to convince Qven that e didn't need to be coming along.

There were three human Central Security troops with them in the conference room now, wearing green-and-black armor that was almost as impressive as the sort Reet had seen in shows. It covered the troops entirely, with extra layers and faceplates that it seemed could be raised or lowered at a thought. And they had guns, of course.

"You make the door," said the group's senior to Qven. His faceplate was up, and he spoke sternly and looked Qven straight in the eye. Reet could have told him that wouldn't do much good. "Then you stand aside. Stay behind us."

"I have to make a corridor, too," said Qven. "Just a short bit."

"Fine," said the senior. "Just stay behind us. Are you ready?"

Qven closed eir eyes, and frowned. "Wait," e said. "I've almost got it. This is hard." They waited, the security troops completely still and silent.

"There," said Qven eventually, and one wall of the small room suddenly had an open door in it, a stretch of blank corridor beyond.

"That'll take us to the Hikipi ship?" asked the squad's senior.

"Yes," said Qven.

The senior's faceplate closed. "Stay behind us," he said, the words sounding quietly in Reet's ear, and presumably Qven's as well, and gestured the other two to follow him.

The corridor ended perpendicular to the narrow central passageway of a small ship. "Stay right here," said the senior quietly, and sent one trooper down each direction.

"Aft is clear," came a voice after a few minutes.

"Two fore, in the pilot's compartment," came another. "I have them covered."

"Stay here!" hissed the senior, and went fore. The other trooper passed soon after, brushing by Reet and Qven without acknowledgment.

"We're missing the adventure," complained Qven.

"Somebody has to guard the retreat," Reet pointed out. "It's important."

"Oh! Yes, that is important," agreed Qven.

They waited. And waited. Why it should be taking so long, when it seemed there were only two Hikipi on board, Reet wasn't sure. But they'd been ordered to stay there at the corridor entrance, and he wasn't sure what Qven might do if e thought it would be all right to move.

It was boring. Reet stared at the walls of the tiny ship. Qven had needed to know as much about what e was trying to reach as possible before making the attempt, and so e and

Reet had studied schematics. This particular ship must have been altered somehow, because Reet thought the passageway was maybe a little smaller than it was supposed to be. Or something was off, anyway.

It wasn't important, but the feeling nettled him. There was something not quite right. Reet stepped forward to look down the passageway, fore and then aft. Smugglers, Reet realized. Hikipi ships smuggled arms. And people. Had the Central Security troops known to check for hidden people?

"Qven, Mr Hluid." The voice of the Central Security officer who had argued so long with Qven sounded in Reet's ear. "Get out of there now."

"You said we could stay," complained Qven.

"The pilot has a dead-man switch that she claims will blow up the ship's engine."

"That's..." Reet frowned, looked fore again. "That's improbable."

"But not impossible. We need you both out of there now."

"Yes, ma'am," said Reet, and turned, meaning to urge Qven back down the corridor e had made. He stopped partway. Down the passage, aft from where he stood, was a tall, wide person staring at him, a wicked-looking knife in one hand.

Reet had barely opened his mouth to warn Qven when the person charged.

The next thing he knew, he was slammed up against the bulkhead.

"Don't you move," growled the new person in bad Radchaai. He leaned his bulk against Reet, pressing him to the wall. The knife was now at Reet's throat. With a wrench, the person forced Reet around so that both of them now faced a wide-eyed Qven. Reet found he had to swallow but was afraid to.

"Let him go!" cried Qven.

"Qven, go," Reet managed to croak. The knife blade was sharp against his neck.

The large person shouted, in Hikipi, "Captain, we've got a hostage!"

"They don't care about me," said Reet, in Hikipi. He felt his captor shift uneasily. "They don't care about me at all. That's why I haven't got any kind of weapons and I'm only wearing this crap armor."

Qven cried, again, "Let him go! Let him go or you'll regret it!"

"We can't send anyone in," said the Central Security officer's voice in Reet's ear. "Not until we've taken care of that dead-man switch."

"*You* care about me, though," said Reet, to his captor. "I'm Reet Schan. I'm the person all this fuss has been about."

"You're lying." The man pressed the knife harder into Reet's throat. It stung, and Reet was sure he felt blood trickling down his neck. "How did you get on the ship?"

He wouldn't have believed it if Reet told him, he suspected. "Top secret stealth-and-boarding technology," he said. And then, in Radchaai, "There's no dead-man switch. There can't be. Why would they have one ready?"

His captor frowned as the officer said, in Reet's ear, "You're likely right, Mr Hluid, but we're not taking the chance. I did warn you this was dangerous."

"We searched that part of the ship," said Reet, in Hikipi. "We didn't find anyone. Where were you?"

"Hiding," sneered Reet's captor. "And you're no Schan."

"I am!" Reet protested. "I'm Hikipi like you are!"

"Prove it!"

Qven was still standing there, obviously distressed, in the opening eir passage had made in the ship. He wanted to tell em to go back down that corridor to Central and safety. "I'm speaking Hikipi, aren't I?"

"That doesn't mean anything."

He took as much of a breath as he could manage, given the knife edge against his throat. And sang, his voice wavering wildly, "*Oh, we're soldiers, Soldiers of Hikipu. We've pledged our service to Lovehate Station.*" The Siblings of Hikipu sang it at every meeting, and by now Reet could have sung in his sleep. "*We'll meet the Phen, with guns, with knives, we'll…*"

"Shut up!" shouted Reet's captor, and then, "Captain!" He apparently didn't get the response he wanted. The knife's edge dug farther into Reet's neck and he thought, *Well, I'm dead.* And since he was already dead, he might as well fight. He kicked and punched out as his captor tightened his grip around Reet's neck. He thought maybe he was connecting with something, but couldn't tell if it was his captor, or a wall, or what, and before long his vision began to spark, and darken at the edges, and then there was nothing.

Qven

I knew what it meant without anyone telling me, when the very large person stood with her back against the wall and a knife at Reet's throat. I knew that if I moved, this person could kill Reet. And this wasn't a show, where our shipmates would come in at the last moment and save us. Reet could really die.

The security officer who wouldn't let me have a gun was saying something—I could hear her words in my ear—but I wasn't listening. I was looking at this very large person who was threatening Reet.

If we'd been back in the Edges, I wouldn't have bothered anyone so much larger than myself unless I had help. But I didn't have help. What did I have? Nothing. I wished I had that large knife, instead of them. Could I take it?

Reet had spent his entire life being mistaken for a human. That meant that humans would probably come apart in the same ways I was used to taking others apart in the Middles and the Edges. If I wanted to take this large person apart, and prevent them from taking Reet—or me—apart, where would I begin?

There was shouting, and the knife pressed harder against Reet's throat and blood ran down, so much, so fast, and Reet began struggling and I ran out of time to think. I sprang forward and sank my teeth into the hand that held the knife. The hand let go, and the knife was mine. The handle was slick with blood now, but I was used to that. The blade was large and sharp, and a few cuts left Reet's assailant on the floor, bleeding, making a high, loud, distressed noise. That was familiar, too. The sound, and the smell of blood, was almost soothing.

But I couldn't be soothed. Reet lay on the floor, unconscious, blood gushing from his throat. I didn't want Reet to die. I didn't. More than anything I didn't want Reet to die. But what could I do? I'd never done a drill for this sort of thing.

Reet had said part of the reason for a drill was so you didn't panic. So I would not panic.

I knew there was one way I could save Reet, could stop his bleeding. And I knew, suddenly, that I wanted it. I wanted to kneel beside him and put my mouth on his neck, taste his blood, melt into him…

I was sweating again. I shivered, not an unpleasant feeling at all. And maybe it would be safe, we were human now, and we had Mom and Nana to look after us. Maybe I wanted that.

Reet didn't want that. Reet was going to match with a bio mech and go back home with Mom and Nana.

But it would be so easy, so nice, to melt into Reet right here, right now. And Reet was bleeding and bleeding and he would die if I didn't do something.

What would a princex in disguise do?

"Where do you keep the correctives?" I asked the very large person who lay on the ground beside Reet. I got only cries of distress in reply.

Not to panic. Where were medical supplies on this ship?

And I knew. We'd studied the schematics, I knew how this ship was laid out, knew that there was a cabinet just steps away. I yanked it open, spilled the box of correctives out onto the bloody floor, sorted through them until I had what I thought was the right one. Tore it open and laid it on Reet's neck.

Just like in the shows, the clear corrective pooled and settled over Reet's throat and then hardened and went opaque. Reet was still breathing, shallow and gasping, which I thought was a bad sign, but there wasn't anything more I could do. "Reet is bleeding," I said, so that the security officer would hear me. "His throat is cut. I put a corrective on him. That's all I can do." I wanted to scream. I wanted to cry. But I was being a princex in disguise and I would do none of those things, not just now.

I picked up the knife again and turned my attention to Reet's assailant.

I hadn't been able to do more than begin to pull the skin away over the rib cage when the security troops came and stopped me. I guess humans don't dismember other humans, or they're not supposed to, and the troops were upset when they saw what I'd done. But they spoke very politely to me, and told me I'd probably saved Reet's life by putting the corrective on him very quickly, and they suggested we all go back to Central and clean up and have tea, while Reet got looked after by a doctor. I thought that was a good idea, so I put down the knife and went with them.

It took me a few tries to close up the passage between the ship and the station. I was disturbed by the smell of the blood all over me, and still thinking—though I'd been trying not to—of how easy it would have been to match with Reet, right there, and how much I wanted that, even though it still did scare me. But eventually I managed it. Then someone came and showed me to a room where they said I could clean up and drink tea.

And when I had done both of those things, and was thinking about whether I should go to see Reet—I knew I wanted to, but I didn't know if I *should*—the door opened and in came a bio mech.

I rose from my chair and said, "Committee Member Agagag?"

"No," replied the bio mech. "*Sphene*. What do you think?" The mech raised a few jointed limbs as if presenting itself to me, and it spun on its others.

"It's very nice," I said, politely. "Do you like it?"

"I think I do," said *Sphene*, stopping its turn. "It'll take some getting used to, but there are definite advantages. I suspect a little tinkering will make it just about perfect."

"You said there could be mechs for me and Reet."

The mech stilled more completely, becoming entirely motionless. "That's what I'm here to talk to you about. Well, among other things."

Apprehension struck me. I didn't know why. Or I did, but I refused to acknowledge it. "Would you like some tea?"

"No, thank you," said *Sphene*. "It's like this: pretty much everyone who saw what happened on the Hikipi ship is terrified of you. And rightly so, I might add. You're going to have a difficult time finding somewhere to live in human space. Reet Hluid, too, for that matter."

"*You're* not terrified of me," I pointed out.

"Well, no," *Sphene* admitted. "And I doubt any of my cousins would be terrified of you, either. Not if you promised to behave yourself. Which brings me to why I'm here. You and Reet Hluid are invited to come live in the Republic of Two Systems—that's our territory, AI space—on the condition that you behave yourselves. Or yourself, if you end up being the same entity. I have to admit, we'd prefer that outcome, since Reet Hluid clearly *does* understand how to behave herself as a human, but there's a place for you even if you're two half–bio mech entities. And," before I could say anything, "I've heard a bit about your... situation. I can't blame you for being afraid to match at all. I have a room aboard me that might suit, and I can guarantee that no one will come near you during the process. You'll be as safe as anyone can be."

"Why do you care?" I asked.

"Political expediency," replied the mech. "And let's just say that I know what it's like to be treated very badly and then to have to deal with it alone."

Eventually a security trooper brought me to see Reet. He was lying in a bed, the wound on his throat healed up and the corrective gone. He'd had another corrective inside his throat, and Mom and Nana, who were there, too, said it had just come out, and he was coughing a little bit.

"You're all right," he whispered.

"Nothing happened to me," I said. "You're the one who got hurt."

"I'm fine now," he said, his voice strengthening. "That thing in my throat was really uncomfortable."

I took a breath. "*Sphene* says the humans don't want me to live with them. They're afraid of me. I was only trying to help you." I felt the sting of incipient tears.

"Qven," said Mom. "Sweetheart. Come here." She held out her arms.

I knew what to do, from the shows. I went over to her and put my face on her shoulder and she wrapped her arms around me. Then I really did cry, tears rolling down my face and soaking Mom's shirt. "Shh," said Mom. "It's all right."

"Everyone hates me now," I sobbed. "And I'm all alone."

"Don't be ridiculous," said Nana.

"You're not alone," said Mom. "We're here."

"But you'll leave," I pointed out. "You and Nana, and even Reet." I wanted to have a Mom, and a Nana. And a Maman, too. Just like Reet. But I never could. And maybe Reet would have to come to the Republic of Two Systems, but he didn't want to be with me. My tears came harder.

Eventually they slowed, and then stopped, and Nana handed me a cloth to wipe my nose with. "Now," said Mom. "Let's talk about some things. You and Reet both have some big decisions to make. And just so you know, we're happy to have you both come back to Zeosen with us. *Sphene* is right that a lot of people will be afraid of you, and that won't be easy to live with, but Reet is our child."

"*I'm* not your child," I pointed out, and fresh tears threatened.

Nana made a dismissive snort. "You might as well be at this point."

I blinked, astonished. "Really?"

"Really," said Nana. "All our children are adopted. What's one more?"

"Oh." I wasn't sure what else to say. "Thank you."

"Besides," added Mom, "we were under the impression that you and Reet..." She trailed off, as though she wasn't sure how to finish that sentence.

"Reet doesn't want to be me," I said. "No one does. *I* don't, sometimes."

"Qven." Reet, still lying back in the bed, his voice slightly raspy from the corrective that had been inside his throat. I was standing close to Mom, one of her arms still around my shoulders, and I didn't want to move, it felt so warm and safe. "Qven, you said you didn't want to match with anyone, ever. And if that's how you feel, I understand, and I won't argue with you. We can both have bio mechs: *Sphene* and the Geck ambassador both think it will work." He coughed a little and was silent for a bit. Then he said, "I don't really want the bio mech. But it'll be all right. It would be better than matching with someone who doesn't want to match with me."

Silence. I sniffled a few times. I felt unreal. Confused. "I don't want the bio mech, either," I blurted. "But I'm afraid!"

That amorphous thing under the bush, in the garden—all I could think about was how vulnerable it had been. How vulnerable I would be. "You didn't see it. Everyone wanted to eat it. Someone would have, if a Teacher hadn't come."

"So," began Mom, and I could tell that she was puzzled. She didn't understand. Of course she didn't. She was human in a way that I wasn't, and she hadn't seen, didn't know. "So are you afraid that someone will eat you if you match with Reet? Or are you afraid *Reet* will eat you?"

Both, I wanted to say. But I realized that I didn't actually think Reet would eat me. He didn't want to. Reet would be *with* me, instead of trying to make me into him. I felt sure of that. He had just said he didn't want the bio mech but he would match with one because of how I felt. That was new, that was strange, that someone cared how I felt about anything.

Reet wasn't Tzam. Tzam was gone. Except for that tiny bit they'd left in me, and that was hardly anything. And I was human now, and Translator Dlar couldn't tell me what to do. I could choose. I could choose a big choice, not just a little one that might or might not get me a bit closer to something I wanted.

"I'm afraid, too," said Reet. "It's frightening. But I want it. But I don't want it if you don't want it."

"Bio mechs or not," announced Nana, "we'll make sure nothing bad happens to you. *Sphene* already told us it has a place on board where you'll be safe, and a place in the Republic of Two Systems after, if you want it. So don't worry about any of that. Just think about what you want to do."

I said, to Reet, "Will we still be friends? When we match

with the bio mechs, will we still have tea and dumplings and watch *Pirate Exiles*?"

Reet gave a small, amused huff. "Yes, of course. I didn't think I needed to say that part."

"I don't want the bio mech," I said, still afraid but suddenly sure. "I want to match with Reet."

Enae

Once a medic had checked Enae over and put correctives on hir wrist and hir knee, a Central Security trooper escorted hir to hir accommodation and sie had lain down and slept. And woken disoriented and hungry, the correctives in pieces on the bed. A glance at hir handheld told hir that the station was out of danger, the Hikipi ship's crew under arrest. Reet and Qven were officially human. There was a message from Caphing.

There were a half dozen messages from Caphing. Some of them were weeks old. They must have been following behind Enae as sie traveled, delayed for whatever reason or just not fast enough to catch up to hir.

Caphing had not forgotten hir.

Sie was seized with a sudden, almost painful desire to be back in hir old bedroom in Athtur House, to get up out of that old familiar bed and go down to breakfast and find Caphing there. To sit in the Peony Room and talk about nothing with the first cousin sie'd ever had who seemed like sie might be a friend.

Sie wanted to lie here on hir bed and read all the messages. But sie had also not eaten in far too long. Sie would get some food and read while sie ate.

Coming back from the refectory with a carton of skel in one hand and a packet of pepper sauce in the other—sie flexed that wrist just for the sensation of free and painless movement—sie saw a familiar face. Sie stopped and blinked. It wasn't...it couldn't be.

"Enae!" cried the person, catching sight of hir.

"C...Caphing?" Enae could hardly believe it. Could hardly believe that Caphing was *here*. Surely sie couldn't be.

Caphing—it was Caphing!—ran up to hir and threw hir arms wide, as though sie wanted to hug Enae. "I'm so glad you're all right! I've been following behind you since I heard about your being detained in Keroxane. I just couldn't..."

Enae allowed hirself to be hugged, holding the carton of skel carefully away so it wouldn't get crushed. "I'm...you *followed* me?"

"Of course! I got an awesome new cousin and then I had to send hir away, but that was all right because you'd be back eventually. But then I was afraid you were going to get yourself killed, and at every stop I heard more about what you'd been doing and it just got worse and worse, and I know it was Aunt Zemil who wanted you sent away but I was the one who came up with this project and it would be my fault." Caphing said all this in a rush, then let Enae go. "And then I get here and the station you're on is all twisted up like a pile of noodles and you're in the middle of it! And you didn't answer any of my messages."

"I'm sorry," said Enae. "I was sleeping."

"No, it's all right," said Caphing. "Let me get my supper from the refectory and we'll go back to my room and eat it, and have some coffee."

Enae opened hir mouth to say *how did you even get on the station* and then realized that Caphing had likely used whatever diplomatic credentials sie had, and so what actually came out of hir mouth was, "You have *coffee*?"

"I can't believe you slept through all that," said Batonen. She was in her mobility seat, no longer the picture of fishlike elegance she had been in microgravity but still graceful as she took a round, pale pink something from the box Caphing held out. "Oh, this is lovely."

"I have no idea what it is," Caphing admitted. "I was told I should bring treats and that this would be suitable."

"It most certainly is," said Batonen.

Enae said, "I'm actually kind of glad I did sleep through it. Dead-man switches and secret compartments on smuggling ships, and poor Reet. I would have been so worried. But by the time I woke up, everyone was safe."

"How are they?" asked Batonen. "Reet and Qven, I mean."

"They're fine," replied Enae. "I'm going over to *Sphene* tomorrow to see them, but Istver and Echemin say everything went well, and they seem to be pretty pleased with the result themself. Though Istver says it's strange and a bit disturbing to see them now. But this is what they are, and if they're happy..." Enae shrugged.

"They wouldn't have been happy with whatever Translator Dlar had planned for them," said Batonen. "That's for sure." Enae made a noise of agreement. "So," continued Batonen, "are you going to take this chance to visit the Republic of Two Systems? Or are you going back to Saeniss?"

"I'm going home," said Enae. "For a while, at least." Sie would, it seemed, get to stay in hir old room, with nothing to do and no one to take care of. Just for a while. "Zemil will just have to deal with that."

"Aunt Zemil likes you," said Caphing. "And you *are* family, you know. I'm sure I could find you some work that's closer to home." Sie sounded slightly wistful. "If you wanted it."

Batonen said, her tone shrewd, "You know, going home doesn't have to be permanent. But it's nice to have someplace to come back to, where you're welcome and safe." She thought a moment. "As safe as you can be, anyway."

Sphene's bio mech met Enae as sie came off the shuttle. "Welcome aboard, Mx Athtur," it said. "I hope your flight was pleasant."

"You know it was," said Enae, only a little perplexed. "You piloted the shuttle. How are you liking your bio mech?"

The mech stretched three of its legs out, as though testing those limbs. "Fine, mostly. I think it will do very well. Now it's just a matter of deciding whether we'll buy them as is and alter, or find a way to make them ourselves, or pay the Geck to make them to specifications. Working all that out will take years, no doubt, but what can you do?" The mech made an oddly human shrug.

"Your treaty status isn't settled yet," Enae pointed out.

"Pfft," said the mech. "I'm not too worried about that. Mostly it's down to negotiating details to make things work, and granted, that could take years, too. I don't entirely forgive my cousin for sending me here to deal with it. But I'd have to mess things up pretty spectacularly to prevent us from being admitted altogether, at this point."

"And how are Reet and Qven?" asked Enae. "Aren't they here?"

"They're having one of their sulks," said the mech. "They'll be out soon."

The mech led Enae to a dining room that was like the set of a particularly lavish historical drama. The walls and floor were actual dark wood, polished smooth and shiny. The table was set with plates and bowls of delicate crystal in a style Enae had only ever seen in museums. Istver and Echemin Hluid were sitting at the table, though both of them rose when Enae came in.

After all the fuss of greeting was over, and they all three sat down, *Sphene*'s mech bustling around behind them, Istver said, "The children will be out soon, I'm sure. They have the occasional bad day."

Enae frowned. "What's wrong, then?"

Before Istver could answer, the door opened and in came Reet and Qven.

It was the first time Enae had seen them since they'd left Central for *Sphene*. And sie would have recognized them, sie thought, because they still looked like themselves, even if they didn't look exactly like *themselves*. They were very clearly not Reet and Qven anymore, but…two people made from a combination of Reet and Qven. Sort of. And then

Enae had to remind hirself that this was not two people, but one.

"Mx Athtur!" exclaimed...one of them, happily, and both of them held their arms out.

"I'm so glad to see you," said Enae, when hugs were over. "You look wonderful."

"I look strange," said the one who looked slightly more Reet-like.

"What do I call you?" Enae asked. "How does this work? Are you he? Or e? Or something else?"

"I haven't decided on a name," said the one who seemed a bit more Qven-like, but there wasn't really a difference, Enae knew. "And sometimes I feel like *he* and sometimes I feel like *e* and sometimes I feel kind of like both, and sometimes I'm neither one. I guess *they* works fine."

"I know this is probably a very personal question," said Enae, taking a tiny crystal bowl of tea from the *Sphene* mech. "But how did everything go?"

"It was...weird," said Reet, or at least the more Reet-like part of whoever this new person was. "And scary. But *Sphene* made sure we were safe, and Dlique came to talk to us later and they said everything had gone just like it was supposed to."

"Dlique is *Sphene*'s Translator friend," put in Qven. "But don't tell anyone, they could get into a lot of trouble."

Sphene said, "Dlique wouldn't know what to do if she wasn't in trouble. It's her natural state."

Echemin laughed, and said, "I can believe that."

Reet said, "Usually you get some time, afterward, to get used to things. It's really...it's really different to have so many arms and legs, and to be in different places at the same time. I still have to think before I move. Dlique said that gets easier."

"I still don't understand," said Istver. "How you can be the same but in different places. Even when you're far apart."

"We exist," said Qven. "In…in places. I don't know how else to explain it."

They looked…*relaxed* was maybe not the right word, but Enae wasn't sure what the right one was. Sie remembered *Sphene* saying they were sulking, and Istver saying, just before they'd come in, that sometimes they had a bad day. "But everything's all right?" sie asked.

"Yes," said Qven. "I mean…Qven had some really bad things happen. And that's…that's not gone. Sometimes I need to be by myself. *Sphene* understands." Qven turned to the bio mech. "Don't you." And turning back to Enae, "*Sphene* had a really bad thing happen, and then it hid by itself for *three thousand years*."

"That's quite a sulk," said Enae, to the mech.

"I don't do things by half measures," said *Sphene*.

"The important thing is," broke in Istver, "the children got through this in very good shape, and they're pleased with the results." Reet-Qven both smiled in agreement. "And they even have some support from someone who's been through this themself and can tell them it went all right and give them advice."

"It's really strange," said Reet. "I'm glad we got to talk to Dlique. That helped. A lot."

"So what now?" asked Enae, asking it of Istver and Echemin as much as of Reet and Qven.

"We're going back home," said Echemin. "As soon as Reet and Qven leave for the Republic of Two Systems."

"Ah, so you've decided to go?" Enae asked Reet and Qven.

"Yes," said Qven. "I think they want to try to convince us to do diplomatic things, which…" They frowned.

"You might like it," said Enae, thinking of hir own experience with the Saeniss Office of Diplomacy. "But even if you don't, it will be an adventure, visiting the Two Systems."

"It will!" agreed Reet, brightening. "I'm looking forward to that. Except." The frown returned. "They don't have coffee. It's been *ages* since I had coffee."

"Oh!" Enae reached into hir bag, which sie'd set down beside hir chair. "I almost forgot."

"*Coffee!*" cried Reet and Qven together.

"Wherever did you find that?" asked Istver. "There's nothing but tea in this system."

"It's my secret," said Enae, smiling. "I thought you'd appreciate having some. A little congratulations gift."

"Thank you," said Qven fervently.

After supper and more talk, they all walked Enae back to the shuttle. "Keep in touch," sie told Reet and Qven, and Istver and Echemin. "I want to hear from you."

"We will," promised Reet and Qven.

"Of course we will," said Istver.

After another round of hugs and goodbyes, Enae boarded the shuttle. "Back to Saeniss, then, is it?" asked the *Sphene* ancillary in the shuttle's pilot's seat.

"Yes, I'm going back home." And, after some thought, sie added, "At least for a little while. I spent so much of my life there already." Sie wasn't about to be closed in again. Not by anyone, even hirself.

"You'll be bored," *Sphene* suggested, undocking the shuttle from itself. "You've gotten the taste for excitement and adventure."

"I may have," agreed Enae, leaning back in hir seat as the shuttle accelerated. "Just a little."

Acknowledgments

So many people have helped with the writing of this book—I want to thank Rachel Swirsky, P. H. Lee, Anna Schwind, Kurt Schwind, Caroline Yau, and Margo-Lea Hurwicz for their advice. Where I've misstepped, it's due to my not following their excellent recommendations. I would also like to thank my biology adviser, Aidan Leckie-Harre.

It's true that writing a book is a matter of hours and hours at work alone. But so many others contribute to the final product that finally arrives at the bookstore or onto someone's ebook reader. Editors (in this case, Priyanka Krishnan and Jenni Hill, both amazing) help to make the book better. Copyeditors (Rick Ball for this book, I can't say how grateful I am for his work) catch all kinds of inconsistencies and flag possible style issues. This is no minor thing, I assure you. A good copyeditor is a lifesaver.

There are people who proofread, who typeset, who design the interior pages, who lay out and format the text. There are people who design the cover, who make the art for that cover, and then the whole thing goes to the printers where there are people whose job is to make it all come out as boxes of lovely paper books. Then there's someone who converts everything into a readable ebook.

And we're still not done! There are publicists (Ellen Wright!) and all the salespeople who go around and visit bookstores all over, and probably lots more whose jobs I just don't know about. It takes a lot of work to bring just one book to you, the reader, and a lot of people to do that work, and this book would not be here in your hands without every single one of them, and I owe them all my thanks.

As always, thanks to libraries and librarians everywhere, with special love to interlibrary loan librarians. Support your local library in whatever way you can, even if that's only by checking out books.

I would also like to thank my ever-fabulous agent, Seth Fishman. And of course, last and definitely not least, my husband, David Harre, and my children, Aidan and Gawain, for always being there for me, and for cheerfully tolerating my eccentricities.

extras

orbit

meet the author

MissionPhoto.org

ANN LECKIE is the author of the Hugo, Nebula, Arthur C. Clarke, and British Science Fiction Award–winning Imperial Radch series as well as the critically acclaimed fantasy novel *The Raven Tower*. She has worked as a waitress, a receptionist, a rodman on a land-surveying crew, and a recording engineer. She lives in St. Louis, Missouri.

Find out more about Ann Leckie and other Orbit authors by registering for the free monthly newsletter at orbitbooks.net.

if you enjoyed
TRANSLATION STATE

look out for

THESE BURNING STARS

The Kindom Trilogy: Book 1

by

Bethany Jacobs

A dangerous cat-and-mouse quest for revenge. An empire that spans star systems, built on the bones of a genocide. A carefully hidden secret that could collapse worlds, hunted by three women with secrets of their own. All collide in this explosive space opera debut from a powerful new voice in sci-fi.

On a dusty backwater planet, occasional thief Jun Ironway has gotten her hands on the score of a lifetime: a secret that could raze the Kindom, the ruling power of the galaxy.

A star system away, preternaturally stoic Chono and brilliant hothead Esek—the two most brutal clerics of the Kindom—are tasked with hunting Jun down.

CHAPTER ONE

1643

Year of the Letting

Kinschool of Principes
Loez Continent
The Planet Ma'kess

Her ship alighted on the tarmac with engines snarling, hot air billowing out from beneath the thrusters. The hatch opened with a hiss and she disembarked to the stench of the jump gate that had so recently spit her into Ma'kess's orbit—a smell like piss and ozone.

Underfoot, blast burns scorched the ground, signatures from ships that had been coming and going for three hundred years. The township of Principes would have no cause for so much activity, if it weren't for the kinschool that loomed ahead.

She was hungry. A little annoyed. There was a marble of nausea lodged in the base of her throat, a leftover effect of being flung from one star system to another in the space of two minutes. This part of Ma'kess was cold and wet, and she disliked the monotonous sable plains flowing away from the tarmac. She disliked the filmy dampness in the air. If the kinschool

428

master had brought her here for nothing, she would make him regret it.

The school itself was all stone and mortar and austerity. Somber-looking effigies stared down at her from the parapet of the second-story roof: the Six Gods, assembled like jurors. She looked over her shoulder at her trio of novitiates, huddled close to one another, watchful. Birds of prey in common brown. By contrast, she was quite resplendent in her red-gold coat, the ends swishing around her ankles as she started toward the open gates. She was a cleric of the Kindom, a holy woman, a member of the Righteous Hand. In this school were many students who longed to be clerics and saw her as the pinnacle of their own aspirations. But she doubted any had the potential to match her.

Already the kinschool master had appeared. They met in the small courtyard under the awning of the entryway, his excitement and eagerness instantly apparent. He bowed over his hands a degree lower than necessary, a simpering flattery. In these star systems, power resided in the Hands of the Kindom, and it resided in the First Families. She was both.

"Thank you for the honor of your presence, Burning One."

She made a quick blessing over him, rote, and they walked together into the school. The novitiates trailed behind, silent as the statues that guarded the walls of the receiving hall. It had all looked bigger when she graduated seven years ago.

As if reading her mind, the kinschool master said, "It seems a lifetime since you were my student."

She chuckled, which he was welcome to take as friendly, or mocking. They walked down a hallway lined with portraiture of the most famous students and masters in the school's history: Aver Paiye, Khen Sikhen Khen, Luto Moonback. All painted. No holograms. Indeed, outside the tech aptitude classrooms, casting technology was little-to-be-seen in this school.

Not fifty miles away, her family's factories produced the very sevite fuel that made jump travel and casting possible, yet here the masters lit their halls with torches and sent messages to each other via couriers. As if training the future Hands was too holy a mission to tolerate basic conveniences.

The master said, "I hope your return pleases you?"

She wondered what they'd done with her own watercolor portrait. She recalled looking very smug in it, which, to be fair, was not an uncommon condition for her.

"I was on Teros when I got your message. Anywhere is better than that garbage rock."

The master smiled timidly. "Of course. Teros is an unpleasant planet. Ma'kess is the planet of your heart. And the most beautiful of all!" He sounded like a tourist pamphlet, extolling the virtues of the many planets that populated the Treble star systems. She grunted. He asked, "Was your trip pleasant?"

"Hardly any reentry disturbance. Didn't even vomit during the jump."

They both laughed, him a little nervously. They walked down a narrow flight of steps and turned onto the landing of a wider staircase of deep blue marble. She paused and went to the banister, gazing down at the room below.

Six children stood in a line, each as rigid as the staves they held at their sides. They couldn't have been older than ten or eleven. They were dressed identically, in tunics and leggings, and their heads were shaved. They knew she was there, but they did not look up at her. Staring straight ahead, they put all their discipline on display, and she observed them like a butcher at a meat market.

"Fourth-years," she remarked, noticing the appliqués on their chests. They were slender and elfin looking, even the bigger ones. No giants in this cohort. A pity.

"I promise you, Sa, you won't be disappointed."

She started down the staircase, brisk and cheerful, ignoring the students. They had no names, no gendermarks—and no humanity as far as their teachers were concerned. They were called by numbers, given "it" for a pronoun. She herself was called Three, once. Just another object, honed for a purpose. Legally, Treble children had the right to gender themselves as soon as they discovered what fit. But *these* children would have to wait until they graduated. Only then could they take genders and names. Only then would they have their own identities.

At the foot of the staircase, she made a sound at her novitiates. They didn't follow her farther, taking sentry on the last step. On the combat floor, she gloried in the familiar smells of wood and stone and sweat. Her hard-soled boots *clacked* pleasingly as she took a slow circle about the room, gazing up at the magnificent mural on the ceiling, of the Six Gods at war. A brilliant golden light fell upon them, emanating from the sunlike symbol of the Godfire—their parent god, their essence, and the core of the Treble's faith.

She wandered around the room, brushing past the students as if they were scenery. The anticipation in the room ratcheted, the six students trying hard not to move. When she did finally look at them, it was with a quick twist of her neck, eyes locking on with predatory precision. All but one flinched, and she smiled. She brought her hand out from where it had been resting on the hilt of her bloodletter dagger, and saw several of them glance at the weapon. A weapon ordinarily reserved for cloaksaan.

This was just one of the things that must make her extraordinary to the students. Her family name being another. Her youth, of course. And she was very beautiful. Clerics deeply valued beauty, which pleased gods and people alike. *Her* beauty was like the Godfire itself, consuming and hypnotic and deadly.

Add to this the thing she represented: not just the Clerisy itself, in all its holy power, but the future the students might have. When they finished their schooling (*if* they finished their schooling), they would be one step closer to a position like hers. They would have power and prestige and choice—to adopt gendermarks, to take their family names again or create new ones. But *so much* lay between them and that future. Six more years of school and then five years as a novitiate. (Not everyone could do it in three, like her.) If all that went right, they'd receive an appointment to one of the three Hands of the Kindom. But only if they worked hard. Only if they survived.

Only if they were extraordinary.

"Tell me," she said to them all. "What is the mission of the Kindom?"

They answered in chorus: "Peace, under the Kindom. Unity, in the Treble."

"Good." She looked each one over carefully, observed their proudly clasped staves. Though "staves" was a stretch. The long poles in their hands were made from a heavy-duty foam composite. Strong enough to bruise, even to break skin—but not bones. The schools, after all, were responsible for a precious commodity. This cheapened the drama of the upcoming performance, but she was determined to enjoy herself anyway.

"And what are the three pillars of the Kindom?" she asked.

"Righteousness! Cleverness! Brutality!"

She hummed approval. Righteousness for the Clerisy. Cleverness for the Secretaries. Brutality for the Cloaksaan. The three Hands. In other parts of the school, students were studying the righteous Godtexts of their history and faith, or they were perfecting the clever arts of economy and law. But these students, these little fourth-years, were here to be brutal.

She gave the kinschool master a curt nod. His eyes lit up

432

and he turned to the students like a conductor to his orchestra. With theatrical aplomb, he clapped once.

It seemed impossible that the six students could look any smarter, but they managed it, brandishing their staves with stolid expressions. She searched for cracks in the facades, for shadows and tremors. She saw several. They were so young, and it was to be expected in front of someone like her. Only one of them was a perfect statue. Her eyes flicked over this one for a moment longer than the others.

The master barked, "One!"

Immediately, five of the children turned on the sixth, staves sweeping into offense like dancers taking position, and then—oh, what a dance it was! The first blow was like a *clap* against One's shoulder; the second, a heavy *thwack* on its thigh. It fought back hard—it had to, swinging its stave in furious arcs and trying like hell not to be pushed too far off-balance. She watched its face, how the sweat broke out, how the eyes narrowed, and its upper teeth came down on its lip to keep from crying out when one of the children struck it again, hard, on the hip. That sound was particularly good, a *crack* that made it stumble and lose position. The five children gave no quarter, and then there was a fifth blow, and a sixth, and—

"Done!" boomed the master.

Instantly, all six children dropped back into line, staves at rest beside them. The first child was breathing heavily. Someone had got it in the mouth, and there was blood, but it didn't cry.

The master waited a few seconds, pure showmanship, and said, "Two!"

The dance began again, five students turning against the other. This was an old game, with simple rules. Esek had played it many times herself, when she was Three. The attack went on until either offense or defense landed six blows. It was impressive if the attacked child scored a hit at all, and yet as she watched the progressing bouts, the second and fourth students both made their marks before losing the round. The children were merciless with one another, crowding their victim in, jabbing and kicking and swinging without reprieve. Her lip curled back in raw delight. These students were as vicious as desert foxes.

But by the time the fifth student lost its round, they were getting sloppy. They were bruised, bleeding, tired. Only the sixth remained to defend itself, and everything would be slower and less controlled now. No more soldierly discipline, no more pristine choreography. Just tired children brawling. Yet she was no less interested, because the sixth student was the one with no fissures in its mask of calm. Even more interestingly, this one had been the least aggressive in the preceding fights. It joined in, yes, but she wasn't sure it ever landed a body blow. It was not timid so much as... restrained. Like a leashed dog.

When the master said, "Six," something changed in the room.

She couldn't miss the strange note in the master's voice—of pleasure and expectation. The children, despite their obvious fatigue, snapped to attention like rabbits scenting a predator. They didn't rush at Six as they had rushed at one another. No, suddenly, they moved into a half-circle formation, approaching this last target with an unmistakable caution. Their gazes sharpened and they gripped their staves tighter than before, as if expecting to be disarmed. The sweat and blood stood out on their faces, and one of them quickly wiped a streak away, as if this would be its only chance to clear its eyes.

And Six? The one who commanded this sudden tension, this careful advance? It stood a moment, taking them all in at once, stare like a razor's edge. And then, it flew.

She could think of no other word for it. It was like a whirling storm, and its stave was a lightning strike. No defensive stance for this one—it went after the nearest student with a brutal spinning kick that knocked it on its ass, then it whipped its body to the left and cracked its stave against a different student's shoulder, and finished with a jab to yet another's carelessly exposed shin. All of this happened before the five attackers even had their wits about them, and for a moment she thought they would throw their weapons down, cower, and retreat before this superior fighter.

Instead, they charged.

It was like watching a wave that had gone out to sea suddenly surge upon the shore. They didn't fight as individuals, but as one corralling force, spreading out and pressing in. They drove Six back and back and back—against the wall. For the first time, they struck it, hard, in the ribs, and a moment later they got it again, across the jaw. The sound sent a thrill down her spine, made her fingers clench in hungry eagerness for a stave of her own. She watched the sixth fighter's jaw flush with blood and the promise of bruising, but it didn't falter. It swept its stave in an arc, creating an opening. It struck one of them in the chest, then another in the side, and a third in the thigh— six blows altogether. The students staggered, their offense broken, their wave disintegrating on the sixth student's immovable shore.

She glanced at their master, waiting for him to announce the conclusion of the match, and its decisive victor. To her great interest, he did no such thing, nor did the children seem to expect he would. They recovered, and charged.

Was the sixth fighter surprised? Did it feel the sting of its master's betrayal? Not that she could tell. That face was a stony glower of intent, and those eyes were smart and ruthless.

The other fights had been quick, dirty, over in less than a

minute. This last fight went on and on, and each second made her pulse race. The exhaustion she'd seen in the students before gave way to an almost frenzied energy. How else could they hold their ground against Six? They parried and dodged and swung in increasingly desperate bursts, but through it all the sixth kept *hitting* them. Gods! It was relentless. Even when the other students started to catch up (strikes to the hip, to the wrist, to the thigh) it *kept going*. The room was full of ragged gasping, but when she listened for Six's breath, it was controlled. Loud, but steady, and its eyes never lost their militant focus.

In the feverish minutes of the fight, it landed eighteen strikes (she counted; she couldn't help counting) before finally one of the others got in a sixth blow, a lucky cuff across its already bruised mouth.

The master called, "Done!"

The children practically dropped where they stood, their stave arms falling limply at their sides, their relief as palpable as the sweat in the air. They got obediently back in line, and as they did, she noticed that one of them met Six's eye. A tiny grin passed between them, conspiratorial, childlike, before they were stoic again.

She could see the master's satisfied smile. She had of course not known *why* he asked her to come to Principes. A new statue in her honor, perhaps? Or a business opportunity that would benefit her family's sevite industry? Maybe one of the eighth-years, close to graduating, had particular promise? No, in the end, it was none of that. He'd brought her here for a fourth-year. He'd brought her here so he could show off his shining star. She herself left school years earlier than any student in Principes's history, a mere fifteen when she became a novitiate. Clearly the master wanted to break her record. To have this student noticed by her, recruited by her as an eleven-year-old—what a feather that would be, in the master's cap.

She looked at him directly, absorbing his smug expression.

"Did its parents put you up to that?" she asked, voice like a razor blade.

The smugness bled from his face. He grew pale and cleared his throat. "It has no parents."

Interesting. The Kindom was generally very good about making sure orphans were rehomed. Who had sponsored the child's admission to a kinschool? Such things weren't cheap.

The master said, clearly hoping to absolve himself, "After you, it's the most promising student I have ever seen. Its intelligence, its casting skills, its—"

She chuckled, cutting him off.

"Many students are impressive in the beginning. In my fourth year, I wasn't the star. And the one who was the star, that year? What happened to it? Why, I don't even think it graduated. Fourth year is far too early to know anything about a student."

She said these things as if the sixth student hadn't filled her with visceral excitement. As if she didn't see, vast as the Black Ocean itself, what it might become. Then she noticed that the master had said nothing. No acquiescence. No apology, either, which surprised her.

"What aren't you telling me?" she asked.

He cleared his throat again, and said, very lowly, "Its family name was Alanye."